'A TRILOGY OF MAGICAL TALES'

By

Ron S King

'A TRILOGY
OF
MAGICAL TALES'

COPYRIGHT 2010 --- Ron S King

ISBN: 978-1-4461-4016-1

www.ronskingbooks.com

FOREWORD.

Having written three original Fairy-Stories and having them published separately, I decided to put the three stories together, a Trilogy and naming the book…

A TRILOGY OF MAGICAL TALES.

Each story is a tale of challenge and has the characters facing all kinds of hardships, entering unknown lands, where anything can happen.

In each story, there are pictures for the reader to colour in with paints and crayons, so that the book will contain hours of amusement and will become a favourite for children and adults alike.

These stories are a learning, there are morals, stories which tell of greed and how good will always win over evil. The reader will find these stories unlike any fairy-tale ever read, with a new and original approach to the world of imagination…

I trust you will enjoy the read and have fun with the painting…

Ron S King.

ILLUSTRATIONS.

All illustrations are drawn up by Kelly Aston, without whom this book would never have been finished.
My thanks to this artist for her commitment and attention to detail.

Kelly has sketched the pictures out, so they can be coloured in by the reader.

THE RAIN MAIDEN

THE KISS-DIAMOND

'THE KISS-DIAMOND'
A MAGICAL TALE

By

Ron S King

OBERON & TITANIA

IN THE BEGINNING.

It was still dark and the Wood-Ghouls seemed to whisper their horrid chants from every tree. The Sun had not come up and the darkness seemed to stick to the world like glue.

I hurried on.

"You are too early!" the chattering Woodpecker told me.

It seemed not to matter that I was on a very important mission, that I was Pucker-Up, the Turner of Good Fortune, a most important Gnome and regarded very highly by the Kiss-Kids Clan.

"It doesn't matter who you are!" exclaimed the Woodpecker, puffing himself up. "You are not allowed into the Flower-Ring, not until Oberon has kissed Titania into the morning.

You know full and well how important that is! Why, until Oberon has given Titania a morning kiss, the Sun cannot rise to wake the Mortals up, on the Earth below."

"Yes!" sang the Bluebirds from the trees. "Even we, the singing choir of Larks and Thrushes are not allowed to sing in chorus, till after the Royal Morning-Kiss."

And so I waited until Oberon, King of all Fairy-Folk, Elves, Gnomes, Nymphs and kind, had laid out the bed of Bluebell petals and then, calling his beautiful Queen, Titania, to lie gently on the bed, he bent to her and kissed her into the morning.

As he did this, I watched the golden ball of Sun rise to the heavens, lighting up the world far below and I heard the happy cries of the Mortals as they arose from their beds.

Then the birds, the Bluebirds, along with Larks and Thrushes, all began to sing, sending up colours of blue and white, to light up the sky.

It was magical and I felt the joy of the Mortals below as they also began to sing.

"You may speak to his Majesty, once the morning procession has finished. Join in at the front." said the Woodpecker.

I joined in the procession, behind the woodland Pixies, who blew trumpets and horns, while giggling Fairies, with tambourines, flutes and bell-triangles, mingled and danced, as birds of all colours, flew and sang above us.

We all followed the King and Queen, as they walked, hand in hand, between bowing trees, till they reach the Grove Of Peace and sat on thrones of sun-kissed gold.

"This is Pucker-Up." informed the Woodpecker, puffing up his green chest, extending his wings.

I walked forward and bowed low, so that Oberon held up his hand. The band ceased to play, the birds falling silent as I began to speak.

"Hail, to a very sweet morning, your Majesties." I said.

THE CHATTERING WOODPECKER

"Hail to you, Pucker-Up." said Oberon, gesturing to the Woodpecker, to fetch me a chair to sit on.

I sat before the King and Queen.

"As you will know, Your Majesties." I began. "I am Pucker-Up, known as the Turner of Good Fortune and Speaker for the Kiss-Kids Clan.

Both, Oberon and Titania nodded, for they knew of me.

"This morning." I continued. "I have a sad tale to report and it is of utmost importance that you help us."

Titania leaned forward, her face concerned.

"Speak on, Pucker-Up." she said kindly.

"As you will know." I continued. "The Kiss-Kids Clan are the holders of the Kiss-Diamond, the light of all love for the world of the Mortals. With much sadness, this morning, I have to report that the Kiss-Diamond has been stolen."

There was silence at this news, then everyone starting talking at once, concerned voices, so that Oberon held his hand up for silence, his face very stern.

"Who has done this?" he demanded.

"I am not sure, your Majesty… Although one of the Kiss-Kids, called Dance-Along, found a Crow's feather by the side of the Rosemary Bush, where the Kiss-Diamond was cushioned." I said.

There was a silence when I said that, because everyone knew, the only ones to wear robes made from Crow's feathers were the Dark-Clan, a tribe of

Satyrs and Pandemonium's, or so we all thought, for no-one had actually seen a member of the Dark-Clan and, having never seen one, we all supposed them to be evil natives who lived to the west of World's End.

"What shall we do? What shall we do?" began to cry the Owl, so that others took up the cry.

"We must get the Kiss-Diamond back!" exclaimed the Woodpecker, above the din.

Oberon called for silence once more.

"We have to get it back." he said. "Else the Mortals will not be allowed to see the Moon-Queen rise in her silver ball, nor the Love-Rain fall, to give the Mortals their colours. We must act right away." he said, rising from his throne.

Everyone quickly agreed, shouting… "We must get the Kiss-Diamond back!"

Holding Titania's hand, Oberon led the party down, through the Pearly Trees and into the Purple Grasslands of the Gophers, up and over the Ginger-Tops, till they reached the lands of the Kiss-Kids. The lands of the Kiss-Kids were grey and solemn, there were no sounds of crying, just a silence of gloom.

"You see, your Majesty." I cried, spreading out my arms. "Do you see how the land lies? That is because there is no reflection of the Sun from the Kiss-Diamond, to make the Love-Fruit grow!

And, as you know, without the Love-Fruit, the Kiss-Kids can't squeeze out the juice as Sky-Rain, on the lands of the Mortals, to light up the beautiful colours of the plants and trees, that paint the landscape." I cried.

Those who heard my words began to cry, holding their heads in their hands.

"Then, without such beauty." I continued. " The Kiss-Kids cannot cry Happy-Tears, which become pearls, which they give to the Moon-Queen, to light up her silver ball as she floats across the Mortals sky at night… And if the Mortals cannot see her Moon-Ball light the heavens, then the Mortals cannot love."

Titania listened in sadness then, she too, burst into tears, so all around began to sob and wail even louder.

Oberon put his hands in the air and called for silence, then asked if anyone had any ideas.

"What shall we do?" he asked.

"This calls for volunteers, to go to the lands of the Dark-Clan and rescue the Kiss-Diamond." shouted the Owl.

"Yes! Yes!" all began to shout and clap their hands.

"Then I call for brave and stout hearts among you. Who will volunteer, to go into the lands of the Dark-Clan and bring the Kiss-Diamond back?" asked Oberon.

For a while, all became silent.

"As Turner of Good Fortune for the Kiss-Kids, I will go!" I shouted, standing up,

"But you can't fly! You're just a Gnome, a Kiss-Kid and we all know Kiss-Kids can't fly!" exclaimed the Woodpecker, afraid to volunteer and jealous of my brave heart.

"Pucker-Up can fly on my back!" shouted the Golden-Eagle, landing on the ground beside me.

I mounted astride its back and, with a spread of its huge golden wings, he took me swiftly up into the sky, then hovered over the assembly.

"You see." I called. "I am ready to go, with the Golden-Eagle carrying me! Who else will come with us?"

"I am ready to go with Pucker-Up and the Golden Eagle!" cried the Woodpecker, afraid to be left out, now puffing out its chest in a show of courage.

"Is there anyone else?" I called.

"I really think you should have another, one who has royal power and diplomacy." said Owl, looking directly at Oberon.

"Yes, your Majesty… You must come with us!" shouted the Woodpecker.

Oberon smiled as he acknowledged those who cheered and sang in praise.

"And I shall go alongside my dear King." said Titania, taking hold of Oberon's hand.

"Then it is settled." said the Woodpecker, continuing… "We will travel together, my Lord Oberon and Titania, Her Royal Highness. Then will come myself, followed by Pucker-Up, astride the Golden-Eagle."

"Don't be so hasty, Woodpecker." cried the Owl, his eyes wide and round with wisdom. "Do you know how long you have got, to rescue the Kiss-Diamond, before the land of the Mortals fall into a Forever-Sleep?"

"Quick!" shouted Blue-Fairy, poking her head out from the petals of the blue rose. "Ask the Dandelion-Clock how long you have got."

Oberon stooped and picked up the Dandelion-Clock and began to blow.

The King of all the Woodland Folk blew twelve times, each puff removing some of the white seed pods, till there was none left to the Dandelion's head. Titania plucked a yellow Cowslip from the earth and, taking the Dandelion from Oberon, deftly made the Cowslip into a hat, which she placed on the Dandelion's head, to keep it warm.

"We have twelve fairy hours to rescue the Kiss-Diamond." I said, then, had another thought.

"Supposing we can't get back in time." I asked.

"What will happen if the Moon-Queen does not receive any Tear-Pearls. She will not be able to rise in the night sky, so the Mortals cannot love?"

There was silence for a while as we all thought hard, then the Owl hooted, so that he was heard.

"I suggest we find the brightest bird, to take the place of the Kiss-Diamond, so that it reflects the Sun and lights up the fields where the Love-Fruit grows and the Kiss-Kids can collect the Love-Fruit. They can then squeeze the fruit to rain colours down on the land of the Mortals. And they can cry Happy-Tears to make the pearls for the Moon-Queen."

"You realise." said the Woodpecker. "If we cannot

get back in the twelve hours, then the chosen bird will turn to stone."

"But we must try, we must get the Kiss-Diamond back, for the sake of the Kiss-Kids and the Mortals, who have faith in all Fairy-Folk." I said.

"Well, I would be the most obvious choice." offered Woodpecker. "For I have the most colourful body, with my deep red head, green chest, blue body and yellow wings, also with a bravest of hearts!" he cried, then considered. "But I have to lead the way, to keep my King Oberon and his dear Queen Titania safe." he finished.

"Well, the Golden-Eagle cannot stay." I stated. "Even though his colour will be all the more golden with the Sun's rays. But he has to carry me on his back."

"What about the Peacock?" hooted the Owl. "Surely the Peacock, with its beautiful eyes is the most colourful bird of all."

Woodpecker tutted with impatience, before saying… "Don't you know the Peacock spends most of its time looking into the Glass-Trees, admiring its tail…It's too vain. And, besides, the Peacock has to stay here, because the Dell-Fairies need the eyes on its tail, to give to the new-born babies."

"Then, perhaps we might ask the Humming-Bird." stated Oberon. "Surely the Humming-Bird is the most beautiful of birds, it has the most beautiful iridescent colours, which light up the world as it sips the nectar from inside the flowers."

"Most true, your Royal Highness." agreed the Owl. "But what happens if none of you come back in time, later than twelve fairy hours. The Humming-Bird will turn to stone and then it cannot collect the nectar, which Mortals need for their porridge in the mornings?"

Again, the Woodpecker tutted, showing disdain. "Look, you silly Owl." he exclaimed. "If we don't get back in time from this most dangerous mission, then the Mortals will not have a Forever-Time, which means they will not want sweet nectar for their porridge!"

"Please, dear friends… Let us not have any disagreements." broke in Oberon. "Let us just ask the Humming-Bird if he will take the place of the Kiss-Diamond, till we get back."

"Will the Humming-Bird come forward!" hooted the Owl loudly.

The Humming-Bird came shyly forward on quick fluttering wings.

"Dear, sweet, Humming-Bird." said Titania. "Will you stay, cushioned by the Rosemary-Bush and allow your body to light the fields of Love-Fruit up, so the Kiss-Kids can harvest the Love-Fruit?"

"I will be happy to serve the Mortals." the Humming-Bird bravely agreed, its small body shining all colours of the rainbow as its wings flashed to the Sun.

The Humming-Bird lay quietly, settling itself in the Rosemary-Bush. The Sun shone brightly, its rays bouncing in reflected glory from the shimmering iridescence of the Humming-Bird, so that it lit up the whole of the Love-Fields, showing the Love-Fruit, which hung in bright red lusciousness from the fruit bushes.

With shouts of joy and clapping their hands, the Kiss-Kids came tumbling out from their Nesting-Houses, beginning to collect the fruit in baskets, their tears starting to fall as soft silver pearl-drops. All the Fairy-Folk cheered loudly, calling out in praise of the brave Humming-Bird, who had put itself in danger, of being turned to stone, for the sake of the Mortals on earth below.

"Now, we must hurry." said Oberon. "For we only have the twelve fairy hours."

"Then… We are ready!" shouted Woodpecker.

"Wait." commanded Oberon, the thought suddenly striking him. "Where exactly are the Dark-Lands?"

Woodpecker, who had started to fly into the sky, now came back down, so quickly that he came to earth with a bang.

Everyone stopped talking as they all looked from one to the other.

"Well?" asked Oberon. "What way shall we go?"

"You go to the Sparkling-River and ask the Otter-Folk." came a small voice.

Everyone turned, hearing the voice of the Tyree-Mouse, its whiskered face poking out from a Coconut Bush.

"I know where the Sparkling-River is!" cried the

Golden-Eagle.

Everyone began to cheer the Tyree-Mouse, so that the little creature blushed even redder than its body, before quickly popping back into the bush.

"One more thing, your Royal Majesty." said the Owl, facing Oberon.

"What is it now?" demanded the Woodpecker, anxious to be off. The Owl ignored the Woodpecker with a grand gesture, talking directly to Oberon.

"Would it not be better if your Majesty and the Queen became Masked. If you left our lands Un-Masked, you may get recognised by the bad Terror-Skins and the like, who will take you away."

"The Owl is right." I said. "Let you and the Queen become Masked, so no-one will recognize you both, till you want others to know who you are."

Oberon took off the opal ring from the middle finger of his right hand and put it on the middle finger of his left hand. Immediately, his face and body underwent a change, so that he looked just like one of the Fairy-Togs, those who worked on the Dragonfly farm.

"Do as I did, dear Queen Titania." said Oberon, so that Titania changed the ring to her left hand and took on the mask and shape of another ordinary Fairy-Tog.

"Now we are ready!" shouted the Golden-Eagle and I felt the powerful flight muscles of the Golden-Eagle tense beneath me and was soon lifted up, high into the air and speeding away to the West.

"Follow me!" shouted the Golden-Eagle.

Below, the crowd waved upwards and I heard the sounds of the cheers grow fainter as we flew, with Oberon, Titania and Woodpecker following behind. It seemed as if the Golden-Eagle flew to the roof of nature's sky, flashing against the Sun, while I held on tight, clutching at the neck feathers with all my might.

"Look!" exclaimed the Golden-Eagle, suddenly swooping down, so that I felt my stomach turn a somersault and I held on even more grimly.

As we approached the Tor-Mountain, I saw an outcrop near its top and from a hole in its centre, there spewed a shower of water which had all the colours of the rainbow, arching out and falling till it splashed itself in a sort of firework display, forming a pool of paintwork far below.

"That's the fount of the Sparkling-River." said the Golden-Eagle. "See how it begins to run from the source-pool? We have to follow its source, between the mountains, till we reach the place where the Otter-Folk live."

From above, we could see the river as it ran, like a silver snake, through tall mountains and tall trees. Now, as we flew lower, we could see white tips riding the waves, while the noise of cheering and whistles seemed to come from hidden cracks and crevices within the rocks and hidden holes in the trees.

PUCKER - UP ON THE EAGLE

"What is that noise?" I called.

"I can tell you." shouted Woodpecker, flying even lower, so that he seemed to skip along the waves. "It is a sight to see!" he shouted, flying back up to join us.

"Those white tips down there are tiny white horses, they are racing along the tips of the waves, each faster than the other, while the cheers and whistles are from Junior-Crackers, tiny Water-Voles and Mice, who work to keep the river-banks and forests clean. From what I heard between the shouts was that the race is always run on Sugary-Tuesdays, which happens to be today."

"And what does the winner get?" I asked, as we flew onwards, leaving the racing and cheers behind.

"I have no idea." replied Woodpecker. "I suppose we can always ask the Otter-Folk, if ever we see them."

"What is that smoke?" said Golden-Eagle, its sharp eyes catching sight of a spiral of smoke coming from behind a banking of bushes.

We flew on, turning right, where the Sparkling-River banked and Golden-Eagle stopped, to hover in the air, so Oberon, Titania and Woodpecker came to a mid-air halt, hovering beside us.

There, on the bank of the river were stretched out six Otter-Folk, lazing on their backs, each with a small white clay pipe jutting from its mouth, from out which spiralled bubbles of smoke.

"Hallo!" shouted Woodpecker, diving down at breakneck speed.

Suddenly, becoming aware of Woodpecker's dive and shouting, the Otter-Folk screamed in alarm, the pipes falling from their mouths as they jumped up and all dived into the river, leaving only silent ripples which widened out into pools of liquid colour.

Landing on the bank, we all stared down at the water, seeing only some rising bubbles and hearing loud popping noises.

"Now what shall we do?" asked Titania, angrily looking at Woodpecker. "If it had not been for your shouting, Woodpecker." she said. "The Otter-Folk would not have left. Now we cannot ask them where the Dark-Lands are!"

"It's not my fault if those Otter-Folk were cowards, who were not as brave as I am." replied Woodpecker.

"Now, let's not argue." said Oberon, disliking rows and disputes. "What we have to do is for one of us to dive into the water, to see if we can find and talk to them."

"Well, I certainly can't dive into the river." said Woodpecker. "I'm a bird and if I get my feathers wet, I will never fly again... And that goes for the Golden-Eagle." he finished, bringing in the Golden-Eagle, to back up his statement.

"Of course, you are right, Woodpecker." soothed Oberon. "And it goes without saying, that the Golden-Eagle cannot dive in, for the same reason."

"Why are you looking at me?" I asked, suddenly

aware that Woodpecker was staring at me with wide eyes.

"Because, Pucker-Up, I do believe it's your turn to do something. I have led the way so far, while the Golden-Eagle has carried you on his back. And we cannot expect our royal King and Queen to dive into the river, for fear they may never come out again." Suddenly, Woodpecker turned to look at the others, before turning back to me with a sly look on his face.

"Unless, of course." he said. "You're scared!"

I had never been so insulted in all my life… Me, Pucker-Up, the Turner of Good Fortune… Accused of being scared!

"I will go into the river." decided Oberon, seeing my face turn red with anger and offering to dive in, before I could have an argument with Woodpecker.

"No, your Majesty." I said quickly. "Woodpecker is right. I have done nothing to help yet and so I will dive in."

Saying this and not waiting for anyone to speak, I went to the bank and, holding my nose, with my eyes closed, I jumped into the river, feeling myself sink.

Holding my breath, I opened my eyes, to behold a swirling mist of brilliant colours, of blues, reds, purples and orange, the blaze of colour so vivid that I could not see an inch in front of me.

My mouth opened, so that I swallowed some of the water and, struggling back to the surface, I spluttered out some of the swallowed colour and climbed onto the bank.

Oberon, Titania, Golden-Eagle and Woodpecker knelt around me, slapping my back till I had brought up the rest of the water.

Gasping, I told them about the swirling mists below the surface, so that we all lapsed into silence, wondering what we could do.

The silence was broken by the sound of music, which came from the bank opposite. As we looked, we saw a most remarkable sight, for, coming into view was the sight of a Cat-Fish dancing with a Dog-Fish, waltzing together to a tune, played on pan-pipes by a small beautiful Angelfish.

"I'll shout over and ask them how we find the Otter-Folk." said the Woodpecker.

Titania held a hand up.

"No, Woodpecker. That last time you shouted, you frightened the Otter-Folk away. I will ask and so, please stay quiet." she said.

Woodpecker muttered under his breath, then stopped when he saw Oberon give him a stern look.

Meanwhile, Titania had walked to the edge of the river bank and sweetly called out… "Excuse me, over there!"

The music stopped, the Angelfish hiding behind the dancers, staring out with frightened eyes.

"What do you want?" answered the Dog-Fish, still holding onto his dancing partner.

"And hurry up!" snapped the Cat-Fish. "It's our Waltz-Love dance time and we don't like being stopped." she finished.

"We want to know if you can tell us how to speak to the Otter-Folk?" Titania called back.

"What do you want to ask the Otter-Folk?" demanded the Dog-Fish, starting to dance with his partner again.

"We want to know where the Dark-Lands are?" Titania answered.

"I've never heard of them… And if I don't know of the Dark-Lands, then the Otter-Folk won't certainly have heard of them!" returned the Dog-Fish.

The Cat-Fish let go of her partner and began to dance on her own. The Angelfish put the pan-pipes to her lips and began to play.

"Don't be so ignorant!" shouted Woodpecker, stamping up and down the bank. "If I could swim, then we would not even have to ask the likes of you!"

"Don't listen to him." implored Titania, pushing Woodpecker so that he nearly fell over.

"Can't you just please tell us how to reach the Otter-Folk?" she begged.

Both, the Dog-Fish and the Cat-Fish had stopped dancing, outraged by the Woodpecker's outburst. But now, as they heard Titania's pleading, they started to dance again. Then the Dog-Fish gently patted the Angelfish on the head, saying…

"Just swim down to the Otter-Folk and advise them that there is a party who wish to see them. Now hurry up and then come back to play the Pan-Pipes."

The Angelfish put her Pan-Pipes down and nodded,

before diving into the river.

We all stared down into the water and waited. It seemed ages before, suddenly, the Angelfish popped up, her head gleaming as colours from the water cascaded from her.

Swimming close to our side of the bank, she said…

"I have just spoken to Officer-Crab, who has instructed me to tell you that you will have to dive right down to the bottom of the river and report to him."

"We can't do that." I said, alarmed. "If we go right down to the bottom, we will drown. We cannot breathe under water."

"Of course you can." smiled the Angelfish. "You simply have to have faith. You will be able to breathe under water, as long as you have faith in yourself. That is the first thing we fish learn at school, to have faith, that we won't drown under water."

"That's right." said Titania. "No-one can fly, not even Fairy-Folk, unless they have faith and that goes for all birds as well."

"That's true." said the Golden-Eagle and Woodpecker, together.

"Then I have faith!" I exclaimed. "I have faith in justice and the need to bring back the Kiss-Diamond, for the love of the Mortals. You may all stand there, if you like but I am diving in!"

"We have faith, don't we, my dear Lord Oberon?" asked Titania, to which the King of all Fairy-Folk kissed her, then said… "We shall all dive in and meet this Officer-Crab!"

"May Golden-Eagle and I wait here, on this river bank till you come back?" implored Woodpecker, "You must know we will lose our flight if our wings get wet."

"Of course, Woodpecker." replied Oberon in an understanding way. "You both have been very brave to come this far and we will be grateful if you both wait here, till we get back and then help us return to our own lands of the Flower-Ring."

"Let us hold hands and jump into the river." I said. "And may we have such a strong faith, that we can breathe underwater."

"Thank you for your help!" called Titania to the Cat-Fish and Dog-Fish on the other bank. The Angelfish had swum back, to pick up the Pan-Pipes, to begin playing, so that the Fish-Folk danced their Love-Waltz, taking no more notice of us.

"Are we ready?" I shouted and, clasping hands with Oberon and Titania, we all jumped into the river.

I felt the water cover me, filling up over my head and I kept my eyes closed for an Ever-Time, before slowly opened them.

We had all sunk beyond the mist of colours and now I saw that the water was like liquid glass, so clear that I could see for miles.

"Isn't it beautiful!" exclaimed Titania, letting go my hand and kissing Oberon on the cheek.

"It's so clear!" exclaimed Oberon, now opening his

eyes, looking around at the shoals of striped Bee-Fish, who played around us with huge darting eyes. The thought suddenly struck me. We were miles under water, yet we were breathing and even talking, as if we were on dry land.

When I spoke my thoughts to Oberon and Titania, they both looked amazed at first, then laughed in delight as they swam in circles, touching the giggling Bee-Fish, who swam between their fingers.

"Halt! Who goes there?" demanded an angry voice, so loud that the Bee-Fish sped away, their yellow and black striped scales changing to a frightened pale white.

We had come to the bottom of the river, our feet sinking into a soft bed of silver sand. Before us stood a most fearsome sight, that of a giant Crab, dressed in a suit of armour, his face an angry red, while his eyes stood out on stalks.

I began to shake, afraid of this Officer-Crab, although both Oberon and Titania showed no fear at all, which gave me the courage to stand up straight.

"What is the password?" demanded Officer-Crab, as one of his eyes swivelled around, to glare back at the rows of soldier Crabs and Crustaceans, who were formed in lines of attention, the larger Crabs moving down till, at the end of the line, stood some Prawns, then Shrimps.

"Stand still!" shouted Officer-Crab, without turning. The eye swivelled back, so that both eyes glared at us again as he asked of us… "Well? What is the password?"

"We don't know any password." said Oberon.

"No password!" spluttered Officer-Crab. "You can't come here without a password!"

"Please… Can we speak to the Otter-Folk?" begged Titania.

Officer-Crab stared at Titania, his eyes now enlarged on their stalks.

"How dare you speak to me without permission!" he exclaimed, drawing his sword from its scabbard.

"I'm sorry." apologized Titania.

"Too late!" shouted Officer-Crab. "Order of the guard, take these spies to the guardroom!"

Two of the Crabs drew their swords and stood beside us.

"Quick march!" ordered one of the guards in a high voice.

"It's madness!" I shouted, most angry that High Royalty, that Oberon and Titania, should be marched away like common criminals.

"Halt!" suddenly shouted Officer-Crab, hurrying to catch us up and standing before us.

"Why didn't you say the password when I first asked you?" he demanded, his eyes seeming to sink back as the stalks detracted.

"Password?" I said, not understanding.

Officer-Crab began to get angry again, his face getting crabby as he glared at me.

"Don't make out you did not know the password was 'Madness'!" he shouted.

"Forgive him, Officer-Crab." said Titania, sweetly. "He was testing you and your troops, making sure you were on your guard."

"I see." said Officer-Crab, somewhat mollified. "But don't do it again, otherwise I might not be so forgiving."

We thanked him for his forgiving nature and he dismissed the two guards, ordering them back into line, before asking us to follow him down the line, inspecting the troops as we went.

"Present Arms!" Officer-Crab shouted, so the soldiers formed two lines, holding their swords up, to form an archway, so we had to duck even smaller as we reached the prawns and then the shrimps, further down the line.

"I will protect you till we reach the Castle! Follow me… Quick march!" said Officer-Crab, saluting.

The castle was a giant Conch shell, turned up on its end so the twirly-whirly top fired itself up, losing itself into a blaze of colours.

The castle was walled around by green Sea-Urchins, which left big gaps as they waved about in the river's currents.

We were led by Officer-Crab who marched us around the walls till we arrived at the gates.

"I will leave you here, at the gates of the courtyard. The Tri-Courtesans will take you into the castle… If ever you get there." said Officer-Crab, saluting us again and raising his sword, before turning about smartly and marching off.

"I wonder what he meant?" said Titania. "What did he mean… If we ever get there?"

Before Oberon or I could answer, out through the gates came three strange half-animal, half fish-beings, all arguing at the top of their voices.

"I say I'm right, though I'm not sure!" argued the Bull-Fish, snorting.

"You might be right, though I might have a different opinion, so we are both right!" exclaimed the Ram-Fish.

"Well, one of us has to be right but which one? We really have to make a decision!" joined in the Goat-Fish.

We waited patiently as the three argued as to who should make a decision. Then Oberon coughed, before saying… "Excuse me. I wonder if you can explain the problem, perhaps I can make a decision for you."

The three creatures stopped arguing, to turn to look at us.

"Are you going to explain or shall I?" queried the Bull-Fish.

"I don't mean to head-butt in but who is going to decide who will explain the problem?" interjected the Ram-Fish.

"Well, let's ask these folk here to decide who will explain the problem." said the Goat-Fish, pointing at us.

At that, the three began to argue all over again.

"Those Tri-Courtesans can never make their minds

up." said a sudden high-pitched voice behind us and we turned to see a Hermit-Crab, walking towards us, carrying a blue-painted shell on his back. As he spoke, the lid of the shell slipped down over his eyes, so that he puffed, pushing the shell up on his back.

"Sorry about that." he said. "I just got this new shell and it's still a bit too big for me. But I shall grow into it." he finished.

"I wonder if you might take us into the Castle, to speak to the Otter-Folk?" asked Titania, in a most charming voice.

The Hermit-Crab giggled, before saying, "Well, you certainly won't get those three to take you into the Castle. Just look at them, always arguing. That's because they all have horns on their heads, you see. So they are always on the Horns of a Dilemma."

"Ah! Now that explains it." I said as we started to follow the Hermit-Crab through the courtyard and up the flight of marble steps.

"Yes." said the Hermit-Crab, as he reached for a large iron knocker, which hung from strands of seaweed and, with a big swing, knocked on the door. "The thing is…" he went on to explain. "If they only had one horn on their heads, they would have been Unique-Horns and, as we all know, Unique-Horns are very special folk indeed. However, those Tri-Courtesans are not so special."

A grill in the gate opened up and we were inspected by a large and unblinking eye.

"Password!" came the demand.

"It's Madness!" I replied.

The door was opened by an Octopus, a rubbery yellow thing covered all over in purple spots, who then stood back, allowing us through, while scratching at his neck with all its tentacles.

"Through that hallway and turn half-left, up the stairs and the next door on the right." said the Octopus, before any of us could speak.

One of his tentacles pointed the way and we began to walk through the hallway.

"Just a moment, come back here!" called the Octopus, his huge eye staring at us.

"What do you want, what exactly is your business here?" he asked.

"We want to talk to the Otter-Folk." replied Oberon as we came back from where we had started.

"Then why didn't you say that in the first place?" demanded the agitated Octopus.

"You will have to take the right-hand side of the staircase, into the adjoining alcove and follow your nose till you see a pearly sort of door… That's it, the Otter-Folk are in there." he finished.

We left the Octopus, who was turning purple and waving his tentacles about in a mass of confusion, following the directions and, finding the pearly door, Oberon knocked, lightly at first, then louder when no-one answered, even though we could plainly hear laughter and loud talking.

Titania turned the handle and opened the door.

THE OCTOPUS

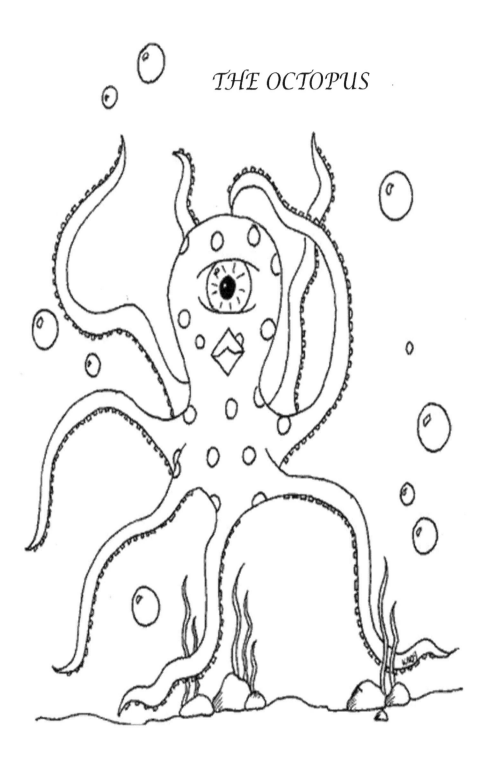

"Come in and take a pipe!" shouted a voice as we entered.

This was followed by shouts of welcome and many white clay pipes being thrown at us.

In the large room were a dozen or more Otter-Folk, stretched out on sofas, each smoking one of the clay pipes, from which a constant stream of bubbled smoke belched out and ballooned themselves up into the ceiling.

The bubbles were being gathered in large nets by groups of pink Puffer-Fish and taken out through a round hole in the centre of the ceiling.

"Who are you and what do you want?" inquired one of the Otter-Folk, putting down his pipe and rising from the sofa.

Oberon stepped forward.

"Are you the King?" he asked, lowering his eyes from the actions of the Puffer-Fish above.

"We are all Kings here. No-one is above the other, although I can blow more bubbles than all the others. So I suppose you can call me the Bubble-King."

"I am Oberon, King of all Fairies and Woodland Folk. And this is Titania, my Queen." offered Oberon, drawing Titania to his side.

"Piffle!" exclaimed another of the Otter-Folk, rising from his sofa and laying his pipe aside.

"I have seen Oberon. Many ages in time ago, I was helped by the Fairy-Folk, when I was imprisoned by a Harridan. Oberon sent his people to rescue me and I saw him then. You are not Oberon!"

Oberon removed the Mask ring from the middle finger of his left hand and un-masked himself by placing the ring on the middle finger of his right hand.

Bidding Titania to do the same, Oberon stood, tall and proud, as the real King of all the Fairies, as did Titania, who had also un-masked herself and stood as her Regal Highness.

"Ah, King Oberon, you have to forgive me. I now see it is you, as I see it is your fair Queen, Titania." said the Otter, bowing low.

"It is right, as the best Bubble-Blower." remarked the newly found Bubble-King. "That I welcome you to our castle and request that you all lay upon a sofa and smoke a few rounds of all-colour Sea-Weed, as a show of good intelligence."

Saying this, the Bubble-King clapped his hands and ordered some of the Puffer-Fish to come down from their duties and bring more sofas and clay pipes. Oberon smiled.

"While I thank you, for your very kind offer." he said. "I am afraid we must desist from smoking the pipes of all-colour Sea-Weed. We are forbidden by the Health-Ministries, to smoke. It is understood that the smoke pollutes the air of the dear lands of the Mortals, so they cannot breathe." he finished.

This brought gales of laughter as the Otter-Folk rolled from their sofas and onto the floor, while the Puffer-Fish came down, to flit between the laughing Otter-Folk, joining in with their high-pitched giggles.

Oberon looked nonplussed, looking first at Titania, then at me. I shrugged, I had no idea what the Otter-Folk were laughing at, or why the Puffer-Fish circled our heads, still giggling.

Eventually, the laughter stopped as the Otter-Folk reclaimed their sofas and, relighting their pipes, they began to puff hard so that the bubbles rose once more to the ceiling, while the Puffer-Fish began to net them.

"You must forgive us." said the Bubble-King. "But our bubbles do not pollute the air of the Mortals. Do you see the Puffer-Fish…Up there." he continued, indicating, by jabbing up with his pipe.

I craned my neck, staring up at the fish as they worked.

"They are collecting the bubbles we make and then take them to the Transformation-Depot. It's there that the smoke in the bubbles is transformed into coloured Mist-Bubbles and released into the river. How do you think we get such a lovely colour to our water? That's why it is called the Sparkling-River. Without such colours, we cannot grow the all-colour Sea-Weed in the first place… And the water is what puts colour into our lives."

"In that case, my friend, we shall be delighted to lay on a sofa and puff your clay pipes." said Oberon, making his way, to lie stretched out on one of the sofas.

Titania and I followed Oberon's example, laying out

and taking the white clay pipe that was offered. The all-coloured Sea-Weed tasted a bit scented and seemed to have a sleepy effect, that I was not sure

whether I dreamed or not as I drifted through a field of pink, white and scarlet carnations.

I was not aware of any bubbles coming from my pipe, though I could see, through the carnations, the stream of bubbles which followed a trail from the pipes of Oberon and Titania, floating up and being collected by the chasing Puffer-Fish.

Perhaps I had fallen asleep, I was not sure, though it seemed ages since we had arrived at the castle. I jumped to my feet, alarmed into action, aware that we had only twelve Fairy-Hours, to rescue the Kiss-Diamond.

"Sire! Your Majesty! Dear Queen! Please wake up!" I begged, shaking each in turn, till eventually, they opened their eyes and brought themselves back down to earth.

The room was empty, though we could hear sounds of plates and cutlery being used in the room next door.

Opening the door, we saw the Otter-Folk, seated on the backs of Tortoises, before a long table, made of old oak planks, salvaged from a shipwreck. On the table was laid a glorious feast, of piled fruit and jelly.

The Otter-Folk were filling their plates and eating as fast as they could go, some even feeding each other, others throwing the jelly, so we had to duck as the jelly flew across the room.

"Excuse me!" called Oberon.

"Ah! So you have woken up?" said the Bubble-King, throwing a huge blancmange at us.

"Eat it! Eat it!" shouted the rest, before continuing to eat again.

"What about the presents?" suddenly called one of the Otter-Folk, the jelly and fruit spilling out from his mouth.

"Yes." said the Bubble-King, standing up and clapping his hands.

A Puffer-Fish appeared.

"Bring the present for King Oberon!" ordered the Bubble-King and waited till the Puffer-Fish reappeared, carrying a small box, covered in seed-pearls.

Taking the box and offering it to Oberon, he said, "Open it, if you please."

Oberon took the box and gently opened it, to see, lying in the box, on a red satin cushion, a tiny brightly coloured Squid.

"Thank you for the present." said Oberon, closing the box.

"Thank you! Thank you! That's not a present, that's a living Life-Saver!" shouted the Bubble-King. "Tie the box to your belt, King Oberon, tie it tight!"

Oberon frowned, not used to being ordered about, although he tied the box to his belt, not seeming to notice the different colours the box seemed to change into, as if the box itself was alive.

"Now where's my present?" suddenly demanded the Bubble-King.

Then, seeing Oberon's blank face said, "It's only right! I give you a present and you give me one back. It's only right, isn't it?" demanded the Bubble-King, this time turning to appeal to the rest of the Otter-Folk.

The Otter-Folk responded loudly, shouting out, "It's only fair. If you give a present, you get one back!"

"But I haven't brought you a present." said Oberon, holding out empty hands.

"Well that's not fair!" exclaimed the Bubble-King.

"Well, you can't leave here till you either give me a Present-Return, or till you have smoked fifty-five clay pipes of all-colour Sea-Weed. Now, have you a Present-Return?"

Oberon scratched at his neck, not sure what to say. We knew we could not stay that length of time, in fact, we could not leave till we knew exactly where the Dark-Lands were and only the Otter-Folk knew where that was.

"I have a Present-Return for you." said Titania, standing in front of the Bubble-King.

"You do? Then where is it? Can you give me it now?" asked the Bubble-King.

Oberon said nothing, though he threw a puzzled look, first at Titania, then at me. I shook my head, for I had no idea what Titania was up to.

"Fetch me a sheet of plaited Seaweed and a Cuttlefish." asked Titania.

The Bubble-King clapped loudly, commanding the Puffer-Fish to do as Titania asked.

The rest of the Otter-Folk began to crowd round, nudging each other and forgetting the piled-up food. The Puffer-Fish returned and presented Titania with the plaited Seaweed and the Cuttlefish.

Taking a pinewood nut from one of her hair-grips, Titania opened the nut and drew out a tiny golden pen, then, squeezing the Cuttlefish, so that it squirted ink, she dipped the pen into the ink and began writing on the plaited seaweed.

"There!" she exclaimed, having finished writing and handing the sheet of Sea-Weed to the waiting Bubble-King.

"Here is your Present-Return." she said.

The Bubble-King climbed onto the table and, waving the sheet of Sea-Weed, called for quiet, so that he might read out his Present-Return to the others.

His voice was loud and clear as he read…

"WHAT IS LOVE?
The mind of the lover pays no mind
Said the wise old owl as he sat in a tree
Love's controlled by emotion, I think you'll find
And feelings are blind to thought you see

So the heart rules the head is what you say
Said the donkey on the ground, playing a game
How can one think about love's state of play
Don't instinctive thought come into the frame

Thinking ain't instinctive said the nosey hare
It's derived from all your senses, a total bind
So what the eye don't see, it ain't really there
If you can't see love then love ain't on your mind

This here love thing then, what's it all about
Chattered squirrel, sitting up there high above
Can't smell it, see or hear it, nothing to shout
Excepting its heartfelt, this thing called love

But it's still a strange thing to be reckoned with
Said the wise old owl as he flapped his wings
I'm just glad I have a heart and love to give
So what is love, if your mind's on other things?"

The Bubble-King rolled up the page and held it to
his chest, beginning to cry.
"That's a most beautiful Present-Return." he cried.
"Read it again!" shouted one of the Otter-Folk and
his demand was immediately taken up by the rest.
Once again, the Bubble-King read out the poem in a
loud and emotional voice.
"I don't understand it. What does it mean?" asked
the Otter, who had demanded a second reading.
The Bubble-King called for silence, holding up his
clay pipe.
"It's a sacred poem!" he exclaimed. "The reason you
don't understand it is because only those with the
sacred knowledge can understand what it means.
And, because we cannot understand the secret

meaning, you have to accept it is truly a beautiful
Present-Return and very true."

All the Otter-Folk began clapping and hailing the poem as a most beautiful work and the very height of truth.

Having finished with their eating, the Otter-Folk left the room, returning to the first room and, settling back onto their sofas, they began to relight and smoke their clay pipes with an added vigour.

"Excuse me." began Oberon. "May we ask our question now, the reason why we are here?"

The Otter-Folk lowered their pipes, so the smoke-bubbles ceased to float upwards, which caused the Puffer-Fish to begin giggling.

"What do you want to know?" asked the Bubble-King.

"We wish to know exactly where the Dark-Lands are, where the Dark-Clan live." replied Oberon.

"I don't know!" said the Bubble-King, laying back and starting to puff on his pipe again.

"Pardon? What do you mean, you don't know?"

I could hear the exasperation in Oberon's voice and chimed in.

"A Tyree-Mouse told us that you knew where the Dark-Lands were." I said.

At this, all the Otter-Folk began laughing, falling from their sofas and rolling around the floor.

Oberon, Titania and I, looked at each other in amazement. Then Oberon raised his voice. "Why are you all laughing?" he asked, now quite angry.

I had never heard Oberon in anger before and his

THE PUFFER FISH

raised voice startled me, as, I'm sure, it did Titania, who stood with her mouth open.

"Don't you know?" spluttered the Bubble-King, wiping his eyes. "The Tyree-Mouse is famous for its lies. That's why it lives underground, so it can undermine the truth!"

We stood, perplexed. What were we to do now?

"Ask Horatio." said the Bubble-King, suddenly, pulling himself back onto his sofa.

"Who is Horatio?" asked Oberon.

"Horatio the Hermit. He's the Crab who keeps changing shells. He keeps storing knowledge in his attic, that's why he needs larger and larger shells, to house his learning. If anyone knows…He will!" answered the Bubble-King, closing his eyes and seeming, now, totally disinterested.

"Where will Horatio be found?" asked Oberon. There was no answer, all the Otter-Folk now engrossed in puffing on their clay pipes, the smoke-bubbles rising thick and fast.

"Pucker-Up… Will you please go and see if you can find Horatio?" asked Titania.

I left the room, retracing my steps, following my nose till I reached the floor below. I found the Octopus writing out proclamations, eight at a time.

"Will you scratch my head?" he asked, as I approached. Seeing my stare, he added, "Can't you see, I'm using all my hands to write these proclamations. I'm trying to think what to write so I need to scratch my head."

"Do you know where I can find Horatio, the Hermit-Crab?" I asked, scratching his head vigorously.
"Ah! That's it." said the Octopus, satisfied with my head-scratching.
"Now I know what to write. Now, what did you want to know?"
I repeated my request and the Octopus began to write, saying, "He will be down at the Shell-Bank, looking for a new home."
"And where might I find the Shell-Bank?" I inquired.
The Octopus stopped writing, its big blue eye wearing a puzzled look.
"If you don't mind." he asked, indicating that he needed his head scratched once more. I did as he requested, scratching his head as hard as I could. He nodded his thanks, before advising…
"Ask the Tri-Courtesans."
I sighed, turning away.
This was getting so ridiculous, no-one seemed to know anything, so that I was going round in circles. I decided not to ask where I might find the Tri-Courtesans. And, even if I found them, I knew they would end up on the Horns of a Dilemma.
Passing out through the door, I skirted past the arguing Tri-Courtesans and wandered down a sandy path which had Cockle shells at even spaces, each bearing the miles to the sea.
I had reached the one which read, 'To the Sea, many, many miles, even more than seven.'

I sat down on the shell, tears beginning to fill my eyes.

I had no idea of the time, or even how long a Fairy-Hour was. Only the Mortals knew about hours and they were so far away.

"What's the matter with you? Have you got sea-salt in your eyes?"

I turned to see a Star-Fish staring at me, changing colours each time it spread its arms and jumped.

"I need to know where the Hermit-Crab, Horatio is." I said, drying my eyes.

"He's down there, three shells along, everyone knows that!" the Star-Fish exclaimed, puffing as its colour changed from red to violet, which caused it to do another Star-Jump.

"Thank you so much." I said, leaving and started to walk further down the path. I had passed another two shells when I heard the high voice of the Hermit-Crab from behind a sand-dune.

"Blast it! When am I going to find a shell which will fit me?"

This was followed by another "Blast it!" as a large Cockle-Shell whizzed over my head.

"Hallo!" I hailed. "Is that you, Horatio?"

Horatio's head popped over the top of the dune, then his body, quite naked of a shell.

"What do you want? Can't you see I am busy?" snapped the impatient Hermit-Crab.

"I need to find out where the Dark-Clan live." I said, adding, "The Otter-Folk said you would know."

"The Dark-Clan?" replied Horatio. "Of course I know where they are. But the knowledge is in my last home and a Boot-Lace Water-Snake has taken root there. That's why I'm looking for another shell." continued Horatio, hefting another shell onto its back and, deciding it was too small and throwing it down onto the sand.

"If I help you remove the Water-Snake, will you tell me where the Dark-Clan live?" I asked.

"If you help me get my house back, not only will I tell you where the Dark-Clan live, I will lead you as far as the Fir-Tree pool." came the answer.

"Thank you, Horatio." I said warmly, feeling at last that I was getting somewhere.

"You're most welcome." said Horatio, now much warmer. "Come, I will show you where my Home-Shell is."

I followed Horatio along a side track and, coming out from between two cracks, I saw the round dome of a purple-dotted shell.

"That's it." said Horatio, pointing. "That's my Home-Shell."

Horatio stood back, then hid behind a rock as I crept forward. Reaching the mouth of the shell, I listened and could hear the echoes of snoring.

"Hallo! Water-Snake!" I shouted loudly, hearing my voice reverberate a thousand times louder as it ran round the inside of the shell.

"What! What is that?"

I heard the hissing voice of the Snake come from

inside the shell and knew I had frightened it with my shouting. Summoning all the breath in my body, I shouted… "If you don't come out, I will shout so loud it will burst your ear-drums!"

My shouting seemed to fill the whole shell with thunder, so loud that the Water-Snake came slithering out, its long green body slithering over the sand in a Zig-Zag line of having Been-Here and Gone.

Horatio came out of hiding, rushing forward to claim his dwelling back, settling the shell on its back and suddenly vanished inside.

"Horatio… Are you there?" I called.

He seemed to be gone for some time and I shook the shell as I became worried.

"Of course I'm here!" exclaimed Horatio, suddenly popping out of the shell, holding a map.

"Here it is." he said, spreading the map out and pointing at a spot which seemed to be covered by Fir-Trees.

"That's where you have to go." he said, pointing at the map, before rolling it up and disappearing back into the shell.

"You said you would lead us to the Fir-Tree pool!" I shouted.

"Did I?" questioned Horatio, his head popping out again. "I must have said that, didn't I? You would not have thought of that on your own, would you?"

I agreed, I would never have thought of saying that and his body came down from the inside of the shell, the shell lifting onto his back and we began to walk back towards the castle.

Oberon and Titania were waiting at the gates of the castle and I introduced them to Horatio, telling them he would be our guide, taking us as far as the Fir-Tree pool.

"Where do we go from here?" asked Oberon.

"Now, that's a simple question." answered Horatio. "We go back from where you came from and start again, everybody knows that!"

I had learned never to argue but to just accept what happened.

"Please lead on, Horatio." I said.

"Wait." said Oberon. "Let us put our Mask-Rings back on our left hands, Titania. We don't want others to recognise us."

We waited till the royal couple had switched ring-fingers, so they had, once again, become unrecognisable, masked as Fairy Togs, then declared themselves ready for the journey.

Horatio took the lead, taking us back along the sandy-bed road, stopping every now and again to examine discarded shells.

"Halt! Who goes there?"

It was Officer-Crab, now all dressed up in a red and yellow uniform, his sword flashing as he raised it.

"It's us, Officer-Crab." I reminded him.

"What's the password." he demanded, seeming not to remember me or my travelling companions at all.

"The password is Madness." I said with a sigh.

"Wrong! It's the wrong word! That was the last password…We have a new one now!" shouted Officer-Crab, waving his sword at us.

"Call out the guard!" he continued to shout. "We have intruders!"

Immediately, the guard came out from behind their rock-fort, lining up, the larger Crabs to the front, behind them came the smaller Crabs, then the Prawns, with the Shrimps hidden to the back.

"More madness!" I exclaimed, as the guard began to advance towards us.

"Halt!" shouted Officer-Crab. "That's the new password… It's More Madness!"

The advancing guard halted and sheaved their swords.

"We need you to help us get through the Deep-Cut, to where the Fir-Tree pool is." said Horatio, coming out from behind Titania.

"The Deep-Cut?" quizzed Officer-Crab, his eyes piercing on their stalks, looking at each of us in turn.

"Will you take us there?" I asked in a very polite voice.

"I'll have to think about that." replied Officer-Crab, giving my request some thought, before replying, "You know it is very dangerous, those rascals, the Mussels and Whelks live in the Deep-Cut and we are at war with them. If we go there, you will have to help us fight them."

"Of course we will fight alongside you." said Oberon, showing more enthusiasm than I felt.

"Good… That's settled then. Now, what about payment for my troops?" demanded Officer-Crab. "Payment?" I asked.

"Yes, payment, of course! My troops don't fight for nothing. You need to pay or we don't go to war!" declared Officer-Crab.

"But we have nothing to pay you with." said Oberon, holding out empty hands.

"Then I can't take you. You don't suppose I want to get my new uniform dirty, do you? I mean, war with the Mussels and Whelks is a dirty business." declared Officer-Crab, brushing down the yellow shoulder pads.

"I have this" said Titania, suddenly taking the hairgrip from her hair, so that her golden hair flooded out in a halo of colour. She opened the nutshell, which contained the golden pen and, taking it out, offered it to Officer-Crab.

"Hmmm." said Officer-Crab, studying the pen, then said "I suppose the nutshell goes with it?"

"Of course it does." replied Titania, immediately offering the nutshell.

"And some of your hair? I'd like some for my pillows." demanded Officer-Crab, taking the nutshell and touching Titania's hair.

"No!" thundered Oberon. "You have enough. Take back the pen and nutshell, Titania. We will go on alone!"

"How dare you!" shouted Officer-Crab.

"Just as I had made up my mind, to take you and

fight for you!" he finished.

"Well, then…Are you going to take us?" demanded Oberon.

"Of course I am. First I will address my men. War is a dangerous business and I need to instill confidence in the troops." replied Officer-Crab, before calling for his troops to line up and listen.

"Troops", he began. "You know some of you may never come back or be injured in this fight with those fierce warriors, the Mussels and Whelks. But we shall steel our hearts and minds, fighting for what we believe in."

Then, telling us to stay behind his advancing troops, he ordered them to march, swords drawn, towards the Deep-Cut. The larger Crabs began to blow on trumpets, making such a racket that I thought this was surely no surprise attack.

We had marched for a while, smartly wheeling left and right turns when, suddenly, rounding a bend in the path, we came upon the sight of the enemy.

They had come from within cracks in the walls and now lined up, the largest Whelks at the front and, behind the Whelks were lined the Mussels, then a line of Winkles. Out in front, with sword aloft stood the largest Whelk, warlike and unafraid.

"Halt!" shouted Officer-Crab and our lines drew up, to face the enemy.

Marching stiffly out, we watched as Officer-Crab and the large Whelk marched forward, to meet each other.

"Captain-Whelk!" saluted Officer-Crab.

"Officer-Crab!" saluted Captain-Whelk.

Then they both lowered their swords and shook hands. I felt emotion swell in me, seeing these two brave soldiers saluting each other in that way, before the fighting and bloodshed.

"How brave they are." I whispered to Oberon.

"Indeed, they are." whispered Titania and she started to cry.

"Fetch the table!" ordered Captain-Whelk in a loud voice, which made everyone jump.

"Fetch the chairs!" ordered Officer-Crab, as an echo. We watched, puzzled, as two large Whelks disappeared into one of the cracks in the wall, then returned, carrying a white plastic table and two chairs, which they placed on the floor, between Officer-Crab and Captain-Whelk, a chair each side of the table.

"Christopher Shrimp!" called Officer-Crab, turning to face his troops.

"Yes, Sir!" said Christopher Shrimp in a small voice, stepping smartly forward and saluting. His hat fell over his eyes and he pushed it back up with the tip of his sword.

"Come to the table, Christopher Shrimp!" demanded Officer-Crab. "And take your place on the chair." Christopher Shrimp was helped up onto the chair and sat still.

"William Winkle!" suddenly called Captain-Whelk, turning to see a small Winkle step out from the back line, marching smartly up to Captain-Whelk, to salute.

"Private William Winkle… Take your place at the table and prepare for battle!" ordered Captain-Whelk.

"Yes, Sir!" William Winkle piped up, before being helped onto the chair and now sat opposite Christopher Shrimp, their eyes locking in determination.

"Prepare for battle!" shouted Officer-Crab.

"Prepare for battle!" echoed Captain-Whelk.

Christopher Shrimp reached over to grasp William Winkle's hand and they began to arm-wrestle, puffing and pulling, tugging and heaving, first one way and then the next, neither soldier willing to give up.

The troops on both sides began yelling and cheering as the struggle continued, with both, Officer-Crab and Captain-Whelk dancing up and down, shouting commands, their swords waving wildly over their heads.

The arm-wrestling suddenly came to an abrupt halt, when, with a loud crack, Christopher Shrimp's arm snapped off, allowing William Winkle to slam the dislocated limb down onto the table.

A loud roar went up from the ranks of Captain-Whelk's men as they saw what had happened.

"We've won the war!" cried Captain-Whelk's men, waving their swords.

"No!" shouted Officer-Crab, striding up to the table.

"Yes! We won!" exclaimed Captain Whelk, fiercely.
"Tell me how you have won?" cried Officer-Crab.
"Private Christopher Shrimp's arm came off, that's
how we won!" shouted Captain-Whelk." holding up
the broken limb for all to see.
"But he has a lot more arms left!" thundered Officer-
Crab.
"That's not fair… Not fair at all! Our William
Winkle only has one good arm… And, anyway, they
are Christopher Shrimp's legs, not arms!" cried
Captain-Whelk.
"I beg to differ, Captain-Whelk!" shouted Officer-
Crab. "What makes you think Christopher Shrimp's
limbs are legs?"
Captain-Whelk drew himself up to full height.
"We can all see that Christopher Shrimp has a boot
on each foot!" he roared.
"What do you mean, you rogue! Christopher
Shrimp's arms and legs are all the same, so his limbs
can be arms or legs… And I say they're arms!"
Captain-Whelk's face went green and rubbery,
"So, now we have soldiers with boots on their
hands!" he exclaimed.
"All's fair in love and war, Captain-Whelk. You
know the rules… It all about a Call-To-Arms!"
At this, the two leaders began to argue bitterly, while
the troops on both sides began to sit down and eat
jam sandwiches.
"Do you think." whispered Horatio to me. "That we
should creep round them while they are arguing?

They can take all night."

I relayed his question to Oberon and Titania, who both immediately agreed, so that we began to edge past the arguing Officer-Crab and Captain-Whelk, who were now shouting straight at each other, their faces turning blue.

Once we had moved beyond their sight, we began to run, stirring up the soft sand, past sleeping Eels, Sardines and an old sunken pirate ship, until we came to the end of the road.

There, in front of us was a steep up-climb of water which, high above, ended in a watery ring of pure blackness.

"Up there is the Fir-Tree pool." said Horatio. "It is a secret pool which lies in the middle of the Fir-Tree forest."

"How do we get up there?" I asked.

"Well, that's easy." replied Horatio. "You just hold your nose and swim up through the black hole. Strange that..." he mumbled. "The water at the top used to be white up there, so I don't know what has happened."

"Are you coming up with us, Horatio?" asked Titania.

"Of course not!" exclaimed Horatio. "How would I survive up there, with no water to breathe in?"

"But I thought you were going to show us how to reach where the Dark-Clan live." I said.

"Did I?" answered Horatio. "I can't remember, though you don't need me. When you get up there, look for the Santa-Man and ask him. He will show you the way."

"Then we have to leave you here and go up to the Fir-Tree forest." said Oberon, taking Horatio's claw in a hearty hand-shake.

"I shall make my way back to the Otter-Castle and find another shell." said Horatio, turning away.

"I suppose Officer-Crab and Captain-Whelk will still be arguing."

We watched him till he was gone from sight and then turned our eyes upwards, to the black watery hole high above.

"The thing is." said Titania. "How do we get up there and can we breathe in the air as we used to? We have been breathing in water for such a long time."

"I think, your Majesty." I said. "We will have to keep that same faith we had when we first dived into the water. I'm sure we will be able to breathe when we get to the top."

Before anyone could answer me, there was a 'Whoosh' sound and we saw a big glass ball, descending from above and we stood back as it landed on the sand.

"Anyone going up?"

A door had opened in the side of the glass ball and a Shrew-Mouse stood at the opening, its fingers on a set of buttons.

"Anyone going up?" it asked again.

"Where are you going up to?" I asked.

"That's a foolish question! I'm going back where I came down from, up to the top, of course.

Now, make up your mind. Anyone going up?" asked the Shrew-Mouse again.

"We're all going up." I said as we climbed into the ball and the door closed with a 'Whooshing' sound.

"Mind the door!" shouted the Shrew-Mouse, pressing a button.

The ball started to rise.

As the ball rose, the water seemed to start draining from the inside, so that our heads appeared above the water-line.

"What's going on?" I asked in alarm.

We had not had time to put ourselves into a faith mode, getting our hearts and minds set so we could be safe.

"It's alright." said the Shrew-Mouse. "This is a Depression-Lift. It changes the air back to normal so you can breathe fresh air."

No sooner had we been assured of being safe, when the ball popped to the surface and lay, bobbing, on top of the black liquid.

"All off, those who want Fir-Tree Forest!" exclaimed the Shrew-Mouse, pressing buttons, so that the door slid open and a ramp moved out, to rest on the far bank.

"Thank you so much." we called out as we walked over the ramp to dry land.

But the Shrew-Mouse had pressed the button, sliding the ramp back into the ball and, with the door closed, the ball made a loud popping noise, before vanishing back under the water.

"Extraordinary" said Titania, peering down into the inky darkness of the pool.

"I don't like the look of this place." said Oberon, staring round. "It smells of dead wood and bogs."

"I must say, this Fir-Tree Forest is rather stark." I replied, seeing only brown, patchy grass and stumps of trees, which seemed to jut out of the earth like broken teeth.

"It's all very eerie." shivered Titania, moving close to Oberon and staring round. "Not a noise of birds or Angel-Songs, not one smell of goodness." she finished, feeling more confident when Oberon put his arms round her.

A noise seemed to come from my left, a sort of snoring sound and I spun round, my eyes sharpening to a bundle of rags, lying at the foot of one of the black tree stumps.

We moved quietly to where it lay.

"What is it?" asked Titania, tapping at the bundle with a dainty foot.

"I have no idea." I answered, giving the bundle a sharper kick. "I don't know what a bundle of stinking rags is doing here in this rotten place."

"Who are you calling a bundle of rotten stinking rags? And I'll thank you for not kicking me and waking me from my sleep!"

Oberon, Titania and I jumped back in alarm as the

bundle of rags suddenly stood up, so we could make out the face of one of the ugliest old Crones I had

ever seen, even when I had once visited the Land of Hideous Faces.

Titania, the first one to gain any sense of balance put out a hand, to touch the Crone on the shoulder.

"I'm so sorry." she said, kindly. We did not mean to offend you."

"Then prove it!" snapped the Crone, sniffing a long, warty, nose, her eyes fierce and as black as Samuel Lumpkin's cat.

"Pardon?" I said, still somewhat shocked at her hideous face and evil smelling clothes.

"I said…Prove it! Prove how sorry you are and how you like me!" said the Crone again, coming forward to look me in the eye.

"I would be happy to prove how sorry we are, dear Crone. Just tell us how we can prove it and we will do as you ask." I said in a gentle way, feeling her eyes burning into mine.

"Kiss me!" she snapped.

I felt her hand, bony and sharp with damaged skin, take hold of mine and I froze.

"Go on then… Kiss me!" the Crone snapped again, her thin lips, dribbling with saliva. "Come on, kiss me!"

"Go on, Pucker-Up, kiss her." giggled Titania, pushing me in the back.

"I will kiss you, if you tell us where to find the Santa-Man." suddenly said Oberon, moving to take

THE OLD CRONE

my place.

The Crone froze, her eyes becoming small and cunning, her hair seeming to change from black to blue. Then, straightening, as if coming to a decision, she cackled, then put her face forward.

"Go on then, kiss me. You are better than that screwed-up little Gnome!"

How dare she call me a screwed up little Gnome! I was fuming! It was true, I was a Gnome and had no argument with that. But I was not a screwed up little Gnome! In fact I was considered quite tall for a Gnome, back in Kiss-Kids land. Why, I even came up to Oberon's belly-button in height.

I know we Gnomes and Fairy-Folk are not supposed to get angry and have bad thoughts or wishes but I wished Oberon would bite the Crone's warty nose right off!

Oberon reached forward, to kiss the Crone on the lips but the Crone poked her tongue out, slithering, like that of a snake's forked tongue, the twin-tips touching Oberon's lips. I saw his lips turn a blue-green colour, while spots began to crawl over his face, turning to blisters and boils, his golden hair started to turn grey and straggly.

"She has bewitched you, your Majesty!" I cried, terribly afraid.

Titania fell to the ground, fainting away at the sight of her beloved King, who seemed, now, to have grown stunted and wizened with a crooked back. The Crone cackled in hideous glee, jumping up and down, then turned, to run and disappear into the stumps of black trees.

I stood still, horrified, not knowing what to do, then shouted in alarm as Oberon, in a fit of madness began to cry out, that he was home and could see all the Fairy-Folk, dancing for him.

I realized that Oberon was in some kind of trance and saw him suddenly rush off, through some black vegetation, towards a swamp, from which rose bubbles of sulphur, that popped and allowed wafts of evil smoke to escape into the dank air.

"Wake up! Please wake up, your Royal Highness!" I cried, kneeling beside Titania and touching at her face.

Her eyes opened, first to stare at me blankly, then widen as she remembered what had happened.

"Where is my Lord Oberon!" she cried, rising to her feet and looking around.

"He has run away, Your Majesty… Over there, in that direction. Please hurry, we must catch him. He is under an evil influence, the Crone has put on him!"   "Help me, Pucker-Up." she said, hitching up her gown and leaning on me so that we ran in the direction that Oberon had taken.

"There he is!" I shouted, espying Oberon. "Look, he's on the side of the swamp and going to jump onto the stepping stone!"

"Oberon! My dearest Lord of all the Fairy-Folk. It is I, your Titania! I beg you, Sire, do not jump onto that stepping-stone! It will sink and you with it, into the swamp!" cried the mortified Titania.

Oberon stopped, turning to look at us. For a moment, he seemed to come to his senses, reaching out to Titania, his face now completely covered in sores and boils, his frame, crooked and bent.

"I have to go back to my home." he cried, turning back to face the swamp. "Look! Can't you see the Owl and Woodpecker? There, there's Cyrese, the Lyre-Player! And there is Joel-Creek, the Drummer-Boy!"

"Your Highness!" I shouted in desperation. "They are mirages, figments of your imagination. There is no-one there! Come away from the bank...Please, Sire!"

"Quick...Tell her to kiss him!" exclaimed a tiny voice in my ear. I turned, to see a tiny Wood-Nymph, her wings shimmering as she hovered just by my right ear.

"Tell her to run up and kiss him!" shouted the voice again, more urgent and, without thinking I shouted, "Quick, Titania... Run to Oberon and kiss him!"

The sudden urgency of my command seemed to stir a reaction in Titania, so that she ran to Oberon's side, hugging him and kissed him full on the lips.

It seemed to me that the darkness lit up with orange flashes as Oberon and Titania glowed with pure love, so bright that it lit the sky for a briefest of whiles, then darkened once more. And the grey of the Fir-Tree Forest dampened our spirits once more.

"What are you doing, dear Titania? Why are you

hugging me and laughing, though tears are streaking your face!" asked Oberon, as if he had just woken from a dream.

"You are back, sweetest Lord, my dearest treasure." said Titania, amid laughter and tears.

"Back? What are you talking about? I have been no-where." replied Oberon, not understanding anything. I saw that his face had now returned to normal, a sweet and kind face, even though it was not the real face of Oberon, for he was still Masked. His body, too, was once again tall and straight, as a Royal frame should be.

"You haven't got time for that now." said the tiny voice in my ear. "You all have to come with me. Tell them to follow me!" ordered the Wood-Nymph, flying round so she was right in front of my nose, making my eyes go funny as I looked at the shimmering light of her wings.

"What is that light?" asked Titania. "And why are your eyes all crossed like that, Pucker-Up?"

"It's a Wood-Nymph." I explained, shaking my head, so the Wood-Nymph moved and tugged at my ear.

"I suppose you can't see her." I continued. "But she saved King Oberon's life and now asks that we follow her." I went on.

"Then of course, we must follow her. Tell her to lead on and will you thank her for saving My Lord's life." said Titania, holding Oberon's hand tightly.

I did as Titania asked and the Wood-Nymph

laughed, sounding like a pealing of bells, which I found most attractive.

"Let us go." she said, pointing to the South and flying ahead, so that we hurried to keep up with the light of her wings.

"Where did the light go?" asked Oberon as we came to a stop.

"I am not sure, one minute she was just ahead of us and now she has gone." I answered, just as puzzled.

"Over here!" came a voice, followed by a Pssst!" There, standing by a stump of a tree, stood a Wood-Sprite, who crooked a finger at us.

"Come on." she said and suddenly seemed to disappear.

"What is happening?" asked Titania.

Both Oberon and I shook our heads, as mystified as Titania was.

"You have to go down the stairs." said the Wood-Nymph, once again appearing in front of my nose and pointing.

"Go to the tree-stump and down the stairs. Hurry now!"

I walked quickly to the tree-stump and saw an opening, with a set of rickety steps leading down into the earth below. Oberon and Titania had hurried to keep up with me and now stood by my side as we peered down, into the darkness.

"We have to go down the steps." I said, trying to appear brave and promptly began to descend, stepping down, into what seemed to be, the bowels of the earth.

As we reached a winding stair, we saw a plaque on the wall, it read, 'The Halfway Stage, Keep Going.' It seemed that we were turning in circles as the stairs wound their way down. Then, suddenly…

"What took you so long?"

The Wood-Sprite who had been by the tree-stump earlier, now stood in front of a yellow door.

"You should have taken the lift." she said as she opened the door.

I was still trying to determine exactly where the elevator was when the bright lights and noise made me blink my eyes so many times, that I thought I was seeing stars.

It was some time before my eyes got accustomed to the brightness, after the gloom of the swampy land above.

The Hall seemed to be an endless expanse, of distant walls and echoes of a thousand voices, which hushed into silence as we made our entrance.

The Sprites all sat in Zig-Zag rows of different colours, forming a star-crossed flag.

The lights were not lights as I had seen before, the dark-leafed vines swaying down from an earthy ceiling, to end with large white bowls upon which sat hundreds of Wood-Nymphs, all fluttering silver wings, so the air blazed with such brightness, that I had to turn my eyes away.

Suddenly, the sound of a million hands, all clapping, thundered around the hall, while excitement seemed to electrify the air.

"Silence!"

A tall Sprite, dressed in an electric blue costume stood up, on what seemed to be a large plastic bag. "Show the strangers to a seat." she said.

The noise stopped abruptly and we were shown to a bench, to sit between some giggling Pixies.

"Welcome to the Under-Land." said the tall Sprite, now seating herself on the bag.

The bag seemed to move, as if there were wriggling worms inside.

"Stop wriggling!" the Sprite commanded sharply and the wriggling stopped.

"Now… Greetings to you all." she continued, smiling at us. "We are so glad you have come to help us. You are so very brave and I do hope it doesn't eat you!"

Oberon stood up, a frown crossing his face.

"Excuse me." he began. "I am not sure what you mean, about being eaten, I mean. We have come here to speak to the Santa-Man. I was told he could tell us exactly where the Dark-Clan live."

The tall Sprite held up her hand to stop the frightened whispers which had started to go round.

"Please don't mention that place again." said the Sprite. "You are frightening the children."

"I beg your pardon, I did not mean to frighten them, though I would like to know what you meant about being eaten. And where is the Santa-Man?" asked Oberon, in a quieter voice.

"They need to be told!" shouted one of the purple Sprites.

With that, the tall Sprite called all the leaders of the different coloured Sprites, so they sat, huddled together, talking in secret whispers, taking quick glances at us every now and then.

As we waited for the meeting of the Sprites to finish, my eyes wandered round the sea of excited faces. A quick movement caught the corner of my eye and I turned. It came from the bag that the tall Sprite had been seated on.

Curious, I walked towards the bag, seeing it wriggle and as I opened it, peering inside, I jumped back. A pair of large brown button eyes stared up at me.

"Are you my new owner?" said a growling voice.

I opened the bag wider and saw the voice came from a cuddly brown Teddy-Bear, squashed in among other new toys.

"No... I'm not your new owner." I said. "Who are you?"

But before the Bear could answer, another voice came from inside the bag.

"If you squeeze me I cry and my eyes close if you lay me down." said the voice.

"Shut up, Dolly. This is my new owner!" snapped the Bear .

The Dolly started to cry.

"That's a bit rude." I said.

"Well." said the Bear. "She always gets the Girly-Mortals to choose her and they give her lots of cuddles. While I always get the Boy-Mortals, who pull me around, so my stuffing comes out!"

"I don't know what you are talking about, Bear, although I am not your new owner. I'm here on serious Kiss-Kids business!" I said, closing the bag and returning to the bench.

"They are toys for the Mortal-Children at Santa-Time." explained the Wood-Nymph, suddenly appearing in a flash of light, to sit on my nose. Before I could say anything, the tall Sprite left the huddle and came towards us, the others returning, to join the ranks of different colours.

"You need to be told." said the Sprite, standing before us. "Especially you!" she continued, pointing at Oberon.

"What do we need to be told?" asked Oberon, standing up.

I had, at last, managed to flick at my nose till the Wood-Nymph flew away, buzzing twice around my head before settling its light onto a roof-beam, high above.

"The Santa-Man is held as prisoner by the Demon, Morpheus, a dreadful black beast who has stripped this beautiful land of all the green Fir-Trees, killing the joy of Santa-Time and so not allowing us to take the toys to the Mortal-Children" said the Sprite.

We sat in silence, till Oberon said, "What can we do? I don't think we can help you to fight this Demon, especially if it will eat us."

"You have to fight the Demon!" claimed the Sprite,

pointing at Oberon once more, before continuing. "You asked where the Dark-Clan live. I tell you this, only the Santa-Man can tell you, only he has the knowledge. So, until you fight the Demon and rescue the Santa-Man, you will not be able to get to where the Dark-Clan live."

"Oh, my Lord Oberon!" begged Titania. "Please don't go to fight this Demon. He will eat you and I will surely fade away!"

Oberon quieted Titania's fears, holding her in his arms and comforting her.

"Shush, my beautiful Queen Titania. You know it is my duty, as it is of all who dwell in Fairy-Land and all-about, to see that the Mortals are safe from harm, that they are well and truly love each other. We must find out where the Dark-Clan live, so we may rescue the Kiss-Diamond. Dearest heart, you know that. Without the Kiss-Diamond, the Mortals are in dire peril. Don't you see, dearest Lady, that I must fight the Demon?"

"Oh, my Sweet Oberon." said Titania, drying her eyes. "I am so ashamed, that I tried to stop you. Of course, for the love and sake of all Mortals, you have to place yourself in this gravest of dangers."

All the Sprites, who were listening to this speech began to sob and moan in sympathy.

"Quiet!" demanded the tall Sprite, standing once more on the bag of toys.

"Do you agree?" she demanded from Oberon. "That you fight the Demon, Morpheus?"

"I agree." returned Oberon, moving away from us, to stand straight and tall.

"And I go with him!" I suddenly heard myself say, moving up to stand beside Oberon.

"Me, too!" declared Titania.

"No, Titania…You must not come with us. Stay here and be safe among the Wood-Sprites." said Oberon

"But I will go with you!" I said, unafraid.

"And I shall be with you." whispered the silvery voice of the Wood-Nymph, descending swiftly from above and hanging onto a strand of my hair, swinging down in front of my eyes.

The Hall was quiet, except for the gentle sobs from Titania, who was now cuddled by Sprites and Pixies.

"Pixie-Light! Take them to the lair of Morpheus!" cried the tall Sprite, indicating a green Pixie, who jumped to attention.

"Come." said the green Pixie, leading Oberon and I towards the door of the Hall, through it and to ascend the stairs, climbing, till we reached the gloomy and dark earth above.

"They're coming! They're coming!"

I was suddenly startled by the sight of the old Crone who, as if appearing from nowhere, ran in front of us, her rags flying out in all directions.

The green Pixie halted, his eyes wide with fear.

"Carry on… Don't be afraid." said Oberon.

But the green Pixie would not go any further, trembling and starting to cry.

"Just point to where we should go and then run back

to the others." said Oberon, gently.

The green Pixie pointed with a shaking finger and quivered.

"Keep to the left and follow the path, till you see the Black-Tree. The Demon lives there." he said, before running back.

Oberon and I continued our journey in silence, following the left-hand side of the path indicated by the green Pixie, till we came to the Black-Tree.

I felt Oberon stop, to join me as we stared at what lay before us. From the dark forest of decaying stumps, there rose a giant tree, as black as the night, with leaves that were wispy, hanging like misshapen cobwebs, from which dripped a poisonous juice. Its branches were loaded, hung with shrunken heads and bones, which whistled eerily as the wind moaned its sound through them.

The flapping of Bat's wings froze my mind as the flitting creatures alighted on the branches, among the bones and heads, then turned upside down.

There was a harsh coldness in the air as I surveyed the ghostly tree, running my eyes from its top, where the Rooks sat, down to the thick trunk, which had gnarled and twisted roots spreading out like grasping fingers.

My eyes centered on the door which was built into the trunk, to rest on the silver key which sat in the lock.

"Tell Oberon, he has to unlock the door and go in." whispered the Wood-Nymph, close to my ear.

Whether Oberon heard the words, I was not sure, though he stepped forward, moving to the door, his hand on the key and turning.

Beyond the door were a series of wooden steps, leading down to a long corridor. I walked behind Oberon, hearing my own breath coming fast and fearful.

"Come in." said a voice, so sweet in its tone. There, I saw a beautiful Witch-Queen, tall and elegant, with dark tresses that tumbled down her back.

"Come in." she said again, a hand held out in welcome.

We entered the large room, bedecked in colourful banners, with a soothe of music seeming to come from the very air itself. I relaxed somewhat, seeing no harm from such a pleasant surrounding, with the beautiful Witch-Queen.

"Sit. Please sit and eat." she said, offering us seats at a table, loaded to a full with delicious fruits and sweetmeats. The smell was such that I sat and reached out for an apple, my mouth already tasting such an appetising lay.

"Don't eat it!" the Wood-Nymph exclaimed in my ear. "It's poisoned!"

"Don't touch the food, My lord." I said, reaching out to push Oberon's hand away. Oberon looked at me, not understanding my alarm.

"The food is poisoned, Sire!" I shouted, jumping up from my seat. Oberon did the same as we prepared for whatever would come.

"You fools!" suddenly screamed the 'Witch-Queen', her dark beautiful eyes turning a glaring red, widening and weeping red tears. The room, which had been warm and musical was now changing into a dark and forbidding place.

I screamed in fear as the face of the beautiful Witch-Queen began to change, her once smiling mouth now thin and evil, open to expose large fangs, a Wolf's mouth, the throat uttering loud savage growls.

The hands became black, with raking claws of steel, which ripped at its clothes, so they fell in shreds on the floor. I gasped in fright, seeing no real body beneath the gown, just a dark, shadowy and sinister shape of a Demon.

"It's Morpheus!" I screamed.

In fear, I backed against a wall and squeezed myself down, making myself as small as possible. Oberon drew himself up and stood, bravely facing the monster, who now roared a terrible cry, its fangs and claws gleaming.

I did not even see it move, the Demon moving at such incredible speed that it had Oberon by the throat, its jaws wide open, ready for the bite.

I suddenly jumped up, not aware of anything except to help my friend, Oberon. Throwing myself at the Demon, I cannot remember a thing, except to feel myself flying through the air, to land with a thud against the wall, the breath knocked from my body. I lay still, feeling the pain as tears filled my eyes. I watched, knowing there was nothing I could do.

"Open the box, Sire!" I shouted.

I had no idea where this thought came from, except that the image sprang to mind, of the gift the Otter-Folk had given to Oberon, the box which was tied to his belt, which contained the Squid.

It was all so sudden!

"Open the box, Oberon!" I screamed, seeing the fangs of the beast about to strike.

Oberon's fingers struggled to open the small box at his belt and then the box sprang open, allowing the Squid to leap out.

It was all so fast, so unexpected. The Squid let out a high shrill sound and then seemed to jump deliberately into the open mouth of Morpheus!

For a moment, nothing happened. It might have been just a Mortal-Second but, to me, it seemed an age.

Then the Demon let out a strangled cry, its red eyes turning yellow, its mouth snapping shut.

Letting go of Oberon, who fell to the ground, it let out a last roar, then there was a loud, thunderous noise, then a blinding flash before the Demon seemed to explode, its huge head bursting apart, its body-shape disappearing in a shower of sparks, to become a cloud of coloured stars, a confetti-shower, sparkling the room before floating down to glitter the earthen floor.

"Collect the dust!" I heard the small voice urge in my ear and I knew the Wood-Nymph had stayed with me through the horror.

"Quick, Pucker-Up! Take Oberon's belt-pouch and

MORPHEUS

put all the dust in it!" cried the Wood-Nymph.
Oberon was standing now, his face pale, though his
eyes shone with a fierce and brave light.
"Give me your belt-pouch, Sire." I said, reaching
out.
"Take it, Pucker-Up. You do as you will, while I
search for the Santa-Man."
The Confetti-Dust lay in a shimmering of high
colours, of all different hues, so that it lit up the
darkness. I began to scoop the dust up with my hands
and quickly filled up the pouch, till it bulged.
"I can't seem to find an opening anywhere." said
Oberon, poking and tapping at the walls in his search
to find any doorway which might lead to where the
Santa-Man was being held.
"Perhaps this is it." I replied, sweeping the last of the
dust into the pouch, to reveal, embedded in the floor,
a large square flagstone which had an iron ring at its
center.
Oberon and I began to tug at the iron pull-ring,
heaving so hard that I thought I would burst.
Gradually, it began to come away from its casing,
giving a terrible moaning sound as it lifted clear.
"What's going on here?"
As the flagstone came away and we had placed it
further back, a large and jolly head popped up from
the opening.
"Are you the Santa-Man?" I asked, as Oberon and I
helped to heave the large man from the hole.
I say Man, though he was not a man such as the

Mortals are. This Santa-Man had Pixie ears for a start and a round red face which was covered in bushy white whiskers. His mouth seemed to burst through the whiskers when he laughed, which was often and very loud, a sort of hearty laugh describes it best.

"Indeed, fellow Good-Men, I am he." he laughed and slapped at himself as if to make sure he really existed.

"What has happened here?" he asked. "I feel as if I have been asleep one hundred round years!"

While Oberon was telling the Santa-Man what had been going on, I began to realise how much the room had changed. It was now alight with a glow of space and love, a very beautiful room indeed.

"Then I have much work to do!" exclaimed the Santa-Man, booming with laughter, having been told of his capture and enchantment by the Demon. Suddenly he swooped and, lifting me high into the air, settled me onto his shoulders in a Flying-Angel and carried me as he and Oberon ascended the stairs, putting me down once we had closed and locked the door of the tree trunk.

"What have you done to my Master? What have you done to Morpheus!"

The old Crone, whom had, earlier, led us a merry dance, now had come from out of a crevice in the ground and ran towards us, screaming and crying, to fall in a heap at my feet, her cries and groans now sounding horrible.

"What shall we do with her?" I asked of the Santa-Man, at the same time, brushing off some of the Confetti-Dust which had clung to my coat.

As I did so, some of the dust sparkled its way down, to fall on the old Crone, who gave a cry, before laying lifeless on the ground, as if she had expired.

"I'm so sorry, Crone." I said, leaning over to help her up.

For, no matter what harm the Crone had done us, I did not forget my Kiss-Kids manners and good heart. Then, as my hand touched her, a most marvellous thing happened, which caused me to jump backwards, almost tripping up.

The rags the Crone was wearing had suddenly turned soft and white, a fairy tunic, while the Crone had changed into a most beautiful fairy, who now stood up and flexed her gossamer wings, before starting to lift herself off the ground.

"Wonderful!" boomed the Santa-Man, slapping me a powerful slap on the back.

"You have released the White-Fairy from the evil spell and now she will be able to sit on top of the Christmas-Tree, that's if it ever gets back to how it was." he finished, somewhat dubiously.

We stood back, staring up at the dark and evil tree, feeling its coldness and unhappy life.

"Pucker-Up." I heard the voice of the Wood-Nymph whisper in my ear. "Give the White-Fairy some Confetti-Dust and tell her to fly up to the top of the tree and sprinkle it all over."

I did as the Wood-Nymph said and, taking some dust from the pouch, I gave it to the White-Fairy, along with the instructions the Wood-Nymph had given me.

We watched as the White-Fairy spread her wings, flying high into the air, some of the dust escaping from her hands, coming down in a cloud of wonderful rainbow hues, streaming out behind her. With a flittering of wings, the Bats rose from the cobweb branches, flying like black mushrooms, to fly off in all directions, while the Rooks cawed in loud and angry cries when they saw the White-Fairy approach their nest at the top of the tree. In screams of rage, they flapped heavy wings and lifted themselves high into the air, then swooped off towards the Swamp-Lands.

The White-Fairy hovered for a short while over the top of the tree, then allowed the Confetti-Dust to fall, spreading itself out as it covered the tree in a glistening river.

"Look! Oh, look at the tree!" I shouted, clapping my hands. "See how the cobwebs are going and how the bones and shrunken heads are changing!"

I could not believe my eyes and watched, astounded as the tree began to change, from black to a most beautiful and spruce green, its pine needles shining to a new light. The bones and shrunken heads were now glass balls, with lit candles inside, burning in marvellous radiance. The bones becoming chocolates, wrapped in gold leaf.

We all 'Ooohed' and 'Ahhhed' as we saw fairy-lights and silver tinsel adorn the tree, along with new toys, which hung from the branches, while Bluebirds and Birds of Paradise flew in and out of the lush greenery, instead of the Bats and Rooks.

The White-Fairy stood on top of the tree, a wand now in her hand, which shone as a silver star.

"We have our beloved Christmas-Tree back!" shouted the Santa-Man, picking both myself and Oberon up and dancing around the trunk of the tree. "Look again! Do you see how the roots have un-knotted themselves and now drive into the good earth, in search of Nutriment-Juice?" I cried, feeling giddy as the Santa-Man took a last twirl, before setting us down.

It was then that I noticed that the door, which had been at the foot of the trunk, was now gone, closed up for good, the silver key lying on the new grass. "May I keep the key?" I asked the Santa-Man, picking the key up.

"By all means, my brave little Pucker-Up, of course you can keep it. It will bring you luck on any Happy-Day of the twenty-first." boomed the delighted Santa-Man, reaching up to grasp a glowing glass ball from the tree.

"I want you to have this." he said, plucking the ball and handing it to Oberon. "It will keep you safe from harm."

"What is it?" asked Oberon, seeing the swirling colours change within the glass ball, feeling it warm and smooth in his hand.

"It's an Illusion-Ball." answered the Santa-Man. "It can change to any shape you wish, a very handy property and my present to you as a Thank-You gift for what you and Pucker-Up have done for us."

As Oberon put the ball inside his tunic, the Santa-Man reached up once more and took down a toy trumpet.

"Come!" he shouted, then began to blow a merry tune on the trumpet and we marched behind him as he led the way back to where we had come from.

It seemed, as we marched, that Fairies, Pixies and Sprites came out from behind black tree stumps and holes in the ground, popping up from nowhere, to join in the singing and dancing, till there was a great following of noise.

"Oberon! My sweetest Lord… You are safe and well!" exclaimed Titania, rushing up, to smother Oberon with glad and happy kisses, so that orange flashes lit up the sky.

Oberon kissed her many times, forgetful of those who watched, giggling and laughing at this expression of love.

"And you, too, my brave Pucker-Up!" she exclaimed, coming over to lightly kiss my cheek.

I blushed, for I was not used to having a royal Queen kiss me in that way.

"Giselle! Giselle!" shouted the Santa-Man, who had stopped blowing the trumpet and now held up a large hand.

"I am here, dear Santa-Man." came a voice and, before us stood the tall Sprite whom we had seen down in the big Hall.

"Dear Giselle…Listen to me carefully. I want you to take some of the Sprites and bring me that big wicker basket, filled with Happy-Face balloons and some Glitter-String. Bring the basket back here and I want all the Christmas-Folk to help, blowing up the balloons."

Giselle led the Sprites off, while the Santa-Man put the trumpet to his lips and we all marched round in a large circle, till Giselle and the Sprites arrived back, carrying the large basket, full of Happy-Face balloons.

The Sprites lay the basket down and, sitting, all the Christmas-Folk began to blow up the balloons, till the air was thick with round, floating Happy-Face balloons, some so light and airy, that they began to lift some of the Pixies and Fairies off the ground, till Sprites clung onto the feet of the up-lifted Pixies and Fairies, keeping them down to earth.

"Now." boomed the Santa-Man. "Tie the balloons with the glitter-string, to the basket… And secure the basket to the ground with a strong anchor." he warned.

"What is the Santa-Man up to?" I asked Oberon, who held Titania to him.

"I have no idea." replied Oberon, shaking his head.

The basket groaned and grunted as it tried to lift itself from the ground, the anchor holding it down. "There, it's ready." said the Santa-Man, looking at Oberon and I.

"In you go." he said, indicating Oberon and myself.

"What do you mean?" asked Oberon, surprised at Santa-Man's demand. "In we go… What?"

"In you go, into the basket." explained the Santa-Man, laughing loud at our expressions.

" I should explain." he said.

"Please do explain." answered Oberon.

"What you and Pucker-Up have to do is to climb into the basket and I will remove the anchor, so that you float up into the air." explained the Santa-Man.

"And when we are up there…?" queried Oberon.

"Why, you and Pucker-Up will sprinkle the rest of the Confetti-Dust all over the land, so it becomes a land of beautiful Christmas-Trees again.
Then the Mortals will have a wonderful Christmas when we plant the trees at night, just before Christmas, while the Mortals sleep."

"How wonderful!" cried Titania, clapping her hands. However, I had some doubts about this plan.

"Might I just make an enquiry?" I asked.

"Please do." replied the Santa-Man.

"I do understand what you want us to do and very pleased to comply. As to getting up there, that's easy. But, how do we get down again, once we have sprinkled all the Confetti-Dust?" I said.

The singing and dancing came to a halt as the Santa-

Man held up his hands and asked if anyone had any suggestions.

"What about if a hundred fairies fly up there and help them down?" asked one Pixie.

"Don't be silly!" said another, rudely. "Why, even a million fairies can't lift a heavy weight!"

Now there was silence as everyone cupped chins in their hands and sat down to think. It was a sad silence, a silence like when Mortal-Children are up to mischief, so that Mortal-Mothers are warned of such mischief their children are up to, or so I am told, that kind of silence.

I felt a familiar tug on my ear.

"What is it?" I asked the Wood-Nymph, not happy at all at being disturbed while I thought about an answer.

"The answer is simple." said the Wood-Nymph, giggling at my impatience and biting at my ear.

"So? What is it?" I asked, pulling my head away.

"When you want to come down, you just pop the balloons, one at a time. You see, with less and less balloons to lift you, you will gradually float back down again. But, be careful that you burst the balloons on equal sides, otherwise the basket will over-tip." explained the Wood-Nymph.

"I have it! I have the answer!" I shouted in glee and explained to the waiting throng, word for word what the Wood-Nymph had told me.

Everyone began to cheer and even the Santa-Man lifted me, once again, into the air, calling me Pucker-

Up the Brainy'!

I was so over-come with the cheers from the audience that I forgot to feel guilty, for using the Wood-Nymph's idea as my own.

"That was my idea!" exclaimed the Wood-Nymph, buzzing angrily in my ear and flew from me in a speed of fire-light.

"Actually, it was the Wood-Nymph's idea!" I shouted loudly.

But it was too late, everyone was already calling it Pucker-Up's Big Idea, writing it down on Fir-Cones, and once the words were in writing, they could not be taken back!

"Come along, Pucker-Up." said Oberon, already in the basket and impatient to be off.

I clambered in beside him and, with a mighty roar from the crowd, the anchor was pulled from its moorings and we began to float up, till those below looked like small ants and our eyes took in the whole view of the countryside.

It looked so grim and grey, with ugly wisps of smoke rising from the ground.

"Start sprinkling the Confetti-Dust!" shouted Oberon, blowing out his cheeks and puffing strongly so that we moved along.

Taking the Confetti-Dust from the pouch, I began to sprinkle it all over, moving from side to side of the basket so all got a fair sprinkling.

"Do you see what is happening down below?" Oberon exclaimed.

I had been too busy, sprinkling the Confetti-Dust, to take notice, so that I now stopped to look.

"Wow!" I shouted in amazement. "The whole world down there is a beautiful scene of greens and blues and browns, and flowers of all sorts. Do you see that river, how lovely it flows…And look, Sire, how the Fish play with the Butterflies."

"It is marvellous!" answered Oberon, leaning out over the side of the basket. "Do you see how the old black stumps of trees are now replaced by tall and green Christmas-Trees!"

"This is magic, My Lord. I can even hear the cheering and singing from down below… Oh My! Look how everything is lit up by that bright golden Sun. And how blue and clear the sky is now!" I marvelled.

"Hurry now, Pucker-Up. Finish throwing the rest of the Confetti-Dust down and let us pop the balloons." said Oberon, already starting to prick the balloons at his end of the basket.

I hurried to finish my task and began to pop the balloons at my end so the equal popping gently lowered us down to a softest landing.

On the ground, we alighted from the basket, amid shouts and cheers, of singing and noisy scenes of Pixies, Fairies and Sprites all holding hands and dancing round in a large circle.

The air smelt so sweet, perfumed by the flowers and new grass, while the trees stood tall and proud. This was surely a beautiful land.

THE SANTA-MAN

I left Oberon, who had set off to find Titania, while I joined in, dancing with the Fairies, Sprites and Pixies, who had formed a band so that music piped its sound to the blasts from the Santa-Man's trumpet. I picked up a tambourine and started banging on it as I danced along to the Celebration-Music.

I was carried along with the music and singing, that it was some time before I realised Oberon had been gone for a while.

Leaving the dance, I set off in search of him and had only just reached the area where the food-tables had been set out, when I saw a most worried-looking Oberon who came striding up, carrying a struggling Elf under his arm.

"What ever is the matter, Sire?" I asked.

"Put me down, you ruffian!" shouted the Elf, his pointed hat falling from his head, so that I saw his pointed ears.

"They have taken Titania!" cried Oberon, putting the Elf down on his feet, though still holding him by the scruff of the neck.

"Who has? What are you talking about, Sire?" I asked again, seeing Oberon becoming more agitated and shaking the Elf, who proclaimed he had done nothing, continuing to struggle.

"The Un-Beautifuls, that's who." cried Oberon. "And this Elf was seen talking to one of them, before they ran off with Titania."

"I only asked the Un-Beautiful if I could go back with her, that's all I asked!" said the Elf, beginning to cry loudly.

"What is going on?" boomed the Santa-Man, coming to where we stood.

Oberon repeated the story, that the Un-Beautifuls had taken Titania away.

The Santa-Man listened to Oberon, first warning the Elf to stop snivelling and be quiet.

"It's unusual for the Un-Beautifuls to act in this way." mused the Santa-Man, as we sat on one of the benches by the tables.

"I've never heard of them being violent before." he finished.

"I wish someone would explain what is going on? Who are the Un-Beautifuls and where did they take Titania?" I said.

"The Un-Beautifuls are a tribe of the most ugliest women, who live beyond the Electric-Waterfall, in the Land of the Flowers." said the Santa-Man. "That's all I can tell you."

"I can tell you all about the Un-Beautifuls!" shouted the Elf, still struggling to break free from Oberon's grip.

"Then tell us, you little wretch!" demanded Oberon.

"Well, if you stop shaking me, so my teeth stop rattling, then I'll tell you all about them." demanded the Elf.

Oberon let the Elf go and waited.

"I am from the Clan of the Wood-Painters." began the Elf.

"We are Elves, who live just beyond the Flower-

Land of the Un-Beautifuls. We have no problems with the women from the Un-Beautiful tribe and can come and go as we please. We paint all the flowers and berries, so the Un-Beautifuls know what beauty is, for they have the most hideous of faces and look for beauty everywhere."

"Why are you here?" asked Oberon.

"I was sent by the Senior Members of the Wood-Painters. We had run out of paint and cannot paint any more flowers or trees. The Senior Members thought the Santa-Man would have some boxes of paint and I could take them back with me."

"We have no paints to spare." said the Santa-Man. "Only enough for the Mortal-Children.

But if you are free to come and go through the land of the Un-Beautifuls, why did you not run back to your own land?" queried the Santa-Man.

"Because I cannot get through the Electric-Waterfall." cried the unhappy Elf, starting to snivel again.

"I asked that woman of the Un-Beautifuls to take me with her but she said she couldn't. Now I am all alone and cannot get back." he finished beginning to wail loudly.

"How far is this Electric-Waterfall?" I asked.

"It's five thousand Cat-Leaps and fifty Rule of Thumb." replied the Elf.

I measured out the distance in my mind. Everybody knows how far a cat can leap, while one Rule of Thumb is the distance between the thumbs when both arms and hands are stretched out. That was quite a distance to go!

"Then I think, My Lord, we had better get going, to rescue the Lady Titania!" I said, rising from the bench.

"And you, Elf, will show us the way." said Oberon, rising and indicating the three of us should leave.

"I hope you travel well." said the Santa-Man, waving us off. "And visit us on the way back, my friends!" he boomed.

We waved our goodbyes to the Santa-Man and all the folk who had come to see us off. I did not see the Wood-Nymph and guessed she was still angry at me for stealing her idea. However, I was much too set on reaching our destination, to worry about not seeing her, to say goodbye.

As we walked through forests and hills, Oberon questioned the Elf about the Elf's men-folk and how they lived, though keeping a sharp eye on him, should he consider running away and leaving us lost. But the Elf seemed more that content to travel with us, seeming more worried should we leave him alone.

I listened as the Elf talked of the Dragon-Mountain, which stood between his land and the lands where the Dark-Clan lived.

Oberon stopped in his tracks.

"The Dark-Clan? You know where the Dark-Clan live?" he asked.

"Why, of course I do." answered the Elf, continuing

to walk and talk as he went on.

"Their lands start just beyond the Dragon-Mountain. Though none of we Elves have ever been to where the Dark-Clan live, it's much too grim and, besides, we can't get past Dragon-Mountain."

As the Elf had finished saying this, he stopped to point ahead.

"See that?" he said. "That's the Electric-Waterfall, the gateway to the Land of the Flowers, where the Un-Beautifuls live."

The forest had opened out to a high mountain and there, in front of us, was a sight as I have never seen before in my life.

From the top of the mountain, stretching across, as far as the eye could see was the most wondrous drop of a Waterfall, tumbling down in a pulsating blue and green, with flashes of lightning crackling out from its source. It roared down at a thunderous pace, its shimmering beauty seeming to plunge to earth, though there was no pool at the bottom, the Waterfall seeming to travel straight down, into the ground.

I ran forward, to feel the freshness of the water, to play under its magical wetness.

"Don't touch it! Please don't touch it, you will burn!" cried the Elf in alarm.

I stopped, returning to where the Elf and Oberon stood.

"What's the matter with it?" I demanded, suspecting a trick.

Saying nothing, the Elf picked up a stick and threw it at the Waterfall. As it hit the water, there was a sharp crack and flames spat out from the sheet of tumbling water as the stick immediately caught fire.

"It's not water." the Elf said. "It's an electro-magnetic force!" he explained.

"Then how do we go through it?" asked Oberon.

"I have no idea." replied the Elf. "Only the women of the Un-Beautifuls know how to pass though its force-field, that's why I wanted to come back with them."

Utterly frustrated, Oberon picked up a rock and threw it straight at the Electric-Waterfall, expecting the powerful electric current to break the rock to pieces.

Instead, we saw the rock burst through the wall, seeming to tear a large hole in the centre. As it went through, the sound of a loud clunk echoed out. Then the hole seemed to close up, the electric buzzing and spitting sparks as it did so.

"Did you see that?" asked Oberon.

"Yes." I answered. "And I do believe I saw some kind of door behind the wall.

"Do you know what I think? I think these rocks are some kind of lode-stone, a sort of magnetic rock which can withstand the electric current." continued Oberon, bending down to pick up another rock and examining it closely.

"There is a door, behind the Electric-Waterfall." chimed in the Elf. "It opens to a tunnel which runs through the mountain, to bring you out to the Lands of the Flowers. I saw one of the Un-Beautiful women open the door with a key." he finished.

"Let the three of us all throw a rock at the Electric-Waterfall and see what happens." said Oberon, hefting the large rock in his hand.

Choosing a large boulder, I waited for the Elf to find a suitable stone, then, as Oberon gave the word, we all threw the rocks at the wall. The rocks burst through with a loud crack, leaving a trail of sparks showering the earth.

Our rocks had caused a large tear in the curtain of the Electric-Waterfall, which was big enough for a small animal to get through and we could see the door, just before the current repaired the rip, so that it crackled and spat once more.

"Did you see the lock, Pucker-Up?" asked Oberon, now becoming excited.

"Yes." I said. "It is seated on the left-hand side." My mind whirled.

"I have an idea, Sire." I said, searching through my pockets and drawing out the silver key which once locked the door in the Christmas-Tree. Holding it up, I went on...

"I wonder if this key will fit the lock."

"We have to try it, to see if the key will unlock the door!" cried Oberon, before turning to the Elf.

"Elf, can you run fast?" he asked.

"I was the fastest runner of all the Wood-Painters, when I was younger." the Elf replied.

"Then I want you to do something for us, which will take a lot of courage."

The Elf looked from Oberon to me, rather dubious. "What do you want me to do?" he asked, suspiciously.

"What we ask you to do is to wait till Pucker-Up and I have thrown a rock each at the Electric-Waterfall, so the rocks tear a hole just big enough for you to jump through. Then you try the key in the lock, to unlock the door for us." said Oberon.

"Why me?" demanded the Elf.

"Because you are the smallest and can get through the tear and, also, because you are a Wood-Painter. Is it not true that the Wood-Painters are well known for their bravery." added Oberon.

"Yes, that's true." said the Elf. "We Wood-Painters are the bravest of Elves. Of course I will try to open the door. Give me the key then."

I handed the Elf the silver key and he stood as close to the Electric-Waterfall as possible, waiting as Oberon and I carefully chose as big a rock as we could manage.

"Are we ready?" asked Oberon.

"I am." I said, lifting my arm.

"I am ready." shouted the Elf, his best foot forward.

"Throw!" shouted Oberon and we both let fly with our rocks, seeing them strike the Electric-Waterfall, to rent a large hole through its fierceness. At the same time, we saw the Elf dash forward, jumping through the hole, to fit the key in the lock. It turned and the door came open as the Elf pulled with all his might.

Then, an amazing thing happened. First there was a blinding flash and the Electric-Waterfall vanished, as quickly as a light goes out when switched off. Before us was just the bare face of the mountain, with the Elf standing by the open door.

Without waiting any longer, Oberon and I ran forward, to join the Elf and go through the door, beginning to walk quickly through the tunnel. Behind us, the Elf had closed the door, which seemed to switch the electric on once more and we could hear the buzz and fusing as the Electric-Waterfall began to operate again.

"Do you see the light ahead?" said Oberon as we ran towards the end of the tunnel with some excitement, not sure of what we would come up against but anxious to rescue the Queen Titania.

"Isn't it beautiful?" breathed Oberon.

We stood at the opening of the tunnel, high up, overlooking large green fields, carpeted with flowers, bluebells and poppies, daisies and violets, the mixture of colours dazzling the eye, under a bluest of azure skies.

"That's why they call it the Land of the Flowers." said the Elf, then pointed an excited finger.

"Look…Look down there!" he shouted.

Below us, close to a clear pool, sat a group of women, lounging in long flowing blue gowns.

"There's Titania!" I exclaimed, pointing her out, so

that Oberon began to run down the grassy hill, calling out to her.

I saw her get to her feet, while the women in blue gowns, quickly rose to their feet and began to run, losing themselves in the tall grass further down.

Oberon had reached Titania and I waited till they had greeted themselves, with kisses and hugs, holding tight to each other.

Once I felt they had enough time to greet each other, I ran down the hill to join them and find out exactly what was going on.

From what I saw, it did not seem that Titania had been badly treated. In fact, she looked very well indeed.

"At first, I thought the Un-Beautifuls were going to harm me." said Titania.

"Especially when they dragged me away from the Celebration Party and the dancing. But they really were very kind and wanted me to show them how to comb their hair and try to be as beautiful as I." she finished.

"But why did they run away when we arrived?" asked Oberon.

"Because they were afraid you would find them so ugly that you would try to kill them. They ran to get their Ostrich fans, which they keep in front of their faces." explained Titania.

As Titania talked, she led us to one of the grass-thatched huts and we now sat on pillows made from Cowslips.

The Elf yawned, for it had been a tiring time for him and now he lay out on the pillows and began to sleep.

Titania left us for a while and returned with some bowls, which were filled with food. We dined as we talked, from Coconut bowls of Nectar-Dew and honey from the wild Honey-Rose with Sugared Chocolate-Raspberries.

"Why are they so ugly?" I asked, having not yet seen the women close up, though already afraid of what they might look like.

"They are not really ugly at all." answered Titania. "The truth is, they have been enchanted by a wild Satyr-Warlock, who put them under a spell, convincing them they are so ugly that they have to wear masks. They are made to sit and paint the likeness of the masks, which the Satyr-Warlock sells to bad Mortals, who use the masks to frighten Mortal-Children when they misbehave."

"And that's why the Un-Beautifuls cannot give us their boxes of Sun-Ray paints." said the Elf, waking up from his sleep and rubbing his eyes. "They need it all to paint those ugly masks for the Satyr-Warlock!" Saying that, the Elf promptly fell back asleep again and started to snore.

"So they are really beautiful, under the masks they wear, their real faces?" asked Oberon.

"Yes." answered Titania. "Though they have such a strong belief, that they are ugly under the masks, that they refuse to take the masks off!"

THE UN-BEAUTIFUL

"That is so sad." I said, feeling really sorry for the Un-Beautifuls.

"That's the power of belief." returned Oberon. "If you don't believe in yourself, then you can never see your inner beauty."

"And there's nothing anyone can do?" I asked.

"The only thing anyone can do to change things is to find something which has a stronger magic, to make the women believe the truth of their natural beauty." said Oberon with a shrug.

"If only we could find a way to convince them." sighed Titania, clearing the empty Coconut dishes away.

Oberon cupped his chin in his hand and I could almost see his mind ticking over. Then he sat up straight and smiled.

"Titania, My Queen." he said brightly. "I want you to go and bring all the women down to the poolside. Explain to them that I have some powerful medicine which will make them all beautiful again. I shall wait there with Pucker-Up till you bring them."

"What are you going to do, My Lord?" I asked, mystified.

"You will have to wait and see." replied Oberon, still smiling.

Leading me to the pool, he asked me to pick a bunch of Daisies, telling me to pick them clean with their stalks. I did as he asked and sat there watching as he deftly made a Daisy-Chain.

We sat till Titania arrived with all the women, who

waved large Ostrich-Feather fans in front of their faces, only taking quick peeps over the top as they saw us sitting there.

"Please, Ladies... Please be seated." Oberon begged, waiting till they had done as he asked.

"I now ask you to trust me." he said, holding up the Daisy-Chain. "Trust me and I will show you a stronger magic than any that bad Satyr-Warlock ever has."

The Un-Beautifuls waved their fans, hiding their faces and whispering among each other. Titania, who sat amongst them, sensed their unease and coaxed them.

"Please have faith in My Lord Oberon's magic." she urged, although not quite sure what Oberon had in mind.

She only knew of her own great faith in him.

"Now." ordered Oberon. "I want you, Titania, and you, Pucker-Up, to go and pluck the most prettiest Daisies, enough for each of the women to make a Daisy-Chain."

Titania and I made ourselves busy, going among the Daisies, plucking them clean to their stems and returned, giving each of the women enough Daisies, to make themselves a Daisy-Chain.

Oberon watched them, seated serenely, then rose as he saw each of them hold up a Daisy-Chain.

"Now, sweet Ladies, watch me carefully, for I will first demonstrate my magic by making myself beautiful with the charm of the Daisy-Chain."

Gently and with a great show of pretence, he placed the Daisy-Chain around his neck. I was not aware of what he was doing but while the Un-Beautifuls watched his face, he had slipped off the ring on his Mask finger, to replace it on his Unmask finger, so that his royal face underwent a change of such beauty that all the Un-Beautifuls gasped in amazement.

"Now, Ladies… I would like you to lower your Ostrich fans and let us see your masks."

I sat with bated breath, hoping not to be too shocked by the ugliness of the Un-Beautifuls.

As the women, one by one, lowered their Ostrich-Feather fans, I was aghast at the hideous appearances of their faces, spiteful with ravages and pits, noses which ran and mouths of thin yellow lines. I averted my eyes, not wanting to look anymore.

"Now, Ladies… I want you all to gently place the Daisy-Chains around your necks as I did and then remove your masks, just as I did. Remember to have faith in the change and your natural beauty." said Oberon in a most gentle way.

Each of the Un-Beautifuls did as Oberon asked, putting the Daisy-Chains around their necks and then put their hands to their faces, to lift away the frightening masks.

I gasped at the difference, for the Un-Beautifuls were, indeed, truly beautiful, each one as pretty as the Daisy-Chains they wore around their necks.

"Now sweet Ladies… I want you all to go and look

at yourselves in the pond, lean over and look at your reflections. Know how your belief in me and the faith you have in yourselves has made you beautiful once more."

It took them some time, to pluck up the courage to look at themselves in the glass of the pool and upon seeing themselves, cried out in joy, dancing on their toes, telling each other how pretty they were.

"How do we ever thank you?" they asked of Oberon. "All I ask is that you continue to have faith in yourselves. It does not matter how a person looks, faith in the self will bring out the natural beauty. Now I want you to go with Titania. She will show you how to plait your hair and enjoy your beauty."

I enjoyed watching Titania show the women how to comb their hair, to unravel the knots, so the hair flowed in plaits and ringlets down their backs. She had also had them discard the blue gowns they had all worn, so that they now wore beautiful dresses of different colours.

Oberon had lit a fire and was burning the masks cast off by the women. Speaking to them, he now called them The-Beautifuls, that they gloried in their new name, calling it to each other over and over again.

"We have work to do." said Oberon at last, clapping his hands for attention.

The-Beautifuls stood, waiting.

"Which of you is the Queen?" he asked.

"We have no Queen here." said one, stepping forward. "For we are all equal as we are now all beautiful."

"Then I shall speak to you all." said Oberon. "I want you all to go and fetch the Satyr-Warlock to me. Tell him that the spell has been broken and you are now The-Beautifuls and I wish to speak with him. You all have the power to do as you wish and, should he not come with you, then drag him here."

The-Beautifuls ran, seeking out the Satyr-Warlock, throwing vine-ropes about his neck and dragging him, crying, to face Oberon.

"Henceforth, evil Satyr... You are banished from this land and will walk, evermore, on tiptoes through the Dark-Lands." thundered Oberon, so that all who listened, shuddered at the threat in his voice.

The Satyr cringed, knowing that he stood in front of the mighty Oberon, King of all the Fairy-Folk.

"Take him away and deliver him from your lands." he ordered.

Some of The-Beautifuls led the Satyr-Warlock away, to put him outside the boundaries of their lands.

It was later and, having woken the Elf from his sleep, Oberon gathered The-Beautifuls around him. He held Titania's hand as he told the women that we had to leave, to continue our journey.

"But first." he said. " I would ask you to give all your boxes of Sun-Ray paints to this brave Wood-Painter, who has served us all so well. You will not need the paints now, having to paint no more masks for the evil Satyr. And the Wood-Painters need those paints to keep all the trees and flowers in colour."

"We will give you all the Sun-Ray paint boxes we have." said one of The-Beautifuls.

"But can you allow Titania to stay with us till you come back from your journey? We need her, to show us how to do our hair properly and to act as beautiful women once again." asked another.

"I cannot say whether Titania can stay or come with us." replied Oberon. "It is up to her what choice she makes."

"Then may we ask her?" asked The-Beautiful.

"Of course you may." replied Oberon.

"It might be better that Her Majesty stays, Sire." I said. "For we do not know what dangers lie ahead. Besides, she does love being with The-Beautifuls."

"Indeed, you are right, Pucker-Up. But, still, it is up to her to make the decision." said Oberon.

Titania was certainly happy, to stay with The-Beautifuls, although I think Oberon saw the sense of my suggestion and inferred it would be better that she stay behind and wait till we came back.

So it was settled and with a sad farewell, we left the land of The-Beautifuls, weighed down with the boxes of Sun-Ray paints, making our way through the fields of violets and clover, towards the forests of the Wood-Painters.

We had not gone far when Oberon had us wait until he had taken the Un-Mask ring from one hand, to exchange it for the other, so that he was now a Fairy-Tog once again.

"I had to wait until we were out of sight of The-

Beautifuls explained Oberon. "For, had The-Beautifuls seen me change back into my disguise, they would have thought the spell would soon wear off and they would be ugly again. This way, they will always be beautiful and I can be Un-Seen as Oberon, the King of all Fairy-Folk.

"And very wise, too, your Majesty." I applauded.

We had travelled quite a distance from the Land of The-Beautifuls, crossing two streams and having to hide from a monster Gerbil, before we came to the forests of the Wood-Painters.

"There!" exclaimed Elf, becoming excited. "Just beyond the next bend is the Enormity-Bridge."

"The Enormity-Bridge?" I asked.

"It's a bridge which takes us into a new time." explained Elf, puffing at the weight of the Sun-Ray paint-boxes.

I was not sure what Elf meant, because, to me, time was never new. Once we got there, in time I mean, time was old. I suppose we could always look forward to a new time in the future, as long as we did not always stay in the present.

I must admit, I did get some strange thoughts into my head at times but, then, that's why the Kiss-Kids made me the Turner of Good Fortune.

"Here we are… The Enormity-Bridge!" exclaimed Elf.

"What kind of bridge is this?" asked Oberon as we stepped onto the wooden runway.

"It lays flat onto the ground, I mean, normally, a bridge crosses over a river or a chasm… It has to cross over something. But this bridge is useless, we might as well walk round it!"

"I am sorry if you don't like our bridge." sniffed Elf. "But, you see, a bridge is to leave one place and end with another. It is an Ending and a New Beginning", he explained.

"Ah, I see what you mean." said Oberon, even though he did not see what Elf meant at all.

We had nearly reached the end of the bridge when we saw a small, busy, creature, standing there at the end. He seemed to be some kind of Pugling, with a belligerent pug face and small round body, attached to four stumpy legs. What was unusual about him was his dress-sense. He wore, on his head, a black beret, pulled to a jaunty angle. On his body was a white smock, while his little legs were covered in striped woollen socks, though they did not cover his feet.

"What is that?" I asked.

"It's a Squabbler." answered Elf, suddenly appearing to lose confidence, his head bowing to the Squabbler, who leaned against the bridge-post, tapping a foot with impatience.

"A merry hail to you, Squabbler!" saluted Oberon in a hearty way.

"Where have you been, Joy-Stick-One?" demanded the Squabbler of the Elf, not even bothering to acknowledge Oberon's hearty greeting.

"I am sorry, Squabbler." replied the Elf, whom now seemed to have a name. "I have managed to get the paint, though I have had such a terrible time of it."
"Don't give me excuses, Joy-Stick-One. Put the boxes down and give me my moustache!" demanded the Squabbler, suddenly taking a paint-brush from behind his ear and holding it out.

I had never heard such rudeness, although we Fairy-Folk were taught never to pre-make judgments on others. So Oberon and I stood silent as we watched the proceedings. The Elf, now Joy-Stick-One, had put his paint-boxes down and, opening one box, took the offered paint-brush and, wetting it with the tip of his tongue, dipped it into the black paint then painted a whirly moustache on the pug-like face of the Squabbler.

"Would you like some eye-spectacles?" inquired the Elf.

"Hmmm. Yes, I think I would." replied the Squabbler and stood still as Elf painted a pair of glasses onto the Squabbler's face.

"That will do." said the Squabbler and, taking the brush and paint-box from Elf, began to march off into the woods.

"Excuse me!" I called, not able to hold in my anger any longer.

The Squabbler stopped, turning to look at me.

"Well, what do you want…I haven't got a lot of time!" he snapped.

"I think." I said. "That you owe this Elf, this Wood-

Painter an apology. He went to a lot of trouble to get those Sun-Ray paints!"

"A Wood-Painter?" replied the Squabbler, scornfully pointing at the Elf. "He's not a Wood-Painter, he's just an Elf!"

With that, the Squabbler turned and continued to walk, till he was lost from sight, disappearing among the trees.

"Well!" exclaimed Oberon. "What was that all about?"

"I suppose I had better explain." said the Elf, sitting on top of the Sun-Ray paint-boxes.

Oberon and I lay down the paint-boxes we carried and sat, preparing to listen to the Elf.

"In the land of the Wood-Painters." he began. "Each of we Elves were given a Squabbler to lead us a Dog's-Life! You see, many years ago, we were unkind to the Mortals. We used to steal their lovely babies, exchanging them for an ugly Grimm-Child and selling the Grimm-Mothers the Mortal-Child. We were found guilty of being evil against the Mortals by the Supreme Guilt Council and, as punishment, ordered to spend the rest of our lives taking care of a Squabbler."

"So, you are not a Wood-Painter at all, just a Dogs-Body." I said.

"I only said that so I would appear important." said the Elf, his head lowered.

"Well, I can't say I feel sorry for you all." I replied.

"Nor me." echoed Oberon. "I think it was a just

punishment!"

"Yes, you are right." said the Elf, shame-faced.

Then continued talking, as we picked up the paint-boxes and made our way into the woods.

"The Squabblers have no names, they are just called Squabblers. Likewise, we Elves are numbered. I am Joy-Stick-One, just known as One for short. The next is Joy-Stick-Two, called Two and so on, down the line, till we reach Joy-Stick-Five-Hundred."

"So you Elves are slaves to the Squabblers?" I said.

"Yes." answered the Elf. "Except Mondays, when the Squabblers have to wash our feet."

"Wash your feet? Why should they have to do that?" I asked, mystified.

"It is decreed they do so, to remind them of humility." explained the Elf.

"A good thing, too." rejoined Oberon.

We had entered the forest, going deeper into the woods, till the Elf said… "Here we are."

"Where?" I asked, staring round.

"Up there." replied the Elf, pointing upwards and I looked up, to see that each giant tree had a Tree-House, perched among its branches. There was a connecting bridge of ropes which went from one house to another, an Air-Roadway.

It was a wondrous sight! I had always wanted to live high, up among the canopies of the forest, where the Birds would sing each morning and the air was fresh.

"How wonderful!" I exclaimed. "So close to the sky!"

THE SQUABBLER

1

"It is beautiful." remarked Oberon staring up. "But how do we get up there?"

"We Elves stay up there, most of the time. We only come down once on a Thursday, to collect the wood blocks which the Squabblers use to paint on." explained the Elf. "Our job is to stay up there, in the houses. Then, when a Squabbler wants to come down, they climb into a wooden bucket, which we let down on a rope, then haul it up when they want to come back up again." furthered the Elf.

"So, how do you Elves get up there?" asked Oberon.

"We have to go to the back of the Long-Hut, where there is a rope ladder which leads up to the Enter-Way, the start of the rope-bridges. Then we make our way to whichever tree-house we live." said the Elf.

"Come along, slowcoach!" shouted the Squabbler, suddenly appearing round a tree and stamping a foot.

"Coming." the Elf called, starting to hurry. "We have to take the Sun-Ray paints to the Long-Hut. The other Squabblers will be there, waiting for the Elves to paint the moustaches onto their faces."

We started to hurry, Elf leading us between an avenue of trees, till we came to a large wooden hut.

We could hear the noise, of shouting voices, long before we got there, getting really loud as we entered.

We did not even have time to look round before the Elves came rushing up to us, quickly relieving us of all the Sun-Ray paint-boxes, running back to the assorted Squabblers, starting to paint their faces with the same swirling moustache that the Elf had painted on his Squabbler.

Some Squabblers were demanding spectacles, then walking around showing others, demanding they offer any criticism of the way they looked.

"How do the Elves know which Squabbler is theirs?" I asked Oberon. "All the Squabblers look alike!"

"The Squabblers have numbers, painted on their berets." answered Oberon.

How strange, I thought… But then, Oberon could see over the top of their heads. That explained to me why the Squabblers kept bending their heads every now and again, like nodding dogs.

I also saw that they constantly squabbled with each other, the room loud with raised and excited voices. That also explained why they were called Squabblers.

"Excuse me!" shouted Oberon in a loud voice.

The room went a deathly quiet as all heads turned to look at us. It was quite embarrassing, though Oberon seemed not to care.

"Who are these people?" demanded one Squabbler.

"And what are they doing here?" shouted another, bobbing his head.

"Joy-Stick-One brought them, said another.

"Put Joy-Stick-One before a Universal-Board!" shouted a third Squabbler.

At that, all the Elves stopped painting moustaches and went under the long tables, which ranged down the centre of the room. Then all the Squabblers started to yodel at the tops of their voices, a tremendous racket.

"Stop!" shouted Oberon, so loud that some of the black berets flew from the top of the Squabblers heads, so that they scrambled about, retrieving the hats and, checking the right numbers, before putting the berets back on their heads.

The hall stayed quiet, all eyes on Oberon.

"I might tell you Squabblers that, had not Joy-Stick-One faced many dangers and fears on your behalf, then you would never have got those boxes of Sun-Ray paints. I think you should all thank him!"

The Squabblers looked at each other.

"Thank an Elf? You are quite mad!" shouted one, coming forward.

"And you are quite rude, Number Fifty-One!" retorted Oberon, reading the number on the Squabbler's beret.

"Do you know who you are talking to?" demanded the Squabbler.

"No." said Oberon. "You all look the same to me, mad Pug-Dogs, who look like French artists!"

"I only happen to be the best Wood-Painter in the forest!" said the Squabbler, pointing at himself in a boastful manner.

"That may be." said Oberon. "But that does not excuse your rudeness to us. After all, we are visitors."

"We did not ask you to come here! We did not invite

you! Anyway, what do you want from us?"

"Pucker-Up and I want to be shown where the Dark-Clan live." answered Oberon.

At these words, all the Squabblers began to shout and argue, till Squabbler Fifty-One turned and held up a hand. The room went quiet and he turned back to Oberon.

"Now I know you are quite mad!" declared the Squabbler. "No-one goes there, or even wants to. It's an evil dark and gloomy place. And, even if you wanted to go, you would not be able to pass the Dragon-Mountain."

"Why can't we get past the Dragon-Mountain?" I asked.

The Squabbler did not answer me, instead he turned. "Joy-Stick-Twenty-Two!" he shouted.

The Elf called Joy-Stick-Twenty-Two came out from under the table and ran to face the Squabbler.

"Fetch me the large periscope." he ordered.

We did not have to wait long before the Elf came back, struggling under the weight of a very large periscope.

"Set it up outside." ordered the Squabbler.

The Elf carried the periscope outside and set it so that its top end could see over the trees.

"Come outside with me." said the Squabbler, so that Oberon and I followed him to where the periscope was set up.

"Take a look through the end of the periscope." instructed the Squabbler.

Oberon put his eyes to the end of the periscope.
"Now, can you see the Mountain?" asked the
Squabbler.
"Yes." answered Oberon.
"Now, run your eyes down to the base of the
Mountain. Do you see that cave?" asked the
Squabbler.
Oberon turned the periscope so that he could see the
large black opening of the cave.
"Indeed, I can see the cave now." he said.
"In that cave." said the Squabbler, ominously. "Lives
a very large and dangerous Dragon. He breathes out
fire, which can kill you at ten paces and will kill
anyone or anything who tries to pass his cave."
Oberon moved away from the periscope.
"Do you know, that Dragon burned up three of our
Elves in the last three Moon-Lights!" said the
Squabbler, prodding Oberon.
"Why would the Elves go near the cave?" asked
Oberon.
"Because, in the area of the cave lies the best wood-
blocks, they show up the true colours when they are
painted on." answered the Squabbler, with some
impatience.
He went on to explain…
"It's important that we paint flowers in the best of
colours, so that the Mortal Flower-Planters know
what the new flowers should look like when they are
born each Spring-Time."
"I wonder why the Dragon burns anyone who goes

near his cave." Oberon mused. "There must be a reason."

"The reason is." retorted the Squabbler, as if Oberon should already know. "The Dragon is lonely and needs a Lady-Dragon for company. That's why he is so angry all the time!"

Oberon stood still, deep in thought.

Then he said, "If I help you, so that your Elves can walk easily past the Dragon's cave, without the Dragon coming out, to burn them up, will you help Pucker-Up and I to reach to where the Dark-Clan live?"

"If you can do that, I will most certainly help you get to the lands of the Crow-Dressers, that's what they are called, those Dark-Clan folk." asserted the Squabbler.

"Good." said Oberon. "Firstly, can you get me four round wooden wheel-blocks, with the face of Pucker-Up painted on them?"

"That's very easily done." replied the Squabbler.

I was quite sure I did not like the idea of my face being used on the blocks, though I said nothing.

"Is that all you want?" asked the Squabbler.

"I can tell you more when Pucker-Up and I have returned." answered Oberon, indicating that was all that was needed to be done, till I had my face painted on the four wheels.

"Sit down." said the Squabbler, having secured the wooden wheels and opened one of the Sun-Ray paint-boxes. He began to paint my face, squinting at

me from time to time and nodding each time his brushed touched the blocks.

I sat patiently till Squabbler Fifty-One had finished painting.

"That really is so very good." I said, leaving the chair and walking round to inspect the face-paintings. They certainly were life-like.

"Would you like a moustache and eye-spectacles painted on?" asked the Squabbler, washing his brushes.

"No thank you." I replied, not very happy with the prospect of seeing me wearing a moustache and spectacles.

"We'll wait till the paint has dried, then you and I, Pucker-Up, will go and pay the Dragon a visit." said Oberon as he and I sat and waited, watching the paint dry, making the faces on the wheels come alive even more.

"Are we ready?" asked Oberon, touching the paint and seeing none come away from the blocks. "Then let's go." he finished, indicating I carry the wooden wheels.

We made our way to the Mountain-Pass, following the Squabbler, who abruptly left us when we had reached the narrow gorge.

"There's the cave." Oberon whispered.

It was very quiet and the mouth of the cave seemed dark and empty.

"Perhaps the Dragon isn't there." I suggested.

"That's where you come in, Pucker-Up." replied

Oberon, pointing at the round blocks.

"I want you to wheel the blocks past the cave, shouting out as you do so." he finished.

While I did not like the idea of putting myself in danger, I knew it was for the benefit of the Kiss-Kids. I also knew that Oberon would be watching, taking note of what happened, so that any plan he had would work.

Creeping as near as I dare and taking each wheel, I shouted as loud as I could, rolling them, one at a time, across the opening of the cave.

No sooner had I done so, than a huge fire-breathing beast with red eyes and evil-dripping fangs, came roaring out of the cave, to set each wheel alight in an instant, burning them to a pile of ashes.

"I have never seen anything so fierce or horrid!" I exclaimed as we made our way back to the Tree-Camp.

Oberon said nothing, his mind working through different ideas till, at last he nodded, beginning to walk quite fast.

When we arrived back at the Tree-Camp, all the Squabblers had been hauled up to their huts. The Elves were asleep, out by the front doors on small wooden mats.

Only Squabbler Fifty-One sat alone in the Long-Hut, his small round eyes watching us as we entered.

"Well?" he demanded.

"I want you to help us with your artwork." said Oberon, as we both sat opposite the Squabbler.

"I can paint anything you like." said the Squabbler.
"Can you paint a life-size Lady-Dragon?" asked Oberon.
"Of course I can." answered the Squabbler in a very sure way. "As big as you like and in any colour!"
"But are you brave, as brave as Pucker-Up?" asked Oberon, looking at the Squabbler, very dubiously.
"Not only am I the best painter here but I am also the most bravest!" said the Squabbler, puffing out his chest, his face more pugnacious then ever.
"Then, shall I tell you what Pucker-Up and I want from you? If you do it, not only will you become a most famous person, but others will sing songs of your deed."
I have never seen a person or thing, so ready to put themselves at such serious risk as did the Squabbler, the lights of a hero shining in his eyes.
"Tell me what I have to do and I will do it!" cried the Squabbler, alive to any plan of action, already seeing himself as a hero.
Oberon kept his voice calm and low, leaning towards the Squabbler as he spoke, so that I could not hear much of what he said.
"I will do it!" exclaimed the Squabbler, banging his fist on the table.
"Excellent!" acknowledged Oberon. "Bring your paints and let us go back to the Dragon's cave."

Retracing our steps back towards the Dragon's lair, I sensed that the Squabbler was having second thoughts about the plan of action, though Oberon, sensing it also, kept up a flow of encouraging words, reminding the Squabbler of the fame which awaited him.

Having reached the place where I had rolled the wooden wheels, we stopped, as silent as any grave. Reaching inside his tunic, Oberon took out the Illusion-Ball, which the Santa-Man had given him. Whispering some words, he placed the ball on the ground. I saw it swirl as the smoky colours rushed around inside the ball and then, suddenly, it started expanding, growing rounder and fatter, until it was as big as Oberon himself.

"Open." ordered Oberon.

The ball seemed to split into two halves.

"In you go." said Oberon to the Squabbler in a quiet voice.

For a fraction of time, the Squabbler hesitated then climbed into one half of the ball, holding tightly onto the Sun-Ray box of paints. The ball closed up with a soft hiss and I could see the Squabbler through the swirling smoke.

"Small." said Oberon and I watched, my mouth open as the ball began to grow smaller, until it was the size of a large pea.

"Now, Pucker-Up, when you rolled the wooden wheels past the cave, I saw there were three Jigs of Time, before the Dragon got to the mouth of the cave and began to burn the wheels up. What I want you to do is run past the cave, as quick as you can, before the Dragon reaches the mouth.

As you run past, I want you to throw the ball as hard as you can, so it goes over the Dragon's head and into the back of the cave."

"That's not a very long time, three Jigs!" I remarked.

"That's why you must run as fast as you can." said Oberon with a smile.

I picked up the ball, it felt so small and light, that I wondered how the Squabbler must be feeling.

"Off you go!" said Oberon, giving me a push, so that I propelled myself across the mouth of the cave, throwing the ball as hard as I could.

I was back, beside Oberon before the head of the Dragon appeared, it nostrils breathing a blast of red hot flame. Its red eyes glared around and, seeing no-one, retreated back into the cave, its tail thumping the ground angrily.

"Dragon!" shouted Oberon, so loud that I jumped in fright.

The Dragon roared to the front of the cave again, its eyes seeking out who had made such a loud noise. Oberon and I kept low, behind a small outcrop.

Coming out of its lair, the Dragon marched up and down, its tail lashing at the air, while the fire belched from its nostrils in a fierce stench.

"Grow and open, Ball!" shouted Oberon, just as the Dragon started to go back into the cave.

Once more the Dragon roared in anger, the flames causing such a stink that the Dragon could not see or smell us in our hiding place.

Oberon kept calling the Dragon, every time it started

THE DRAGON

to go back into the cave, then, nodding his head and seeming to count, Oberon shouted, "Ball, grow small!"

Then Oberon stopped shouting and the Dragon, hearing it all go quiet, went back into the cave, then seemed to make the most sweetest of sounds, almost a loud purring and cooing.

Oberon rose to his feet and suddenly, showing no fear of the slightest concern, walked easily to the mouth of the cave.

Only the sounds of delight came from the cave, there was no sign of the fire-breathing Dragon.

"Pucker-Up." Oberon called to me. "Will you just pop into the cave and pick up the ball, please."

I trusted Oberon, for he was my friend and we had travelled many places together. Should he wish me to be burned alive, then so be it.

Gallantly, I walked forward and entered the cave. I saw a most remarkable sight, for there, on the far wall of the cave, was a beautiful life-sized painting of a beautiful female Dragon. In front of the painting lay the Dragon, its eyes had lost all fierceness, the fire gone, just a pale stream of pink and velvet smoke scenting the air of the cave. Its mouth was soft and making all sorts of Love-Calls, not seeming to care about me as I walked past it, to retrieve the ball and carry it back to the waiting Oberon.

"Thank you, Pucker-Up." said Oberon, taking the ball and laying it on the ground.

"Grow big." he ordered and the ball began to grow,

until it reached the large size once again, where it split into two halves and out stepped the Squabbler, a very pleased smile on its pug-like face.

"Am I famous now?" he asked.

"I assure you, Squabbler Fifty-One, your name will go down into an Always Summer-Time." replied Oberon, at the same time ordering the ball to go back to its original size.

The ball shrivelled back, so that Oberon picked it up and put it back into a pocket in his tunic.

It seemed that the Squabblers were not allowed to have a Celebration-Day, though it was allowed that they would have a day off from painting flowers, to paint whatever they liked, every Squabbler Fifty-One Day, in recognition for Squabbler Fifty-One's bravery.

"As the hero, I shall paint a double-chin to my face." said Squabbler Fifty-One. "And only me, because I am the hero and famous. No-one else can have a painted double-chin!"

"Now, what about your promise, to take us to where the Dark-Clan live." said Oberon, once Squabbler Fifty-One had painted a double-chin on his face.

"Well that's a bit tricky, for two reasons." said the famous Squabbler.

"The first reason is that no-one can fly over the Mountains, because of the black clouds which hug the top. Anyone who gets near the black clouds will be sucked into dark holes and will never be seen again."

"Then we can walk." said Oberon, quickly.

"And that's the second reason why it will be tricky. The entrance to the Dark-Clan lands is a narrow passage which has a floor covered by the Zithering-Tapers, snakes of such venom, that even a touch with one of their tongues will kill you." reported the Squabbler.

Oberon considered this, his brows drawn.

"So." he said. "No-one can walk where those snakes are."

"That's right." rejoined the Squabbler. "Only we Squabblers can walk where the Zitherers are." he added.

"You mean, you can go through the path without being bitten?" asked Oberon, his eyebrows raising.

"Of course." said the Squabbler, adding, "The Zitherers hate our skin, so they don't bite us!"

"Why can't you carry us through the Zitherers?" I asked.

"Are you mad?" shouted the Squabbler, giving me a look. He began to laugh, pointing at us.

"Look at the size of you both!" he laughed. "How do think I can carry you around. Why, even an Elf could not carry your weight!"

"Then how many Squabblers would it take to carry me?" asked Oberon.

The Squabbler stopped laughing, to stare at Oberon, becoming serious, his eyes considering.

"I would think it would take four of us, at least." he answered, wrinkling his pug face up in thought.

"Then could twelve Squabblers carry both of us?" asked Oberon, leaning forward.

"Easily!" bragged the Squabbler. "Twelve of us can carry both you and the little Gnome, plus another two Gnomes!" bragged the Squabbler, enjoying my look of anger.

I disliked being called a little Gnome, as if I was nothing. But a glance from Oberon reminded me of my place and the fact that I was, indeed, a little Gnome.

"Yes, I think you are quite strong and capable." said Oberon to the Squabbler, voicing appeasement. "But can you carry a dug-out, a boat made from a tree, as well as us?"

"We Squabblers don't need a boat? Why would we want to carry a boat?" asked the Squabbler.

"But, can you carry us, along with a boat?" insisted Oberon.

I listened to the talking, losing any sense of where the conversation was leading. But I knew of Oberon, that he was a wily leader, a shrewd King, indeed.

"Yes." answered the Squabbler. "If we had to."

"Then get the Elves to chop down a tree and cut the inside out so they make a boat, a dug-out. When it is done, we can test your strength." finished Oberon.

With this competitive thought ringing in his ears, Squabbler Fifty-One went to a tree cupboard and brought out a large megaphone and, bringing it to his lips, shouted, "All Elves who are not off sick, or have other important work to do, will you come down to the Long-Hut immediately! This is Squabbler Fifty-One talking, your hero and famous Squabbler!"

Immediately, Elves began to rise from their sleeping mats, to descend down the rope-ladders, filing in order till they were all standing to attention in the Long-Hut.

"Elves? Who has ever made a boat out of a tree?" asked Squabbler Fifty-One.

"What is a boat?" asked Joy-Stick Five, taking off his pixie-hood and scratching his head.

"Of course!" exclaimed Squabbler Fifty-One. "The Elves are Wood-Folk, they are from the woods and forests, they have never seen the sea or the boats which sail on them."

Oberon went to a drawing-board and began to draw, explaining exactly what a boat looked like and how it should be cut from a tree.

He wrote down the measurements, of twenty Side-Kicks in length and two Side-Kicks wide.

"I will take charge, personally." said Squabbler Fifty-One, as he began to order the Elves into teams, of Who would do this and Who would do that.

"Follow me, Elf-Workers." he shouted, leading them towards the Inter-Tower Connection, where the tallest trees were.

The boat was not perfect, although this is what one would expect from Elves who had never seen a boat before. Nor, do I suspect had Squabbler Fifty-One seen a boat before, because he presented the boat with such an element of pride, saying, "We have really made you a most beautiful boat."

The fact is, I would have never wanted to put to sea in such a contraption!

"It looks a most beautiful boat." admired Oberon, this admission of seeing such beauty brought tears of happiness to Squabbler Fifty-One's eyes and I had to hide a smile.

"Shall we Squabblers paint it?" asked Squabbler Fifty-One, bringing out his Sun-Ray paint-box.

"No, thank you." replied Oberon. "It is such a beautiful shape and with such natural colour, it needs nothing more done to it."

"Not even a moustache on its front? Everything should have a moustache painted on it, even a pair of spectacles, if it needs it!" exclaimed Squabbler Fifty-One in a sulky voice.

"Ah, yes. I see what you mean." Oberon agreed, allowing that the boat needed to have a moustache, going so far as to allow that it needed spectacles.

"That's marvellous." said Oberon, admiring the painted moustache and spectacles which adorned the boat.

"Now, Squabbler Fifty-One." Oberon continued. "I want you to get another eleven of your strongest Squabblers, with you at the front, as the hero and most famous, of course. And I want you and all the rest to upturn the boat so it sits over you all, like a Turtle-Shell, so you can walk and run with all your legs poking out at the bottom, like a Caterpillar."

It took twenty-two goes before Squabbler Fifty-One and the chosen Squabblers could walk, with the upturned boat on top of them, without all tripping each other up and falling over.

But, eventually, they could walk and run at a trot with some sense of reasonability.

"Now." said Oberon. "Here is the test of your strength. Pucker-Up and I will climb onto the boat, to see if you can stand our weight, not only stand it but run with us on board."

"Get ready, fellow Squabblers." urged Squabbler Fifty-One, as Oberon and I climbed up, to straddle the boat.

"Now run!" ordered Oberon, so that the little legs of the Squabblers all started moving at once, the Caterpillar moving off at speed.

However, we had only gone a short distance when the legs of the Squabblers lost union and we all tumbled down in a clattering heap.

"Try again!" shouted Oberon as we picked ourselves up.

It took another thirty and a half tries, before the tiny legs ran in time and Oberon was satisfied, about the strength of the Squabblers and our safety aboard the upturned boat.

"Now, here is the plan." said Oberon, as he faced the Squabblers, seated before him.

"I want you, Squabbler Fifty-One, to lead your men, along with Pucker-Up and myself, to the entrance of the Dark-Clan lands. As you have informed us, there will be the Pathway of Zitherer-Snakes, a path full of hundreds of poisonous reptiles, which will kill me and Pucker-Up if they bite us.

Because they will not bite you Squabblers, you will be running through the snakes, carrying the upturned boat, with Pucker-Up and myself straddled on top. Once we have passed the 'Pathway of Zitherer-Snakes, you can let us get off the boat and wait there for us till we come back with the rescued Kiss-Diamond, that's if we come back." finished Oberon.

"That is so easy!" shouted Squabbler Fifty-One boastfully. "We Squabblers can easily carry you both over the snakes!"

"Then let us go to the Pathway of Zitherers and test ourselves!" replied Oberon, already starting to walk, instructing the Squabblers to pick up the boat and lead the way to the lands of the Dark-Clan.

We had left the woods and were on a bare stretch of desert, when we came to a pair of towering rocks which had, between them, a small channel of land which was covered with a sprawling mass of hundreds and hundreds of snakes, which spat and hissed, showing large and venomous fangs, dribbling toxic juices.

"This is the Pathway of Zitherer-Snakes, which leads to the Dark-Clan lands." said Squabbler Fifty-One.

I could see, beyond the snakes, that the sky was low and dark, with swirling clouds and black holes, drawing in whatever was carried up by the winds. It all looked bleak and threatening, with rumbles of thunder, followed by flashes of lightning, in the distance.

I must admit, I was not very happy, at the thought of entering this savage land, though, having Oberon with me, gave me the strength I needed. I stayed very close to him.

"Right, Squabblers!" ordered Oberon.

"Lift the boat over your heads and get in step! That's good. Now, lower the boat, so Pucker-Up and myself can climb aboard."

The boat was lowered and, once Oberon and I had straddled the top, Oberon gave the order to rise, so that I felt myself lifted.

"Right! Together, Squabblers, let's run!" shouted Oberon and we moved off at a pace, Oberon and I hanging onto the boat with all our strength as the little legs of the Squabblers ran between the snakes, the snakes seeming to part, dividing into two separate waves as the Caterpillar ran through.

"Let the boat down now, Squabblers!" shouted Oberon as we reached the other side of the Pathway of Zitherer-Snakes. The snakes had closed ranks once more and I shuddered at the sight of the heaving venomous carpet.

I was now more aware of the closeness of such a threatening atmosphere, of the darkness, which seemed to cling to my body like a cold and chilling damp. I shuddered again as I looked up at the black clouds, rumbling above.

"Wait here, brave Squabblers." said Oberon as he

THE DARK-LANDS

indicated that I should go with him.

I turned as we began to walk, to see the Squabblers had seated themselves in the boat and were either eating sandwiches or starting to fall asleep.

"What way shall we go, Sire?" I asked, as we skirted a bubbling pool of tar.

"We walk in the open." replied Oberon. "The easiest way to be found is to walk in the open." he finished.

"But don't we want to creep in and rescue the Kiss-Diamond?" I asked.

"After all, how are we to rescue the Kiss-Diamond if we are captured by the Dark-Clan folk?" I queried.

"Where is the Kiss-Diamond being held?" Oberon asked.

"I've no idea." I replied, thinking hard. "If we don't know, how will we find it?" I asked, puzzled.

"The creatures from these Dark-Lands will tell us." said Oberon, starting to shout,

"Hallo!" he called. "Is anyone at home?"

Oberon's shouts seemed to enliven and enrage the thunder, which began to roar, as forked lightning and a wildest wind threw a tempest at us. Even so, with all this going on around us, I could hear Oberon's shouts.

"Come out and find us!" he shouted.

"There's a cave over there, where the road forks!" I shouted, above the noise. "Let's stay there till the noise dies down."

And with that, I began to run, reaching the cave and sat on a rock, just inside the mouth.

"Boo!"

I jumped in fright at the sound, turning to see a puce-faced little Anagram, dressed from head to foot in Crow's feathers, staring at me, before poking a tongue out.

I will admit, I did not know what an Anagram was, or what it looked like, never having seen one, but the name just sprang to mind, as a good idea comes when the mind spins a yarn.

"Boo!" said the Anagram, then poked out a yellow tongue once more.

"That's rude." I said.

"No it's not. That's how we Crow-Dressers greet strangers."

"Crow-Dressers?" I said. "Aren't you called the Dark-Clan?"

"Huh!" snorted the small figure. "That's what those who have never seen us think. They call us names because they don't know what we look like… We are called Crow-Dressers!"

"I do beg your pardon." I replied. "From now on I shall call you folk the Crow-Dressers."

By now, Oberon had arrived at the cave and stood, staring at the little figure, who had then turned to him, to say "Boo!" before poking its tongue out.

"It's an 'Anagram' I said. "It calls itself a Crow-Dresser, though I think Anagram sounds so much better."

"I don't understand it." said Oberon, scratching his head. The Dark-Clan folk have such a fearsome reputation, yet here we have a harmless little cherub, whose worst weapon is to poke its tongue out at us." he finished.

"Boo!" said a loud voice and Oberon turned to see a full-grown Crow-Dresser standing alongside two others, all dressed fully in Crow's feathers.

"I am Popular." said the first, poking out a yellow tongue. "And these two are named Confident and Peculiar." he continued, pointing at the other pair, who both poked out a tongue.

Oberon, far cleverer than I, realised that the word Boo, along with the poking out of a tongue was considered a greeting.

"Boo!" he exclaimed and poked out a tongue.

The three folk all returned the greeting once more, first to Oberon and then to me. I tried so hard not to giggle and poked my tongue out at the small Anagram I had first seen. It hid behind Popular, peeking out at me from time to time.

"As for thinking that we Dark-Clan folk are the very devils." said Popular. "That's because you pair are the first to ever come into our lands and actually see what we look like. You have to understand that most folk are afraid of the Unknown and what they have never seen, so they fear it."

"I most heartily agree with what you say." said Oberon, bowing, then continued, "Though it is said that you Dark-Clan folk have stolen the Kiss-Diamond from the land of the Kiss-Kids, which is the very reason why we are here. We mean to get it back!"

"Please call us Crow-Dressers and not Dark-Clan Folk." asked Popular. "We dislike the name Dark-Clan, it is not our faults that the land seems so dark and ominous. That is why we live underground, in caves of Anonmite, because of the dangerous weather above."

Oberon nodded, agreeing the name, Crow-Dresser, seemed far nicer and said "Boo!" when the Crow-Dressers poked a tongue out.

"Please follow us." said Popular

Oberon allowed us to be lead deeper into the cave, until it opened out into a series of large cavernous halls, each full of Crow-Dressers, milling about and who stared at Oberon and I, before saying "Boo!" then poking out a yellow tongue.

"You have to understand." said Popular, leading the way, which also attracted a large following of all kinds of Crow-Dressers. "We need light in these places, an extraordinary amount of bright light, so we might survive."

"Indeed, I do respect what you say." returned Oberon, poking his tongue out at some passing Crow-Dressers.

"Though I must remind you, the Kiss-Diamond is stolen property and, while we are not interested in exactly who stole it, you will also understand that the Kiss-Diamond is very important to the Clan of the Kiss-Kids, who need it to light up and grow the Love-Fruit, the juice of which paints the colours of the land of the Mortals. Without the Kiss-Diamond, the Kiss-Kids cannot cry the Pearl-Tears which the Moon-Queen needs, to light up her silver ball for the night sky, so the Mortals can continue to love each other."

The Crow-Dressers listened intently to every word Oberon had said.

"But what are we to do?" asked Confident, in an agitated state. "I mean, if we give you the Kiss-Diamond back, then we cannot survive at all, the Crow-Dressers will go to the lands of the Non-Existent, never to be seen again."

I looked at Oberon, very uncertain what to do.

"Sire?" I asked "What shall we do?"

"Before you speak." said Peculiar. "Let us take you to a very special place and show you what keeps us to this land.

"Of course, we will need permission from the Tri-Umphants, our most senior members." he finished, ushering us forward with a sweep of his hand.

"Yes." spoke Oberon. "Let us gain permission, so you can show myself and Pucker-Up exactly why the Kiss-Diamond is so important to you."

The door to the Court of the Tri-Umphants was securely closed, so that the three Crow-Dressers, Popular, Confident and Peculiar, all knocked three times, each calling out for permission to enter the court.

The door was swung open by a tiny Crow-Dresser, who wore a green hat, which reminded me of a

Parakeet. He hung onto the door handle as it opened, so that he continued to hang suspended with both feet kicking out.

"Will someone throw that Mercant out!" demanded a stern voice, so that another Crow-Dresser, larger and wearing a yellow hat, walked to the door and, lifting the tiny Crow-Dresser from the handle, carried him beyond the door with a warning not to come back. The Mercant, whatever he was, walked through the gathered crowd, poking his tongue out and laughing madly.

"What do you want?" demanded the middle Tri-Umphant.

At the far end of the hall seated at a table, on a rostrum, were three large Crow-Dressers, adorned in fancy robes of red and blue dyed Crow's feathers.

"We need permission to enter the Nesting-Hall!" shouted Popular, edging forward, that we followed his lead, edging closer to the rostrum.

The demand was met with a sudden tutting and very concerned faces from the Tri-Umphants.

"No-one, except the Dung-Collectors and the Feather-Hoarders, are allowed to go into the Nesting-Hall!" shouted the middle Crow-Dresser, after holding a heated debate with the other two.

"This stranger wants the Kiss-Diamond back!" shouted Popular.

"What!" was the astounded answer.

This time the three Tri-Umphants jumped up and down, hooting and throwing their coats over their heads.

"Throw them in the Tar-Pool!" cried the Crow-Dresser on the left.

"Throw them into the air, so the Black-Holes get them!" cried the one on the right.

"Let's just call them Mercants and throw them out!" exclaimed the middle one, to which the three all began to clap hands.

"While I much prefer the third suggestion, of simply being thrown out." said Oberon, coming right up to the table. "I will have you listen to me before you do."

The three Tri-Umphants blinked, their eyebrows raised, while they blew small bubbles of consternation.

"Why…Why… You…" spluttered the middle Crow-Dresser, before falling out of his chair. The other two sat silent, speechless.

Oberon waited till the middle Crow-Dresser regained his seat, before continuing.

"Then I shall just speak." said Oberon.

He began to speak, telling the Tri-Umphants of our travels and the reasons why we had to make this journey, so we could rescue the Kiss-Diamond.

As Oberon talked, the Tri-Umphants listened, their actions less agitated, sitting quietly as Oberon finished talking. This time they conferred in soft, whispering, voices.

"You have to understand." said the middle Crow-Dresser, at last. "We just cannot allow you to take the Kiss-Diamond. The magical light and heat from the Kiss-Diamond keeps the Crows nesting and laying their eggs, so that we can go on eating and wearing the Crow's feathers, the only cloth which our soft skin can bear. The dung from the Crows feeds the Mushrooms, which is our only diet, without which we would all perish. We have no wish to go to the land of Non-Existent, surely you understand that."

"And I have no wish to see you all visit the dreaded land." replied Oberon. "But supposing I can give you a diamond of special importance, a diamond so bright, that it will light up your very skies!"

The Tri-Umphants conferred, though noisily this time, with hurried moves.

Now, they seated themselves and bowed towards Oberon.

"We have come to a decision." said the middle Crow-Dresser, nodding his head along with the others.

"You will be allowed to see the Kiss-Diamond and make an exchange for a better stone. But…" here he wagged a finger. "If you cannot make the exchange to our satisfaction, then you forfeit the existence of this little Gnome, beside you. Is that a deal?"

"I accept the decision." answered Oberon. "You will see that I speak the truth and you will be delighted with the exchange!"

I truly hoped that Oberon did speak the truth, for I had no wish to visit the land of Non-Existent, wherever that was!

"Then, Popular." said the middle Crow-Dresser. "You may lead the stranger down to the Nesting-Hall, along with the little Gnome. You will also be accompanied by a set of Crow-Guards who will carry out the Act of Dis-Satisfaction on the little Gnome, should the exchange fail."

I really was not happy at all as Oberon and I were lead down dark corridors and through a closed courtyard, accompanied by four Crow-Dressers, all large and unsmiling.

I dare not look at Oberon in case he showed a sense of having lost our fight to rescue the Kiss-Diamond.

"This way." commanded one of the guards, instructing all the rest to stay where they were. Oberon and I were lead through another door until we stood facing a very heavy grating, a portcullis, which was raised by a loud grinding machine. Behind it was another door which was opened by a guard from within.

The first thing to strike my eyes was the sight of the Kiss-Diamond. It sat in the centre of the cavern, on a podium of blue velvet. The light blazed from its core, a white blast of heat which lit up the walls and ceiling to a full glory.

Above us, the noise of the cawing Crows was loud and raucous, as they landed, to feed the baby Crows, then leaving the large nests, which were seated in the nooks and crannies of the rock walls, to fly out through a roof-space.

Eggs shells seemed to come flying out from the nests as new-born fledglings called for the Mother-Crows to feed them. The dung-droppings littered the floor, though, strangely, there was no smell.

I gazed round and upwards, now aware of exactly what the Crow-Dressers meant, about needing the Kiss-Diamond so much, for I knew that, without light and heat, the Crows would die.

Oberon walked forward, his eyes first taking in the sights and sounds, then centering on the Kiss-Diamond which sparkled its heat.

"Wait there, Pucker-Up." he commanded and I stood where I was, as he moved, to touch the Kiss-Diamond. It crackled, as if greeting an old friend. I reasoned that the Kiss-Diamond had recognised Oberon as being the King of all the Fairies, Pixies, Elves and all Wood-Folk.

Reaching out, Oberon took the Kiss-Diamond from its stand and I gasped in fear as the blinding light suddenly dimmed, so that the Crows began to call out, wild black wings flapping in alarm.

"Oberon!" I cried out, feeling my heart pumping fast.

"Quiet!" ordered Oberon, without turning round.

I felt I was doomed and swayed in faint.

Then Oberon stepped back, to be at my side and I saw he had the Kiss-Diamond cradled in his hands. The light in the cavern had gone out completely and I closed my eyes, feeling the extreme cold of the Dark-Lands.

"Become the Kiss-Diamond, even more so, that you light the dark of these lands!" I heard Oberon say and I opened my eyes to see the Illusion-Ball laying on the podium.

At Oberon's command, there was a blinding flash and an explosion which shook the cavern, so loud that I fell over.

My eyes closed tightly as the blinding white light raked the walls and ceiling, causing the Crows to cry out in alarm, then settle as a warmth began to comfort them.

The world was alive to the light and heat and, once I had got over the shock, I forgot myself and hugged Oberon's knees in gratitude.

"I knew you could do it, Sire!" I cried. "I just knew!"

The guard, who had been standing at the door, began shouting, "The light is bright! The light is bright!" before he fell into a heap on the floor.

The noise of my shouts brought the other guards running into the room and, seeing the brightest of lights and feeling the heat, ran off, down the corridor, shouting that a miracle had happened and that all was saved.

Popular was now joined by Confident and Peculiar, who first stood in amazement at the changes within the cavern, before directing we all report back to the Tri-Umphants.

"What I don't understand, Sire." I said as we made our way back to the Court of the Tri-Umphants. "Is that, if the Illusion-Ball could become so bright, far more powerful than the Kiss-Diamond, why did we not just take the ball back and place it in the Rosemary-Bush instead?"

"Because, Pucker-Up' replied Oberon, stopping to look at me. "There is a place for everything and everything in its place!" he exclaimed.

"What does that mean?" I asked, puzzled.

"It means that one should never want more than what makes one happy." said Oberon, walking on, so that I had to run to catch him up.

Coming out into the main square, we saw crowds of Crow-Dressers, all singing and dancing and who, on seeing Oberon and I, began to cheer us and walk behind us as though we were first in line of a royal procession. I felt so proud.

The Tri-Umphants had changed places three times, before sitting back in the places they had started from.

Each cried out a loud, "BOO!" then poked out a tongue. This time I followed Oberon's example and did the same, not feeling silly at all. I suppose it is true that, when in the Crow-Dressers lands, do as the Crow-Dressers do!

"This is a happy time for we Crow-Dressers." said the one in the middle. "And we have to make a reward to you, in recognition of all the good fortune you have brought to our lands."

Saying this, he lifted a Money-Pouch and held it out. Oberon bowed his head then walked forward, gratefully accepting the gift.

"Keep it safe, for it is no ordinary pouch, it is a Continuation Purse, very rare and extremely valuable." said the Crow-Dresser.

"Tell them the news!" exclaimed the Crow-Dresser, seated on the right. "Go on, tell them!"

"When I am ready!" replied the middle one, upset that another was trying to steal his thunder. He sulked for a smallest of times, muttering, "I will when I'm ready."

I heard a great roar come from the crowd beyond the door and then the door burst open, so the throng began to pour into the court, led by Popular, Confident and Peculiar.

"What is this!" shouted all three judges, pounding on the table with small silver gavels.

"Come and see, Tri-Umphants! Come and see what has happened to our lands beyond the caverns. The lands are in full colour, all blues, greens, reds and yellows! The Sun is no longer a black ball of thunder, it is golden, while the black clouds are now like a blue blanket! Oh, come, you must see our lands and feel the warmth! Come!"

It seemed that Oberon and I were forgotten, as was the good news we were supposed to get, as the Tri-Umphants rose from their seats and began to run after the crowd. We listened, hearing the cheers grow dimmer.

"I think, Pucker-Up, our work is done here." said Oberon belting the Continuation-Purse round his waist.

I heard the chink of coins.

"I think there is something in the purse, Sire." I said. Putting his hand inside the purse, Oberon pulled out three gold coins, looking at them as they glowed under the light.

"Here." he said, handing them to me. "As a reward for your bravery."

We Kiss-Kids had been taught to accept whatever is given with a grateful air, so I gratefully accepted the gold coins, bowing before placing them securely inside my tunic.

Oberon patted the purse with a smile, when I heard another chink. Puzzled, Oberon put his hand into the purse and pulled out three more coins.

Holding them in one hand, he withdrew another three gold coins, then another three.

Putting them all back inside the purse he declared that this was, indeed, a Continuation Purse, continuing to replace the three gold coins, whenever the purse was empty.

"It is time for us to go back, to make our way back so we can collect my dear Titania from the Lands of The-Beautifuls and make our way back home and replace the Kiss-Diamond to the Rosemary-Bush."

As we walked out into the bright sunlight, we were greeted by a large, cheering, crowd of Crow-Dressers, who followed us, calling us Saviours and Magic-Men, declaring the day be a holiday, a day called the Day of the Diamond Light.

Oberon begged the crowd to leave us, that we could

continue our journey homewards. He made a short speech, standing on a rock and thanking them for their generosity, then signed a gold plaque with his name, so that the Dark-Lands be, hereafter, named as The Light-Lands of Oberon.

"Going home will be easier than our travels, coming here." said Oberon, starting to walk.

"I would have thought, Sire, that, being the same distance, it would be about the same in difficulty." I remarked.

"It is easier going back than coming forward because you're coming forward when you're going back!" said Oberon and laughed gaily at my puzzled expression.

Leaving the Crow-Dressers to their dancing and celebrating their new Naming-Day, we walked to where the Squabblers sat by the boat.

"We never thought we would see you again." said Squabbler Fifty-One, rising to his feet, before indicating the brightness of the sky over the Dark-Lands.

"We thought that light was from the fires which were burning you and the little Gnome." he finished.

Oberon smiled, even winking at me, so that I smiled back, enjoying our secret joke.

"It is time to return to your Wood-Lands, Squabbler Fifty-One." said Oberon. "Have your Squabblers pick up the boat and let us return."

It was then, I realised that the Path of Zitherer-Snakes was clear of all the poisonous reptiles, the way ahead was as clear and empty as any road of safe travel.

"Do you see, My Lord?" I said, pointing at the clear-way."

"Yes. That was strange." said Squabbler Fifty-One, breaking in to the conversation. "It happened quite suddenly, when the Sun got turned on over the Dark-Lands. It lit up the pathway and all the snakes sidled away in quick order, to escape the light, hiding under the rocks and in the crevices!"

"Then we shall not need to ride on the boat." said Oberon, beginning to cross the pathway.

I quickly followed him, at the same time, poking my head round, this way and that, for fear the snakes would suddenly rush out and bite me.

"We will bring the boat with us." shouted Squabbler Fifty-one, ordering the other Squabblers to pick up the boat and hurry after us.

"We will use it as our Totem-Pole, back at the Wood-Lands, to remind everyone of my bravery!" he exclaimed.

Joy-Stick-Twenty was the first to see us from his vantage point, high up in the trees. His excited shouts brought the Squabblers and Elves running, to greet us as we entered the Long-Hut.

"Be seated!" ordered Squabbler Fifty-One as we entered. "And I will tell you of my bravery. And the other Squabblers who helped, of course." he added as an afterthought.

The Squabblers and Elves sat quietly as Squabbler

Fifty-One recounted his exciting adventures, somehow seeming to forget that he and the other Squabblers were left just after we had passed the Pathway of Zitherer-Snakes. It would seem that his story got longer and longer until it reached a fantastic amount, so that even Oberon and I stood in rapt attention as Squabbler Fifty-One explored every avenue of his imagination.

Having finished his inventive tale, he stood, bowing to applause which thundered from the many clapped hands and throats within the Long-Hut, then held a hand up, to stem the applause, indicating that Oberon had something to say.

Oberon stood to the front, waiting till the noise had died down, then looked round, at those who sat before him. Putting a hand into the Continuation-Purse, he withdrew a gold coin and held it up to the light.

"Do you see this?" he asked.

The heads of the Squabblers and Elves all nodded.

"Will one of these gold coins buy the freedom of one Elf?" he asked, turning to face Squabbler Fifty-One.

"Indeed, it will!" answered Squabbler Fifty-One eagerly, for he had never seen a gold coin before, or ever owned one, though he knew the coin would buy many things.

"Elves?" asked Oberon, turning back, his eyes searching out the Elves in the audience. "If I give you each a gold coin, to purchase your freedom from the Squabblers, would you dearly promise never to steal babies from the Mortals, to sell to the Grimms?"

"You can trust us!" shouted Joy-Stick-One, standing up. "We will never do such a thing in all our lives!" he rejoined.

"Then I take you at your word of honour, Elves." said Oberon, before scouring the audience again, his eyes picking out the Squabblers.

"And you, Squabblers. If you receive the gold coins from the Elves for their freedom. Do you promise to treat them as equals, allowing them to sleep within your Tree-Huts, rather than on wood blocks outside your doors?"

The Squabblers roared in agreement, standing up to applaud this generous offer.

"Then I want all the Elves to line up outside. Line up so that I can give each of you a gold coin, which you can give, in return for your freedom, to your personal Squabbler."

The line of excited Elves queued up and Oberon proceeded to dip into the Continuation-Purse at his belt, drawing out the coins and giving them, one by one, to the grateful Elves, who handed the coins to their former employers, the Squabblers, who, in return, shook the Elves by the hand and hugged them.

"Now we have to go." said Oberon, giving the last of the Elves their coins. Hearing the cries of gratitude grow fainter, Oberon and I left the happy Squabblers and Elves, talking together and laughing.

Following the trail, Oberon and I left the forest and walked swiftly onward, till we came, at last to the Enormity-Bridge.

"Wait a while." said Oberon. "I need to change the ring over to my right hand, so that I become Un-Masked. The-Beautifuls must see me as I was when I left them."

I waited as Oberon did this, suddenly changing, so I saw him as Oberon, once more, the King of all the Fairies.

"Now." he continued, mounting the bridge, so that I followed him. "Let's go and find Titania."

As we drew to the top of the hill, we could see The-Beautifuls down below. They sat in circles, giggling and laughing, so that we heard the merry sounds from where we stood. Some of The-Beautifuls were sitting around the pool, crushing the petals of flowers, making coloured paints and placing them into the Sun-Ray paint-boxes, while others sang as they sat, making Daisy-Chains.

"Look!" I shouted, pointing out Titania, who, seeing us, came running up the hill, calling out Oberon's name. Some of The-Beautifuls had also seen us and ran with Titania, calling out and laughing.

"Oh, my beautiful Queen Titania!" shouted Oberon, lifting up his Queen and showering her face with kisses, while she, in a delirium of delight tried to do the same to Oberon.

How wonderful, to be back, to have Oberon and Titania together again. However, though I laughed at their playful antics, I was not too happy with those tall and beautiful women who kept patting me on the head, as though I was some kind of child. I would have them know, back in Kiss-Kids land, I was considered quite tall and handsome as well.

"Please, Ladies, Leave Pucker-Up alone." laughed Titania, seeing me duck and shy away from the patting hands.

"Come, dearest Oberon." she cried, taking him by the hand and leading him down the hill. "Come, tell me all about your journey to the Dark-Clan lands and, tell me, My Lord, did you get the Kiss-Diamond back?"

"Indeed, I did, sweetest Titania. It is safe and well, beneath my tunic, which is why we need to hurry back to the lands of the Kiss-Kids and relieve the poor Hummingbird, by replacing him with the Kiss-Diamond."

The-Beautifuls begged Oberon and Titania to stay, calling for them to join in with the singing and dancing. But Oberon was in a hurry to return home and begged to be excused.

"But you may all join me, Ladies." he said. "To go as far as the Electric-Waterfall and, from there we must leave you all. I also beg you to remember to wear a fresh Daisy-Chain each day, that your natural beauty shines through."

All together, The-Beautifuls came, singing in such a lovely tune that I began to cry. With Oberon, Titania and myself, they came down the track and through the cave which ran through the Mountain, till we reached the door which lead out the other side, down which the electric current formed a terrible wall of fused and sparkling colour.

We could hear the roaring crackle of the Electric-Waterfall, and heard it suddenly snap off as I opened the door. Beyond the door lay the sight of the path which we had used to reach the Waterfall after leaving the Santa-Man.

"All clear." said Oberon, leading Titania out through the door, with me quickly following. Titania ran back and kissed all The-Beautifuls, then, just as quickly, ran back to catch us up.

Once we had reached a safe distance, Oberon called out, " Close the door up, sweet Ladies."

The door shut tight and, immediately, the fall of the Electric-Waterfall caused a crashing sound as it raced down the mountainside, once again forming an un-passable wall of electric current.

"I will miss them." said Titania, sadly.

Oberon stopped her, raising a finger.

"We have to change our rings back to the Mask finger." he said, removing his ring, to become a Fairy-Tog once more. Titania also changed her ring, from right to left-hand finger.

"Now, Titania and Pucker-Up, let us go and find the Santa-Man!" said Oberon.

The land of the Fir-Trees was alive to the eye, with rows and rows of Christmas Trees, vivid in a beautiful and lush green, each tree adorned with coloured ball and lights, with parcels and chocolates, ready to be planted in the homes of the Mortal-Children at Christmas times.

The land was alive with happy voices, of singing, as the Helper-Elves worked to make each tree prettier than the last.

"How are you, dear friends?" boomed the large and jolly Santa-Man, on seeing us approach. He ran to greet us, hugging Oberon first, then Titania and myself next, almost smothering me with his large body, so that I found it hard to breathe.

"Come downstairs, into the Great-Hall for something to eat and drink, some Mince-Pies and Brandy-Snaps!" he invited.

"No thank you." replied Oberon. "For, you know we have to get back home as soon as possible with the Kiss-Diamond, so that the Kiss-Kids can get on with their work and the Mortals will be able to enjoy your beautiful trees."

"Of course, I understand." said the Santa-Man.

"However." said Oberon to the Santa-Man. "Before we set off back home, I want to make you a present of this Continuation-Purse. Tie it around your waist and when you need gold coins, you simply put your hand into the purse and draw the coins out. It never runs out and you can buy all the presents and toys you want for the Mortal Children's special day at Christmas."

"Thank you, my very dear friend!" cried the Santa-Man, taking the Continuation-Purse and tying it around his large waist.

"And may all Fairyland be kind to you." he finished, wishing them a Fairy-Farewell.

"You may accompany us to the Down-Well if you wish." said Oberon.

"Gladly." answered the Santa-Man.

So, with the Santa-Man accompanying us on our trek back to the Down-Well, we all laughed and made very merry.

"It's wonderful to see the water in the pool so clear." said Titania, remembering how, when we had first arrived, the pool was a filthy black.

We all agreed, now looking into the crystal depths of the pool, then jumping back as the glass bubble suddenly whooshed up and sat bobbing on the water.

"Any one going down?"

The door of the glass globe had slid open, allowing the walk-way to slide out, reaching the bank.

"Anyone going down, back to where I just came up from?" shouted the Shrew-Mouse, its finger, ready on the button.

"Oh, it's you lot." said the Shrew-Mouse, eying us with sharp and beady eyes. "Hurry up and climb aboard!"

We had said our goodbyes to the Santa-Man, who waved to us, right up until the board slid back into the glass ball and the door hissed shut.

"Going down!" shouted the Shrew-Mouse, so that, with a bubbling pop, the ball started to submerge and we lost sight of the jolly Santa-Man.

"Remember to have faith, that we can breathe under water." Oberon reminded us, as the water started to rise inside the glass ball.

I closed my eyes and wished myself the most faith in all the world, as I felt the water rise, first over my feet, then my legs and body, till it rose to cover my head. I opened my eyes, for, when one prays to have faith, it's always done with the eyes firmly shut.

"I wonder if Horatio, the Hermit-Crab is still around?" I mused, taking a deep breath and breathing easily under the water.

"We shall see." said Oberon. "Though we shall not have time to visit the Otter-Folk, we have to get back to make things alright again.

At this, we all agreed, there was no time at all for Dilly-Dallying.

"All out, who want the bottom!" shouted the Shrew-Mouse, his finger pressing a button, so the door slid open and we stepped out onto the sandy bed of the cavern floor.

"Thank you." we said, each in turn, to the Shrew-Mouse. Though he just twitched his nose and shouted loudly, "Anyone going up?"

The door closed and we watched the glass ball bubble its way up to the top again.

"Look! There's Horatio!" I cried, espying the Crab, who had such a large shell on his back, that he could hardly walk.

"Hallo, Horatio!" I cried, walking up to him.

"I'm so very busy, building up my library of books,

that I have no time for talking." said Horatio, popping in and out of his outsize shell.

"In fact." he went on. "I have to write a book about the books I already have upstairs. And I've already written two about the first lot. They just keep coming. Sometimes I wish people would not write books, or that people never want to read them, of course."

"I shall never write a book, Horatio." I promised, leaving him to continue popping in and out of his shell.

"Poor old Horatio." I said to Oberon. "I doubt he will ever find a shell large enough for his library." Oberon had no time for small talk, only finding long words for the biggest conversation, though he stopped talking as we rounded the corner to a loud sound of cheers.

"It's Officer Crab and Captain Whelk!" I cried. The two Officers were seated opposite each other at the table, hands gripping tightly as they arm-wrestled each other, grunting and moaning as their arms went, first this way and then that, while the soldiers of both sides, shouted and cheered in full cry.

It seemed that no-one was interested in us as we simply walked on by, so that we continued until we came to the upward shaft, which would lead us back to where we had left Woodpecker and the Golden-Eagle on the riverbank.

"Remember, Titania and Pucker-Up." said Oberon, as we stared up the watery shaft and seeing the blue of sky beyond.

"When we float up and reach the top, we can, once again, breathe in the fresh air. It is important that we all keep a very strong faith." he finished.

It seemed to me that faith is so very important, because, without it, you just can't go anywhere or do anything. I suppose, when you consider it, the Mortals would have to have such a huge amount of faith in we Fairy-Folk, as to be able to love and have fun.

"Let us hold hands now and float to the top." said Oberon, grasping hold of Titania's hand, then mine, in such a tight grip that I closed my eyes, to stop the tears coming out.

I felt the strange sensation of rising, slowly and surely, lifting, as though in a dream.

"Here they are!" I heard a voice shout and opened my eyes to see Woodpecker and the Golden-Eagle, leaping about in a huge joy of happiness.

"Help us out of the water!" demanded Oberon and the Woodpecker, with a wild flapping of wings helped, first Oberon, then Titania, out of the pool, while the Golden-Eagle had gripped me with its talons, careful not to hurt me, lifting me up into the air, then gently setting me down on the ground.

"You were certainly quick!" exclaimed Woodpecker to Oberon, once we had caught our breath.

"Not much longer than a Cat's-Whisker."

I will admit, with Woodpecker saying that, I had never really considered giving Time a second thought. Now, when I thought about it, I wondered how long it had been, for us to get the Kiss-Diamond back.

And how long had we left before the Hummingbird turned to stone and all was lost.

"We have to get home, Sire." I worried.

"Yes, you are right, Pucker-Up. Let's not waste any more time. And, Woodpecker, before you ask and bathe us with your questions, we have got the Kiss-Diamond back!" said Oberon, now dry and lifting himself from the ground, ready to fly, holding Titania's hand, so she did the same.

"Climb aboard." said the Golden-Eagle, so that I mounted onto his back and felt the fan of his giant wings as he spread them.

"Goodbye!" called a small voice, just as we took off. On the other side of the riverbank, the Angelfish had stopped playing the Pan-Pipes, just long enough to wish us goodbye.

"Come on. Keep playing! Why do you keep stopping, we will never finish our Love-Waltz!" snapped the Dog-Fish, hugging the Cat-Fish and starting to waltz again as the Angelfish began to play once more.

I gripped tight onto the Golden-Eagle's feathers as we rose, looking back, at the dancing Cat-Fish and Dog-Fish, who got smaller and smaller, till they vanished from view, the view ahead being taken up by the sweet sight of our Homeland, as we followed the course of the Sparkling-River once more.

Reaching the fount, where the river spewed out its source, we turned left and saw the beautiful sight of the Flower-Ring.
We were home!

The bands were out and the crowds of assorted Fairy-Folk covered the land as we descended.
I had to cover my ears for a while, to get used to the noise of cheers and a shouting of voices, welcoming us back home.
It was then I noticed that both, Oberon and Titania, had changed their ring-fingers in flight, so that they were both Un-Masked, now in all goodness of beauty.
"We have no time for speeches!" shouted Oberon to the cheering crowds.
"We have to get back to the lands of the Kiss-Kids, to where the brave Hummingbird sits upon the Rosemary-Bush."
The Lemming's Pipe-Band led the way, their trumpets and pipes raising a merry tune, followed by the Elves and Pixies, who danced to a high degree of happiness. Then came the Centaurs, riding Unicorns, as a Guard of Honour, while Mushroom-Gatherers and Holly-Folk brought up the rear in a grand mixture of colours and voices.

In the lands of the Kiss-Kids, the air seemed to lay in heavy heart, the Kiss-Kids hiding in their homes and not willing to come out, even to reap the Love-Fruit, which hung from lowered bushes, as though ashamed of what was produced.

The Love-Fruit was smaller than normal and missing the lush redness of the ripe strawberry colour. The land seemed sad and lost.

"Look at the poor Hummingbird!" I said, on seeing it laid, quite low in the Rosemary-Bush, its high plumage now looking drab and lifeless.

"Quick, someone, give the Hummingbird some Nectar from the Honeysuckle and dew of the sweet Orchids!" shouted Oberon, lifting the poor bird from its seating and placing the Kiss-Diamond in its place. There was silence, as the crowd pressed closer, not a sound. Suddenly, there was a brilliant flash of power and the world lit up as, first, the sky turned a vermillion red, then into a cobalt blue which mirrored the blue of a thousand Mortal-Children's eyes.

The Sun blazed its gold in rays of dazzling beams and the land was greener than ever before as the Kiss-Diamond sparkled and flashed in the sunlight, sending out its diamond rays in all directions.

The Love-Fruit burst into a juicy redness, plump with succulence, the juice dripping from its source, while the cheers and shouts of jubilations came from a thousand throats as the Kiss-Kids ran from their homes, the tears of joy falling as liquid pearl-drops from their cheeks.

I saw Titania begin to cry and I felt my heart burst open, my own tears of joy falling as milky pearl-drops.

The Fairy-Land Folk played their trumpets and pipes all through the night, while the Hummingbird, now full of Honey-Dew and Nectar, from the Honeysuckle and Orchids, flew in happiness, joining in with the birds, led by the Woodpecker, in a sweetest of birdsongs.

I was made a High-Honour of all Kiss-Kids land, higher even than that of Turner of Good Fortune, nearly as high as Oberon's title, that of King of all the Fairies and Woodland-Folk.

And though I lived as befits one in High-Honour, I gained more joy, when looking down, through the blue and white gauze netting of the sky, to see the Mortals at play and Mortal-Children kissing the cheeks of their Mothers and Fathers. Especially at night, when the Moon-Queen rides her silver ball through the night sky, knowing that all the Mortals in their Earth-Land, loved each other.

I am Pucker-Up and extremely happy!

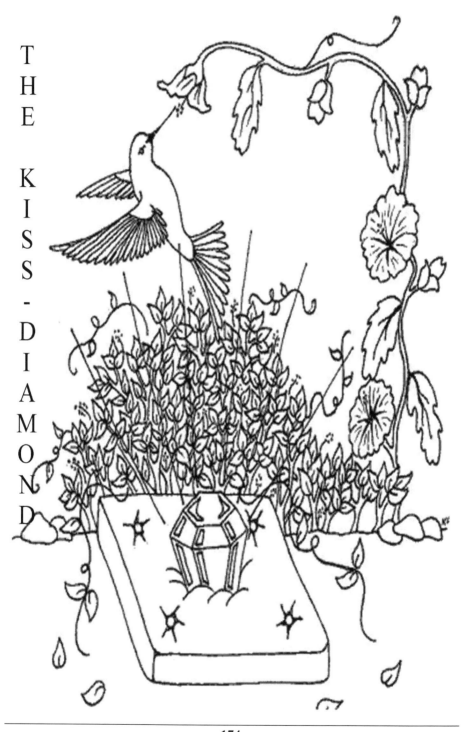

THE KISS - DIAMOND

THE END.

THE MERMAID

'THE SOUL-PEARL'
A MAGICAL TALE

By

Ron S King

ILLUSTRATIONS.

FOREWORD.

This magical tale is about three friends who set out to find the truth of 'Reality-Colours', which will light up their world and lift the sharpness of black and white, to give colour to the flowers and trees.

The friends have to travel to far-away places and meet many strange characters, some friendly, some who are set on holding the friends back from gaining the 'Soul-Pearl' which is the key to the 'Reality-Colours'.

As you read, you will meet such characters as Warty-Toad and the Wishful-Hopefuls, and you will travel with the three friends through strange rooms which hold exciting and dangerous challenges.

We ask that you read the story and colour in the pictures as you travel along with our heroes. Above all, we trust you will enjoy the magical tale…

Ron S King.

CREDITS.

All credit goes to the illustrator, Kelly Aston, who has taken the time to draw out the wonderful illustrations which compliment this book.

Ron S King.

THE SOUL-PEARL

It began, as all good stories do, at its very beginning.

It began at the start of a fine August morning, a nice time, just after the Merry-Closing of July, and everyone was minding their own business.

The last week of every month was a very busy time, everyone getting ready for the month ahead, although, as Nipper-Crab said… "Why is everyone in such a rush to get to the next month, hurrying up, to reach August as soon as July is here? I mean… I was enjoying July, it rained quite a lot and the air was warm, which was just right for water off a Duck's back!"

"I'll tell you why, Nipper-Crab." spoke up Slippery-Fish. "It's because if we rush into the future, then we can put the past behind us!"

Nipper-Crab said nothing for a while, concentrating on walking in a straight line, rather than walking sideways and getting side-tracked.

"But if we keep putting the past behind us, what does that do for us?" said Nipper-Crab at last, hopping on his giant claw and digging his heels in.

"What we get is history." replied Stinger-Scorpion, coming up to join them. "The past tells us where we have been." he continued. "And if we know what our past has been, we can use it to judge what we do in the future… We learn from it, don't you see?"

Nipper-Crab wrinkled his nose. At times he could be very cantankerous, quite crabby, and this was one of those times.

"Then what is the point of wishing and hoping, if we already judge what we will do in the future, because of what has happened in the past!"

"This is all very confusing." said Slippery-Fish, pulling at a loose scale, then pushing it back into place. "I mean…" he went on "If we know what we can do about our future, because of the past, what is the point of believing that all's well which ends well!"

The three friends stopped beside the Sand-Dune, their minds on this problem.

"I believe." said Nipper-Crab, at last… "What's done is done… And we have to believe that, and then get on with the future as best we can."

"But, if that's so, Nipper-Crab, then why have we got a Wishing-Well in the garden?" asked Stinger-Scorpion. "What is the point of it all, what's the point of making a wish, that something will happen in the future…?"

Stinger-Scorpion stopped talking as a shout went up. "It's time! It's time… Henrietta-Turtle's babies are ready!"

Everyone began running after Henrietta-Turtle as she scuttled her way down towards the beach.

"Quick!" called Stinger-Scorpion, breaking into a run, urging his friends to follow him. "Let's get down to the beach before the Storm-Troopers, the

Seagulls, get there and begin to eat the babies!"
"Grab a Cockleshell and put in on your head." yelled Nipper-Crab. "That will stop the Seagulls from pecking your heads."

Down on the beach, Henrietta-Turtle was running here and there, calling out to her babies as their little heads popped up from the sand.

"Come on, Babies!" she called. "Run as fast as you can, down from the beach and into the sea, where the Seagulls can't get you!"

From out of the sky, the Seagulls screeched and called as they dived and swooped, trying to reach the baby Turtles as they raced over the sand, down towards the sea.

"Throw sand at them!" called Stinger-Scorpion to all the folk of Cuttlefish-Avenue and, snatching up a Cockleshell and placing it firmly on his head, began to throw handfuls of sand at the diving Seagulls.

"There are too many of them!" cried Slippery-Fish, gasping as the wind from the Seagulls wings caused the thrown sand to blast back into his face.

"Look! Look up there!" shouted Nipper-Crab, pointing up to where there appeared a 'V' formation of Kestrels, banking in a steep turn and beginning to dive-bomb the Seagulls. The air became a battleground of screeching and screaming birds.

"Hurry, my little darlings!" exclaimed Henrietta-Turtle, ushering the last of the baby Turtles down and into the sea, and, with a wave to those gathered on the sandy shore.

THE BABY TURTLES

Henrietta-Turtle followed her babies, diving and disappearing beneath the waves.

Seeing the baby Turtles vanish into the safety of the sea, the Seagulls gave a last screaming voice of anger, before peeling away from the fight and wheeling away, back to their homes on the land of the High-Cliffs. The Kestrels dived low, over the cheering crowds below, waving their wings and dancing in the air with victory-rolls and loud whistles, till, having seen the last of the Seagulls, they tipped their wings and drew up into formation, before flying Westward, into the Sun-Clouds.

"Come on, everyone!" ordered Solly-Starfish, allowing the gold badge to flash in the sunlight. "As Mayor of Cuttlefish-Avenue, I order you all to start digging up the empty baby Turtle shells, so we can use them for the windows of our new Round-Houses. Then we have to tidy up the sand, smooth it all over so the sea can kiss it as the tide comes in."

Everyone began to dig for the shells, careful not to crush them and, once that was done and shells taken away in seaweed baskets, everyone began sweeping the sand into a tidy, neat blanket.

"I wish…" began Nipper-Crab. "I was the Mayor. Do you think I might be the Mayor at some future date?"

Both, Stinger-Scorpion and Slippery-Fish, scratched at their heads, then shook them. The excitement of the baby Turtles and the clearing up had left them now wondering what to do next. "Shall we carry on talking about the past and the future?" asked Slippery-Fish.

"No-one knows what is in the future and that's that!" exclaimed Nipper-Crab. "Let's talk about something else."

"Well, I thought it was a jolly good thing to talk about." said Slippery-Fish, while Stinger-Scorpion laughed and poked Nipper-Crab hard, saying… "I bet the Stick-Insect-Guru will know."

"Who?" … "That strange Guru who lives down in the Mournful-Cave?" asked Nipper-Crab, pushing Stinger-Scorpion away.

"The very same Guru. I've heard it said that he knows a lot about strange things and chants groaning sounds from out of his mouth."

Nipper-Crab looked at Stinger-Scorpion in a disbelieving way, and said… "I don't believe you, I really don't."

"Then let's go and ask him!" exclaimed Slippery-Fish. "What do you think, Stinger?"

"Are you mad, Slippery? No-one has ever been to see him… In fact Johnny-Maggot once told me that the Stick-Insect-Guru doesn't exist. Mothers just tell their children that, so they behave themselves. Johnny-Maggot says there is no such person as the Stick-Insect-Guru."

"You're just afraid. Let's just go to the mouth of the Mournful-Cave and shout down… Let's see if anyone is there." taunted Slippery-Fish.

"What do you think, Nipper?" asked Stinger-

Scorpion.

He really hoped that Nipper-Crab would refuse to go, so that they could all go home for tea.

"I don't see what harm it will do." answered Nipper-Crab, dancing a sideways shuffle, then they began walking up over the sands and then down, towards the Sugar-Trees of Barley-Forest.

Without a word, Slippery-Fish and Stinger-Scorpion followed Nipper-Crab, walking through the Foul-Bog, until they came to the dark opening of the Mournful-Cave, the three of them peered into the darkness before they drew back and sat on one of the fallen tree stumps.

"Well?" asked Stinger-Scorpion at last… "Who is going to call into the Mournful-Cave?"

"Let's toss a coin to see who goes and shouts." suggested Slippery-Fish.

Don't be silly, Slippery! We haven't got a coin between us." replied Stinger-Scorpion.

"What is a coin?" asked Nipper-Crab, mystified.

"It's a round thing that the Silly-Folk invented." snorted Stinger-Scorpion, then brightened.

"I have an idea." he said… "Let's hide our hands behind our backs and then pull them out, and the one who has the most fingers showing is the one who has to shout into the cave."

Each of them agreed and putting both hands behind their backs, they waited, till Stinger-Scorpion shouted out… "Go!"

THE BUCKET-BOYS

Only Slippery-Fish pulled his hands out from behind his back and held them out.

"You are IT!" exclaimed Stinger-Scorpion, pointing at Slippery-Fish and dancing up and down.

"But that's not fair!" argued Slippery-Fish… "I was the only one who held out my hands!"

"Well, Slippery… It was not worth Nipper-Crab or me holding our hands out because you would have had far more fingers than us."

Slippery-Fish glared at his two friends, very upset. "I might have had no fingers out so how would you know I would have had most fingers out?" he asked.

"To put it simply, Slippery." said Nipper-Crab. "Everybody in Cuttlefish-Avenue knows about 'Fish-Fingers'!"

"Everybody in the whole world knows that fish have 'Fish-Fingers'!" chortled Stinger-Scorpion, now laughing so hard that he fell off the log and puffed himself upright.

"Well, that's not fair!" shouted Slippery-Fish, seating himself firmly and refusing to move.

"Then it's up to me, to go and shout down into the Mournful-Cave." said Nipper-Crab, side-stepping towards the mouth of the cave.

Slippery-Fish and Stinger-Scorpion watched Nipper-Crab walk towards the cave and both rose from the log, ashamed that they had let their good friend walk into certain danger.

Together, they caught up with Nipper-Crab, standing behind him as he began to shout down into the darkness.

"Hallooooo, down there! Is there anyone at home?"

"Will you please be quiet!"

The three friends jumped back, startled at the voice which suddenly came back at them from inside the cave.

"Hey… You three… Why are you running away? ... Don't be afraid!"

Stinger-Scorpion stopped and turned, his eyes searching back into the darkness of the cave.

"Who are you?" he shouted, motioning Slippery-Fish and Nipper-Crab to come back and join him.

"I am Jackie-Boy Woodmouse and my friend is "Sidney-Boy Woodmouse." came the answer.

"Come out and let us see you!" shouted Nipper-Crab, now more venturesome and standing before the mouth of the cave, blinking into the darkness.

From out of the darkness appeared two of the strangest creatures that Nipper had ever seen. They had the shell-like bodies of Woodlice, while each had the head of a Mouse.

"Wood-Mice!" exclaimed Stinger-Scorpion. "I've heard about you people, though I never believed you existed."

"Of course we exist!" said Jackie-Boy Woodmouse, quite offended.

"We are sorry to doubt you existed." quickly broke in Slippery-Fish. "What are you doing here, living in that dark cave?"

"We are 'Bucket-Boys'." answered Sidney-Boy

Woodmouse.

"Bucket-Boys?"… What do you do?" asked Nipper-Crab.

"We are in charge of the Bucket… I'm the Down-Boy." said Sidney-Boy Woodmouse.

"And I'm the Up-Boy." broke in Jackie-Boy Woodmouse.

"You will have to explain." said Stinger-Scorpion, somewhat bemused.

"Who have you come to see?" asked Sidney-Boy Woodmouse.

"We have come to see the Stick-Insect-Guru." admitted Stinger-Scorpion, adding… "That's if such a person exists."

"Of course he exists." spluttered Jackie-Boy Woodmouse.

"And this means…" added Sidney-Boy Woodmouse. "If you want to see him, I would have to lower you down into the cave in the bucket."

"And when you wanted to leave, I would have to lift you out… That's why we are called the Bucket-Boys." finished Jackie-Boy Woodmouse.

As the Bucket-Boys spoke, they lit candles and led the three friends deeper into the cave. The passage ended at a deep well, over which sat a large winch which carried a large bucket.

"Get into the bucket." ordered Sidney-Boy Woodmouse, his hands on the handle of the hoist and edging it to the side. "I don't think I want to get into the bucket." said Nipper-Crab, cautiously peering over the edge of the drop.

"Come on… Make up your minds. We can't stand here all day, you know." said Sidney-Boy Woodmouse, peevishly.

"Don't be such a coward!" exclaimed Stinger-Scorpion, beginning to climb into the bucket. Slippery-Fish hesitated for just a moment, and then also climbed into the bucket.

"Okay!" shouted Sidney-Boy Woodmouse, beginning to turn the handle so the bucket began to move out. "Only two to go down!"

"Wait!" suddenly shouted Nipper-Crab, grabbing hold of Sidney-Boy Woodmouse's arm. "Let me get into the bucket."

"Three going down!" shouted Sidney-Boy Woodmouse, bringing the bucket back and waiting for Nipper-Crab to clamber aboard. Then, with quick turns of the handle, the bucket began to descend into the darkness… Lower and lower.

It seemed ages before the bucket reached the bottom, resting with a soft bump.

"Go down that little tunnel to your left."

The voice of Sidney-Boy Woodmouse floated down from out of the darkness, so that the three friends climbed out of the bucket and began to walk down the tunnel.

"Bucket coming up empty!" came the floated voice of Jackie-Boy Woodmouse, as the bucket started to rise back up.

The tunnel opened out into a large clearing, well-lit

by candlelight and seated in front of a small fire, sitting on a box was the strange figure of the Stick-Insect-Guru. He wore nothing except a white loincloth around his waist, with a matching white turban on his head. He sat very still, his eyes on the fire, saying nothing.

"Is he the Stick-Insect-Guru?" asked Stinger-Scorpion of the other two. The three stood before the seated figure, not knowing what to do or say.

"He looks like a Guru." said Nipper-Crab.

"How do you know, Nipper? I mean, we've never seen a Guru before, have we?"

"Of course I'm a Guru!" exclaimed the Stick-Insect-Guru, suddenly coming to life and standing up. "And I know why you are here." he finished.

The three friends moved back, alarmed, till Stinger-Scorpion plucked up enough courage to say... "Why are we here then?"

"You were going to ask me about the future. What do you want to know?" said the Stick-Insect-Guru.

"We want to know, if we can act on the future by what has happened in the past... Why do we need to have wishes and hopes for the future ... Why is there a Wishing-Well in the middle of Cuttlefish-Avenue?"

"He has to be the Stick-Insect-Guru! He has to be a Magic-Man... How else can he know why we are here, what we wanted to know?" asked Slippery-Fish, quite afraid.

Both Nipper-Crab and Stinger-Scorpion stood with

their mouths open, flabbergasted.

"Please don't be afraid, said the Stick-Insect-Guru gently. "I will tell you why there is a Wishing-Well in the middle of Cuttlefish-Avenue. First, I can tell you that the Wishing-Well has always been there, put there by the Wishful-Hopefuls, a tribe of Angel-Like qualities who were said to have come down from space, many ages ago. They put that Wishing-Well there for a special reason, till a time when there would come three brave Wise-Beings, who would give light to their world."

"I don't understand." said Stinger-Scorpion, scratching his head and staring at Nipper-Crab and Slippery-Fish, who simply shrugged, not knowing what to make of it all.

"Then I shall make you understand." said the Stick-Insect-Guru and, standing up, he removed his turban and took, from within its folds, a small green bottle. "Please open your mouths." he ordered, then, seeing their looks of alarm, he said… "I promise this will not harm you, you will have to trust me."

Stinger-Scorpion opened his mouth wide, poking his tongue out. Seeing their friend offer an open mouth, Nipper-Crab and Slippery-Fish did the same, closing up their eyes.

"I am going to just dab a small drop of this liquid on your tongues from this eye-dropper. You will not feel a thing." promised the Stick-Insect-Guru.

As he spoke, he moved to each of them, dipping the eye-dropper into the bottle and seeping a drop of the liquid onto their tongues.

"I can't taste anything." said Nipper-Crab, closing his mouth and smacking his lips.

"Me neither." said Stinger-Scorpion and Slippery-Fish quickly agreed that he could taste nothing.

"So? What happens now?" demanded Stinger-Scorpion.

"Follow me." said the Stick-Insect-Guru, leading them back along the tunnel until they came to the Up-Shaft.

"Bucket-down!" came the voice of Sidney-Boy Woodmouse, followed by the sound of the handle being cranked and the appearance of the large bucket.

"Climb into the bucket." ordered the Stick-Insect-Guru. "When you get to the top go to the entrance of the cave and look out at what you see, look and smell, then come back down here to me and I will explain further… Now, off you go!"

Stinger-Scorpion, Nipper-Crab and Slippery-Fish climbed into the bucket.

"Bucket up!" came the voice of Jackie-Boy Woodmouse, as the bucket started to rise, lifting them up till they could climb out, making their way to the cave entrance.

"What is that?" cried Stinger-Scorpion, his eyes wide in awe and fear.

Nipper-Crab had fallen down in some kind of fit, while Slippery-Fish covered his eyes, his mouth wide open, though no words came out.

THE GURU

"He has bewitched us!" screamed Nipper-Crab, suddenly rising and covering his eyes with his hands. He ran blindly, followed quickly by Stinger-Scorpion and Slippery-Fish, bumping into the rocky sides as they made their way back down the tunnel to where the Bucket-Boys stood waiting.

"Quick! Lower us back down to the Stick-Insect-Guru!" cried Stinger-Scorpion, pulling the stricken Slippery-Fish, as they reached to where Nipper-Crab stood, still shaking.

"Bucket down!" shouted Sidney-Boy Woodmouse, herding the three into the bucket and beginning to lower them down into the depths of the cave. They ran through the small tunnel, to where the Stick-Insect-Guru waited, his thin arms spread out, his mouth making 'Shushing' noises, to calm them down.

"What have you done to us?" wailed Slippery-Fish.

"My eyes went into my mind and I saw all strange lights!" exclaimed Stinger-Scorpion.

"Was that the magic water you put on out tongues?" cried Nipper-Crab.

The Stick-Insect-Guru asked the three upset friends to be seated, and, raising his turban, brought out the small green bottle.

"This, my friends." … he began, holding the bottle up, "Is called Charmed Eye-Opener. I was left it many years ago by one of the Ancients, a last member of the Wishful-Hopefuls. I was told to leave my home and move down here, to live as a Guru and wait until three Wise-beings would visit me, asking about the Wishing-Well.

"But what was it we saw outside the cave?" broke in Stinger-Scorpion.

"What you saw was Reality-Colours, true colours of what the world is really like. All your lives, you and all the folk of Cuttlefish-Avenue have lived in a world of black and white. None of you has ever seen colours until now. What you saw was the beautiful colours of the blue sky and green grass, with trees and butterflies as they should look. Because you could suddenly see colours, you were also able to smell the scent of flowers and of the sea, wonderful perfumes and dazzling rainbows."

"But it frightened us so much." responded Stinger-Scorpion, adding… "What happens to these Reality-Colours now? Do we see them all the time, or do they just go and leave us seeing in black and white?"

"If you listen to me, I shall explain just why I showed you what colours look like and how they will brighten up your lives." replied the Stick-Insect-Guru. He went on… "I had waited for you three Wise-Beings to visit me so that I could show you the Reality-Colours and then tell you that you have to travel to the Lands of the Westward-Sun, to find the Soul-Pearl and bring it back to Cuttlefish-Avenue, to bring it back and to place it in the Wishing-Well, so that all the folk of Cuttlefish-Avenue can drink of the waters and are then all able to see their world in Reality-Colours, just as you have seen for the briefest of moments, to see the vibrancy of nature and to taste the sweetness of the food."

"We will become Heroes!" exclaimed Nipper-Crab, suddenly alive to the idea of bringing back the Soul-Pearl.

"But what exactly is the Soul-Pearl and where are the Lands of the Westward-Sun?" asked Slippery-Fish, somewhat dubiously.

"I will be honest with you, my friends." replied the Stick-Insect-Guru. "I have no idea exactly what the Soul-Pearl is or what it looks like. I can only tell you that the Lands of the Westward-Sun lie to the West, across the sea. I do believe you are the chosen three and you will find a way to reach those Lands and bring back the Soul-Pearl.

Stinger-Scorpion suggested the three of them huddle together, in conference, to discuss the situation. The Stick-Insect-Guru waited patiently as they whispered together, then…

"We have discussed the idea and have decided to go and look for the Soul-Pearl." said Stinger-Scorpion, in an important way, then added… "But, first, we have to find a boat which will carry us over the sea to the Lands of the Westward-Sun, wherever that is."

"Then you may take your leave, my wonderful friends… And I wish you a 'Bon Voyage' and with much luck. I know you will bring so much joy and happiness to the folk of Cuttlefish-Avenue." said the Stick-Insect-Guru.

"Will we still be able to see those Reality-Colours,

when we leave the cave?" enquired Nipper-Crab.

"I'm afraid not." replied the Stick-Insect-Guru. "You only had a tickle of the juice on your tongues, which only lasts a very short while. Once you put the Soul-Pearl into the Wishing-Well and drink the water, those beautiful Reality-Colours will always be yours to have.

"Bucket down!" came the voice of Sidney-Boy Woodmouse.

The three friends had taken leave of the Stick-Insect-Guru and now climbed into the bucket, to be raised up to the top of the shaft.

"Bucket-Up." shouted Jackie-Boy Woodmouse.

The bucket was raised and the three friends climbed out.

Sidney-Boy Woodmouse and Jackie-Boy Woodmouse watched the three friends walk away from the cave, and, yawning, they returned to their beds and went fast asleep.

"So what do we do now?" asked Nipper-Crab, quite at a loss as to where to go and what to do about getting a boat.

The three friends had wandered down to the beach and then back into Cuttlefish-Avenue, searching for anyone who owned a boat. No-one seemed to have such a thing and had never considered owning one, considering no-one had ever sailed in the sea on a boat.

It was as they walked, by now getting rather dispirited, that they heard the sounds of happy laughter coming from the garden of Mrs Feather-Watertight. "That's it, my darling babies!" she laughed.

"A good sweet time to you." said Slippery-Fish as they watched Mrs. Feather-Watertight pouring water into a shiny new tin bath, then place her baby Ducklings into the water, to see them laughing and playing as they swam.

"A good sweet time to you, Slippery-Fish… And to you both, Nipper-Crab and Stinger-Scorpion." replied Mrs. Feather-Watertight, not taking her eyes off her swimming babies.

"I see you have a shiny new tin bath." said Slippery-Fish.

"Indeed, I have, Slippery-Fish. My old tin bath had a hole in it and the water ran out from it. My darling babies were so upset, with nothing to swim in."

"Might I ask you, Mrs. Feather-Watertight, what you did with your old tin bath?" asked Slippery-Fish.

"I've thrown it out, onto the sandpit, for other children to put sand in and play with." came the reply.

"If that's the case." said Slippery Fish. "I wonder if my friends and I can borrow it for a while? We would be happy to pay you a few Cockleshells for its usage." continued Slippery-Fish.

"Of course you can have the old tin bath!" exclaimed Mrs. Feather-Watertight, before turning her attention back to her Ducklings.

"Why do you want the tin bath!" exclaimed Stinger-

Scorpion.

They had walked down to the sandpit and emptied the tin bath of the sand and now the three friends stood, staring at the hole in the bottom of the bath. "Don't you see?" exclaimed Slippery-Fish. "This tin bath will make an excellent boat for us to set sail in and search for the Lands of the Westward-Sun."

"But it has a hole in the bottom of it." said Nipper-Crab, emphasising it by lifting the tin bath on its end and poking his finger through.

"Quite right, Nipper." spoke up Stinger-Scorpion. "It's alright for you, Slippery… And you, Nipper, you can both swim, but I will drown when the tin bath gets full of sea-water through that hole."

"That's easy!" said Slippery-Fish. "You never gave me a chance to explain… We can plug the hole by using a small Octopus. They are very squashy little things and excellent at plugging holes."

With that explanation satisfying both Stinger-Scorpion and Nipper-Crab, they found a small Octopus and gently filled up the hole with its head, while its arms held it fast to the bottom of the bath. With that, the three friends carried the tin bath down to the sea and set it in the shallows, ready to set sail.

"Wait!" cried Nipper-Crab, just as they were getting in. "What about the High-Water-Tide, out there? … I mean no-one has ever been out to sea before and that High-Water-Tide looks really high.

The three now stood, staring out to sea, looking into the distance to where the water seemed to reach nearly to the sky, giant angry waves which rose, then crashed themselves back into the sea.

"Even if we had giant paddles, I doubt if we could get over that High-Water-Tide." said Stinger-Scorpion, dubiously.

"I have an idea!" suddenly exclaimed Nipper-Crab, nipping at the air with his giant claw.

"Well, what is it?" said Stinger-Scorpion, still staring out to sea.

"Slippery-Fish is a Fish, isn't he?"

"We know he's a Fish, Nipper… What about it?"

"Well." answered Nipper-Crab… "Fish can swim. We can put some sea-weed reigns on Slippery and he can tow us out to sea and over the High-Water-Tide!"

"But I have never been out to sea before!" wailed Slippery-Fish, beginning to shake.

"Remember who we are, Slippery." reprimanded Stinger-Scorpion sharply. "We are the Wise-Beings, chosen to bring the Soul-Pearl back to Cuttlefish-Avenue and place it in the Wishing-Well.

"Yes." joined in Nipper-Crab. "Surely you want to help us give the folk of Cuttlefish-Avenue the beauty of Reality-Colours?"

Slippery-Fish hung his head in shame and nodded that he would be ready to tow the bath, with Stinger-Scorpion and Nipper-Crab seated inside, out to sea and over the High-Water-Tide.

Getting some sea-weed, Stinger-Scorpion tied it around Slippery-Fish's waist, and then climbed into the bath.

"Away we go, Slippery!" shouted Stinger-Scorpion, as Slippery-Fish began to swim out towards the High-Water-Tide. The closer to the rise of the sea wall, the higher it seemed to climb.

"You'll never get over the top!" shouted Nipper-Crab.

Suddenly, the air seemed to be full of Flying-Fish, calling and laughing, jumping high over the tin bath which began to rock and lurch as it neared the rising water.

"You'll never do it!" the Flying-Fish called.

"Go away!" shouted Stinger-Scorpion, standing up to wave away the laughing Fish, so the bath rocked violently, nearly tipping up.

"Sit down!" screamed Nipper-Crab in fear, gripping hard to the sides of the bath.

It was then that they had reached the High-Water-Tide, which rose up so high in the air that it blocked everything out. There was a loud roaring sound and it was as if a giant hand had picked the tin bath up and hurled it backwards, so that the bath was thrown back onto the beach, to land with a thump on the sand, tipping out Stinger-Scorpion and Nipper-Crab in a bundle, to have Slippery-Fish flying through the air, landing on top of them.

It was some time before the three friends could gain their breath and untangle their crumpled forms. The tin bath lay on its side, a few more dents dimpled its sides, although the small Octopus still bunged itself into the hole, its arms gripped tight.

"What shall we do now?" asked Slippery-Fish, having stood the bath upright and was now untying the sea-weed from around his waist.

"I have no idea." answered Nipper-Crab… "But one thing I do know is that I will not be going out to sea in that bath again!"

"Me neither!" affirmed Slippery-Fish, seating himself on the sand.

"I think." said Stinger-Scorpion. "We need to speak to the Stick-Insect-Guru to ask what he thinks we should do."

"Then you will have to go on your own, Stinger." said Nipper-Crab, tiredly, seating himself beside Slippery-Fish.

Feeling a sense of failure, Stinger-Scorpion made his way back to the Mournful-Cave and now stood peering into the dark mouth of the cave. There seemed to be no-one there and Stinger-Scorpion moved deeper into the cave. There was nothing there except two large Oysters, side by side, which had their lids shut tight.

"Hallooo! Bucket-Boys!" shouted Stinger-Scorpion, now peering down the shaft.

"What is it?"

Suddenly, the top shells of the Oysters had sprung open, to expose the two Bucket-Boys, who had pushed blankets aside and were sitting up.

"You made me jump!" exclaimed Stinger-Scorpion, turning round to see the Bucket-Boys.

"What are you both doing inside those Oyster shells?" he asked.

"These are our beds, we sleep inside the shells... Now, what do you want? It had better be important, otherwise we are going back to sleep." grumbled Sidney-Boy Woodmouse.

Both Sidney-Boy Woodmouse and Jackie-Boy Woodmouse had risen from their Oyster beds and stood, yawning loudly.

"I need to see the Stick-Insect-Guru... It is very important." replied Stinger-Scorpion.

"At this time of night?" said Jackie-Boy Woodmouse. "He may be asleep and we can't disturb him."

Stinger-Scorpion frowned. "It's still day-time!" he exclaimed.

"Well, we can't know that... We don't know when it's day or night in the dark of this cave. It all looks the same to us." replied Jackie-Boy Woodmouse. The other Bucket-Boy nodded, beginning to yawn again.

"Well, it's day-time... Now are you going to let me down, so I can see the Stick-Insect-Guru, or not?" demanded Stinger-Scorpion, grumpily.

"I suppose I will have to." replied Sidney-Boy Woodmouse, going to the bucket and heaving it to the edge of the shaft, so that Stinger-Scorpion climbed aboard.

"Bucket down!" shouted Sidney-Boy Woodmouse as he started to lower the bucket down into the well.

The Stick-Insect-Guru sat, as he had before, warming himself in front of the fire. Seeing Stinger-Scorpion, he arose, his face concerned.

"What is it? What is the matter?" he asked.

"I'm afraid I have some bad news." began Stinger-Scorpion and continued to explain how the High-Water-Tide had been too strong for the tin bath and had thrown them back onto the beach.

The Stick-Insect-Guru took his turban from his head, scratching at the bald dome with a stick finger, deep in thought. Then, replacing his turban, his face brightening, he said… "You will have to go and ask the Weather-Man for his help. You can tell him that I, the Stick-Insect-Guru, have sent you. He will help you get past the High-Water-Tide."

"How do I find this Weather-Man?" asked Stinger-Scorpion, relieved that the Stick-Insect-Guru had provided the answer.

"Listen carefully, my friend." urged the Stick-Insect-Guru. "You will have to take the Bush-Lane and walk through the Barley-Grove, till you reach the Rising-Oak. When you reach there, you will have to call out for the Moaning-Weasel. He will guide you to where you can meet the Weather-Man."

Slippery-Fish snored loudly, asleep in the tin bath, the Octopus splattered on top of his head, rather like a fried egg which had been thrown with some force. Nipper-Crab had been standing at the shore's edge, idly throwing stones into the sea. Now, on seeing Stinger-Scorpion coming towards him, he moved to meet him, enquiring about the meeting with the Stick-Insect-Guru. Stinger-Scorpion told Nipper-Crab about the meeting and how they would have to find the Weather-Man, to have help with over-riding the High-Water-Tide.

"I think its best that we leave Slippery here, guarding the tin bath, while you and I go and track down the Weather-Man." said Stinger-Scorpion.

Looking down at the sleeping form of Slippery-Fish, Nipper-Crab heartedly agreed… And, together, the two set off, walking briskly towards the uphill climb of Bush-Lane.

Bush-Lane was the birthplace of all Butterflies and the sighs and soft whispers which came from the bushes to each side of the path, which had such an effect as to make Stinger-Scorpion and Nipper-Crab walk in silence, gently, as if they walked on a fine, cloudy mist.

At the top of the hill, they came to Barley-Grove, an Avenue of tall Barley-Sugar trees, whose tops leaned towards each other, as to form an umbrella which darkened the walk below. Having entered Barley-Grove, the two friends were suddenly aware of scurrying sounds and scratching noises.

Suddenly they were confronted by small red Squirrel-Folk, who descended from the tops of the trees, each clutching small begging-bowls, which they held out.

THE BARLEY-BEGGARS

"Sugar, please… Sugar for our trees." They all began begging, pulling at Stinger-Scorpion and Nipper-Crab.

"They are Barley-Beggars." exclaimed Stinger-Scorpion, pushing the small creatures away from him. "I've heard of them and its best we take no notice of them, Nipper."

They continued to walk through the Barley-Grove, unheeding of all the cries for Sugar. Giving up their begging, the Barley-Beggars ran back up into the trees and called out bad names.

"You are both mean… Misers! You are both miserable, ugly creatures!" they called.

"Ignore them, Nipper." advised Stinger-Scorpion. "You know the old saying, that sticks and stones may break our bones, but names will never hurt us!"

Once the Barley-Beggars saw that their name-calling caused no reaction from Stinger-Scorpion and Nipper-Crab, the Barley-Beggars became quiet and Barley-Grove became peaceful once more.

"What do you want?"

The two friends had reached the Rising-Oak, an open space, where they were stopped by a small Weasel, who rose from a bed of oak leaves, to stand in front of them. He had a long straggly beard which nearly reached the ground, and was dressed in a flowing cloak which had strange patterns of moons and stars on it. On his head he wore a pointed hat with the same designs on it.

"I asked you pair… What do you want?" he said

again, his voice croaky and whiney.

"You must be the Moaning-Weasel?" said Stinger-Scorpion.

"Yes, I am! And you're not helping me with silly statements. I have enough to put up with, what with my aches and pains and the price of sand!" exclaimed the Weasel, leaning heavily on a stout stick.

"Forgive us." said Stinger-Scorpion, feeling sorry for the Moaning-Weasel, even though he was not exactly sure what the price of sand had to do with anything.

"Why should I forgive you? And, more to the point, what do you want?"

"We want to see the Weather-Man." joined in Nipper-Crab.

"Why?" demanded the Weasel.

"It's really none of your business." replied Stinger-Scorpion, unhappy at the rudeness of the Moaning-Weasel.

"We have been sent here by the Stick-Insect-Guru and I think the Weather-Man will be quite upset if he hears you were not helping us." said Nipper-Crab.

"Why didn't you say that in the first place? If you had opened your mouths and told me, I would have had less to moan about." sniffed the Weasel.

"Well, you know now… So are you going to lead us to the Weather-Man?" asked Stinger-Scorpion.

"I have to be careful about bothering the Weather-Man. The last thing I want is to get soaked by the

Rain-Sponge. How do you think I got all these aches and pains? It was the water and the damp, that's how."

"Well, I'm sorry about the Rain-Sponge and your aches and pains, but we are not to blame for them."

"Will you now lead us to the Weather-Man?" demanded Stinger-Scorpion.

"What is the Rain-Sponge?" asked Nipper-Crab.

The Moaning-Weasel made no reply and, bending on his stick, he walked to the centre of the clearing and drew a large circle on the ground.

"Watch me and learn." he demanded.

Stinger-Scorpion and Nipper-Crab watched in amazement as the Moaning-Weasel suddenly looked up to the sky, his thin arms raised, his fingers working as if he was playing a piano. His feet began to dance up and down, while his thin voice croaked out a strange sound. He then jumped up and down, chanting loudly, before stopping to grasp his stick and gasp for breath.

"Come into the circle and do the Rain-Dance, just as I did." croaked the Weasel.

"Why should we do that stupid dance?" demanded Stinger-Scorpion.

"Are you mad!" shouted the Weasel in panic, his weak eyes scouring the sky. "Do you want us to get the Rain-Sponge soaking us?"

"I think we had better do it." said Nipper-Crab, moving into the circle.

Stinger-Scorpion joined him, beginning to giggle.

"I feel silly doing this… But let's get on with it." he said.

"Now… Follow my steps and sing as I do." said the Weasel and started to hold up his arms. Stinger-Scorpion and Nipper-Crab did the same, copying the Moaning-Weasel's steps and lifting their voices at the same time. Faster and faster they went, till, at the end they all fell down on the ground, puffing and panting.

Regaining his breath and picking up his stick, the Moaning-Weasel bid both the two friends to stand outside the circle, while he stood in the centre.

"Stand clear." he ordered, and then tapped three times on the ground with his stick… "Going up!" he shouted.

The ground seemed to suddenly open up. There was a loud humming sound and then a huge glass dome rose from the ground, spinning and humming. Continuing to rise up, like a Lighthouse, rising from the ground, its base an ivory tower, rising high into the air till its glass dome top vanished into the clouds.

Just as sudden, it hissed to a stop and the two friends, who had been standing with mouths open, became aware of a door in front of them.

"Open the door!" floated a voice down to them and they realised it was the voice of the Moaning-Weasel, who was still on top of the glass dome. "Open the door and go up the stairs." came the voice.

THE MOANING WEASEL

"Go up the winding staircase till you get to the top of the tower and there you will see the Weather-Man." Stinger-Scorpion gingerly opened the wooden door and peered in, seeing the staircase which wound itself round the wall, going ever upwards in a spiralling ascent.

"I think, Nipper, it would be better if you went up the stairs, to see the Weather-Man."

Nipper-Crab, who had been peering over Stinger-Scorpion's shoulder, looked dubiously at Stinger-Scorpion.

"Why me?" he asked.

"Because, Nipper, I don't have a head for heights and you much prefer to walk sideways. So you can stay close to the wall as you climb and go up with a sideways style."

"Well, what do I say to the Weather-Man when I meet him, Stinger? You always know what to say, while I get lost for words and start going around the houses. I find it hard to go right to the point of what I want to say."

Stinger-Scorpion agreed with Nipper-Crab, although he still insisted that Nipper-Crab should be the one to climb the stairs.

"You have to remember just who you are now, Nipper. You are a Wise-Being. You are blessed and must not show any nervousness at all. Simply ask if the Weather-Man can assist us in getting over the High-Water-Tide." assured Stinger-Scorpion.

Assured by his friend's words, Nipper-Crab began to

climb the stairs, climbing higher as he side-stepped each tread, ever-upwards.

At last, Nipper-Crab had reached the highest level and came to a silver door. Opening the door, he stood still, his eyes taking in the scene. The room was large, circular in shape, its walls were made of panels of glass, windows which had different moving pictures in them, of animals and strange places. In the centre of the room stood a giant red-faced Walrus, his whiskers twitching, his eyes of a fierce black. Around him were an assortment of buckets and boxes, each labelled with pictures of Rain, Lightning-Bolts, Thunder-Clouds and the Sun.

"No... No... No! You did it wrong again!" roared the Weather-Man, picking up a bucket and rushing over to one of the windows. Inside the window was a picture of a Goola-Gong-Bird, trying to dance, its wings flapping helplessly.

"That's not a proper Rain-Dance!" roared the Weather-Man at the picture of the Goola-Gong-Bird, and, reaching into the bucket he carried, the Weather-Man brought out a soaking wet pink sponge and threw it at the window. Immediately, the picture clouded over and the Goola-Gong-Bird now stood in unhappy stance, drenched from head to foot in a downpour of rain.

"It's only a dance... A stupid dance to please me... And they can't get it right!" continued to shout the Weather-Man, rushing in a circle, from window to window.

THE WEATHERMAN

"Look there! Look at that fool. He thinks that holding a Toadstool over his head will save him from a soaking!" he shouted, pointing at a picture, then running to one of the boxes and, opening it, drew out a streak of Lightning-Bolt.

Rushing back to the window, he drew back an arm and threw the bolt at the picture. Immediately, the Pie-Toad dropped the Toadstool-Umbrella, shocked as the Lightning-Bolt lit him up in a blaze of white flashes.

"That got him!" exploded the Weather-Man, then, as if suddenly seeing Nipper-Crab standing there, he glared at him.

"Who are you and what do you want?" he demanded.

"The Stick-Insect-Guru sent me, Sir." Nipper-Crab stammered, forgetting in his fear to go round the houses, and coming straight to the point.

"What? The Stick-Insect-Guru? Is he still down that ghastly Mournful-Cave?" demanded the Weather-Man, his eyes roving around the window panels. Then, without waiting for an answer, he demanded…

"So? Stop stammering and tell me what you want… I haven't got all day!"

"My friends, Stinger-Scorpion and Slippery-Fish want…"

"Look at that! Discrepancies everywhere! No Rain-Dance, no-one ever asking for the Sun!"

Without waiting for Nipper-Crab to finish talking, the Weather-Man had grabbed the Sponge-Bucket and rushed over to the window with the pink sponge and Nipper-Crab watched as the sunbathers began to run for cover as the rain began to pour in sheer torrents.

"Do you see what I mean?" demanded the Weather-Man angrily, coming back to stand in front of Nipper-Crab.

"Now." he said… What was it you and your friends wanted from me?"

"We want you to help us get over the High-Water-Tide" answered Nipper-Crab in a small voice.

"The High-Water-Tide, you say? Speak up there!" demanded the Weather-Man, peering right into Nipper-Crab's face.

"We need to get to the Lands of the Westward-Sun and this means we have to sail in out boat past the High-Water-Tide. The Stick-Insect-Guru suggested you could help us."

Nipper-Crab tried hard to keep his voice in control, though it rose into a high waver by the time he had finished speaking.

"He did, did he? And can you tell me how I am supposed to help you and your friends get over the High-Water-Tide?" said the Weather-Man, impatiently.

"I don't know, Sir." answered Nipper-Crab, beginning to wish he was back on the ground.

Once again, the Weather-Man's focus was distracted by the sight of an Ostrich, who had fallen over as he tried to do the Rain-Dance. Roaring with rage the

Weather-Man had rushed over, trailing water from the sponge, before splashing the offending picture with a deluge of water.

"What is the matter with them?" he exclaimed. Nipper-Crab stood silent, watching as the Weather-Man raged, saying nothing till the Weather-Man's rage had died down.

"Sometimes I feel like just walking out and letting the weather take its own course." finished the Weather-Man, calming his nature by putting the wet sponge on his head and squeezing it so that water streamed down, turning his red face to a pale blue.

"You are doing a marvellous job." said Nipper-Crab, putting admiration into his voice, hoping the Weather-Man would deal with his problem.

"Well at least you can see just what I have to put up with… I get no thanks at all. Now then, you say you need my help to get you over the High-Water-Tide?" Nipper-Crab nodded quickly when the Weather-Man spoke.

"Indeed, I do, Sir." he answered.

"Where about is your boat situated?" asked the Weather-Man, mopping at his face with an old towel.

"On the beach, Sir… By the Sand-Dune."

The Weather-Man walked over to one of the windows, standing for a while as he watched the pictures of two Penguins pulling a sledge, loaded with parcels, up a snow-packed hill. Nodding and grunting, the Weather-Man walked to a box, and opening it, he drew out some snow, and going back to the window, he threw the snow at the screen, watching as the scene blurred as a Snow-Storm began to block out the picture of the two Penguins. "That's better." the Weather-Man grunted, and then pressed a button, and the picture vanished. He twirled a knob at the side and a quick flutter of pictured scenes went on and off until a picture came into view, which Nipper-Crab instantly recognised as the beach where sat the tin bath, with Slippery-Fish sound asleep inside it.

"What's that on his head?" asked the Weather-Man, peering intensely at Slippery-Fish.

"It's an Octopus." explained Nipper-Crab, not really sure why the Octopus should be asleep on top of Slippery-Fish's head.

Seemingly satisfied with the answer, the Weather-Man asked... "How many of you are going to be in that boat?"

"Three of us, Sir... There's me and Slippery-Fish, as well as Stinger-Scorpion."

The Weather-Man considered the information, "You'll need a mast and sail for the boat before you start off. Now, here's what I shall do. I will blow a wind which will carry your boat out to the High-Water-Tide, then really blow hard, so that the wind takes your boat right over the top of the High-Water-Tide. Do you understand?"

"Yes, Sir." quickly answered Nipper-Crab, starting to move towards the door.

"Just a moment… Where do you think you are going?"

Nipper-Crab froze, standing stock still.

"I haven't finished yet!" said the Weather-Man, motioning Nipper-Crab back to the centre of the room.

"There is only one thing I want from you and your friends in return." said the Weather-Man, peering intently into Nipper-Crab's face.

"Anything, Sir… just tell me what you want us to do and we'll do it for you." Nipper-Crab promised.

"Here's what you must do for me, in return for my help… Before you set sail, I want to see you and your two friends do the Rain-Dance for me. Is that a promise?" asked the Weather-Man.

"Of course we will, Sir. We would be highly delighted to do the Rain-Dance for you." promised Nipper-Crab.

Suddenly the Weather-Man turned, his face turning a brightest red, his whiskers twitching violently.

"Look at that!" he roared, rushing across the room, to point at a picture of four young Pigs, sitting on a haystack with pipes smoking in their mouths.

"Bucket! ... Where's my bucket and Lightning-Bolt. I'll give them a big surprise for smoking under-age!" Nipper-Crab opened the door and crept out, drowning out the noise as he closed the door behind him.

"What happened?" asked Stinger-Scorpion, as Nipper-Crab joined him outside the tower.

"He is quite mad, that Weather-Man." said Nipper-Crab, then went on to explain what had gone on during the meeting with the Weather-Man, also stating that they would need a mast and sail for the boat.

"Coming down!"

Both Nipper-Crab and Stinger-Scorpion jumped back as the voice of the Moaning-Weasel floated down and the whole round tower began to shake, then spin round as it started to sink gradually back into the earth from where it had risen. The glass dome whirred and revolved then vanished beneath the earth, which smoothed itself out, as if nothing had ever been disturbed, leaving the sight of a panting Moaning-Weasel laying there.

"Now, do you see why my old bones play me up? Why I moan so much?" cried the Moaning-Weasel, and, rising with the aid of his stick, crooked a finger at Stinger-Scorpion and Nipper-Crab, saying...

"Come into the circle, both of you, and do the Rain-Dance with me."

"No thank you." replied Stinger-Scorpion, starting to walk away.

"Wait, Stinger." called Nipper-Crab. "I would suggest that we do the Rain-Dance. I have seen what the Weather-Man does if you refuse. Please do the Rain-Dance with me and the Weasel."

Stinger-Scorpion saw that his friend was very serious indeed, so that he joined them in the centre of the circle, and held up his arms in readiness.

"Ready, everyone? … After me… One, Two, Three!" shouted the Moaning-Weasel, beginning to tinkle his fingers and sing.

The Rain-Dance was finished and both Stinger-Scorpion and Nipper-Crab thanked the Weasel. He took no notice but went to where his bed of Oak leaves was and lay down, promptly falling asleep.

"Let's get back to the boat and get ready to make sail." said Stinger-Scorpion, and they began to walk towards Barley-Grove.

"Just a moment." said Stinger-Scorpion, suddenly. "I just have to go back and collect something."

Nipper-Crab waited as Stinger-Scorpion walked back from where they had come, soon returning, carrying the Moaning-Weasel's stick.

"Why have you taken the Moaning-Weasel's stick?" asked Nipper-Crab.

"Well, Nipper… It will make an excellent mast for our sail." answered Stinger-Scorpion.

"But won't the Moaning-Weasel miss it… Won't he need it?" queried Nipper-Crab, feeling the guilt rise up inside him.

"Well, he will miss it. Nipper." agreed Stinger-Scorpion. "But look at it this way… It will just be one more thing that the Moaning-Weasel can moan about!"

Now that certainly made sense to Nipper-Crab and the feelings of guilt quickly subsided.

They had reached the Barley-Grove, though no Barley-Beggars came down from the trees with their begging-bowls. They had seen Stinger-Scorpion carrying the stout stick and decided that he would beat them if they came out of their hidey-holes. Instead, they remained hidden, simply shouting out insults and name-calling.

"Look at that Scorpion with his big stick!" We are not frightened of him… Or that silly Crab! … Hey… Misers! Measly-Mouths!" shouted the Barley-Beggars.

"Take no notice of them." advised Nipper-Crab, seeing Stinger-Scorpion start to wave the stick up in the air.

Moving on and leaving the name-calling behind, Stinger-Scorpion and Nipper-Crab walked back through Bush-Lane, their eyes taking in a sweet time, of baby Butterflies coming out from cocoons, to lie on the leaves of the bushes, allowing their wings to dry, then spread in flight, while proud Butterfly Mothers sat with soft proud eyes. The air became alive to 'Coos' and 'Sighs', as the babies took flight and filled the sky.

Stinger-Scorpion and Nipper-Crab stood quietly, waiting until all the baby Butterflies had spread out and upwards, disappearing into the sky. Then the two friends made their way to the beach, to where Slippery-Fish still lay in the tin bath, snoring loudly.

"Lift Slippery forward, Nipper, and try to do it gently, so he doesn't wake up." said Stinger-Scorpion, quietly, at the same time peeling the Octopus from Slippery's head and setting it down on the sand, where it scuttled away, to settle in a shallow pool.

Nipper-Crab did as Stinger-Scorpion asked, easing Slippery forward, while Stinger-Scorpion went behind and removed a quantity of fish-scales from the back of Slippery-Fish.

"We need these to make a sail for the boat, Nipper." said Stinger-Scorpion quietly.

Nipper-Crab felt, once more, that well of guilt creep into his heart, even though he understood they did need a sail for the boat.

"Help me glue these scales together and fix them to the mast... Then we can wake Slippery up, ready to set sail."

Together, Stinger-Scorpion and Nipper-Crab glued the scales together, making a fine, shiny sail, tying it to the stick which Stinger-Scorpion had stolen from the Moaning-Weasel. Jamming the stick-mast into the hole in the bottom of the tin bath, both stood back to gaze at the finished boat.

"It looks great!" exclaimed Nipper-Crab, and then watched as Stinger-Scorpion started to shake Slippery-Fish awake.

"Come on, Slippery... We have to set sail!" he shouted.

Slippery-Fish woke with a start, staring round blinking his eyes sleepily.

"What's going on?" he asked, trying to make sense of being shook awake.

"Wake up, Slippery! We are about to set sail for the

Lands of the Westward-Sun!" shouted Stinger-Scorpion. "We need you to help us push the boat down towards the sea… Hurry up, slowcoach." Grumpily, Slippery-Fish climbed out of the tin bath and began to help push the boat down towards the sea.

"It has got very chilly… My back is very cold!" exclaimed Slippery-Fish suddenly, looking around for the cause of the chill.

"That's because the Weather-Man has started to blow a wind so that the boat sails out towards the High-Water-Tide." said Stinger-Scorpion. Nipper-Crab could not help giggling, so that Slippery-Fish looked at him suspiciously.

"Jump in!" shouted Stinger-Scorpion as the boat began to float and then move out to sea.

The three friends jumped into the boat and settled down as the wind began to pick up, breezy at first, then the boat beginning to rock and lurch as they moved out into deeper water, seeing the High-Water-Tide rising menacingly in front of them.

"Wait!" suddenly screamed Nipper-Crab, standing up. "We have to go back… We forgot to do the Rain-Dance for the Weather-Man as I promised!"

"It's too late for that now, Nipper. Sit down, you are rocking the boat!" shouted Stinger-Scorpion.

"We must go back!" wailed the unhappy Nipper-Crab, now lying down in the bottom of the boat.

THE WATERSPOUT

The wind had seemed to whip itself up, creaming the sea into angry white whirls, growing stronger, then to rage as a downpour started, a deluge of water which had the three crying out in fear, hugging the bottom of the boat.

Above the roar of the wind and the rain came a thunderous voice… "You did not do the Rain-Dance for me! You promised you would… Now you all have to pay!"

"It's the Weather-Man!" cried out Nipper, his voice lost to the savagery of the storm, which now whipped the waves up into a fury.

The wind raised its voice and howled in screams of torment as it picked up the water, spouting it high into the air, spiralling ever higher, taking up whatever lay in its path.

The tin bath flew, as light as a straw, caught up in the maelstrom of twisting and circling violence, lifting up and rising into the air with such force, that Nipper-Crab, Stinger-Scorpion and Slippery-Fish had no time to think, to reason out what was happening to them. They had their eyes closed, feeling as though their stomachs were being torn out in a whirling storm of madness.

Then it was over. The three friends seemed to drift, lost in some kind of space, in a deathly drifting of quietness. Stinger was the first to open his eyes and look around him. The bath was gone, spewed out from under them and hurled back down into the sea. He lay quiet for a while, then patted outwards with his hands, feeling a soft quilting under him, as if he lay on a duvet of soft white sheepskin. Above him was just the wide expanse of sky, nothing more.

"Nipper... Slippery?" he whispered, reaching out to touch them.

"Are we dead?" asked Nipper-Crab, opening his eyes, bit by bit.

"I'm not sure, Nipper. Try not to move too much. I think we are floating on something soft, just feel the stuff we are laying on." said Stinger-Scorpion.

"What happened? Where's the boat?" asked Slippery-Fish in a small frightened voice.

He had kept his eyes closed, listening to his friends talking. He reached out with his hands, finger-walking the softness beneath him.

"We're not sure, Slippery, what is going on. The boat is gone." replied Stinger. "Just lay still, till we know where we are." he finished.

"Do you mind moving off my head?"

The small voice seemed to come from the sheepskin beneath them.

The three friends lay very still, afraid to move, their eyes wide and staring.

"It would appear that we have three large bodies laying on us." spoke up another tiny voice.

"Who said that?" whispered Stinger-Scorpion fiercely, his eyes swivelling from Nipper-Crab to Slippery-Fish and back again.

"I did!"... And get your muddy, wet, feet off my new suit!" came the voice, just a bit louder, indignant.

At that, Stinger-Scorpion took his life into his hands and rolled over, feeling the sheepskin rise and fall under his body.

"We're lying on a cloud… Up in the sky!" he exclaimed, sitting up and, moving to the edge, peered over to see the sea far below.

"We're in Lord-Land-Heaven!" whispered Nipper-Crab and closing his eyes once more, he lay very still.

"Are we Stinger? Are we in Lord-Land-Heaven?" croaked Slippery-Fish, feeling his life's blood leaving his body.

"No, we're not, you two!" fiercely asserted Stinger-Scorpion, beginning to gain confidence and bouncing his body on the sheepskin. "I told you, we are floating on a cloud, in the sky." he finished.

At that, both Nipper-Crab and Slippery-Fish opened their eyes and sat up.

"Then whose voice was that we heard?" inquired Nipper-Crab, pinching at the fleece-like quilt.

"It wasn't a voice." said Stinger. "It was just our imagination, caused by our fear. Fear does that, it let's us hear voices and the more we fear then the louder the voices!"

"Then you had better believe it!" said a voice, much louder this time, so that Stinger-Scorpion, Nipper-Crab and Slippery-Fish quickly lay down, flat on their backs, their eyes wide and round, afraid to move.

"I think they heard you this time!" chortled another voice, and this was followed by a thousand little voices, all raised in laughter and whistles.

"Who are you?" quavered Nipper-Crab, not daring to open his eyes.

"We are the Puff-Clouders!" shouted a thousand voices in unison. "That's who we are and that is who you are laying your big fat heavy bodies on!"

"Why can't we see you?" All I can see is a big white cloud." said Stinger, now opening his eyes and sitting up.

"Turn over and have a good look!" said a voice. Stinger-Scorpion rolled over onto his stomach and peered down at the sheepskin, settling his eyes to the brightness. It was then, at first, he made out the white mass that seemed to be wiggling and jiggling about, as if the fleece had a life of its own.

"Look closer… You have to squint and adjust your eyes, to see us!" demanded the voice, followed by many giggles from all over the quilt.

Stinger-Scorpion squinted his eyes, adjusting his sight, and then gasped in amazement.

"You are blobs of cotton-wool!" he gasped again.

"Cotton-wool? Look closer… Go on, take a real close look." said one of the blobs.

This time Stinger-Scorpion squinted real hard and saw what the white cloud was made of. The cloud was made up of thousands of little folk, all dressed in clothes, in woolly suits and hats, which looked, and felt, like cotton-wool. They all had their arms linked together so that, from a distance, they looked like a fluffy white cloud.

"Do you see now, what you are laying on? We are the Puff-Clouders and when we join arms, we become Cloud-Cuckoo-Land!"

Nipper-Crab, who had been listening to the conversation between Stinger-Scorpion and the Puff-Clouder, now sat up, trying to be as light as he could. "But if you let go of each other, we will fall back down into the sea." he said in a shaky voice.

"Of course you would!" exclaimed another of the Puff-Clouders.

Nipper-Crab felt a ripple of movement beneath him and lifted his body up.

"It doesn't matter where you move to, you will still be sitting on some of us." laughed a voice beneath him.

"I'm sorry." replied Nipper-Crab. "I can't help moving… But do you ever let go of each other?" he finished.

"Of course we do, we have to. Each night, when the Dark-Angels pull the black satin sheet over us, we let go of each other and light our little candles, then we float off into the dark of night… We become the Star-Lights." said the Puff-Clouder, while a thousand little voices agreed with whistles and cheers.

"You mean?" said Stinger-Scorpion suddenly grasping what the Puff-Clouder meant… "Is that, when the night falls, you all become twinkling lights in the night sky, what we below see as stars in the sky?"

"I don't know what you folk see from down below at night, though, when the morning comes and the Light-Angels come and draw the dark curtain away, we all link arms again and sing songs and laugh together." said a Puff-Clouder.

"Do you know what time, or when the night will come, when the Dark-Angels will come and you all let go and become Star-lights?" asked Nipper-Crab.

"I don't know what you mean by the time. There's no time here. I only know that when it's warm and the sun plays out in a round gold way, the Dark-Angels come earlier." explained the Puff-Clouder.

"So we don't know when these little cotton-wool blobs will float apart, and we will fall back down into the sea?" worried Slippery-Fish, then added...

"I only know its jolly cold on my back!"

"Excuse me!" exclaimed an angry Puff-Clouder to Slippery-Fish. "We are not cotton-wool blobs, we are Puff-Clouders... And the reason your back is cold is because you don't have any of those fishy clothes on your back, you are back-bald!"

"Where have my back-scales gone?" demanded Slippery-Fish, looking from Stinger-Scorpion to Nipper-Crab.

"Don't worry about that just now, Slippery." smoothed Stinger-Scorpion. "We have bigger things to worry about, like what happens to us when the night falls."

"Exactly." said Nipper-Crab. "When the night falls,

it won't be the last thing which falls!"

"Oh, you'll be alright." said one of the Puff-Clouders.

"We will?" said Stinger-Scorpion, somewhat dubiously.

"Of course you will because, first of all, you will be able to float for a while. After all, the sky is a mirror-image of the sea, so you can float on both!" explained the Puff-Clouder.

"But we will eventually fall down and drown, won't we?" said Nipper-Crab, becoming despondent.

"But you will be able to float long enough to catch the Shooting-Star, which always stops here once the Dark-Angels have been." said the Puff-Clouder, giving the three friends new hope.

"A Shooting-Star? How do we get on it and where will it take us?" asked Slippery-Fish, now forgetting the missing scales from his back.

"It's not really a Shooting-Star." answered the Puff-Clouder. "It's a Sky-Train, called the Orion-Express, and it will take you wherever you all want to go."

"A Sky-Train? I've never heard of that before." said Stinger-Scorpion, lying down again and feeling the comfort of the soft quilt beneath him.

He closed his eyes, now aware that the Puff-Clouders had started to sing, in such a sweet harmony that all worries seemed to disappear and soon he was fast asleep.

Nipper-Crab and Slippery-Fish also lay, soothed by the magical harmony of the lullaby, till their eye-lids closed and they drifted into a smiling and gentle world of dreams.

Such beautiful dreams do not come often, dreams of magic and fairies, of tinkled laughter and flowers, of perfumes and glorious colours. It is said that only lovers and poets dream in colour… And Stinger-Scorpion, Nipper-Crab and Slippery-Fish dreamed of love and soft flowing words.

The thing about beautiful dreams is that they seem to last less than a blink of an eye, so quick although they leave gently, leaving the dreamer with a smile to wake up with. And so the three friends each woke up smiling, with eyes open, yet trying to retain the memory of the dream.

"I had such a marvellous dream." said Stinger-Scorpion, sitting up. "It was all about love and fairies."

"And me too!" exclaimed Nipper-Crab, rubbing at his eyes.

"So did I!" said Slippery-Fish, so that they all started talking at once, deciding, in the end, that the singing by the Puff-Clouders had lulled them into an enchanted sleep.

Beneath them, there was silence, not one sound from the Puff-Clouders, although there seemed to be a kind of electric expectancy in the air.

"Look!" said Nipper-Crab, suddenly turning round and pointing.

From the East, coming silently towards them, were two large Angels, dressed in black flowing robes.

They seemed to spread out, each holding the corner of a black satin sheet, which spread itself wide, darkening the sky in a night's shift.

"It's the Dark-Angels, bringing in the night sky." said Stinger-Scorpion, hardly daring to breathe.

"Yes." agreed Nipper-Crab, seeing the night darken the sky above them, then spread its sheet till he could hardly see his hand in front of his face.

"I can feel the Puff-Clouders moving beneath me." whispered Slippery-Fish, so that the three became aware of shifts and ripples of movement, which left them feeling a floating sensation.

"Look! Look!" whispered Nipper-Crab in awe. "The Puff-Clouders have un-linked arms and are separating… Do you see? Each has lit a small candle, and they are drifting into the dark sky, lighting up the black, like twinkling stars."

"Oh, don't you see!" exclaimed Stinger-Scorpion. "Those Puff-Clouders have become Star-Lights! They are what we see when we are down on the ground, and we see them as twinkling stars."

"Aren't they beautiful?" said Slippery-Fish, watching as the Star-Lights lit up the night.

"I'm still chilly." reminded Slippery-Fish, shivering slightly.

The Star-Lights had gone, leaving behind wisps of white cotton fleece, which floated in the air.

"Help me collect the cotton-wool." said Stinger-Scorpion, having an idea.

They collected up the wisps of fleece and Stinger-

Scorpion rolled it up into a ball, and then strung it out so that it formed a pad.

"Stop floating around and stay still, Slippery." instructed Stinger-Scorpion and pushed the pad firmly onto Slippery-Fish's back.

"Does that feel warmer, Slippery?"

"That is so much better." replied Slippery-Fish, now smiling.

"Hey!" said Stinger-Scorpion, suddenly. "Do you realise that we have nothing beneath us! We are just floating in the night air."

"Where is that Orion Express, the Puff-Clouders told us about?" said Slippery-Fish, swishing about in the air as if he was swimming.

"How long do you think we can stay up here, floating about, before we fall down into the sea?" worried Nipper-Crab, starting to wave his arms about.

"I'm not sure, but…"

Stinger-Scorpion's words were cut off by the noise of an approaching Sky-Train, its engines steaming out blasts of hot white air, and a screeching of air-brakes.

The Sky-Train puffed angrily beside the three friends.

"Will ye be getting on or not?" came a voice, followed by the top half of a little Leprechaun, leaning out of the engine window.

"Either in or out, which is it to be now?" he demanded, and then vanished from view, to be heard shovelling coal into the heat-box and stoking the fire. Stinger-Scorpion, Nipper-Crab and Slippery-Fish quickly climbed into the carriage, closing the door and seating themselves, then waited.

There was a sudden lurching, a hiss of steam and the Sky-Train began to speed through the night, its whistle blasting out warnings, steam snorting out in gusts from the nostrils of the engine chimney.

"And where will you happy fellows be going?" asked the Leprechaun, seating himself between them.

"How did you get in here?" asked Nipper-Crab, jumping up in alarm at the sudden appearance of the train driver.

"And more to the point!" exclaimed Stinger-Scorpion. "Who is driving the train?"

"Ah, me lads… Be sure and the train is going round in circles, seeing as it has no instruction as to where it should be heading." said the Leprechaun, then standing he raised his hat and introduced himself. "Meet me in a merry greet, lads… I am Patsy O'Leary, at your service… Known on the Sky-Track as Tommy."

"I am Stinger-Scorpion and these fine folk are Nipper-Crab and Slippery-Fish." said Stinger-Scorpion, introducing himself and his two friends. Nipper-Crab stared at Tommy curiously, not sure what to make of this strange little Leprechaun.

"So what do we call you, Patsy or Tommy?" he asked at length.

THE
SKY-TRAIN

"Call me O'Leary." decided the Leprechaun, touching at his hat, then added… "Would you fine fellows care to ride up front, in my cab?"
Without waiting for an answer, he rose, opened the door and climbed out into the night, inviting the others to follow him to the front of the Sky-Train, then climbed inside. It seemed as if the three friends were walking on air, anxious to climb into the Engine-Cab in case they fell into the sea.
"You can shovel coal in." he ordered Nipper-Crab… "And you can do the stoking." he finished, pointing at Slippery-Fish.
"What do I do" asked Stinger-Scorpion, feeling left out of the action.
"You can drive the train with me." instructed O'Leary, turning to tug at a cord, which set the whistle blasting.
"Turn that wheel." said O'Leary, pointing, and Stinger-Scorpion turned the wheel.
There was a loud hissing, a gush of smoke from the funnel, and the Sky-Train began to move, picking up speed as it whistled its cry into the night.
"We've left the coach behind!" cried out Nipper-Crab, staring back at the coach, which then seemed to disappear into the night.
"It doesn't matter, me darlin' lad." laughed O'Leary. "We won't be needing that, seeing as we are all up in the front of the train"
"Where are we going?" asked Slippery-Fish, continuing to poke at the tender-fire.

"We're still going round in circles." declared Nipper-Crab, looking out of the side window.

"That's because no-one has said where you want to be going to." answered O'Leary.

"We want to go to the Lands of the Westward-Sun." said Stinger-Scorpion.

No sooner were the words out of Stinger-Scorpion's mouth, than the Sky-Train seemed to rear up and took off at an enormous pace.

"Hang onto your hats, lads!" shouted O'Leary.

It did not matter that the three intrepid travellers wore no hats, the Sky-Train sped off into the night, climbing high over a soft-cheese Moon and through Tunnels, which O'Leary described as Worm-Holes. It seemed that going through the Tunnels brought new emotions and feelings, which had all of the passengers reeling with laughter, drinking in the magic of the ride and drunk on the experience.

It seemed the ride was endless and the magic began to wear off.

"How long will it be before we arrive at the Lands of the Westward-Sun?" shouted Stinger-Scorpion, as they came out of the pitch black Tunnel into a lighter shade of grey. Below lay a pasture, alive with Unicorns, while winged Horses galloped through the sky, coming quite close to the Sky-Train.

"When do you want to arrive?" answered O'Leary, staring at his wrist as if he wore a watch.

"Watch out for that Asteroid!" he suddenly shouted, snatching at the wheel and turning it.

"I think O'Leary is quite mad." whispered Slippery-Fish to Nipper-Crab. "Do you think we will be able to get off this Sky-Train?" asked Stinger Scorpion. "Well, there's nothing we can do while we're on the train. I mean, we can't jump off into nowhere. All we can do is hang on and see what happens." answered Nipper-Crab.

"Here's the Terminal-Tunnel!" shouted O'Leary, pulling at the chord so the whistle shrilled loudly as the train entered a very dark and large Worm-Hole. The whistle-blast echoed back from the walls, making a roaring sound, which caused them all to put their hands over their ears. The Tunnel wormed and twisted, so that the passengers felt they were on a roller-coaster, even turning upside-down. And, just as sudden, the train-ride was over. The Sky-Train had shot out of the Tunnel like a cork from a bottle, coming out of the dark into bright sunlight.

"All out!" shouted O'Leary.

The train had pulled into a small railway station, hissing steam and puffing as it stood in wait.

"All out!" shouted O'Leary again, even though he had seen Stinger-Scorpion, Nipper-Crab and Slippery-Fish alight from the train, and they were now standing on the platform, staring about them.

"Where are we?" shouted Stinger-Scorpion to O'Leary.

But the little Leprechaun was not listening, eager to pull away from the station. The whistle shrieked and, with a huge gust of smoke, the train vanished into the sky.

"You are at the main station of the Lands of the Westward-Sun." said a voice, so that the three friends quickly turned, to see a large Toad who carried a shopping-bag over one arm, his hands washing themselves, making him seem somewhat crafty.

"Who are you?" demanded Slippery-Fish, his face showing distaste. He really had no time for Toads, they seemed to think themselves so superior to Fish, simply because they could live on both water, and land, while Fish could only live in water.

"My name is Squire-Warty-Toad." said the Toad, bowing low, though his eyes took in Slippery-Fish, with a similar dislike.

"Then we shall call you Warty." said Slippery-Fish.

"I wonder, Warty-Toad, if you might acquaint us with what is going on and what part you take in it?" said Stinger-Scorpion, stepping between them, his voice soft and compromising.

"Thank you, Stinger-Scorpion… I shall, indeed, acquaint you of what is happening. First, allow me to welcome you to the Lands of the Westward-Sun. This welcome is extended to you through me by my Masters, the Wishful-Hopefuls."

"We have heard of the Wishful-Hopefuls. The Stick-Insect-Guru told us about them. Were they expecting us? I mean, how did you know Stinger-Scorpion's name?" asked Nipper-Crab.

Warty-Toad cast large, bulbous, eyes at Nipper-Crab

and blinked hugely, before saying… "I am forbidden to say too much, Nipper-Crab, except to tell you that the three of you were expected to be here when I arrived."

"So, what do we do now?" asked Stinger-Scorpion.

"I have to take you to the Palace of Rooms." explained Warty-Toad, then, removing the large shopping-bag from his arm, he held it out, offering it to Stinger-Scorpion.

"The Palace of Rooms?" queried Slippery-Fish, gazing around at the deserted railway station. There were no other buildings in sight, that he could see. "And what is that shopping-bag for?" he asked, touching it gingerly.

"I have no idea." said Warty-Toad. "Excepting that I was instructed by my Masters to hand it to Stinger-Scorpion on his arrival."

Stinger-Scorpion opened the bag, peering into it. It was empty. Gazing at Warty-Toad with quizzical eyes, he demanded… "And where is this Palace of Rooms?"

"There." replied Warty-Toad, pointing to the sign, which read 'Waiting- Room'.

"That's just a musty old station Waiting-Room." muttered Slippery-Fish, not fully trusting the Toad.

"There are times, Slippery-Fish, when you must not trust your eyes, times when things are not always what they seem." said Warty-Toad, his large eyes blinking.

"Come on, let's go into the Waiting-Room, we have

nothing to lose." said Nipper-Crab, taking the lead and walking towards the Waiting-Room, his friends in tow.

The Waiting-Room smelt aged and damp, as if no-one had been there for a hundred years. Along either side of the room were spaced a row of dust-covered seats. The room was empty, and the three friends gazed about them, then at each other, having no answers.

"So, what are we supposed to be looking for, Warty-Toad?" asked Stinger-Scorpion, turning around, and was surprised to see that Warty-Toad had vanished.

"Where has the Toad gone?" asked Nipper-Crab, mystified. "He was here a moment ago."

"Go through the other door, at the end of the room." came Warty-Toad's voice, seeming to come from out of thin air.

"Other door? There's only the door we came in, there's no other door!" exclaimed Slippery-Fish. "I knew we should have not have trusted that Toad. Toads are so distrustful!"

Just as Slippery-Fish had said those words, continuing to grumble, there was a quick gust of wind and then a door suddenly appeared, and opened, at the far end of the room.

Peering in, the three friends saw that the door opened to a long corridor, with other doors leading off on either side.

"What are we supposed to do?" queried Nipper-Crab.

THE WARTY TOAD

KHD.

"I don't trust it." spoke up Slippery-Fish.

"I think my friends." said Stinger-Scorpion, bravely stepping into the corridor. "We are supposed to go to each door and open it, to see what lies within… Starting with this one first." he continued, turning the gleaming door handle and stepping straight in. Nipper-Crab and Slippery-Fish stood outside the room, staring in, their eyes wide in amazement.

"Goodness gracious!" exclaimed Nipper-Crab as he watched Stinger-Scorpion begin to pick up the priceless treasures.

"We're rich!" shouted Slippery-Fish, rushing into the room, to join Stinger-Scorpion and Nipper-Crab, who stood in the middle of the room, their hands full of gold pieces.

"Just look at what is here." breathed Nipper-Crab, taking up a golden crown and seating it on his head.

"There's a fortune here!" cried a jubilant Stinger-Scorpion, grabbing a handful of gold-dust, throwing it up into the air, so that it showered all three in a rich golden dust.

"What is that!" exclaimed Nipper-Crab, suddenly, seeing shadows scurry across the room, hearing whispering and whistling sounds.

"Yes, I saw something, like little whisks of fur flying about." said Slippery-Fish, feeling quite afraid, forgetting the treasure and going towards the door.

"There it is again, that noise, it's coming from behind the pile of Gold Bars, over there." whispered Stinger-Scorpion, beginning to creep towards the sounds.

"Be careful, Stinger." warned Nipper-Crab, not daring to follow Stinger-Scorpion and then watched Stinger-Scorpion suddenly jump, and vanish behind the pile of Gold Bars.

The scampering sounds and squeals became loud, while the voice of Stinger-Scorpion was raised, between shouts and laughter.

"Come and see!" shouted Stinger-Scorpion. "Look at what I have!"

Running now, Nipper-Crab and Slippery-Fish saw that Stinger-Scorpion had his hand raised, holding up a very indignant Gerbil, whose cheek pouches were puffed out, crammed with Diamonds and Pearls.

"There's a whole pack of them, stealing all our treasure! They all ran into that hole by the skirting-board… All except this one I've caught." said Stinger-Scorpion, shaking the Gerbil so that its mouth opened and the Jewels fell to the ground. Letting the Gerbil go, it fell to the ground, giving one last angry outburst, then ran and vanished through the hole.

"We have to stop them stealing all our treasure." said Nipper-Crab, beginning to place some of the Gold Bars in front of the hole, blocking it up.

Now the three friends turned their attention back to the Gold and Silver, their eyes wide with greed.

"Look! Look up there!" shouted Slippery-Fish, his eyes on a large Crown, which was alive with Gold and Jewels, that had a Diamond as big as a fist, sitting at the top of it. The three friends stared up at the shelf, to where the Crown sat, their minds on how to reach it.

"I want it!" shouted Nipper-Crab, trying to jump up, and not reaching high enough.

"Let me stand on your shoulders, Nipper." said Slippery-Fish.

"No, let me stand on your shoulders, Nipper!" said Stinger-Scorpion.

This began an argument, the air full of greedy voices.

"Where has it gone?" wailed Slippery-Fish, pointing up at the bare shelf. The Crown had disappeared, while the three friends had been arguing.

"We should not be arguing, there's plenty of treasure down here. Forget the Crown and let's collect up all those Jewels and Precious Metal." calmed Stinger-Scorpion.

"You're right, we are letting greed get the better of us." responded Nipper-Crab.

"Shall we share it out?" asked Slippery-Fish, starting to make a pile of his own, choosing the biggest gold items.

"There's your problem, Slippery." said Stinger with a smile. "You just don't stop to think, do you?"

"Well, what is there to think about Stinger." replied Slippery, pulling a face. "All we need to do is to share it out equally, that's no problem, is it?"

THE GOLD ROOM

Nipper-Crab stood up, watching his two friends, knowing that Stinger-Scorpion had some kind of point to make.

"Go on then, Slippery. You take your share while Nipper and I watch you carry it out of this room." Slippery-Fish thanked Stinger-Scorpion for his consideration, greedily pooling his share of the gold, piling it up, and then starting to collect it into his arms.

Stinger-Scorpion and Nipper-Crab watched Slippery-Fish as he tried to collect his hoard up, watching, as each time he picked up an item, he dropped one, till, in frustration, he threw the gold onto the floor, giving up.

"See what I mean, Slippery?" said Stinger-Scorpion, adding… "We cannot carry it all on our own, there's too much!"

"But we can't leave some of it behind!" exclaimed Nipper-Crab.

"Neither shall we, my friends." smiled Stinger-Scorpion, holding out the shopping bag.

"Why?" he asked, "Would the Toad give me this large shopping-bag?"

"Ah!" exclaimed Nipper-Crab. "He was testing us; he wanted to see if we would use it, to carry all the gold in the bag. I'm so glad the Toad gave you the bag Stinger, otherwise we would have only carried what we could in our arms. Only you would have realised how tricky and crafty that Toad was!"

"Exactly!" said Stinger-Scorpion, laughing. "Now

let's open this bag and fill it up with all the gold, and then we can find a stick and push it through the handles, so we can all carry the bag."

With great zeal, the three friends began to start filling the bag with the gold, hastily gathering up the most precious first.

It seemed they had only just half-filled the bag, when there was a loud ripping sound and the collected gold fell through a large hole in the side of the bag, falling onto the floor with a resounding bang.

"What do we do now?" asked Slippery-Fish, examining the big hole in the side of the bag.

"I'm not sure what we can do." said Nipper-Crab in a small dejected voice.

"Well, perhaps it was meant to be, that we are not able to take the treasure. Perhaps this is a lesson we have to learn, and, anyway… What good would all this treasure do us? Let's face it, we really have no use for gold back in Cuttlefish-Avenue, do we?" decided Stinger-Scorpion.

"I do believe you are right, Stinger!" exclaimed Nipper-Crab, dropping a golden Tiara. "We don't buy or sell anything back home, we share everything."

"Let's leave this foolish gold here and forget about it." said Stinger-Scorpion, throwing the torn bag down on top of the gold.

"And good riddance to bad rubbish!" finished Slippery-Fish, making his way to the door.

"Hallo, you three." said Warty-Toad, eyeing them as

they appeared back in the corridor.

"Did you know about the gold in that room?" demanded Stinger-Scorpion, staring hard at Warty-Toad.

"Gold?" replied the Toad, his face bland. He then smiled and shook his head. "I have no idea what is in that room, I only do as I am instructed… And may I ask what has happened to the bag I gave you?"

"That shopping-bag was really weak! We tried to use it to carry some gold and it split its side!" declared Nipper-Crab.

"I would suggest that you go back into the room and get the bag. You might well have use for it later on." suggested the Toad.

There was something in the way Warty-Toad spoke, which seemed to make Stinger-Scorpion uneasy, so that he nodded and turned the handle of the door, going into the room.

"Where has it all gone?"

Stinger-Scorpion's shout had Nipper-Crab and Slippery-Fish hurrying into the room, and the three stood dumbfounded at the sight of an empty room. Everything was gone, except for the shopping-bag, and a piece of crockery lying beside it.

"The gold has all gone, simply vanished." said Stinger-Scorpion to Warty-Toad as the Toad entered the room.

"Why are you all concerned? Did you want the gold after all?" inquired the Toad.

Stinger-Scorpion shook his head, indicating that he

had no wish to have the treasure, turning away, about to exit the room.

Nipper-Crab followed, although Slippery-Fish stayed, to pick up the shopping-bag and examine it. The bag was complete, there seemed to be no tear in it at all. Turning it around in his hand, Slippery-Fish was aware that Warty-Toad was watching him.

"There is something funny going on in here." he muttered, starting to walk from the room, carrying the bag.

"What about the piece of crockery?" asked Warty-Toad, pointing to the piece which lay on the floor.

"Well, it's no good to us." replied Slippery-Fish.

"Are you sure, Slippery-Fish? Perhaps it just might be more important than the gold." suggested Warty-Toad.

Saying nothing, Slippery-Fish picked up the piece of broken crockery and, putting it in the bag, left Warty-Toad standing there as he left, to join his two friends in the corridor outside.

"I really am not sure where we are supposed to go from here or what we are supposed to be doing." said Stinger-Scorpion, then, seeing Slippery-Fish carrying the bag, said… "What have you got in that bag, Slippery? Don't tell me that you have some of the gold in there?"

"No, Stinger, there's no gold. I just have that old piece of broken pottery, I felt we should save it. Do you see how the split in the bag has mended itself?" said Slippery-Fish, offering the bag up for Stinger-

Scorpion and Nipper-Crab to examine.

"There has to be a reason for the strange things going on in our lives." remarked Nipper-Crab, searching for signs of repair to the bag and finding none.

"Perhaps we have to remember what started it, how we met the Stick-Insect-Guru and so began this journey. Our being here has to have a purpose, it has to have something to do with the Reality-Colours, those wonderful views we saw outside the Guru's cave."

"Of course, you are right, Stinger." said Nipper-Crab. "It has to be fate which caused the 'Weatherman' to send that Water-Spout, and us, landing up here."

"Then its right that we should go on and see what lies behind each door." recommended Stinger-Scorpion.

"And do you notice that, while the doors are all numbered, only seven are marked out in heavy black letters, while all the others are written in white?" remarked Slipper-Fish, then… Hey! Do you see the door we have just come out of? It was marked in black as number ONE. But now the number has vanished, there is no number at all!"

"And where is Warty-Toad? I left him in the room when I came out and now the door is locked." finished Slippery-Fish, pushing and pulling at the door. It was locked tight.

"All this is very strange." muttered Stinger-Scorpion,

beginning to walk further down the corridor, past the doors with white numbers, until he reached a door which had a bold number TWO marked on it in black.

"This is the next one we should try." he said, starting to open the door, then jumped back as the noise of shouting and loud laughter blasted out from inside the room.

Shutting the door quickly, Stinger-Scorpion looked at his two friends.

"I'm not sure we should go in there." he said, shaking his head.

"I think you should, Stinger-Scorpion. I think you should all go inside and see what is going on in there."

Warty-Toad had suddenly appeared, making the three friends jump at the sound of his voice.

"How did you get here? How did you get out of that locked room?" gasped Nipper-Crab, nervously.

"Ah, my friends." replied Warty-Toad, mysteriously. "I come and I go… But you should not question me, you should question your own bravery.

"We are aware of our bravery, Warty-Toad, though we are also aware of our safety." retorted Nipper-Crab, clicking his large claw.

Nipper-Crab hated to have his ego questioned and moved to open the door.

"Come on." he said to Stinger-Scorpion and Slippery-Fish. "Let's show that Toad how brave we really are!"

He opened the door wide and the three friends entered the room, to a blare of trumpets, as a row of small Squirrel-Monkeys stood with trumpets raised to their lips.

"Hail to our guests!" shouted a voice as the trumpets finished their welcome and the Squirrel-Monkeys marched out through a small opening to the side. "Come, guests… Come and seat yourselves, eat, drink and be merry."

At the far end of the room was a large table, weighed down with all kinds of sumptuous foods and drink. Seated on a large throne sat a happy-faced Sea-Lion, who sat wearing just a large bib around his neck and a small golden crown which sat precariously on top of his head.

"Yes, Guests, sit and enjoy a feast with us." welcomed the Queen, lounging back on a sofa, being fed grapes by a chattering Capuchin-Monkey.

The fear that Stinger-Scorpion had first felt vanished at the strange sight before him and the sight of the table groaning with delicious food.

Indicating that Nipper-Crab and Slippery-Fish should sit at the table, Stinger-Scorpion seated himself, beginning to eat hungrily and suddenly aware that he had not eaten for quite a while.

Both Nipper-Crab and Slippery-Fish sat warily, watching Stinger-Scorpion put the cake into his mouth, seeing the cream oozing out from the sides and then aware of their own hunger, reached out to grasp a cake each and began munching.

THE KING'S BANQUET

"Good! Good!" exclaimed the King Sea-Lion, his crown wobbling on top of his head, clapping his hands as he watched his three Guests eat heartily. "More food!" he shouted, clapping his hands. "More wine and lemonade, more fruit and cakes!"

"Music!" suddenly called out the Queen Sea-Lion, accepting a banana from the Capuchin-Monkey. The small side door opened and from it erupted a line of Squirrel-Monkeys, wearing little red waistcoats and matching Fez hats. They carried silver trays loaded with more fruit and cakes, balancing the trays as they presented the food, first to the King Sea-lion, then to the Queen and, lastly, to the three guests, who snatched at the food greedily, eating as fast as they could.

"Where is the music and dancers!" exclaimed the Queen, standing up so suddenly that she knocked over the Capuchin-Monkey, just as he was about to pop a slice of orange into her mouth. He screamed in anger and she calmed him, patting his head, then re-sat, allowing the Capuchin-Monkey to continue feeding her.

The Squirrel-Monkeys collected scraps of food, clearing up what was left over, then, going out, they quickly returned with more trays full of fresh fruit and cakes, and leaving once more, they marched out in single file, closing the door behind them.

From beyond the door came a tune and rousing voices, of whistles and flutes, of chanting and hand-clapping. The three friends stopped eating, to see the door widen itself, allowing a highly coloured Troupe to come out, a grand display of Forest and Jungle friends, Animals of all kind, Squirrel-Monkeys and Capuchin-Monkeys up front with clashing cymbals and whistles, followed by the bigger Chimpanzees and Teddy-Bears, all in striped suits of dazzling colours. Then came the big Trunk-Elephants and Tawny-Camels, with Bass-Drums and boom-boom Tom-Toms, thumping out the base notes.

The whole ensemble formed a semi-circle in front of the table, blasting out the noise in such excitement, that the Queen Sea-Lion, forgetting her station, jumped to her feet and began to twirl and whirl, happily laughing and clapping her hands in time to the music.

At first, the mouth of the King Sea-Lion dropped open, allowing jelly to fall onto his chest, as he saw his Queen begin to dance, then, in happy move, he too jumped up and began to dance.

"Get up you three!" shouted Warty-Toad, suddenly appearing on the table amid the plates, his eyes wide and urgent, to have Stinger-Scorpion, Nipper-Crab and Slippery-Fish up and joining in with the dancing. "Come on!" shouted Stinger-Scorpion, rising to the rhythm, beginning to twist and shake, so that Nipper-Crab and Slippery-Fish were up too, twirling and twisting, clapping their hands in joyful excitement. The dancing continued for some time until, exhausted, the King and Queen sat down, panting and puffing, while two of the Squirrel-Monkeys began fanning them with large banana leaves.

The Troupe began to leave, the music losing its heavy sound as they marched out through the door, which then returned to its small size, leaving only the Squirrel-Monkeys behind, who began to play a slow hypnotic sound on the flutes.

Stinger-Scorpion sat, along with Nipper-Crab and Slippery-Fish and began to start eating again, feeling their stomachs beginning to bloat. But the food was so delicious that the three continued to stuff themselves.

There was no sign of Warty-Toad, having vanished once the three had started to dance.

"Dancers! ... Where are the Dancers?" shouted the Queen Sea-Lion, between burps, the little Squirrel-Monkeys wiping at her with a lump of orange peel.

Now, from the door, came three Blue-Meerkats, dressed in pink ballet clothes, with yellow clogs on their feet. Coming to the table and bowing low, they suddenly jumped in unison, landing on the middle of the table, sending plates flying in all directions.

The music began to hot up, picking up the beat, so that the Blue-Meerkats started to clog-dance, the metal clogs sending out sparks, so that Stinger-Scorpion, Nipper-Crab and Slippery-Fish had to duck out of the way as the shower of sparks flew.

Fascinated, they watched the dance, the whirling and feet-pounding, the sparks and music as it reached full crescendo, as they continued to eat and swell their stomachs into pot-bellies.

The music slowed and the Musicians began to slowly march towards the door, followed by the Blue-Meerkats, who, having jumped down from the table, swayed their slim bodies, their sharp eyes alive to the sound. Then all was quiet as the door finally closed. The two Squirrel-Monkeys had also left, so the Queen Sea-Lion, still burping, slid to the floor and, opening a trapdoor, she dropped herself through the opening and vanished.

"Eat heartily, as good Guests should." invited the King Sea-Lion before, he too, slid unceremoniously to the floor, to open the trapdoor and vanish below, the door snapping shut.

"Look!" exclaimed Nipper-Crab, walking over to where the trapdoor had been. "It has vanished, the floor has sealed over, and the trapdoor has gone!"

"Come back here, Nipper, come back to the table." said Slippery-Fish. "There is plenty of food left and with no-one here, we can finish it all!"

"That's right… Finish it all up!" exclaimed the Warty-Toad, suddenly appearing on the table.

"Where do you keep going to?" asked Slippery-Fish, putting a large slice of Pumpkin Pie into his mouth.

"Take no notice of the Warty-Toad." said Nipper-Crab, slicing up a piece of apple crumble and devouring it… "This food is wonderful." he finished, before concentrating on the rest of the apple crumble.

"Do you notice something?" offered Stinger-

Scorpion, holding his stomach… "It doesn't seem to matter how much food we eat from the table, it always seems to be full up."

Nipper-Crab and Slippery-Fish looked up from their eating, to examine the food on the table and nod in agreement, before continuing to eat.

Warty-Toad sat among the dishes, his eyes wondering from Stinger-Scorpion to Nipper-Crab, then to Slippery-Fish, seeing them scoff the food greedily, seeing their stomachs swell till they could eat no more.

"I can't move!" exclaimed Slippery-Fish, slumped back in the chair and feeling quite sick and uncomfortable. "I've eaten too much!"

"So have we!" agreed Stinger-Scorpion and Nipper-Crab, their faces beginning to turn green.

"That is because you are all gluttons!" shouted the Warty-Toad, turning round to point at each of them.

"Can you help us, Toad?" begged Stinger-Scorpion, trying to move, but too full and heavy, so he held his bulging stomach and groaned.

"You have to help us." implored Nipper-Crab and Slippery-Fish, both helplessly fed-up.

The Warty-Toad hopped down from the table and reached beneath it, coming back with a large bottle, marked Caster-Oil. Unscrewing the lid, he poured a big dose into a ladle.

"Open your mouth, Stinger-Scorpion. Now, I know this is not going to be nice but it will cure your stomach pains from over-eating."

Stinger-Scorpion did as the Warty-Toad instructed, pulling a face and gasping as Warty-Toad tipped the ladle up, the Caster-Oil gurgling its way down his throat.

"Now then, Nipper-Crab… you are next, open your mouth."

Slippery-Fish watched as Nipper-Crab swallowed the medicine, seeing Nipper-Crab's face screw up at the horrible taste.

"Now you, Slippery." ordered the Warty-Toad, then screwed the cap back onto the bottle and waited till the medicine started working, seeing the swollen stomachs of the three friends begin to slim down to normal shape.

"Perhaps that will teach you all not to be so greedy; such gluttons!" said the Warty-Toad, when all three had gained their shapes and were able to move.

"I think it would be nice if the three of you would offer to do the washing-up." continued the Warty-Toad, eyeing all the dirty plates, cups and spoons.

"Where's the sink and the drying-cloths?" asked Stinger-Scorpion, starting to collect the dishes.

"Through that side door, where all the Musicians and Dancers came from." answered Warty-Toad.

"I've never had to wash up before." grumbled Slippery-Fish.

"Nor I." said Nipper-Crab, following Stinger-Scorpion to the side door.

Stinger-Scorpion opened the door and stared in amazement. There was no-one there, the Musicians and Dancers had vanished, although there was no other entrance from which they could leave.

Instead, there was a large bowl, full of hot water, on a table, with drying-cloths laid beside the bowl.

"You fetch the crockery, Slippery. Nipper and I shall do the washing-up." ordered Stinger-Scorpion, starting to scrub at the dirty dishes.

Outside in the dining-room, Slippery had started to collect the dishes, taking them out and laying them on the table.

"What is this?" he said, picking up a piece of broken crockery.

All the crockery had been taken out, where Stinger-Scorpion and Nipper-Crab had finished washing them and it was then that Slippery-Fish had found the broken piece of crockery, holding it up.

"Put it in the shopping-bag, Slippery... Along with the other piece." said the Warty-Toad, handing the bag to Slippery-Fish, watching as Slippery-Fish did as he was told.

Satisfied that all had been tidied and cleaned, the Warty-Toad walked to the main door and held it open.

"I think we should leave." he said, holding the door open so that Stinger-Scorpion, Nipper-Crab and Slippery-Fish left the room and waited as the Warty-Toad closed the door.

"Now what shall we do?" asked Nipper-Crab, staring up the corridor. The three friends stared up at the rows of doors, their eyes on the door numbers.

"Shall we go to the next door, Toad?" asked Stinger-Scorpion.

There was no answer and the three friends turned, to see that Warty-Toad had vanished.

Slippery-Fish pulled the shopping-bag up over his arm and waited for Stinger-Scorpion to decide what they should do next.

"Well, there's nothing for it, my friends." decided Stinger-Scorpion. "Let's just go to door number three and find out what lies there, shall we?"

Without waiting for Nipper-Crab or Slippery-Fish to answer, Stinger-Scorpion walked down the corridor until, reaching door number THREE, he turned the handle and opened the door. The room appeared empty, just a small bare room.

"There's nothing in there." said Stinger-Scorpion, turning to face Nipper-Crab and Slippery-Fish, who had caught up with him and now peered over his shoulder, into the empty room.

"That's most strange." said Nipper-Crab. "I would have thought, after the last two rooms, there would have been something there."

"Perhaps the three of you should go into the room and close the door behind you. You don't want the water to leak out, do you?"

Once more, Warty-Toad had suddenly appeared, his bulbous eyes blinking as he talked.

"I wish you wouldn't keep doing that, Toad… Appearing from nowhere and making us jump!" angered Slippery-Fish. "And anyway… What do you mean about the water leaking?"

"Just enter and close the door." replied Warty-Toad, gesturing with a hand.

At that, the three friends entered the room and, closing the door behind them, stood just inside and waited.

It was as if a soft mist seemed to come down, giving the room a green glow, then came the sound of waves, seeming to lap gently to the beach, to be followed by the sounds of music from sweet Water-Pipes. The three friends peered through the mist, beginning to see shapes as the mist cleared and the sound of a beautiful voice reached their ears, making their hearts thump wildly, as if the voice was drawing them towards the singer.

Slowly the mist cleared.

"She's beautiful." sighed Stinger-Scorpion.

"Her voice is beautiful." whispered Nipper-Crab.

"I have never seen such beauty." said Slippery-Fish, feeling his heart jump at the sight of the beautiful Mermaid, who sat upon a rock, her tail gently lapping the waters below. In her hands she held a Harp, plucking gently at the strings, while her voice floated its beauty across the stretch of water, to where the three friends stood entranced on a beach of white sand.

The voice grew even sweeter, and Rainbow-Fish rose from the sea below the rocks, to harmonise to her voice, adding to the beauty of the scene.

"I don't know how the room has changed, to change

into this scene, but I can't take my eyes off the Mermaid." said Stinger-Scorpion, feeling a most strange feeling stirring in his heart.

"She is so lovely, Stinger… Look! She is calling to us, see how she raises her arms and calls to us?" sighed Nipper-Crab.

"I am in love with her." said Slippery-Fish, simply stating what his heart felt.

"I wish I could get over to her, but she is too far out and I can't swim." declared Stinger-Scorpion, moving back as the waves lapped closer.

"I could certainly get to her, though I would have to crawl along the bottom of the sea." said Nipper-Crab, then added… "But I think I would look rather silly, having to crawl along… And I might get my large claw jammed in the rock as I climbed up to her.

"I can easily swim out to her, after all, I am a Fish." said Slippery-Fish, gazing out at the Mermaid as she sat, a beautiful Siren, out to sea, on a rock.

"Yes. I suppose you could, Slippery. It would be quite easy for you to do that. But, then, if I were a Fish, I would not want to leave my friends standing on a beach while I went out to sea, just to make them jealous." remarked Nipper-Crab.

"Nor I. You are right, Nipper… I would not wish to swim out and leave my friends." added Stinger-Scorpion.

"I'm so sorry Nipper and Stinger." apologised Slippery-Fish. "I have no wish to make you both jealous."

THE MERMAID

Anyway, what would a beautiful Mermaid like her want with an ugly Fish like me?"

Stinger-Scorpion and Nipper-Crab both nodded in agreement. The beautiful singing Mermaid would not fancy any one of them.

It was while they stood, discussing the whole point of this room and the scene about them, that the Mermaid suddenly placed the Harp onto the rock and dived into the water, beginning to swim towards the shore. The Rainbow-Fish swam alongside her, still singing and laughing.

"Look! See, she is swimming towards us!" exclaimed Stinger-Scorpion.

"She is lovely, see how her hair lays out in the water as she swims, like a golden fan." sighed Nipper-Crab.

"She is coming closer! Look she is waving at us!" shouted Slippery-Fish, waving back at her and, forgetting his friends, left the shopping-bag on the sand, beginning to swim out towards her.

"Where are you going, Slippery?" shouted Stinger-Scorpion.

"Come back here, to your friends!" shouted Nipper-Crab, feeling quite angry that Slippery-Fish should be the only one who could swim out to meet the Mermaid.

Stinger-Scorpion and Nipper-Crab watched from the shore as they saw Slippery-Fish reach the Mermaid, seeing them swimming further out to sea, to playfully swim around each other, then sit talking on the rock.

"I hope Slippery falls off the rock!" exclaimed Stinger-Scorpion angrily, not exactly sure why he was so angry.

"Yes, Stinger!" added Nipper-Crab. "A really bad fall! I would not have left my friends."

While both, Stinger-Scorpion and Nipper-Crab, stood complaining, they saw Slippery-Fish and the Mermaid dive off the rocks and begin to swim together, then, as the Rainbow-Fish swam around and sang, they saw Slippery-Fish dance on the waves, holding the Mermaid around the waist, his eyes closed in love.

"Look, Nipper! Did you see the Mermaid give Slippery a kiss? She kissed him on the cheek!"

"Slippery was always such a show-off!" exclaimed Nipper-Crab, now very angry indeed.

He did not want to watch but could not turn his eyes away as he watched the Mermaid and Slippery-Fish hugging as they danced on top of the waves.

"Where are they going now?" asked Stinger-Scorpion, as they saw the dancing couple suddenly dive, with tails flashing in the sunlight, diving down deep into the sea.

Stinger-Scorpion and Nipper-Crab watched and waited to see the Mermaid and Slippery-Fish come back up again. Nothing happened, even though they waited for quite a while.

"What kind of friend was he?" questioned Stinger-Scorpion at last. "I would never have left my friends,

no matter how pretty the Mermaid was!" he added.
"I hope Slippery has got stuck under a big rock, or a mad-eyed Shark has got him!" said Nipper-Crab angrily.
"Why are you both so jealous?"
Warty-Toad had appeared beside the angry friends, his large eyes staring out to sea, a smile on his wide mouth as he asked the question.
"Jealous! Who's jealous?" demanded Stinger-Scorpion, refusing to look at Warty-Toad.
"Well, I am certainly not jealous, whatever being jealous means." added Nipper-Crab,
"Then why are you both angry, and tell me why you have both turned green with envy?" asked Warty-Toad.
"I have no idea why I am angry." replied Stinger-Scorpion. "I'm just upset that Slippery has run off with the Mermaid."
"Nor Me." said Nipper-Crab, now aware that he and Stinger-Scorpion were both bright green.
"See how feelings are, when they affect you, such feelings of jealousy can turn you green with envy and turn you against your best friends." said Warty-Toad.
"I must admit, Warty-Toad, I have never felt such feelings before. In Cuttlefish-Avenue, where we live, no-one is ever jealous of anyone else. We are all the same." said Nipper-Crab, beginning to feel sorry for the bad things he had said about Slippery-Fish.
"I am also very sorry." added Stinger-Scorpion,

feeling his anger going and the green leaving him. "Let us hope that Slippery is really enjoying himself and having a great time under the sea with his new friend." said Warty-Toad.

Both Stinger-Scorpion and Nipper-Crab agreed, thanking Warty-Toad for making them see sense and for getting them over their jealous feelings.

"Now what shall we do?" asked Nipper-Crab, turning towards the door. "Shall we just go on without Slippery?"

"It's up to you both." said Warty-Toad.

"What do you think, Stinger?" asked Nipper-Crab, reluctant to leave and yet feeling they had to keep moving.

"Do you think Slippery will be alright, Toad?" asked Stinger-Scorpion.

But Warty-Toad had magically vanished again, so the two friends stood on the beach, unsure of what to do.

It was as they stood, undecided, that the Mermaid appeared, rising up from the sea in silver light, rising up high above the sea and disappearing into a golden mist of skylight. The Harp, which lay on the rock, changed into something which looked like another piece of broken crockery, small and white on top of the rock.

"What's happening? Where's Slippery?" asked Nipper-Crab, quite alarmed at what he had seen.

"I think, Nipper, you had better go into the sea, go down to where Slippery last dived down. See if you can find him and bring him back here." said Stinger-Scorpion.

Nipper-Crab walked out into the sea, his body sinking beneath the waves as he reached deeper water. Stinger-Scorpion watched anxiously, seeing the trail of bubbles breaking the surface, then came Nipper-Crab, his large claw gripping Slippery-Fish, who seemed to be in some kind of hypnotic sleep.

"Thank goodness you found him, Nipper!" exclaimed Stinger-Scorpion. "Bring him onto the beach and we'll wake him up."

"I found him asleep inside a giant Clam-Shell." gasped Nipper-Crab, bringing Slippery-Fish onto the beach, where the two friends began to shake him, waking him up.

Slippery-Fish coughed for a bit, his eyes blurrily opening and then he sat up quickly, looking around him.

Both, Stinger-Scorpion and Nipper-Crab, patted him, so pleased he was unharmed and seemed no worse for his adventures.

"It was awful!" gasped Slippery-Fish. "I was held prisoner by a giant Conger-Eel, who told me I was to be punished for making my friends jealous and for deserting them. I was held prisoner, till Nipper came and got me out, opening the Clam with his powerful claw!"

"It does not matter any more." said Stinger-Scorpion. "We have all learned a lesson here and we are still the best of friends."

At this, they all hugged each other and laughed. "Wait!" suddenly exclaimed Slippery-Fish. "There is one more thing I have to do before we leave this room."

Without saying anything else, Slippery-Fish walked quickly down to the sea and dived into the water. They watched as he swam out and, reaching the rock, clambered up to take the piece of broken crockery.

Holding onto it, Slippery swam back to where his friends waited and, picking up the shopping-bag, Slippery-Fish placed the piece inside, to lay with the other two pieces within.

"I think." he said, smiling. "It is time to leave this place and move along."

Together, the three friends walked to the door and, opening it, they walked outside, leaving the room to suddenly lose its scene, the sea and the rock, to become dark and empty once more.

"Well, that was a lesson to us all. I'm beginning to think there are lessons for us to learn behind the rest of the doors we have to enter." mused Nipper-Crab, as the three friends walked further down the corridor.

"Then let's stop right now and make a pact, that we will never be jealous of each other, no matter what happens!" stated Stinger-Scorpion, so the three held hands and swore never to ever be jealous or angry with each other from this time.

Having sworn on their honour, the three friends wandered down the corridor, moving down to see how many doors there were which displayed large black numbers. There were four more doors, numbers four, five, six and seven.

"I wonder what will happen when we have been through all the rest of the doors?" said Slippery-Fish, holding tight to the shopping-bag.

"I think there is only one person who has the answer to your question." said Stinger-Scorpion.

"Who is that?" asked Nipper-Crab.

"It has to be Warty-Toad! He's the only one who seems to know anything."

"Of course, you are right Stinger." said Slippery-Fish, staring around, and then saying… "I wonder what he is doing now, whereabouts he is?"

"Here I am!" shouted Warty-Toad, suddenly popping up from nowhere and startling them so they jumped in alarm.

"Then can you tell us exactly what is going on, Toad?" demanded Stinger-Scorpion, composing himself.

"All I will tell you, my friends, is that I am only with you to urge you on to higher things, to lead you through to seeing what feelings you will experience, once you gain the Soul-Pearl. That's all I will tell you." said Warty-Toad.

"So… Do we get the Soul-Pearl in the end?" questioned Nipper-Crab.

"That's the thing about Toads." whispered Slippery-Fish. "They make a lot of noise, without really saying anything at all."

Warty-Toad made no reply, he just gave a smile and vanished.

"I suppose we had better open this door and see what lies ahead." said Stinger-Scorpion, his hand on the door-knob and turning it, so that the three friends entered the room.

Nipper-Crab closed the door gently and then stood alongside his friends.

Their eyes saw the large banner immediately, a large red banner which stretched from one side of the room to the other, from floor to ceiling. On it, in big black letters, were the words… 'HAIRDRESSING COMPETITION'

From behind the banner came sounds of voices and sharp snipping sounds.

Walking up to the banner, the three friends stopped and listened to the noise, not sure whether to lift the banner and pass beneath, or to shout and see if anyone came out from the other side.

"There's no-one here who can cut hair as well as me." came a voice from the other side of the banner… "I pride myself on being the best there is. If there is any person here, who thinks that he, or she, is a better Hairdresser than me, let them step forward!" the voice continued.

"I think we will have to go and introduce ourselves." said Slippery-Fish.

"I agree with you, Slippery." said Nipper-Crab, adding… "Whoever he is, he sounds very big-headed and quite a show-off, too proud for my liking."

Stinger-Scorpion, another who disliked show-off's, lifted the bottom of the banner, allowing his friends to pass under it, then moved in, dropping the hem of the banner behind him.

Before them was a table, with three large Tortoises seated on chairs. They all wore large black top-hats and had their names painted on their backs.

"Cedric-One, Cedric-Two and Cedric-Three." whispered Nipper-Crab, giggling. "They are all called Cedric."

Each Tortoise held a set of cards with numbers on them, holding up different numbers each time a whistle blew. In front of the table was set a Barber's chair, on which sat a small Poodle-Dog, sitting quietly, while a Lion, with a massive mane, began trimming the hair of the Poodle.

The Weasel in the corner blew the whistle in a long shrill blast, so that the Tortoises stopped, lifting their numbers up, to look at the three friends.

"Sit down there, over on those chairs and await your turn." ordered Cedric-One, turning back to the Lion, who began clipping again.

"Ten points for that snip!" shouted Cedric-Two, holding up a number '10'.

"Eight points for that curl!" shouted Cedric-Three, holding the card up.

"Commended ten points!" called Cedric-One.

"Will you be quiet!" shouted Proud-Leo, stopping his work, to point rudely at Stinger-Scorpion, who was whispering to Nipper-Crab.

"Quiet please." ordered Cedric-Two, and then the three judges held up their cards as Proud-Leo snipped and cut the Poodle's fur, till it shone in perfect shape.

"Excellent!" shouted Cedric-Three, as all Judges stood, holding up their cards, awarding ten points on each.

"There, you see." said Proud-Leo, preening his large mane. "There is no-one as good as me. I have style and flair, I am a creative genius!"

"You are a show-off and too proud for your own good!" shouted Stinger-Scorpion, unable to control himself.

"I will not lower myself to argue with a lowly Scorpion." said Proud-Leo, then, turning to the three Judges, he said "Let the Scorpion try to cut a Poodle's fur! See if he's any good! If he gets more points than me, I will cut off my mane... But if I win, then he has to bow down to me and beg forgiveness."

"Fetch another chair!" ordered Cedric-One.

"Bring a shaggy Poodle!" ordered Cedric-Two.

"Blow your whistle, Weasel!" ordered Cedric-Three.

The whistle shrilled loudly as another chair was brought onto the stage by a grey Water-Rat, followed by another, who led a scruffy Poodle.

"Come on Scorpion!" shouted Proud-Leo, and then sat down as Stinger-Scorpion approached to pick up the scissors.

Seating the Poodle on the chair, Stinger-Scorpion began to cut, the fur falling from the Poodle in great chunks.

"One point for the bad cut!" shouted Cedric-One, waving his card wildly.

"No points at all… It's a disgrace!" called out Cedric-Two.

"I agree! No points at all!" declared Cedric-Three.

"Take the Poodle away, before he makes it go bald!" shouted the Weasel, blowing the whistle so loud that the pea popped out of the whistle and rolled across the floor, to be eaten by the Poodle, as it was being led out by the grey Rat.

The Weasel continued to blow the whistle, though no sound came out of it.

"I have to admit." giggled Nipper-Crab to Slippery-Fish. "Stinger has made a mess of that Poodle… It looks like it's been dragged backwards through a hedge!"

"Shush, Nipper… Don't speak too loud! Oh, look… Poor Stinger has to kneel down in front of that Proud-Leo and apologise."

"Oh, gosh!" exclaimed Nipper-Crab, then, turning to Slippery-Fish, pushed him out of the chair.

"Go on, Slippery… Go out there and show them how to trim a Poodle." he said.

"I don't know how to trim hair, Nipper." wailed

Slippery-Fish.

"What's that!" demanded Proud-Leo, taking his eyes off Stinger-Scorpion, who was knelt before him. "Is there another fool who wishes to pit himself against me?" Proud-Leo demanded, his eyes raised, as he stared at Slippery-Fish, who now stood up.

"Yes... I challenge you, you over-bearing proud Lion. I will challenge you to a hair-cutting duel!" shouted back Slippery-Fish, hearing Nipper-Crab cheering behind him.

"Judges! You heard this lowly character... Fetch another Poodle. I shall cut first."

"Fetch a Poodle!" ordered Cedric-One, waving his cards in the air.

The grey Rat came onstage, leading a big brown Poodle, so straggly, it looked as if it had not been cleaned for a year.

"That's it, Rat. Sit the Poodle down on the chair... And you, Fish-Face... Just watch me and see how it's done!" said Proud-Leo, beginning to snip away with great gusto and flamboyancy.

Slippery-Fish watched, feeling quite angry that Proud-Leo had called him Fish-Face. It was true, of course, Slippery-Fish did have a Fish-Face, but it was very rude to say it.

"It's like calling someone Big-Nose, isn't it?" he said later, to Nipper-Crab. "It may be true but you don't say it, do you?"

And Both Nipper-Crab and Stinger-Scorpion had agreed with him.

"A great snip!" called Cedric-One, holding up a card with number 10 on it.

"That is the best haircut you have done so far, Proud-Leo. The Poodle is a masterpiece, the way you have styled it… Ten points for you!" shouted Cedric-Two, waving his card.

"You are a master hairdresser, Proud-Leo! No wonder you are so proud!" added Cedric-Three, showing another ten points.

"Look at the Lion posing!" shouted out Nipper-Crab to Slippery-Fish. "Go on, Slippery… Go and wipe that smug look from his face!" urged Nipper-Crab, jumping up and down.

"Fetch another Poodle." ordered Cedric-One. Proud-Leo stood haughtily to one side, arms folded, watching. In the far corner, Weasel, finding another pea for the whistle, blew a magnificent blast, which made everybody jump.

The next Poodle for the cut sat in shivering dejection as Slippery-Fish picked up the scissors, not sure what to do.

"Go on, Slippery! You can do it!" called Stinger-Scorpion, having risen from the floor and feeling low after having knelt humbly before Proud-Leo, making an apology.

Slippery-Fish began to cut at the Poodle's fur, watched carefully by the three Cedric-Judges and Proud-Leo, not happy at all.

"Look at that clump he's cut off!" shouted an excited Cedric-One, waving a card which had no number on at all.

"Has he cut the Poodle's tail off? I'm sure he has!" shouted out Cedric-Two, gesturing wildly.

"I'm sure it's the Poodle's ear!" called out Cedric-Three, jumping up and down.

"Look at the state of the Poodle!" said Proud-Leo, walking forward and pointing at the unhappy Dog, noting too, that it appeared to have a tail and one ear missing.

"You are disqualified, Fish-Face!" shouted Proud-Leo, while the Weasel began blowing the whistle for all he was worth.

"Foul!" ordered Cedric-One, shaking a fist, his top hat tumbling off the top of his head and rolling away. The Weasel stopped blowing the whistle, running to catch up with the top hat and, seating it back on the top of Cedric-One's head, he patted it down firmly, then moved to Cedric-Two, then Cedric-Three, patting at each hat, making sure they were firmly on their heads.

"You have to bow down and beg Proud-Leo's forgiveness." said Cedric-One to Slippery-Fish, all watching as Slippery-Fish had to do as he was ordered.

Proud-Leo stood above Slippery-Fish, very proud indeed.

"It's your turn, Nipper."

Nipper-Crab turned quickly, to see that Warty-Toad had suddenly appeared and now dug him in the ribs as he spoke.

"You must be joking, Toad." replied Nipper-Crab. "I cannot cut fur nor do any fancy tricks with Poodles. And I don't fancy having to kneel in front of that stuffy proud Lion."

"How do you know what you can or can't do till you've tried it?" remarked Warty-Toad.

"I don't need to try… I already know I can't cut fur." replied Nipper-Crab, beginning to get angry.

"So, you are just going to sit there and let your friend's down, are you? After all, both of them had a go and they did try… And look at you… You have that big cutting claw. Nipping and snipping away. You don't even need scissors!"

"Are you willing to try to beat me, Crabby?" asked Proud-Leo, standing before Nipper-Crab, jeering at him. "Or do you need that ugly Toad to help you?"

"Get me a Poodle ready!" shouted Nipper-Crab, angry and ready, striding towards centre-stage, his large claw snapping open and shut, like a pair of demented scissors.

"Fetch a Poodle!" ordered Cedric-One.

A large Grey-Rat, wearing a gleaming monocle and sporting a bulbous red nose, came out from a side door, pulling an unwilling shaggiest Poodle ever seen.

"Let the Crab begin!" ordered Cedric-Two.

"Blow the whistle, Weasel." instructed Cedric-Three, as the Rat lifted the Poodle up onto the chair. The whistle shrilled through the room, which started all the Poodles, in the side room, barking and calling out names.

"Shut the door and keep those dogs quiet!" ordered Cedric-One as he saw Nipper-Crab raise his large claw.

Nipper-Crab felt as if he floated, he was as light as a Buttercup, lost to the task of hair-dressing. His claw became a sharp pair of scissors, with a mind of its own, clipping and snipping, so that the fur flew and the Poodle began to take on a marvellous shape. Stinger-Scorpion and Slippery-Fish watched in amazement as Nipper-Crab, a strange gleam in his eye, trimmed and fancied the Poodle, so that it seemed gloriously ready to enter any show-ring.

"Ten points!" shouted out Cedric-One, bouncing up and down, his card waving.

Cedric-Two ran around to the front of the table, declaring…"I have never seen such beauty! You are a Master-Cutter, Mister Crab, and I will give you ten points!"

Cedric-Three sat still, his eyes moving from the beautifully groomed Poodle, to Nipper-Crab, who seemed in a daze, staring at his claw, which continued to open and snap closed. Suddenly Cedric-Three held up his card.

"He's given Nipper ten and a half points!" exclaimed Slippery excitedly, beginning to jump up and down.

"I knew you could do it, Nipper!" declared Warty-Toad, a secret smile dimpling his face.

Proud-Leo sat down on the floor and began to cry, tears staining his golden mane.

"Now it's your turn, Stinger." said Nipper-Crab, handing Stinger-Scorpion a pair of scissors. "You can cut all the golden mane from Proud-Leo's head. He won't be so proud then." Nipper-Crab added. Stinger-Scorpion took the scissors and walked over to the weeping figure of Proud-Leo.

"Now, Proud-Leo." began Stinger-Scorpion. "I have no intention of cutting off your hair. All I ask of you is to learn that pride comes before a fall. You will learn to be a bit more humble after this."

Proud-Leo nodded quickly, holding Stinger-Scorpion's hand and kissing it.

"I will never be so proud again, nor will I treat others badly. Thank you so much, Stinger-Scorpion… And you, Nipper-Crab and Slippery-Fish."

"Nipper-Crab… Will you please stand on the soap box, so I can present you with the prize." ordered Cedric-One, placing the box in front of the table.

Standing on the box, Nipper-Crab watched the three Judges stand in a row.

"Please present the prize." said Cedric-Two, handing the prize to Cedric-Three.

Cedric-Three held up the prize for all to see, and then handed it to Nipper-Crab, saying… "You are a very worthy winner, Nipper-Crab."

Nipper-Crab thanked the Judges for his award, then, climbing down from the soap-box, he handed the prize, a piece of broken pottery, to Slippery-Fish.

"Put it into the shopping-bag, along with the rest of the broken pieces, Slippery." he said.

Going to where the bag lay, Slippery opened it and put the piece of crockery carefully in with the rest of the pieces.

As the three friends walked from the room, Warty-Toad patted Nipper-Crab on the shoulder and said... "I'm proud of you."

"Thank you, Toad." returned Nipper-Crab, turning round to see that Warty-Toad had done his vanishing trick again, gone in the blink of an eye.

"I wish the Toad wouldn't do that." said Slippery-Fish, looking around.

"I have an idea there is a lot more to that Toad than we think." offered Nipper-Crab, then added... I really do believe he had something to do with my scissor-work. It was as if Toad had caused my claw to work without me doing anything. My claw seemed to have a life of its own."

"Indeed, it's strange how the Toad seems to turn up, just as we get caught up in things, as if he is watching us from an invisible place, seeing us while we can't see him." declared Stinger-Scorpion, as he walked further down the corridor, his eyes on the door numbers.

Nipper-Crab and Slippery-Fish looked round in an uneasy way, trying to see if they could spot Warty-Toad.

"Door FIVE." declared Stinger-Scorpion, stopping outside a door and pointing at the number.

"I suppose we might as well go inside and see what is going on in there." said Nipper-Crab. Stinger-

Scorpion nodded and, turning the handle, pushed the door open.

The door opened into a field of well-cut grass, and on each side sat row upon row of cheering crowds. To the left there sat rows of large Grey-Rats, wearing grey knitted woollen suits and sporting baseball caps, which had the words… 'The Bully Boys' emblazoned on them.

On the opposite side of the field, equally noisy, there sat rows of small Brown-Mice, wearing Bowler-Hats with the word, 'Champions' written round the brim.

"It seems there is to be a game of some sort." said Slippery-Fish.

"Yes, Slippery, it looks like it." replied Nipper-Crab, craning his neck, to get a better view.

"But if that's so, where are the players?" asked Stinger-Scorpion.

"Isn't that the big Grey-Rat, who led the last Poodle into the Hair-Dressing competition?" asked Nipper-Crab, suddenly, pointing out the Grey-Rat who had now walked out into the middle of the field.

The Grey-Rat wore a large red baseball cap, which shone as red as his big bulbous nose, which he constantly wiped with a blue and white polka-dotted handkerchief. One eye appeared over-large, magnified behind a black-rimmed monocle.

"Yes… It is the same Grey-Rat! I wonder what he is doing here and how did he get here from the last room?" exclaimed Stinger-Scorpion.

Before the others could make an answer, there was a

blast of bugles, which seemed to cause great excitement from the Grey-Rats, who jumped to their feet, cheering wildly as a team of large Grey-Rats ran onto the field, starting to do exercises.

"That's it, Bully-Boys!" shouted out Big-Red, wiping at his nose with the handkerchief… "Let's finish off those weaklings, the puny Brown-Mice!" he shouted, jumping up and down.

Again, the bugles blared a greeting and onto the field ran a team of small Brown-Mice. This set the rows of watching Brown-Mice cheering wildly and throwing their Bowler hats into the air.

Then a whistle shrilled, so that both sides sat themselves down in an air of expectancy.

"Isn't that the same Weasel, that one who had the whistle in the last room?" queried Slippery, pointing out the Weasel who stood at the far end, the whistle held firmly to his mouth.

"It certainly is." assured Stinger-Scorpion.

"What on earth is going on? I mean, if they are going to play a game, then I can't see any ball… And anyway, what does this have to do with us?" asked Nipper-Crab.

"Did you see that? Big-Red just pushed that little Mouse over!" said Nipper-Crab.

"Yes, I saw it… Big-Red just pushed the little Mouse over for no reason, the big bully!" cried out Slippery-Fish, quite angry at what he had just seen.

"For no reason!" added Stinger-Scorpion, feeling just as angry, and then added… "He's just a big bully!"

Their angry shouts added to the cries which came from the rows of Brown-Mice, who shook their tiny fists at Big-Red, who began to laugh, wiping at his nose.

"I've a good mind to go down there and punch him right on the nose!" exploded Stinger-Scorpion.

As the words came out of Stinger-Scorpion's mouth, Weasel had run onto the field, between the line-up of the Grey-Rats and Brown-Mice.

The noise from the crowds on both sides of the field died down, then roared again as the Weasel blew the whistle loudly, running from the field as the game began.

"What kind of game is this?" shouted Nipper-Crab, watching as the Grey-Rats began to run towards the Brown-Mice, barging into them and knocking them down.

"This is not fair, not fair at all!" shouted Stinger-Scorpion. "Look at those poor little Mice, they are crying and hurt… Stop it, you bullies!" he shouted.

"And look at Big-Red… He is tying one little Mouse up with his handkerchief… Can you see that, Slippery?"

"Yes, I can, Nipper… Those big Rats are just bullies! Let's go down on the field and help the little Mice. After all, we are bigger than those Grey-Rats. Let's see how they like it if we bully them."

"Come on, then!" called Stinger-Scorpion, starting to make his way down towards the field.

THE PUSH-OVER MATCH

"Wait!"

Above the noise from the crowds and from the field, came the shout from Warty-Toad.

Stinger-Scorpion stopped them, seeing who called, and came back to where his friends were.

"What do you want, Toad?" demanded Stinger-Scorpion, his eyes looking back to the field, seeing the Grey-Rats continuing to push over the Brown-Mice, each time they got up.

"Are you angry, Stinger? You as well, Nipper and Slippery?" asked Warty-Toad, holding up a hand.

"Of course I'm angry!" snapped Stinger-Scorpion, as both, Nipper-Crab and Slippery-Fish, nodded their heads.

"Of course we are all very angry, Toad. We don't have bullying at Cuttlefish-Avenue." added Nipper-Crab.

"Of course we all are, Toad. Look at the way those bullies are hurting those little Mice." said Slippery-Fish.

"So, you think that, by going down there, onto the field and bullying the Grey-Rats, you are not being bullies yourselves?" asked Warty-Toad.

"What else can we do?" asked Stinger-Scorpion.

"Firstly, my friends, you have to lose your anger. Without being angry, you can look at the situation calmly and decide what the best way is to deal with those bullies." said Warty-Toad.

"Then, what do you suggest?" asked Nipper-Crab, and then turned as the Weasel ran onto the field, blowing the whistle in short blasts.

"It has to be half-time." said Slippery-Fish, as they watched the Grey-Rats run from the field, while the Brown-Mice hobbled their way to an exit on the other side of the field.

"So what do we do?" asked Nipper-Crab again, turning his eyes back to Warty-Toad.

"The important thing is to think with a calm head and not allow anger make you all hot-headed." replied Warty-Toad.

The three friends nodded, feeling the anger flow from them and they stood, prepared to listen to what Warty-Toad had to say.

"Tell me, my friends." began Warty-Toad. "Why is it that the Grey-Rats can easily push the Brown-Mice down?" he finished.

"That's easy to see!" exclaimed Stinger-Scorpion. "Look at the size of the Grey-Rats, they are twice the size of the Mice!"

"Yes, the Grey-Rats are a lot bigger and also because they have a leader, Red-Rat, who tells them what to do." explained Warty-Toad.

"Yes, Toad, we do understand that, but what can we do about it?" asked Nipper-Crab.

Warty-Toad smiled, looking at each of his friends with large blinking eyes.

"What I suggest is that you go down to the Brown-Mice. Pay them a visit in their Dressing-Room and offer to help them." said Warty-Toad.

"Oh yes? And how exactly are we to help them,

Toad?" asked Stinger-Scorpion, raising his eyebrows.

"Why don't the three of you just go down to the Brown-Mice Dressing-Room and see if you can't feed them up a bit? That might help." replied Warty-Toad.

Nipper-Crab nodded, deciding to do as Warty-Toad had suggested. There was something about Warty-Toad which was very mysterious and Nipper-Crab felt certain that Warty-Toad was there to help them.

"Come on, Stinger and Slippery, let's do as the Toad suggests." said Nipper-Crab, beginning to lead the way down to the Brown-Mice Dressing-Room.

"I hope you are right, Toad." said Stinger-Scorpion, turning to Warty-Toad… But Warty-Toad had vanished again.

Stinger-Scorpion shrugged and, along with Slippery-fish, followed Nipper-Crab down to the Dressing-Room.

The room was quiet, except for the Mice, who moaned as others patched up their hurts with sticking plasters and bandages. No-one spoke or even looked up as the three friends entered the Dressing-Room.

"Whose in charge?" asked Stinger-Scorpion, looking around, as the Mice sat on the bench. No-one answered.

"There must be someone in charge here." said Nipper-Crab.

"We don't have anyone in charge." spoke up one Mouse at last.

"What is your name?" asked Slippery-Fish, looking at the Mouse who had spoken.

"I am called White-Ear, on account of me having one white ear, while everything else is brown." replied the Mouse.

"Then we will put you in charge, White-Ear, on account of you being able to speak up." added Stinger-Scorpion.

"What is the game all about, why are allowing the Grey-Rats to push you down?" queried Nipper-Crab.

"It's not a game. We have to go out onto the field every Saturday and allow the Rats to push us around. It's called Saturday-Push-Over and we are called the Push-Overs." advised White-Ear, keeping his eyes down.

"But why do you allow it?" asked Stinger-Scorpion, mystified.

"Because, if we don't allow the Grey-Rats to push the team around, for all the Brown-Mice to see, then the Grey-Rats will come to our Villages and push everybody around and bully all the children. So, sooner than that, we allow the Grey-Rats to just push our team over," explained White-Ear, tears springing to his eyes.

"What can we do to help these Mice?" whispered Slippery-Fish. "If we go out onto the field, the Grey-Rats will go to the Villages and make the lives of the Mice a misery.

"You are right." said Stinger-Scorpion, sadly.

"There's not much we can do to help the Brown-

Mice."

"Unless, of course, we feed them up." said Nipper-Crab, remembering what Warty-Toad had said, his eyes on the bag of grain which lay in one corner.

"What do you mean, Nipper?" asked Slippery, seeing Nipper-Crab go to the bag and open it.

"I'll explain later, Slippery. Now, what I want all you Brown-Mice to do is line up and have your bowls ready. I will give you all some food which has to be eaten before you go out on the field for the second half. White-Ear, you take charge and have your food first." ordered Nipper-Crab.

White-Ear ordered the rest of the team to line up, and then stood at the front, his bowl held out as Nipper-Crab filled it. Seating himself on the bench, White-Ear began to eat the grain, as Nipper-Crab filled the bowls of each Mouse, so that they joined White-Ear on the bench, their mouths busy in chewing.

"Oh gosh… Look at White-Ear!" exclaimed Stinger-Scorpion, his mouth falling open as he saw White-Ear begin to grow, larger and larger.

"Look!" They are all getting bigger and bigger!" gasped Slippery-Fish as all the members of the team nearly reached the ceiling, bulging with muscles.

"How do you feel, White-Ear?" asked Nipper-Crab.

"I feel so strong. We will crush those Grey-Rats!" said White-Ear, his voice loud and courageous as he flexed his muscles.

"No! You can't do that, White-Ear." said Nipper-Crab. "If you do that, then you become the bullies, instead of the Grey-Rats. You have to remember just how you felt, being bullied."

"Yes." agreed White-Ear." "We shall just go out there and frighten the Rats, so they never bully us again. But I wish to do only one thing." said White-Ear, determined.

"What is that?" asked Stinger-Scorpion.

"As the leader of the team, I want to be able to go out onto the field and push Big-Red down, just once!" demanded White-Ear.

"Well, that sounds reasonable." commented Stinger-Scorpion, and all agreed that this would be reasonable.

The shrill whistle sounded. It was time for the second part of the Push-Over. The Grey-Rats jumped up and down to the cheers of their Supporters, demanding that the Brown-Mice team come out onto the field.

Big-Red pushed his monocle back to his eye and blew his nose loudly, waiting for the team of Brown-Mice to come back onto the field.

Suddenly, Big-Red stared in amazement, the monocle popping from his eye, as the Mice team, led by White-Ear, came bounding out onto the field, big and powerful.

The Weasel dropped his whistle and ran, followed by the rest of the Grey-Rats, who ran, screaming in fear as the Brown-Mice chased them.

Big-Red tried to run, his cap falling and becoming lost in the muddy field, his handkerchief floating up into the air as White-Ear caught up with him and, with a mighty shove, pushed Red-Rat over, then stood with his foot on Big-Red's chest, pinning him to the mud.

"Now, all you Grey-Rats listen to me!" shouted White-Ear loudly. "I want us all, the Brown-Mice and the Grey-Rats, to be friends, and to never see each other as 'Push-Overs' ever again!"

The whole field erupted into cheers and shouts of agreement, then White-Ear helped Big-Red up from the ground, shaking hands, and they left the field together as the crowds of Brown-Mice and Grey-Rats invaded the field, all laughing and shaking hands.

Stinger-Scorpion, Nipper-Crab and Slippery-Fish stood at the edge of the field, watching for a while and then began to make their way towards the door.

"Here." said Nipper-Crab, holding out a piece of broken crockery to Slippery-Fish. "Put it in your bag, along with the other pieces.

"Where did you get that from?" asked Slippery-Fish, taking the broken piece and placing it in the shopping-bag.

"I found that in the bottom of the feed bag, after I had fed all the Mice." said Nipper-Crab, with a smile. "And I knew it needed to join the rest of the pieces you already have in the shopping-bag.

Stinger-Scorpion opened the door and, together, the three left the noise and cheers behind as the door closed.

"I really am not sure what is going on with us." said Slippery-Fish, as he joined Nipper-Crab, to wander down through the corridor.

"I mean." he added... "Why are we here, going through these doors and seeing all those funny things going on. And why?" he asked... "Do I have to carry this shopping-bag around, with useless pieces of broken crockery inside, what's the point?"

"It's no good moaning, Slippery. There has got to be a point to it all and, don't forget, there are only two doors left, number SIX, which Stinger is entering now, and number SEVEN. After that, we might get to the bottom of it all." he finished.

They began to hurry, catching up with Stinger-Scorpion, who held the door of number SIX open, waiting impatiently.

The door opened into a darkened hallway, eerily quiet, so that the three friends peered through the door opening, unsure of what to do.

"This could be a trap of some sort." offered Slippery-Fish, drawing back.

This statement seemed to have an effect on both, Stinger-Scorpion and Nipper-Crab, so that all three now drew away from the door and stood, looking at each other, undecided as to what to do.

"What is it? Why aren't you going into the room?" The three friends spun around, very nervous at hearing a voice which seemed to come out of thin air.

"Well?" asked Warty-Toad, appearing beside them.

"What is the matter?"

"You made us jump!" exclaimed Stinger-Scorpion, indignantly. "I wish you wouldn't keep doing that, Toad!"

"Take a look yourself, Toad." broke in Nipper-Crab, pointing towards the door, happy at Warty-Toad's appearance.

"Ah, I see." remarked Warty-Toad, peering inside the darkened hallway. "You fear the un-known, simply because the inside is different from the other rooms you have entered."

"I'm not afraid of the dark!" exclaimed Stinger-Scorpion, angrily, entering the dark hallway and feeling his way through the gloom.

"There, you see, my friends, how a person will walk into danger when his bravery is challenged." said Warty-Toad.

"Is Stinger in danger?" asked Nipper-Crab.

"Why not go inside and see. Stinger might need help in there." answered Warty-Toad.

"Come on, Slippery. Let's go and help our friend!" exclaimed Nipper-Crab, taking Slippery-Fish's arm and drawing him along.

"Are you alright?" called Slippery-Fish, nervously peering into the dark.

"Yes." came Stinger-Scorpion's voice from out of the darkness. "I seem to have found another door here and I am turning the handle now."

Then the hallway was flooded with a pale light, which came from the inner room. Stinger-Scorpion stood, framed in the doorway.

"Come and see." he called.

Inside the room there sat an old wizened Crocodile, leathery skinned, wearing an old waistcoat that sported a watch and chain across the chest. On his head sat a Turkish Fez-Hat with a long tassel.

"Who is he?" queried Slippery-Fish.

"Please be quiet." said the Crocodile, his glasses nearly falling from his long nose.

The three friends stood watching as the Crocodile threw some clay on the Potter's wheel and began to pump his foot on the pedal so the wheel began to turn, his hands working the clay, fashioning a cup and saucer. He held the cup and saucer up to the light and threw them back onto the table, squeezing the clay and began to model again.

"I'm the 'Plate-Spinner'." he said suddenly, stopping the wheel and turning to face the three friends.

But the three were not listening, their eyes held fast to the large clay figure of a semi-clad female.

"That's Venus in Clay." instructed the Plate-Spinner, following their gaze to the alcove where the figure stood.

"She's very lovely." said Stinger-Scorpion.

"So beautiful." echoed Nipper-Crab.

Slippery-Fish just stared, not saying a word.

"Don't you want to learn how to make cups and saucers?" asked the Plate-Spinner, throwing some more clay on the Potter's wheel and starting to fashion more cups.

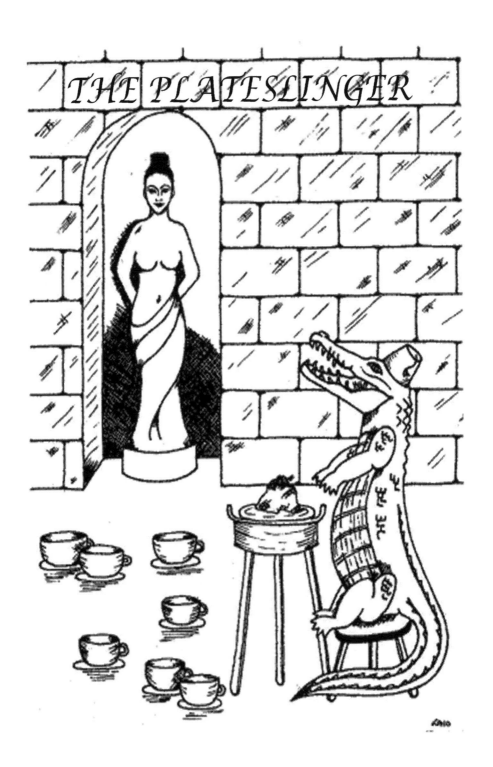

"I would rather make a model of this beautiful Venus." remarked Stinger-Scorpion, not taking his eyes from the vision before him.

"So would I." said Nipper-Crab.

"Me as well." added Slippery-Fish.

The Plate-Spinner stopped his work, turning to look at the three friends, who seemed mesmerised by the figure before them.

"It's no good being lustful over a clay figure." he said, the glasses sliding down his long snout so that he pushed them back up, the tassel on his Fez swinging as he shook his head.

"Why can't we make our own model of Venus?" insisted Stinger-Scorpion.

"Come on then." replied the Plate-Spinner, moving to a long table and placing three lumps of fresh clay at intervals.

"Here you are. Now the three of you can make your own Venus from the modelling clay." he said, pointing to the table.

Taking their eyes from the clay Venus, the three friends moved quickly to the table and began to pinch and mould with the damp clay, each totally enwrapped in their work.

"Have you finished?" asked the Plate-Spinner, after some time.

Stinger-Scorpion stood back, nodding, not completely satisfied how his Venus had turned out.

"What do you all think of each other's work?" asked the Plate-Spinner, as Nipper-Crab and Slippery-Fish stood back, their eyes going from one figure to the next.

"Well, I'm not best pleased with my Venus." said Stinger-Scorpion. "But it has to be better than the Venus made by Slippery. Look, she has one eye lower than the other and a mouth almost up her nose! And the Venus made by Nipper is no better, I mean look at her, her head is too big while her nose has fallen off!"

"Oh, so I suppose yours is better, Stinger!" exclaimed Nipper, patting the head of Stinger-Scorpion's Venus with a hard hand, squashing it flat. Slippery-Fish began laughing so much that he fell onto the table, which tipped up, causing the three heads to topple from the table and splatter onto the floor. This caused the three friends to shout and roar with laughter, slapping each other on the back in good companionship.

"You see how silly it all is, how you have become infatuated and lustful over something which is not real?" exclaimed the Plate-Spinner, scooping up the fallen clay and placing it once again onto the table. Then, walking over to the alcove and, resting a hand on the head of Venus, he said… "Let me show you something, my friends."

With a swift and sharp tug, he pulled the head from the figure of Venus. Going back to the Potters Wheel he dampened the head with water and began to squash the head and begin re-moulding it. The three friends stopped laughing, now watching the Plate-

Spinner as he worked.

"What's he making?" whispered Slippery-Fish.

"I have no idea." Nipper-Crab whispered back.

"I have no idea at all, although I would rather have seen the head back on the clay Venus." whispered Stinger-Scorpion.

Suddenly, the Plate-Spinner stopped working, standing up to point at what he had fashioned from the clay.

"Do you see now, what I have changed the Venus head into?" he asked.

"It's a big clay 'Goblet'." said Nipper-Crab, inspecting the work.

"Yes, I can see it's a large cup." remarked Slippery-Fish. "Don't you think so, Stinger?"

"I quite agree with you both." agreed Stinger-Scorpion.

"Now watch what happens to the cup when I glaze it white and fire it in the kiln." said the Plate-Spinner, taking hold of the cup.

The three friends watched as the Clay-Spinner dipped the cup into a tub of white glaze-paint and, walking over to a hot oven, he placed the cup inside.

"That's called a kiln." explained the Plate-Spinner, pointing at the oven. "It bakes the clay so that it becomes pottery."

They all sat down and waited till the glazing was finished.

"Ah, it's ready now!" said the Plate-Spinner and, opening the oven door, he took out the cup, which now shone in a white porcelain glaze.

"This." he said, holding the cup for the three friends to see… "Is called a Chalice."

"That sounds quite magical." said Nipper-Crab, taking hold of the Chalice which the Plate-Spinner offered him.

"It's quite light for such a large cup." said Stinger-Scorpion, taking the Chalice and, after weighing it in his hands, handed it to Slippery-Fish.

Slippery-Fish held the Chalice closer, staring at it and feeling most strange, as if the Chalice had become hot, heating in his hands until he could hold it no longer.

The sound of the Chalice hitting the floor was like a baby screaming, smashing into a million fragments. There was a long silence as the three friends stood, staring down at the pieces of broken Chalice which littered the floor.

"I'm so sorry." said Slippery-Fish, beginning to cry.

"Don't cry." said the Plate-Spinner, touching Slippery-Fish with a comforting hand.

"I rather think it was meant to be, that the Chalice was meant to be broken. Here…" he added, handing Slippery-Fish an empty bucket. "Put all the pieces into the bucket for me."

Slippery-Fish knelt and began to pick up the pieces of broken Chalice, placing them into the bucket.

"Have you got it all?" asked the Clay-Spinner, taking the bucket which Slippery-Fish offered.

"I believe I have." answered Slippery-Fish, scouring

the ground with sharp eyes.

"There's a piece over there!" exclaimed Stinger-Scorpion, pointing to a piece of broken pottery which lay just under the table.

"This is not the same as the other pieces." exclaimed Slippery-Fish, picking up the piece and examining it closely.

"Where is your shopping-bag?" enquired the Plate-Spinner, suddenly.

"It is there." answered Slippery-Fish, pointing to the bag, which hung from the back of a chair.

"Then might I suggest that you add that piece of broken pottery to the other pieces in the bag?" suggested the Plate-Spinner.

"I don't know why we have to carry that shopping-bag about with us." moaned Nipper-Crab.

"What is the point of those broken bits of pottery?" he continued.

"I want to carry the shopping-bag." asserted Slippery-Fish, "There's something about those bits of broken pottery which have a special meaning!"

"I wonder…" began the Plate-Spinner, in a quiet voice. "If you have ever tried fitting all those pieces of broken pottery together?"

"I doubt if they fit together, they are all different shapes and sizes." said Stinger-Scorpion, scoffing at the very idea that the pieces would fit.

"How do you know, if you have never tried?" asked the Plate-Spinner, taking no notice of Stinger-Scorpion's scoffing, looking at Slippery-Fish instead.

"I suppose I could try it, there is no harm in trying, Stinger." said Slippery-Fish, turning to appease Stinger-Scorpion.

They all stood around the table, watching intently as Slippery-Fish took out all the broken pieces of crockery and laid them out.

"It's like a jig-saw puzzle." said Nipper-Crab, picking up a piece and examining it.

"Well, Slippery-Fish seems to know what he's doing." said the Plate-Spinner, as Slippery-Fish, his tongue poking out in concentration, began to put the pieces together, bit by bit... Until...

"Look! It's a ball! It's a big round ball!" exclaimed Nipper-Crab, and they all stood back, to stare at the ball which now sat on the table.

"It would look much better if it was glazed, it will hold its shape." said the Plate-Spinner and, taking the ball, he dipped it into the chalky glaze, and placed it carefully into the oven.

"Let it bake in the kiln for a while." said the Plate-Spinner, sitting down.

"Hello, all of you, what are you up to?" said Warty-Toad, arriving from thin air and now looking at the three friends with a smile.

"We are waiting for the ball to harden." said Slippery-Fish, going on to explain what had been happening.

The Plate-Spinner had brought some food to the table and they ate, listening as Slippery carried on with his explanation.

"Most interesting." said Warty-Toad, when Slippery-Fish had ended his story.

"I will be very interested in seeing the ball when it comes out of the oven."

"Then, I shall bring it out of the kiln." said the Plate-Spinner, walking over to the oven and opening the door. From out of the oven, he drew the ball, which sizzled and smoked from the heat. Then the heat died away and all eyes lay on the gleaming, perfect ball, which the Plate-Spinner then laid on the table.

"It's a giant Pearl!" breathed Stinger-Scorpion, staring at the luminous globe.

"It's more than that." exclaimed Slippery-Fish. "It's the Soul-Pearl!"

No-one spoke, not for the longest time.

"I think you should put the Soul-Pearl into your shopping-bag, Slippery." said Warty-Toad, at last. "Put it into the bag and let's move on to the last room down the corridor."

The Plate-Spinner smiled, turning back to the Potter's wheel and, throwing some clay onto the wheel, began to make a new head for the beautiful Venus.

He did not look round as the three friends and Warty-Toad shut the door behind them.

"This is the last room." said Stinger-Scorpion, pointing up at the door number.

"Number SEVEN" read Nipper-Crab, and then added... "I wonder what we can expect in this room, and has anyone thought about how we are to get home again?"

"I have wondered how we are to get home." said Slippery-Fish, holding the shopping-bag away from him. "This bag is getting really hot and when I looked into the bag, the Pearl was glowing. I think it is going to burn me." he added, sitting the shopping-bag on the floor.

"Here, let me carry it for you, my skin is always wet and clammy, so it will stand the heat." said Warty-Toad, picking up the bag. "And, as far as getting back to Cuttlefish-Avenue... Well, I think you will all get home safely." he added.

"Come on, Stinger... Let's go inside and see what is there." spoke up Nipper-Crab.

Stinger-Scorpion nodded, and then turned the handle.

Before them lay a beautiful scene, of rolling hills and the soft singing of birds, which flew across the skies. There was a sweet sense of peace about the whole outlay, a gentleness which caused the three friends to stand at the door opening, breathing in the warmth of the air.

"This is so beautiful." said Stinger-Scorpion, at last, walking through, to stand on the grass and take deep breaths.

Nipper-Crab and Slippery-Fish followed Stinger-Scorpion, beginning to walk through fields of flowers and down the path, towards the Stream, which gurgled and ran slowly between the grassy banks.

"Perhaps you and I might go for a swim, Toad." suggested Slippery-Fish, turning back to look at Warty-Toad. But Warty-Toad had gone again.

"Warty-Toad has vanished again!" shouted Slippery-Fish in alarm.

"I shouldn't worry, Slippery." said Stinger-Scorpion, unconcerned. "He is always doing that. He will come back again, like he always does."

"But the Toad has the Soul-Pearl!" exclaimed Slippery-Fish.

"Then we just have to hope the Toad keeps it safe for us." replied Nipper-Crab, standing on the grassy bank, idly watching some fish, which played a game of 'Kiss-Chase'.

"It's so peaceful here." sighed Stinger-Scorpion, sitting down on the bank of the Stream, and then laying down, allowing the sun to warm his face.

"Look! See those three large Lily-Pads, floating towards us!" shouted Nipper-Crab. "Shall we catch them and take a ride downstream?"

"What a great idea, Nipper… Here they come! That's it, Nipper… grab them before they float past. That's great! We have three Boats… get up, Stinger!"

"All aboard!" shouted Slippery-Fish.

And the three friends each lay on a large Lily-Pad, floating idly downstream, losing themselves to the soft ripples of the waves as the 'Lily-Pad' boats gently rocked, while the birds whistled beautiful tunes.

The three friends slept as the Lily-Pad Boats sailed gently on.

"Hey! Lazy-Bones!"

The shouts came from the other side of the Stream. Nipper-Crab awoke and sat up quickly, hearing the shouts and, sitting on the Lily-Pad, looked around.

"Wake up, you two!" shouted Nipper-Crab to Stinger-Scorpion and Slippery-Fish, so they too sat up and looked around, sleepily rubbing their eyes.

"What is it? I was having a marvellous dream." said Stinger-Scorpion, blearily.

"Do you see who is on the other side of the Stream?" asked Nipper-Crab, pointing.

"It's the Toad!" exclaimed Slippery-Fish, focusing his eyes.

"And who, or what, is that with him?" asked Stinger-Scorpion, squinting in the sunlight at the shape which stood next to Warty-Toad.

The figure that stood next to Warty-Toad was tall, and seemed to have a body, although it seemed as if the shape could be seen through, invisible, yet not invisible, whole, though not whole… And all the while, the ghostly shape seemed to have a shimmering shine to it.

"Who is that with you, Toad?… Or rather, what is it?" shouted Stinger-Scorpion, somewhat afraid.

"Is it a Ghost?" called Slippery-Fish.

"Is it an Angel?" enquired Nipper-Crab, hopefully.

THE
BRIDGE

"We are the Wishful-Hopefuls." shouted Warty-Toad, in a voice which did not seem to be like his normal voice at all.

"Wishful-Hopefuls? What do you mean, Toad?... You are Warty-Toad. We know that!" exclaimed Stinger-Scorpion.

"Watch!" said Warty-Toad.

And the three friends watched as, before their eyes, they saw Warty-Toad disappear, and the shape of another ghostly form took his place.

"It is I… Warty-Toad, but in my true form as a Wishful-Hopeful." came the voice.

"It is the Toad, in a new shape… Look, he's holding up the Soul-Pearl for us to see. What shall we do?" asked Nipper-Crab of Stinger-Scorpion and Slippery-Fish, who simply stood with their mouths open.

"What do you want us to do?" called Nipper-Crab, speaking up for the three of them.

Now, a very strange thing happened. As the three friends watched, the two formless shapes seemed to close and merge into one large shape, more shiny and visible, with eyes which glowed a piercing black. The new shape pointed.

"Do you see that pile of wood? … On your side of the Stream's banking?" asked the Wishful-Hopeful. The three friends turned, to see a large pile of wood, stacked high on the banking, along with Hammers and Nails.

"What is all that wood for?" asked Nipper-Crab,

having got over the shock of seeing the two shapes merge into one.

"That wood, Nipper, is for the three of you to build a Bridge, which will allow you to cross over the Stream and come to me!" called the Wishful-Hopeful.

The three friends drew their Lily-Pads to the bank and climbed out, beginning to inspect the wood.

"Why do we need to build a Bridge when we can make a small Raft and float across?" asked Stinger-Scorpion.

"It's no good asking him, Stinger… the Wishful-Hopeful has gone." said Nipper-Crab, pointing across to where the Wishful-Hopeful had been."

"Do you think it will be alright if we just sit on a plank of wood and paddle across?" asked Slippery-Fish. "Or will that be seen as being lazy?"

"Yes I agree, I don't see why we can't just sit on a plank of wood and paddle across." said Stinger-Scorpion, beginning to drag a plank of wood down to the Stream.

"Well, there's no point in working hard when you don't have to." decided Slippery-Fish, now helping Stinger-Scorpion to get the plank into the water.

"I'm not so sure." said Nipper-Crab, uneasily, and then stepped back quickly as the plank sank under the waves.

"Look at that!" gasped Stinger-Scorpion. "The wood just sank! I've never heard of wood sinking before!"

"But why do we have to get to the other side of the

Stream at all? It's so nice here, just lying in the warmth of the Sun and sleeping?" said Slippery-Fish, beginning to lie down again.

"I really do suggest we try." said Nipper-Crab, feeling very uneasy about the wood sinking.

"Well, I agree with Slippery." decided Stinger-Scorpion, stretching out on the grass and closing his eyes. "I don't see why we should do all the work and, anyway, if the Wishful-Hopeful has magic powers, let him come over here to us!" he added, and then began to snore.

"Lay down, Nipper, and enjoy the sunshine." said Slippery-Fish, then, he too, began to snore loudly.

Nipper-Crab sat on the grass, moodily staring out, his eyes on the opposite side of the stream.

Suddenly, he shivered, realising it had become quite chilly. Looking up, he saw the sky darken and angry Rain-Clouds begin to gather directly over where the three friends were.

At the same time, Nipper-Crab saw that the Sun shone brightly, while the birds all sang, across the other side of the Stream.

"Wake up! Wake up, Stinger… And you too, Slippery!" he shouted, as the storm broke, and the rain began pouring down in huge lashes, soaking them all quickly.

"What's happening?" gasped Slippery-Fish, running for cover beneath a nearby tree.

"I have no idea… But look over the other side of the Stream, the sun is shining brightly!" shouted Stinger-

Scorpion, joining his friends beneath the over-hanging branches.

"Hurry, you three, and build the Bridge!" came a voice from across the stream.

The three friends looked over, to see the Stick-Insect-Guru, seated in a bucket, which was carried by the two Bucket-Boys.

"We can't come out into the rain!" Stinger-Scorpion shouted back.

"We'll drown!" exclaimed Slippery-Fish.

"What can we do?" asked Nipper-Crab, in a most unhappy voice

"Do you understand what you have done? You have upset the Weatherman with your laziness, and you still did not do the Rain-Dance for him. I would suggest if you want the rain to stop pouring, you will have to do the Rain-Dance." shouted the Stick-Insect-Guru, leaning out from the side of the Bucket.

"Yes, we shall do the Rain-Dance straight away." shouted Stinger-Scorpion, then, turning to Nipper-Crab, he said… "You start doing the Rain-Dance and we will join in."

"But I've forgotten how to do it!" wailed Nipper-Crab, desperately trying to recall the steps of the dance.

"You must remember, Nipper. Think back to how the Moaning-Weasel showed you, in the circle!" said Stinger-Scorpion, trying to help Nipper-Crab remember.

The memory of how the Moaning-Weasel had shown

him how to do the Rain-Dance began to clear itself, till he could see in his mind how the steps went, the dance and the words which were sung as he danced. Slowly, Nipper-Crab began to raise his arms, the fingers and thumbs opening and closing, like castanets, his eyes closed, to retain the memory, while his mouth opened, so that strange words of the dance came out.

"That's it, Nipper!" shouted Stinger-Scorpion, excitedly. "Come on, Slippery, follow Nipper and do as he does!"

From across the Stream, the Stick-Insect-Guru watched as the three friends danced together, now shouting out the words with heads thrown back, arms raised to the sky.

"That's it!" shouted the Stick-Insect-Guru, encouraging the dancers, getting so excited that he almost fell out of the Bucket.

"The rain has stopped!" exclaimed Nipper-Crab, finishing the Rain-Dance, so the three friends fell to the ground in exhaustion.

"What are those strange lines in the sky?" asked Slippery-Fish, pointing upwards.

The three friends stared up at the sky, seeing the white brightness of a clear sky, with bending grey lines arching through the brightness.

"That's called a Rain-Bow!" shouted the Stick-Insect-Guru, from across the Stream. "You can't see the Reality-Colours of the Rain-Bow, not until you stop being lazy and build your Bridge, so you can get over to this side of the stream."

Getting to their feet, the three friends began to sort the planks of wood out, and then set to work, constructing a bridge which would span from their side of the Stream, to the other side.

On the other side, the Stick-Insect-Guru watched from the other side of the Stream as the three friends began to work, swinging their hammers and nailing planks together. The Bridge began to take shape, reaching out over the water.

"That's the way!" shouted the Stick-Insect-Guru, adding… "I will see you three when you get back to Cuttlefish-Avenue, when you bring the Soul-Pearl back with you and I can be free from the depths of the Mournful-Cave.

"Wait, Guru!" called Stinger-Scorpion, stopping his work and looking across the Stream. "We have not got the Soul-Pearl! Warty-Toad took it with him, before merging into a Wishful-Hopeful. Anyway, we have no idea how we can get back home to Cuttlefish-Avenue."

"The way will become clear, once you have crossed to this side. Now I must go back to the Cave." said the Stick-Insect-Guru.

With that, the Stick-Insect-Guru tapped on the side of the Bucket.

"Going down." said Sydney-Boy Woodmouse. Suddenly, the ground opened up beneath them, the bucket, along with the Bucket-Boys, disappeared down into the opening.

The three friends stood and watched as the earth then smoothed itself, filling the hole through which the bucket had vanished.

"Let's get on with building this Bridge, and see what lies over there, on the other side of the Stream." said Stinger-Scorpion.

The three friends set to work, even harder, and working through the rest of the day and the night, they eventually finished the Bridge and, testing each step, they walked across and stood, gazing around them, on the other side.

"Now what happens?" asked Nipper-Crab.

"Now what happens, Nipper-Crab, is that you follow me."

Before them appeared the Wishful-Hopeful, now more refined, so that the three friends could see a most friendly and beautiful face behind the white veil.

The three friends stood, quite afraid of the sudden appearance of the Wishful-Hopeful.

"Where did you come from and how did you know my name?" quavered Nipper-Crab, not quite daring to stare up into the face behind the veil.

"I have watched you all, from the start of your journey. It was I who caused you to go to the Mournful-Cave, to speak to the Stick-Insect-Guru. I knew the three of you would have the courage to find the Soul-Pearl and take it back to the people of Cuttlefish-Avenue." said the Wishful-Hopeful, in a gentle voice.

"What do we do now?" asked Stinger-Scorpion, becoming bolder and feeling that the Wishful-Hopeful only had their best interests at heart.

"I want us to all hold hands and for you to walk with me. Do not be afraid and have Faith in Me." replied the Wishful-Hopeful, holding out his hands.

Joining hands, the three friends were lead towards a large black rock, walking ever closer, so that they feared they would walk straight into it.

Just as they reached the rock, it opened up, like sliding doors, splitting into two parts, and they passed between the split, coming into a large Hall, misty and magical, which seemed to have a bench that stood behind a Font and a Pedestal, on which sat the Soul-Pearl.

"Please sit, my friends." said the Wishful-Hopeful, letting go the hands and indicating the bench.

The three friends sat, their eyes on the Soul-Pearl, not saying a word.

"Before I give you the Soul-Pearl, my friends... I need to explain to you exactly why you had to travel the journey and why you had to go through all those rooms, until you reached here."

The three friends turned their eyes from the Soul-Pearl, to the Wishful-Hopeful, who stood before them.

"All your lives, you and your friends in Cuttlefish-Avenue have only seen things in black and white, never knowing what Reality-Colours were, or what they gave." said the Wishful-Hopeful.

THE SOUL-PEARL

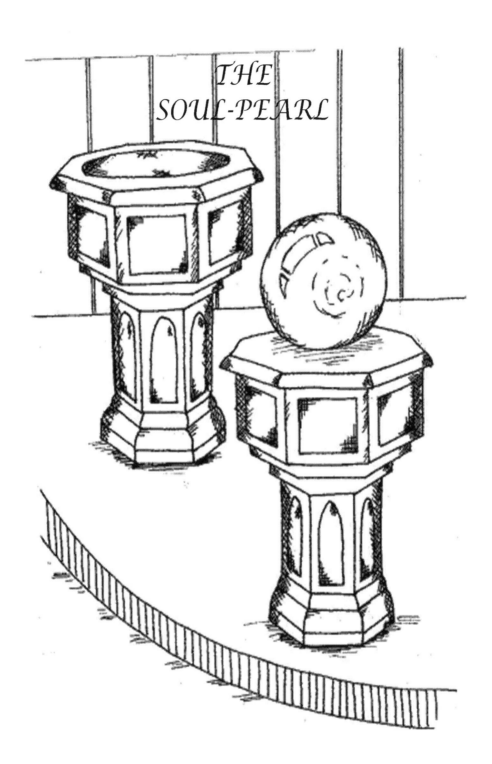

"You, Stinger-Scorpion… And you, Nipper-Crab… And you, Slippery-Fish. You were all sent on a journey of discovery. Those seven rooms which you went through, they were for you to learn from. It was important for you to understand what happens when you all become aware of what feelings and emotions you undergo when you are exposed to Reality-Colours."

The Wishful-Hopeful reached over and took the Soul-Pearl in his hands. It shimmied in the light as he held it.

"This Soul-Pearl will give you the power of seeing Reality-Colours." said the Wishful-Hopeful, continuing… "But, when you see in colour, then you are alive to all kinds of feelings."

"I am not sure we understand." spoke up Stinger-Scorpion, in a timid voice.

"You will not fully understand till you see Reality-Colours. But I tell you, when you see Gold, you only see it as a piece of dark rock. But once you are able to see Gold in its burnished Reality-Colour, you will see its beauty and then desire it. The same in whatever you see, once it is exposed in colours, the beauty will drive you wild with a need to own and show-off in ownership." said the Wishful-Hopeful.

"So, those seven rooms we went through were to show us what to expect when we see things in Reality-Colours?" said Nipper-Crab.

"Indeed." replied the Wishful-Hopeful gently, adding… "Each of those rooms exposed you to each of the Colour-Sins, those sins you can expect once you have Reality-Colours. If you remember each room you came across… Each exposed you to the emotions of Greed and Envy, Anger and Pride, Lust, Gluttony and Laziness."

"Yes, I see that now!" exclaimed Slippery-Fish.

"There, you see." said the Wishful-Hopeful. "Understanding that Reality-Colours enliven the imagination, giving visions of wealth and power and dreams, makes you all Wise-Beings and the High-Teachers, to those who have to learn such Wisdom, before becoming alive to Reality-Colours."

"I am wise to it all!" exclaimed Stinger-Scorpion, standing up, joining the others.

"It will be so. Once we get back to Cuttlefish-Avenue, we shall explain the seven Colour-Sins, before they see Reality-Colours!" announced Stinger-Scorpion.

"Then you are ready to have the secret of the Soul-Pearl, the Pearl of Wisdom." said the Wishful-Hopeful, handing the Soul-Pearl to Stinger-Scorpion. Stinger-Scorpion held out the Soul-Pearl, feeling it warm, seeing it vibrate and pulse in luminosity.

"Nothing is happening." said Nipper-Crab, as he and Slippery-Fish stared at the Soul-Pearl.

"Look at it carefully." instructed the Wishful-Hopeful.

Stinger-Scorpion rested the Soul-Pearl back on the Pedestal and the three friends inspected it very carefully, moving around it, peering sharply.

"I still can't see anything, can you, Stinger or Nipper?" said Slippery-Fish.

Neither Stinger-Scorpion nor Nipper-Crab could see anything different to the Soul-Pearl and said so.

"Please, do not look at the Soul-Pearl as you would normally look at things." said the Wishful-Hopeful. "A normal look is just a glance. I ask that you allow your eyes to stay on the Soul-Pearl, as one would look into a Crystal-Ball."

Slippery-Fish peered, rather than stared, at the Soul-Pearl, seeing its milky luminosity cloud, then clear over, so that he began to see a hair-line crack which encircled the Soul-Pearl.

"I can see a join in the middle of the Soul-Pearl!" he said excitedly.

"That's good, Slippery-Fish." said the Wishful-Hopeful, adding… "Now pick up the Soul-Pearl and twist both parts."

Stinger-Scorpion and Nipper-Crab held their breath as Slippery-Fish picked up the Soul-Pearl and did as the Wishful-Hopeful directed, twisting both parts.

"Look!" exclaimed Nipper-Crab excitedly… "It's coming apart!"

The Soul-Pearl had opened into two parts, opening to expose what lay inside.

"Look!" cried Stinger-Scorpion. "It's the Chalice! It's the same one that the Plate-Spinner made, the same one which Slippery dropped and smashed!"

The three friends stared at the Chalice in amazement.

"How did it get into the Soul-Pearl?" asked Stinger-

Scorpion.

"This Chalice." said the Wishful-Hopeful, removing the Chalice from the Soul-Pearl and holding it up… "Is really what you seek. The Pearl is simply a container, rather like your bodies, your frames, which carry the Chalice of Emotions that allow you to see Reality-Colours."

"I am not sure I understand you." said Stinger-Scorpion… "But what happens now?"

"Take this Chalice, my friends, and go to the Font. Dip the Chalice into the water, and then bring the Chalice back here." replied the Wishful-Hopeful, handing the Chalice to Stinger-Scorpion.

Carefully, Stinger-Scorpion took the Chalice and filled it with water from the Font, handing it back to the Wishful-Hopeful.

"Now, my friends." said the Wishful-Hopeful. "I want you all to close your eyes and I will hold the Chalice up to your lips, where you shall take a drink. When I tell you, you shall open your eyes to all the Wonders of the World. But I shall warn you to remember all the lessons you have learned, before you drink, and become Wise-Beings."

The three friends stood straight and closed their eyes, sensing the nearness and warmth of the Wishful-Hopeful as he passed from one to the other. Each felt the wetness of the water, feeling the Chalice on their lips. Each drank from the Chalice, their eyes still closed.

"Now, Wise-Beings… You may open your eyes."

came the words from the Wishful-Hopeful.

The lights seemed to explode, as they opened their eyes, swirling into a multitude of star-bursts, brilliant colours which burst new highlights, and the three friends cried out in amazement as the World about them became a rainbow of natural brightness, all shapes, and dimensions of colour.

"Do you see now?" asked the Wishful-Hopeful, holding up the Chalice. "Do you feel how your emotions swirl and swivel with new feelings, seeing the truth of this World?"

For a longest of times, the three friends could not speak, except to stare around them, seeing reds, blues, yellows and greens, a world away from the black, white and greys they were used to.

"It's so wonderful!" gasped out Stinger-Scorpion, at last, realising now that those long stalk-things with black heads on them, were the most gorgeous flowers, of many brilliant colours.

Such brilliance also gave a sharpening to the sense of smell, so that Nipper-Crab breathed deeply, for a first time, gaining a sense of perfume from the flowers and in the air.

"Do you see this Chalice?" asked the Wishful-Hopeful, holding it aloft.

"Do you see its colour now? Instead of the black shape, you now see the colour of Gold."

"It is beautiful!" exclaimed Slippery-Fish, adding that he would like to own it.

"That is the power of colour, my friend." said the

Wishful-Hopeful. "When it appeared colourless, you had no desire to own it. Now, you see the raw beauty of Gold, you desire it and might fight for it, had you not learned not to be greedy… A Wise-Being has no wish to own, but to share."

In that instant, on hearing the words which came from the Wishful-Hopeful, Stinger-Scorpion, Nipper-Crab and Slippery-Fish knew that they had no desire to own Gold, or any other richness. They had the riches of the world, for they shared the natural beauty of colours with all forms of life… They were now the Wise-Beings.

"Your work is done here. It is time for you to return to Cuttlefish-Avenue, so you can teach the folk and allow them to see Reality-Colours." said the Wishful-Hopeful in a gentle voice.

"Can you please explain how we can allow the folk to see Reality-Colours? And how are we to get back to Cuttlefish-Avenue?" asked Stinger-Scorpion.

"When you get back to your people, you will remove the Bucket from the Wishing-Well, replacing it with the Chalice, so that the folk can lower the Chalice into the water and then raise it up and drink from the Chalice, instructed the Wishful-Hopeful.

"I understand that. But, how do we get back to Cuttlefish-Avenue?" insisted Stinger-Scorpion.

The Wishful-Hopeful smiled.

"Open that door to your right." he said.

Stinger-Scorpion opened the door, and then stood back in sheer amazement as bursts of colour seemed to fire off like rockets, spraying flashes of illumination, filling the Hall with coloured sensations.

"I have never seen such brilliance!" shouted Nipper-Crab, speaking at last.

"What is it?" asked Slippery-Fish, reaching out, as if trying to touch the colours.

"That, my friends." explained the Wishful-Hopeful. "Is the beginning of the Rain-Bow. It begins here, the Fount of Colour. But, more importantly… Do you see where the Rain-Bow ends?"

Peering through the exaggerated colours of the Rain-Bow, Stinger-Scorpion pointed in excitement, calling Nipper-Crab and Slippery-Fish to come and see.

"Look, both of you! Look down there! The Rain-Bow ends in Cuttlefish-Avenue, in the town centre. It reaches straight down into the Wishing-Well!"

For a time, the three friends stood in the doorway, staring down to where the Rain-Bow ended, in the Wishing-Well.

"Look!" laughed Nipper-Crab, pointing down. "There's Solly, the Mayor… And there, can you see the Townsfolk walking about, like the smallest of Ants?"

"Isn't it strange how they draw water up from the Wishing-Well and drink it, yet they cannot see the Rain-Bow, or any colours!" exclaimed Slippery-Fish.

"That's because they have not drunk the water from the Chalice." said the Wishful-Hopeful, joining them to peer down at the scene far below.

"And that will be our job, as Wise-Beings, to explain about the seven Colour-Sins, and then allow them to drink." added Slippery-Fish.

"What happens if one of the Townsfolk drinks the water from the Chalice before we can warn them about the Colour-Sins?" asked Stinger-Scorpion.

"Then they never get to see any colours, they become the Greys. The Greys have no sense of guilt or conscience. Only Reality-Colours can produce Emotions and only Emotions can give a sense of guilt, conscience, of empathy and sacrifices." said the Wishful-Hopeful.

"Gosh! I have the power of Reality-Colours and I am a Wise-Being. I fully understand the sense of Emotions and can really feel sorry for those who are emotionless. I would hope that I can help everyone become wise in this way." said Stinger-Scorpion, taking his eyes away from the scene below.

"I was wondering." broke in Nipper-Crab. "How are we to arrive back home? To join the folk down there?" he added, pointing downwards.

The three friends turned, to look at the Wishful-Hopeful, who had smiled, then walked through a wall into another room.

"Come through and join me, my friends."

His voice came through the wall and the three stood, looking at each other. Then Stinger-Scorpion walked directly at the wall and both, Nipper-Crab and Slippery-Fish, saw him pass straight through the solid brick.

Quickly, they followed Stinger-Scorpion, joining him and the Wishful-Hopeful in a small room.

"Do you see what this is?" asked the Wishful-Hopeful, pointing to the tin bath which sat in one corner.

"Bless me!" exclaimed Slippery-Fish, instantly recognising it. "That's our old Boat!" he shouted.

"How did it get here?" asked Nipper-Crab, scratching his head. "And look at the colour of it. It is silver all over!"

"And there's the mast, still intact!" remarked Slippery-Fish, inspecting it, and then realising the sail was made from the scales from his back.

"No wonder I was always feeling chilly, especially on my back!" he exclaimed, looking accusingly at Stinger-Scorpion and Nipper-Crab.

"We are sorry, Slippery." they both apologised, now feeling guilty over stealing the scales from Slippery-Fish's back as he had slept, on the beach.

"Kneel down, Slippery, and I will plait them back." said Nipper-Crab, first removing the white fleece he had put on earlier, then carefully put the scales back into place, so that Slippery-Fish felt his back warm up immediately."Can you tell us if the Boat will get us home and, if so, how does it do that?" asked Slippery of the Wishful-Hopeful."It is perfectly simple." The Wishing-Hopeful replied.

"You just sit in the Boat, all three of you, and ride down the Rain-Bow."

RIDING THE RAINBOW

"We won't fall out, will we? I mean, it's a long way down." said Stinger-Scorpion, looking at the tin Bath, dubiously.

"I assure you, my friend." replied the Wishful-Hopeful. "There is no chance of that."

"Then let us go!" exclaimed Nipper-Crab, anxious to leave and return to Cuttlefish-Avenue.

Together, the three friends lifted the Bath and walked straight at the wall so that they once again felt the full force of sheer colour which flooded the room.

"If you set the Boat down here and seat yourselves in it, you may start your journey home." said the Wishful-Hopeful, indicating a place close to the door opening.

"Hold on tight!" shouted Stinger-Scorpion to his two friends, feeling the Boat rise and begin to float.

"Do not forget to take the Chalice with you." said the Wishful-Hopeful, handing Stinger-Scorpion the Golden Cup, then added… "Go well, Wise-Beings!" Then he seemed to change shape, becoming blue smoke and drifting away, to mix with the colours of the Rain-Bow.

There was no sound, nor any real sensation of movement as the Boat rode the downward path of the Rain-Bow. There seemed to be flashes of brilliant colour changes, from reds to greens and yellow, a series of mood flashes, which gave the three friends different feelings, of joy and enthusiasm.

"Where have you three been?" asked Jeremiah Duckworth, jumping up from beside the Wishing-Well, and letting go of Winnie Shrew's hand. Winnie Shrew began to run away, crying out in alarm at the sudden appearance of the three friends, who had climbed out of the tin Bath.

Jeremiah Duckworth stared at the three friends, suddenly aware that they appeared different, seeing each of them having some kind of shimmering white light around them.

"What are those marks on your foreheads?" asked Jeremiah Duckworth, pointing at their heads.

"Gosh!" exclaimed Stinger-Scorpion, looking first at Nipper-Crab, then at Slippery-Fish. "You have both got a Gold Star on your forehead!" he exclaimed.

"So do you, Stinger!" said Nipper-Crab. "We must have got them as we came down the Rain-Bow."

"How did you get here? You just appeared!" said Jeremiah Duckworth, still staring at them in a puzzled way.

"Of course." said Nipper-Crab, smiling. "Jeremiah cannot see the Rain-Bow. He has no knowledge of colours."

"Jeremiah." instructed Stinger-Scorpion… "Go to the Mayor's house and ring the Town's Bell, so that all the folk of Cuttlefish-Avenue know we need them to gather here, at the Wishing-Well."

Jeremiah ran and the three friends heard the Town's Bell clanging away, with Townsfolk calling to each other and coming from their homes, all running towards the Wishing-Well.

Stinger-Scorpion reached over the top of the Well and untied the Bucket, to replace it with the Golden Chalice, and then wound the handle so the Chalice descended into the water.

"It's full of water now." said Nipper-Crab, peering down into the Wishing-Well, indicating that Stinger-Scorpion should draw the Chalice up.

"What is going on here?" demanded the Mayor, leading the folk, to crowd around and stare at the three friends.

"I will ask you, friend Mayor, to be seated, along with the rest of you." said Stinger-Scorpion, indicating the rest of the Townsfolk.

The Mayor was not too happy at being asked to seat himself, fearing a loss of authority. At the same time, he was wary of offending these three friends, who seemed to shimmy under the strange white light. Suddenly, there came murmurings from the back of the crowds, which parted as the figure of the Stick-Insect-Guru appeared, carried in the Bucket by the Bucket-Boys.

"Do you not see, Mayor?" said the Stick-Insect-Guru. "That these three are Wise-Beings. Do you see the marks on their foreheads?"

The Mayor knew better than to offend the Stick-Insect-Guru. So he bade the rest of the Townsfolk to do as he did and sit down.

SOLLY STARFISH

"Now, my friends." said the Stick-Insect-Guru to the three friends, seating himself at the same time…
"Please tell us what you have learned from the Wishful-Hopeful, and what you have in that Chalice you have in your hands.
Thanking the Stick-Insect-Guru for his help, Stinger-Scorpion began to tell the Townsfolk about the Reality-Colours and the seven Soul-Sins and of the new sense of Emotions and Feelings which colours would give.

"Now, my friends." said Stinger-Scorpion, holding the Chalice up high… "Come and drink…"
The Townsfolk of Cuttlefish-Avenue all queued up behind The Stick-Insect-Guru and Solly the Mayor. Slippery-Fish lowered the Chalice into the Well, scooping up the water, passing it from mouth to mouth as all the Townsfolk drank.
Cries of amazement came from every mouth, and with eyes open wide, all the Townsfolk saw the Reality-Colours and felt the swirl of Emotions caused by the seven Soul-Sins, knowing, now, how to behave as all people should.

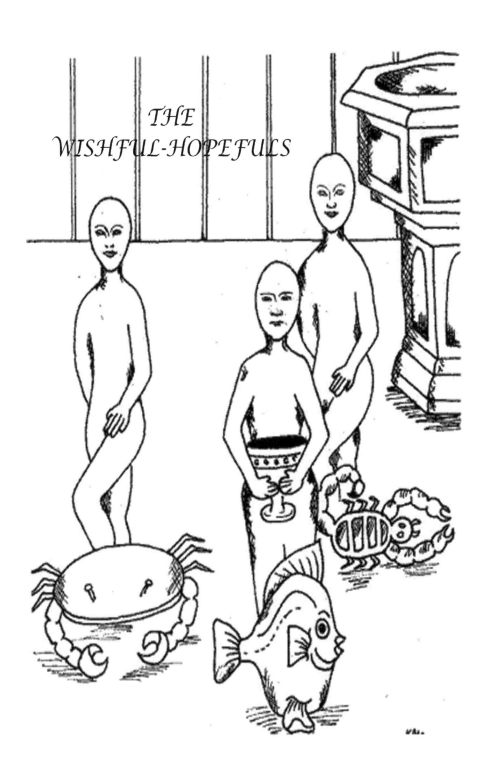

THE END.

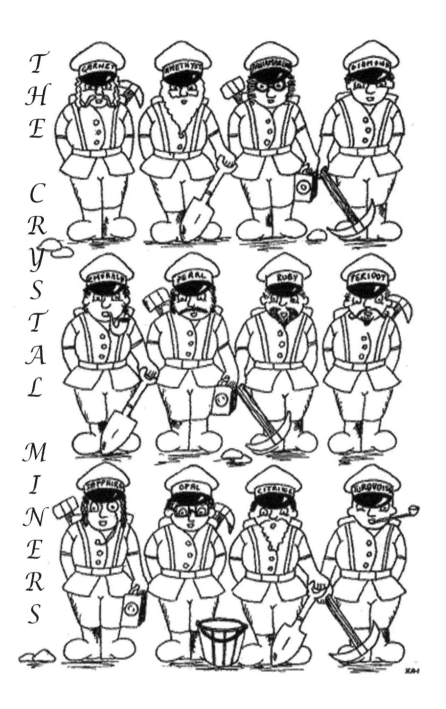

THE CRYSTAL MINERS

'THE EMERALD FIRE'
A Magical Tale
By
Ron S King

'THE EMERALD FIRE'

COPYRIGHT 2010 --- Ron. S. King.

FOREWORD.

Skyrover-Turquoise, one of the Twelve 'Magi' from the land of Celestial Dream, discovers that the 'Emerald Crystal-Moon' has lost its 'Fire-Dust' and he has to travel to the 'Flatlands', taking his Assistant, Juniper-Emerald, to find out exactly why the 'Emerald Crystal-Moon' has lost its power.

The journey takes Skyrover-Turquoise and his Assistant to a strange land, to meet such characters as the 'Ash-Kids', who yodel and call out, 'Hoity-Toity' as a welcome. Then to meet the 'Miners', who drink 'Char-Tar Tea' in the 'Char-Tar Tea Room', also to meet the 'Junior-Miners' who drive 'Ladybird' machines.

This book is an extraordinary tale of twists and turns, which set an almost impossible task for Skyrover-Turquoise... The trust is that you join in with the experience and settle back to enjoy the ride...

Ron S King.

CREDITS.

All credit must go to the illustrator, Kelly Aston, who gave all attention to the drawings which truly enhance this book.

May I, as the author, extend my thanks to you, Kelly, trusting I will continue to make use of your fine drawing pen…

Ron S King.

ILLUSTRATIONS...

FRONTPIECE... The Crystal Miners.

IN THE BEGINNING…

Skyrover-Turquoise wandered the giant telescope through the sky, once again feeling the same sense of wonder he always felt, as his eye took in the rich colours of the Crystal Moons. Moving the telescope from one Moon to the other, he could not see them all, knowing that the sky above only showed the Crystal Moons as each one came into view, one every hour, although, with his special telescope, he could see three at a time as they moved into line. Skyrover-Turquoise watched as the Crystal Moons pulsed their colours, pulsating and throbbing, each Moon sending out its magic in rays, which moved outwards, like ripples in a stream, to move out and meet the rings from the next Moon, so the sky seemed alive with a brilliance of different crystal shades, each blending and melting into violets and purples, colouring the sky.

Humming under his breath, Skyrover-Turquoise turned the handle, wandering the telescope, his eyes beginning to enlarge into twin Turquoise pools of excitement as the telescope took in his own Crystal Moon of December-Turquoise.

He smiled, spending a while, gazing at the colour of his Birth-Stone, the Turquoise of the Crystal Moon.

THE
CRYSTAL TELESCOPE

His eyes dimmed back into normality as he roved the telescope onto the next Crystal Moon, a clear and beautiful January-Garnet, pulsating its red rings in a rippling display.

"Excuse me, Master Skyrover-Turquoise."

Skyrover-Turquoise turned away from the telescope, to look at his Assistant, Juniper-Emerald.

"You are early, young Juniper-Emerald. Is it the time to eat?"

"No, Master... I'm sorry to disturb you in your work." replied Juniper-Emerald.

"Well? If it's not Eating-Time, what is it... What do you want?" asked Skyrover-Turquoise, turning away from the telescope and giving Juniper-Emerald a look of irritation.

"I come to inform you, Master, the last year's Birth-Children are waiting for you, in the classroom." replied Juniper-Emerald.

"Gosh... Is it that time already? It only seems like yesterday that I helped register their births. Are you sure the children are last year's Birth-Children... There's no mistake?" grumbled Skyrover-Turquoise.

"There's no mistake, Master... I checked each of them for 'Sky-Eyelights' and they all passed the test. They are last years Birth-Children, Master." replied Juniper-Emerald in an urgent voice.

"Well, come along then!" said Skyrover-Turquoise, beginning to hurry from the room, with Juniper-Emerald running after him and, passing Skyrover-Turquoise, he reached the classroom door, to open it, allowing Skyrover-Turquoise to sweep into the classroom.

"Quiet for the Master!" shouted Juniper-Emerald, so that all talking ceased as the children sat upright in their seats.

This was the first time the children of 'Last Year's Birth' had seen Skyrover-Turquoise, sitting quiet, looking at the tall figure with awe.

"Good Morning, Children." said Skyrover-Turquoise, standing in the front of the classroom, his eyes looking at each child in turn.

"Good morning, Master Skyrover-Turquoise." replied the children and watched as Skyrover-Turquoise drew down a large drawing-board from the ceiling and began to draw.

"The large circle I have just drawn." began Skyrover-Turquoise, "Is our world, which we know as Celestial Dream. Now, Children, please write down the name of our world, even if you already know what our world is called."

The children opened their books and wrote down the name, whispering the name to themselves as they wrote.

Skyrover-Turquoise waited till all the children had finished writing and were sitting upright once more in their seats.

"Right, Children." he said. "Our world has twelve Crystal Moons, which pass directly overhead, one at a time, at every hour."

Here, Skyrover-Turquoise stopped, to draw twelve

smaller circles around the larger globe of Celestial Dream.

"Now, each Crystal Moon is a month of the year and has a special name. I shall start with the first month, which is the month of the Garnet. Now, Children, write these names down as I mark each name of the Crystal Moons on the board."

The children began writing, copying what Skyrover-Turquoise wrote.

"After the Garnet Crystal Moon, comes the next Crystal Moon, which is called Amethyst Crystal Moon, then follows the other Crystal Moons, Aquamarine, Diamond, Emerald, Pearl and Ruby, followed by Peridot, then Sapphire and Opal, then Citrine and the last is Turquoise." Skyrover-Turquoise stopped writing and walked slowly round the classroom, looking at what each child had written. He nodded, satisfied the children had got the names right, returning once more to the front of the classroom.

"It is important…" he began talking again. "That you children learn the names of each Crystal Moon, because, each Moon is linked to the other, so no matter what Crystal Moon is your Birth-Moon, all of us, who live on this world of Celestial Dream, needs the knowledge contained within each Crystal Moon so we have understanding of each other."

The children sat, listening intently to every word that Skyrover-Turquoise spoke. He nodded, satisfied he had their attention, then began his instruction again.

"Each of you twelve Children were born last year, under the influence of the twelve Crystal Moons. Each of you, each child looks the same, except for your eyes, which are the colours of the Crystals of that month. And each of you were given the special powers of that Crystal and each of you also shares the last name of that same Crystal."

Here, Skyrover-Turquoise stopped, his eyes roving over the children, then he said…

"You can see, Children, my eyes are Turquoise in colour, which tells everyone I was birthed at the month and Rise of the Turquoise Crystal Moon, so my name is Skyrover-Turquoise and my eyes are the colour of Turquoise. I was given the 'Gift' of 'Good-Judgement', which I share with everybody in this world."

Skyrover-Turquoise stopped talking, watching as the children wrote down what he had said, then continued.

"What surname and 'Gift' I have is also given to you, Oliver-Turquoise. For you were birthed at the time of the Turquoise Crystal Moon's Rising." he said, pointing out the boy, so the other children turned, seeing the boy had eyes of a brilliant Turquoise colour, the same colour as the Master, Skyrover-Turquoise.

"And each of you are birthed under a different Crystal Moon's Rising. Can each of you tell me your Crystal Moon's Birthstone?" asked Skyrover-Turquoise.

All the children's hands went up and Skyrover-Turquoise pointed to each in turn, so they spoke, one at a time.

"You first." he said to a girl, so she stood up to answer.

"My name is Agatha-Garnet and my eyes are the colour of Garnet. I was birthed at the Rising of the Garnet Crystal Moon. My 'Gift' is 'Ambition' and to give others 'Aspiration'."

"And the next one." instructed Skyrover-Turquoise, as the girl sat down.

"My name is Johnston-Amethyst and my eyes are the colour of Amethyst. I was birthed when the Crystal Moon of Amethyst was Rising and my 'Gift' is to instill the power of 'Dreams' and 'Inspiration'."

"My name is Angela-Aquamarine. My eyes are the colour of Aquamarine and I was birthed at the Rising of the Aquamarine Crystal Moon. My 'Gift' is to share the sense of 'Clear-Sight'."

Angela-Aquamarine sat down in her seat, the boy next to her quickly rising to his feet.

"My name is Jimboy-Diamond and my eyes are the colour of Diamond. I was birthed at the Rising of the Diamond Crystal Moon and I was given the 'Gift' of 'Good-Taste', to share what is good and acceptable with all others."

"And the next." said Skyrover-Turquoise, hurrying the children.

"My name is Tarina-Emerald and my eyes are the

colour of Emerald. I was birthed at the Rising of the Emerald Crystal Moon and given the 'Gift' of 'Logic' and 'Clear-Thought'." said Tarina-Emerald, sitting down as another boy rose from his seat.

"My name is Jarrow-Pearl and I have eyes the colour of Pearl. I was birthed at the Rising of the Pearl Crystal Moon and was given the 'Gift' of 'Calming-Emotions', to share with others."

"And the next child." said Skyrover-Turquoise, anxious to be back to the telescope, back on 'Sky-Watch'.

"My name is Janina-Ruby and I have eyes the colour of Ruby. I was birthed at the Rising of the Ruby Crystal Moon and was given the 'Gift' of 'Creativity', to share among the rest of those who dwell in Celestial Dream."

"My name." quickly spoke the next child. "Is Lancelot-Peridot and my eyes are the colour of Peridot. I was birthed when the Crystal Moon of Peridot was Rising and given the 'Gift' of 'Good Co-Habitation' to share the idea of living happily together."

"My name is Ima-Sapphire and I have eyes the colour of Sapphire. I was birthed when the Crystal Moon of Sapphire was Rising and given the 'Gift' of understanding how to 'Relate' to others, which I will share."

"Well, whose next?" inquired Skyrover-Turquoise, when no-one stood up.

This brought a tustled-haired boy quickly to his feet.

"I am sorry, Master." he apologised, before hurriedly saying… "My name is Shelaca-Opal and I have eyes the colour of Opal. I was birthed when the Crystal Moon of Opal was Rising and given the 'Gift' of understanding the joy of 'Sharing' with others."

"And my name is Annabelle-Citrine and I have eyes the colour of Citrine. I was birthed when the Crystal Moon of Citrine was Rising and given the 'Gift' of 'Enthusiasm' and 'Good- Spirit', to share with others."

"And…The last child?" queried Skyrover-Turquoise, looking around the classroom.

A boy rose to his feet. "My name is Oliver-Turquoise and my eyes are the colour of Turquoise. I was birthed at the Rising of the Turquoise Crystal Moon and I was given the 'Gift' of 'Good-Judgment', which I share with you, Master, and all others."

Skyrover-Turquoise smiled at this remark and bade the child sit down.

"Before you all leave the classroom, Children, I want you all to remember how important it is that we all share our given 'Gifts' with each other. If one person on Celestial Dream does not share the 'Gift', then it is like the spokes of a wheel… If one spoke falls out, then another follows, until the wheel cannot go round in a complete circle and it collapses. Do you all understand?"

"Yes, Master." agreed all the children, nodding their heads and touching each others hands, so their eyes glowed.

"My Assistant, Juniper-Emerald, will stay behind, to teach you about the colours of the Crystal Moons and how they glow. Once you have written down all he tells you, then you may all go to your homes." said Skyrover-Turquoise, leaving the classroom and hurrying back up the stone staircase towards the 'High-Dome' which housed the giant telescope.

It was a while later, as Skyrover-Turquoise sat at his desk, charting the course and times of the circling Crystal Moons, his Assistant, Juniper-Emerald entered the room, carrying the books in which the children had written the lessons of the day.

Sitting at the smaller of the two desks, Juniper-Emerald began to mark the work, stopping every now and again, rubbing at his eyes. When he had finished marking the books, Juniper-Emerald walked over to the telescope and began reading out the 'Seconds', timing the course of the Crystal Moons as they 'Rose' overhead, calling out the times to Skyrover-Turquoise. Once again, the young Assistant stopped, to rub at his eyes.

"What is wrong with you, Juniper-Emerald?" asked Skyrover-Turquoise, motioning his Assistant to leave the telescope and come closer. "Why do you keep rubbing at your eyes?"

"I keep getting 'Soft-sight', Master. My eyes keep dimming, then glowing again." replied Juniper-Emerald, allowing Skyrover-Turquoise to stare into his eyes.

"Yes, that's most strange. I can see how your eyes seem to lose their sparkle now and again. I suggest you go down to see Master Antavios-Garnet and let him look at your eyes… Yes, report to the Optician and see what he says…Off you go!" said Skyrover-Turquoise, sending his Assistant on his way.

Once Juniper-Emerald had left the room, Skyrover-Turquoise, wearing a troubled frown, quickly walked over to the telescope and set its sight on the circling Crystal Moons, clucking his tongue with impatience as he waited for the Emerald Crystal Moon to 'Rise'. The Crystal Moon which was 'Rising' at that time was the Aquamarine Crystal Moon, which meant Skyrover-Turquoise would have to wait another two hours before the Emerald Crystal Moon would 'Rise' overhead.

Skyrover-Turquoise waited impatiently as, in the next hour, he saw the Rise of the Diamond Crystal Moon, watching its path as it crossed overhead, shedding its colours on the land below, then begin to fade as it passed over.

At last!

Skyrover-Turquoise, straightened himself, straining as he put an eye to the lens of the telescope, watching the 'Rise' of the Emerald Crystal Moon, seeing the clear picture, to sit upright in shock.

"What is going on?" he cried, wiping at the eyepiece and staring through the lens again, blinking hard, then taking another look, nearly falling off the seat.

"The Crystal Fire-Dust of the Emerald Moon has

been blown away!" he cried, leaving the telescope, running to the red box on the far wall and, pulling open the door, pressed the alarm bell, keeping his finger hard on the button, so the sound of the alarm pealed a loud shrieking thoughout the halls and the rooms, the sound which would quickly summon the rest of the 'Twelve-Magi' to assemble in the Great-Hall. Letting go the button, Skyrover-Turquoise ran, hurrying along the hallways and, descending the steps, he ran through the doors of the Great-Hall, where some of the 'Twelve-Magi' had already assembled.

"What is going on, Skyrover-Turquoise? Why have you summoned us here?" demanded Dreamteller-Amethyst, as she seated herself behind the large curved desk.

Other 'Magi' ran into the Hall, asking what the urgency was, before sitting, so that all the seats were taken, except for the one reserved for Skyrover-Turquoise, who stood in front of them, his hands raised.

Everyone was talking, voices urgent as they called to each other, asking what the problem was.

"I am afraid I have some grave news to tell you all and I want you to be quiet." said Skyrover-Turquoise in a loud voice, waiting till the eleven 'Magi' became quiet, settling in their seats as he began speaking.

"Today, as I trained my telescope on the Emerald Crystal Moon, I saw that it was dying. The Emerald

'Fire-Dust', which gives the Crystal Moon its power, has been blown away from the Crystal Moon's surface."

"I wondered why my eyes were beginning to dim!" shouted Articulate-Emerald, rising from the desk and waving his arms.

At this, all the 'Magi' began shouting at once, asking what could be done about such a happening.

"Stop shouting! Please be quiet and let us consider what we can do!" exclaimed Skyrover-Turquoise, walking up and down in front of the desk.

The 'Magi' sat again, whispering to each other, then waited for Skyrover-Turquoise to speak.

"We all know what will happen if the Emerald 'Fire-Dust' is gone. It would mean those born at the time of the Emerald Crystal Moon's Rising, will lose the gift of 'Clear-Speech' and no-one would be able to understand what they were saying. This also means they would lose the colour of Emerald from their eyes, so they would not be able to stay with us but banished to where the Land meets the Sky, the 'Endless Horizon', where they would be no more."

"We would lose a spoke in the wheel, the wheel would begin to wobble!" exclaimed Sharedgames-Opal, beginning to panic.

"How did this happen?" asked Looksharp-Aquamarine, as he calmed Sharedgames-Opal by patting her on the back.

"I can only assume." replied Skyrover-Turquoise "That the wind from the last Solar-Storm blew the covering of Emerald 'Fire-Dust' away, so that the Emerald Crystal Moon lost its glow." explained Skyrover-Turquoise.

"But surely the 'Miner' of the Emerald 'Fire-Dust' has to mine some more 'Dust', to spread it over the Emerald Crystal Moon?" queried Worthwhile-Diamond.

"Well, that's what's supposed to happen." replied Skyrover-Turquoise, stroking thoughtfully at his chin.

"Then I suggest one of us ought to visit the Emerald 'Fire-Dust' Miner and see why he hasn't been doing his job!" shouted Dramaticus-Ruby. At this, all of the 'Magi' rose from their seats, shouting agreement.

"What you say is right, Dramaticus-Ruby." said Skyrover-Turquoise, waving the fearful 'Magi' to be seated again, then going over to Dramaticus-Ruby and, standing before him, he said…"But you know, it needs all twelve of the Crystal Moon 'Miners' to agree to only one of us speaking to any one of the 'Crystal Moon Miners', that's their code."

"Then I suggest we send Skyrover-Turquoise and his Assistant, Juniper-Emerald, to speak to all the 'Miners', that he gets their permission to speak to the 'Miner' of the Emerald 'Fire-Dust'." spoke up Nobarriers-Citrine.

Again, everyone agreed to the suggestion and Skyrover-Turquoise joined the others behind the desk, all joining hands as was the rule of 'Agreement'.

"Because only Skyrover-Turquoise will be going, with only his Assistant, Juniper-Emerald to help, we will all have to allow ourselves to become 'Infused', to have our 'Gifts' melted into Skyrover-Turquoise, so that he has the sole power to use our 'Gifts' as he will." declared Loveaspect-Sapphire.

"I need to think about all this…And I can't think clearly!" suddenly exclaimed Articulate-Emerald. The rest of the 'Magi' turned to look at Articulate-Emerald, who sat, covering his eyes with his hands.

"Quick!" said Skyrover-Turquoise, hurrying around the desk and reaching Articulate-Emerald, took the hands away from his face, to see that the Emerald colour to his eyes had started to dim, while his 'Gift' of 'Clear-Speech' had began to lose its sense, so he began to talk in a way which no-one understood.

"Fetch a blindfold to cover his eyes, that will calm him down and stop him from losing all sense of sight and speech." he shouted.

Loveaspect-Sapphire hurried out from the 'Great Hall', with Skyrover-Turquoise keeping Articulate-Emerald's eyes covered with his hands, till Loveaspect-Sapphire came running back with the blindfold, quickly tying it round Articulate-Emerald's face, so that he sat quiet and still in his seat.

"I think we should hurry and get started!" shouted Aspiration-Garnet, rising from his seat and leaning over the desk.

"Then let us hurry to the 'Infusion-Chamber', so I

can begin my journey." said Skyrover-Turquoise, waving his hands.

"I ask that you, Loveaspect-Sapphire, take Articulate-Emerald's hand and help bring him with us to the 'Infusion-Chamber'." said Skyrover-Turquoise.

With that, Skyrover-Turquoise led the eleven 'Magi' through the main hallways and into the 'Echo-Hall', where sat the 'Infusion-Chamber', a large tube-like structure which had round portholes down either side.

Skyrover-Turquoise stood at the entrance to the chamber, holding open the door so the 'Magi' could climb in and take their seats. He waited as Loveaspect-Sapphire helped Articulate-Emerald to his seat, then set about closing the door.

"You understand, Skyrover-Turquoise, by infusing our 'Gifts', you leave us inside the 'Infusion-Chamber' without the energy to move outside again, not until you return, to defuse the energy and give us our 'Gifts' back?" said Softfeeling-Pearl.

"Of course, I realise the danger and will return once the mission is accomplished." replied Skyrover-Turquoise, in a calm and reassuring voice.

"It has also to be remembered, Skyrover-Turquoise, that you can only use our 'Gifts' the once." said 'Nobarriers-Citrine'.

"Yes, my friend, I do understand that... Now, it is time to get on with the 'Infusion'." replied Skyrover-Turquoise.

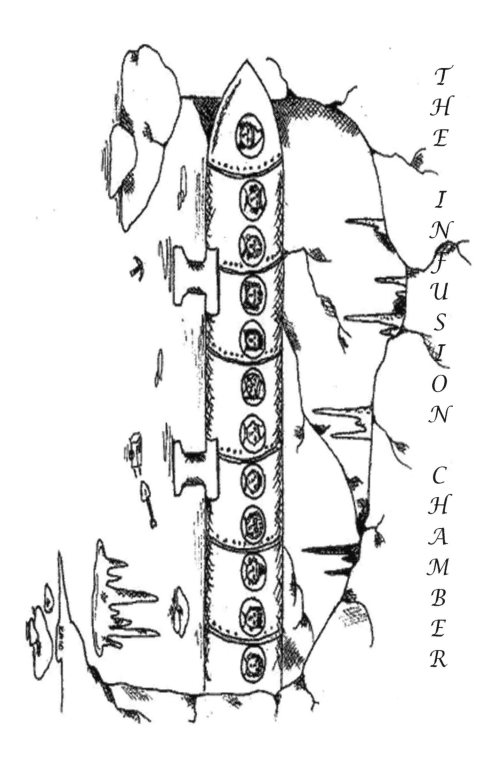

The eleven 'Magi' drew down the headsets which hung above them, settling the ear-pieces and sat, peering out through the portholes as Skyrover-Turquoise closed the door. It hissed into the 'Lock' position, causing a red light to flare and flood the 'Echo-Hall'.

Skyrover-Turquoise moved down the chamber, waving at those who nodded back through the portholes, then entered the single chamber which was attached to the end of the 'Tube'.

Seating himself in the 'Command' position, Skyrover-Turquoise reached up and, pulling down the head-set, placed it firmly onto his head pressing a series of buttons. The chamber began to throb, with low pulsing sounds, that grew louder, to give a loud humming sound. Then the compartment was flooded with a green ghostly glow, which drifted in smoke for a while, then cleared away. Skyrover-Turquoise picked up the microphone and, switching on the button at its base, tapped at it and, hearing the echo of sound, began to speak.

"I am ready." he said, speaking into the microphone, his words carried through into the headsets of the 'Magi', seated in the main part of the 'Infusion-Chamber'.

"Before we start." began Skyrover-Turquoise. "Can one of you use the 'Mind-Draw', so that I can 'Infuse' the 'Gift' of ' Clear-Speech' from Articulate-Emerald."

Loveaspect-Sapphire reached up and opened a small

cabinet door, reaching in and taking out a box which contained the 'Plunging-Needle. Connecting the 'Plunger' into a red tube, she then inserted the 'Needle' into Articulate-Emeralds' arm.

Immediately, Skyrover-Turquoise felt the 'Infusion', the 'Gift' of 'Clear-Speech' fill his mind and he smiled.

"Now…" he said. "As you all know, to 'Infuse' your 'Gifts', you have to say what 'Gifts' you have, which are then transferred to me. Are you ready and willing to 'Infuse' your 'Gifts'?"

Aspiration-Garnet was the first to reply, closing his eyes.

"I am the 'Magi', Aspiration-Garnet and I surrender my 'Gift' of 'Ambitions' to Skyrover-Turquoise." Aspiration-Garnet pressed a button and relaxed as he felt the spirit run from him, so that he slumped down in his seat, his eyes losing their colour.

"I am the 'Magi', Dreamteller-Amethyst and I surrender my 'Gift' of 'Dreams' to Skyrover-Turquoise." said Dreamteller-Amethyst and she, too, pressed a button, to slump down, losing all colour to her eyes.

Each of the Magi followed in this fashion, each surrendering their 'Gifts', each slumping in their seats and losing consciousness.

As each 'Magi' surrendered their 'Gifts', Skyrover-Turquoise felt the spirit of each 'Gift' fill his soul, as if he was ballooning up, his mind swelling as if he could see a galaxy of new worlds, hear a million voices and knowing all there was to know.

He sat, taking in the 'Gifts' of the other 'Magi'.

The 'Gift' of 'Clear-Sight' from Looksharp Aquamarine.

The 'Gift' of 'Good-Taste' from Worthwhile-Diamond.

The 'Gift' of 'Emotional-Calm' from Softfeeling-Pearl.

The 'Gift' of 'Creativity' from 'Dramaticus-Ruby'.

The 'Gift' of 'Good Co-Habitation' from 'Welltogether-Peridot'.

The 'Gift' of 'Relationships' from 'Loveaspect-Sapphire'.

The 'Gift' of 'Sharing' from 'Sharedgames-Opal'

And, lastly…

The 'Gift' of 'Broad-Horizons' from 'Nobarriers-Citrine'.

The noise of the humming grew so loud that Skyrover-Turquoise had to cover his ears, waiting till the noise stopped, till no sound came from within the chamber, or from the inside of the main 'Tube', where all the 'Magi' had turned, as if to stone, with ghostlike faces, staring with sightless eyes out through the porthole windows.

Feeling as though he could fly and light-headed with knowledge, Skyrover-Turquoise removed the headset and opened the door. Stepping down from the compartment, he stared at the white faces of the sightless 'Magi' as he passed the portholes, moving out of the 'Echo-Hall' and walking swiftly through the maze of hallways until he reached the 'High-Dome', opening the doors, to find his Assistant, Juniper-Emerald, slumped by the side of the telescope, who squinted and rubbed at his eyes, which had lost most of their Emerald fire. Juniper-Emerald tried to speak, his mouth making sounds which could not be understood.

"Quiet." hushed Skyrover-Turquoise, moving to a drawer and taking out a scarf. "We have much work to do, Juniper-Emerald." he said, tying the scarf around Juniper-Emerald's eyes.

"Hold onto my coat." Skyrover-Turquoise demanded.

Juniper-Emerald mumbled something and, holding tightly to Skyrover-Turquoise' coat, followed his Master blindly.

"We have to make our way down to the 'Magnetic Train'." said Skyrover-Turquoise, leading his Assistant up the flights of stairs and out into the fresh air of Celestial Dream.

"Here we are!" exclaimed Skyrover-Turquoise. "Mind how you get into the train, watch the step. That's right... Now sit down and buckle up with this strap."

Skyrover-Turquoise helped Juniper-Emerald into the train, seating him in the passenger seat and helping him buckle the strap across his chest.

THE MAGNETIC TRAIN

"We are going to the lands of the 'Miners', though I have no idea where they live." said Skyrover-Turquoise, more to himself than to Juniper-Emerald. "All I can do is print the destination into the train's computer and hope we get there." Juniper-Emerald tried to speak, though his words began to get jumbled, so that he spoke in 'Gobblygook'. Skyrover-Turquoise patted Juniper-Emerald on the shoulder, still continuing to speak to himself.

"I don't know anything about the 'Miners'." mused Skyrover-Turquoise, pausing to type the command-words into the computer… "Except they are the ones who mine the 'Fire-Dust', which is spread over the Crystal Moons, so we can live happily together on Celestial Dream." Skyrover-Turquoise realised, as did all the 'Magi', that, without the 'Miners', life on Celestial Dream would not exist.

As those thoughts crossed his mind and before he could seat himself properly, there was a roar of energy and the 'Magnetic-Train' seemed to leap into the air, the flashing panel on the front showing the train was set on a course of 'Magnetic-North'.

The power and speed of the surge pushed Skyrover-Turquoise backwards and he managed to fall into his seat, fumbling wildly with the strap, buckling himself in. Both, Skyrover-Turquoise and Juniper-Emerald, drew in deep, gasping, breaths, feeling the speed of the train forcing them back, making it hard for them to breathe.

Juniper-Emerald shouted strange words and reached

out, grasping Skyrover-Turquoise' arm in panic. Skyrover-Turquoise reached over and, using the 'Gift' from the 'Magi', Softfeeling-Pearl, placed a hand on Juniper-Emerald's forehead, giving the alarmed Assistant a sense of healing, of 'Calming-Emotions'.

Immediately, Juniper-Emerald felt a sense of pure calm settle over him and he smiled, settling back into the seat.

The 'Magnetic Train' seemed to quieten in its movement, almost gliding now, though the lights were still not on, leaving the train in darkness. "It's getting quite warm now…Can you feel the heat?" said Skyrover-Turquoise, more to himself than to Juniper-Emerald, who seemed to be asleep, a smile on his face.

"I think it will soon get even warmer." continued Skyrover-Turquoise, lifting his head to one side, as if listening, though it was more that he 'Felt' they were on a downward thrust, gaining sense of the journey, that it seemed to be going straight down, through the centre of Celestial Dream, going through the core, which meant it would get even hotter. Skyrover-Turquoise knew that he should not worry, knowing they would be protected by 'Magnetic Streams', which would deflect the raw heat.

Skyrover-Turquoise knew the train ran to true magnetic 'Lay-lines', like invisible tracks. He smiled, as if to assure himself and settled down, already feeling the warmth as the train peaked its run, running its way through the fiery core of Celestial Dream.

The warmth and inner 'Gift' of 'Calming' caused Skyrover-Turquoise to close his eyes and soon, he too, was sound asleep.

"Hoity-Toity!"

The sound of someone shouting and the noise of a fist banging on the side of the Magnetic-Train caused both, Skyrover-Turquoise and Juniper-Emerald, to awake with a sudden jolt, both sitting up in their seats. Skyrover-Turquoise stared out at the sight of a dirty child's face, which peered intently through the window.

"Hoity-Toity!" shouted the child again, this time tapping sharply on the window with a metal poker. "Whose to speak to me? Are you 'Mind-Spirits?'" demanded the child, once more giving the window a hard rap with the poker, so that Juniper-Emerald jumped back in alarm.

Skyrover-Turquoise rose from his seat and moved towards the door of the train.

"What is it? Who is shouting and knocking?" asked Skyrover-Turquoise.

Juniper-Emerald began to cry, pulling at the blindfold and talking 'Gibberish', so that Skyrover-Turquoise went back to where his Assistant sat and 'Shushed' him, telling him to remain calm and be quiet. Juniper-Emerald quietened and put his hands to his ears, as if trying to block out the sounds of the poker as it rapped on the window again.

"Stop it!" demanded Skyrover-Turquoise, waving a stern finger at the child, who stepped back, though his cheeky face wore a wide grin. Skyrover-Turquoise opened the train door and stepped outside. The train had drawn to a halt inside a huge cavern, which was dark and grimy with smoke. There was an acrid smell of sulphur in the air and Skyrover-Turquoise slowed his breathing down, so he found it easier to take breaths in this grim atmosphere. Looking around, he saw that the cavern walls were pitted with small caves, too small for a normal person to enter.

"So? Hoity-Toity… And who are you? Are you a 'Mind-Spirit'… Come to frighten the 'Ash-Kids'?" asked the child as Skyrover-Turquoise climbed down from the train.

"I can assure you that I am no 'Mind-Spirit', nor even a 'Ghost-Apparition'! My name is Skyrover-Turquoise, a Celestial Dream 'Magi'." said Skyrover-Turquoise, bowing grandly, then asking… "And whom might you be?"

"Me?" asked the child, making the cavern echo with his laughter. "I'm an 'Ash-Kid', an 'Ash-Raker'." The 'Ash-Kid' became serious, studying Skyrover-Turquoise, his head cocked to one side.

"But you are different, you aint no Hoity-Toity, or even one of us 'Ash-Kids'!" he exclaimed, continuing… "And you certainly aint no 'Miner', neither. I knows that because I saw one once, through the 'Ash-Grill'. That 'Miner' was small, with a funny hat and coloured eyes, even though you have coloured eyes as well… Not like us 'Ash-Kids', whose all got black eyes, from the soot and 'Ash-Raking'. "

Skyrover-Turquoise stood silent, allowing the 'Ash-Kid' to talk, although it would seem the child spoke so quickly, seeming not to stop for breath, that it might be he would never stop talking.

Suddenly, the 'Ash-Kid' stopped talking and, turning, he cupped his hands together, to let out a loud yodelling sound, which echoed all around the smokey interior of the cavern.

Within minutes, there came tumbling out from the mouths of the caves, hundreds of the small children, till it seemed the cavern was full of shouting and laughing 'Ash-Kids', each as dirty and ragged as the next and all demanding to know who the stranger was.

"Hows we to know his calibre?" said the 'Ash-Kid' who seemed to be the leader.

"He aint no 'Mind-Spirit', that's a certain thing, 'cause he don't look frightening enough…Is you all agreeing my point?"

The 'Ash-Kids' crowded round, shouting their agreement.

Some of the 'Ash-Kids' had gone to the train and were now staring through the windows at the huddled figure of Juniper-Emerald.

"Here's another little 'un. He's not a Hoity-Toity or nothing." one of the 'Ash-Kids' shouted, so that a

few of them began banging at the windows with their pokers, demanding that Juniper-Emerald come out .
"He's got no face in his head!" said the leader, coming to the door and, opening it with a tug, stared in at the frightened figure of Juniper-Emerald.
"Why aint he got no face?" demanded the leader, returning to face Skyrover-Turquoise. "He has a face," replied Skyrover-Turquoise. "It's just that he can't see very well."
"Well, drag him out and lets have a look at his face." ordered the 'Ash-Kid', pointing with his poker.
With that, some of the 'Ash-Kids' entered the train and grabbing Juniper-Emerald by the arms, began to pull him out. Juniper-Emerald became quite alarmed and shouted out.
"He's talking all 'Gobblygook' and 'Gibberish' talking!" shouted one of the 'Ash-Kids', poking his head out of the train door.
"Leave him alone!" shouted Skyrover-Turquoise, holding up his arms and rising to full height, a very imposing figure. The 'Ash-Kids' fell quiet, overawed, those in the train, coming out, to join the others who suddenly sat on the ground in a circle, surrounding Skyrover-Turquoise. As they watched, Skyrover-Turquoise walked to the 'Magnetic-Train' and calmed the frightened Juniper-Emerald down, leading him from the train, so they both stood and faced the seated 'Ash-Kids'.
"This." said Skyrover-Turquoise, indicating his Assistant "Is Juniper-Emerald."

"Why aint he got no face?" shouted the leader of the 'Ash-Kids'.

"I told you before." said Skyrover-Turquoise, pulling the scarf away from Juniper-Emerald's eyes, so the 'Ash-Kids' gasped as they saw the eyes of the Assistant were white and sightless.

"He has also lost the power of 'Good Speech'. That is why my Assistant has come with me to find out exactly why there is no 'Emerald Fire-Dust' covering the Emerald Crystal Moon, because, without the 'Fire-Dust' all those who were birthed in the month of May will not be able to see or speak properly."

The 'Ash-Kids' began to whisper to each other and Skyrover-Turquoise knew they had no understanding of what he was saying.

With quizzical eyes, the 'Ash-Kids' shook their heads and waited.

"Can anyone tell me where I can find the Crystal Moon 'Miners'?" asked Skyrover-Turquoise, in a sudden change of direction, hoping to get a straight answer.

"Hoity-Toity!" exclaimed the leader of the 'Ash-Kids', now rising to his feet and waving his poker about.

"Them folks is up there, above the smoke and over the gratings." he finished, thumbing upwards.

Skyrover-Turquoise silently thanked the 'Gift' of 'Clear-Speech' which had been 'Infused' into him, understanding that what the 'Ash-Kid' had said was, the 'Miners' lived above ground.

"And how do I get above the smoke and over the grating?" he asked.

At this, all the 'Ash-Kids' stood up and began yodelling, pointing at Skyrover-Turquoise, then pointing at their own heads and rolling their eyes, as if indicating he was mad.

Skyrover-Turquoise waited for the noise to die down and the 'Ash-Kids' sat again, all except the leader, who did the speaking.

"It's a biggest secret." said the 'Ash-Kid', his grimy face smiling, while his eyes opened wide. "We is just the 'Ash-Kids'. We gets to clean up the ashes here, in the 'Work-Pits' and enjoy parties afterwards. The 'Miners' looks after us and we looks after ourselves!" he said.

Suddenly all the 'Ash-Kids' rose to their feet, shouting… "Let's have a party!"

"Hoity-Toity!" shouted the leader in agreement… "Let's have a party!"

With that, the 'Ash-Kids' began shouting and yodelling, holding hands and dancing, until the leader shouted loudly… "Party is to begin !" Still yodelling loudly, the 'Ash-Kids' ran, disappearing into the small cave-openings in the cavern walls, then returning with yellow buckets full of ash, still smoking blue puffs of Dim-Fire.

They piled it into a heap in the centre of the cavern. Seating themselves in a circle, the leader indicated that Skyrover-Turquoise and Juniper-Emerald should sit with them.

Skyrover-Turquoise watched as the 'Ash-Kids' took handfuls of the ash and began to roll it in their hands, making small balls, which they began to eat, making delightful noises, as if they ate chocolate and cream cakes.

"Eat! Eat!" exclaimed one of the 'Ash-Kids', handing Juniper-Emerald one of the balls of ash and, before Skyrover-Turquoise could stop him, Juniper-Emerald bit into the 'Ash-Ball' and began chewing. "Eat some!" said the 'Ash-Kid', holding out one of the 'Ash-Balls' to Skyrover-Turquoise who, still unsure, took a small bite from the ash. "Goodness!" exclaimed Skyrover-Turquoise, at once gaining the taste of raspberry jelly and custard, a favourite of his, so that he quickly ate the whole of the 'Ash-Ball' and began to roll some more of the ash, giving some of the balls to Juniper-Emerald and then eating more himself.

The cavern was full of noise as the party continued, all the 'Ash-Kids' filling themselves up with the very best of food, seeming to be ever-hungry, though Skyrover-Turquoise, as an adult, soon found himself to be full and needing to find a way to the ground above.

Leaving the party, Skyrover-Turquoise explored the cavern, finding that all the 'Cave-Holes' were too small for him to pass through, all except one which, on entering, Skyrover-Turquoise found it led to another large cavern with steep sides, which narrowed until he could see a small opening at the top, the sky appearing cloudy and red above.

Returning back to the party, Skyrover-Turquoise asked about the other cavern and the red sky at the top of the steep slopes.

"Hoity-Toity!" exclaimed the leader of the 'Ash-Kids', his mouth full of 'Ash-Ball'.

"Now he sees a red top-hole in the ceiling." he laughed.

At this, all the 'Ash-Kids' began to laugh and yodel and it was then Skyrover-Turquoise realised that, because he had the 'Gift' of 'Clear-Sight', he was the only one who could see the opening.

He also realised the 'Ash-Kids' had lived underground all their lives and only saw grim darkness.

"If I wanted to climb up and touch the roof of the cavern next door, how could I do that?" he asked.

"Hoity-Toity! It's madness to a touch of 'Brain-Gone', that's what it is!" shouted one of the 'Ash-Kids', at which they all began to yodel.

Skyrover-Turquoise knew it was better to laugh with them and even touched at his own forehead, rolling his eyes as if he were mad.

"You can always make some steps out of this ash." said an 'Ash-Kid', standing up and proceeded to press some of the ash together, shaping a step and standing on it.

"That way." he went on "You can go up to all kinds of madness!"

Skyrover-Turquoise jumped up with a delighted smile, clapping his hands and joined all the 'Ash-Kids' as they laughed and yodelled. "Quickly! Collect all the ash you can manage and watch me climb up into an 'Upside' madness!" he shouted. Everyone was delighted with this new game and ran to their cave-holes, returning with buckets full of ash and, following Skyrover-Turquoise into the next cavern, they deposited the ash on the floor by one of the steep slopes.

Some of the 'Ash-Kids' stayed to watch, while others ran for more ash, shouting and yodelling as Skyrover-Turquoise pressed and shaped the ash into steps, mounting each as he made them, climbing ever higher.

"Look at this 'Up-Go' madness!" they all shouted as Skyrover-Turquoise seemed to reach the top and now stood up, to touch the roof of the cavern. What the 'Ash-Kids' could not see was that Skyrover-Turquoise has reached the top of the slope and now peered over the rim, to see a flat land, in which were raised twelve gushing volcanos, each 'Whooshing' out blasts of different coloured smoke, which clouded the sky and land with a technicoloured mist.

At times, the mists seemed to clear and, as Skyrover-Turquoise watched, above the volcanos, there appeared the Crystal Moons and, as each of the Crystal Moons rose above a volcano, the volcano

THE ASH STEPS

erupted, to blast out a cloud of 'Crystal Fire-Dust', which covered the Crystal Moon.

Skyrover-Turquoise watched as the Garnet Crystal Moon rose straight above one of the volcanos, then saw the blast of 'Garnet Fire-Dust' erupt, spraying the Garnet Crystal Moon with the 'Dust', so the Garnet Crystal Moon reflected its colour brightly, continuing on its circle, round to the other side of the world, to where the land of Celestial Dream lay. So... This was how the Crystal Moons got their colours... At last Skyrover-Turquoise knew the secret!

Skyrover-Turquoise stood on the highest ash-step, watching as each Crystal Moon passed over one of the volcanos, each receiving a blast of 'Fire-Dust', all except one Crystal Moon, the Emerald Crystal Moon, which, as it passed over a volcano did not gain any 'Fire-Dust'eruption at all, the smoke simply drifting up from the volcano's mouth in a lazy curl. Here, said Skyrover-Turquoise to himself, was the problem, understanding that he would have to find out why the 'Miner' of the Emerald 'Fire-Dust' was not shovelling the 'Dust' into the fire of the volcano, so it would erupt and blast out the Emerald 'Dust'. Descending the steps, Skyrover-Turquoise stood among the 'Ash-Kids', while they, still laughing and pointing at their heads, followed him to where Juniper-Emerald sat.

Seating himself next to Juniper-Emerald, who still gorged himself on the 'Ash-Food', Skyrover-

Turquoise asked the leader of the 'Ash-Kids' if he minded looking after Juniper-Emerald whilst Skyrover-Turquoise went on a journey of discovery. "Where do you go on this 'Travelling-Distance'?" asked the 'Ash-Kid'. "Are you living in the 'Up-Go' world of confusion?"

Skyrover-Turquoise smiled.

"I promise you all." he said. "If you take very good care of my young friend then, when I get back, I will give you a marvellous present."

At this, all the 'Ash-Kids' jumped to their feet and began to laugh and yodel.

"I will take good care of him." promised the leader, seating himself again and beginning to make some more 'Ash-Balls', handing them to Juniper-Emerald. Leaving the party, Skyrover-Turquoise returned once more to the 'Ash-Steps' and began to climb and, reaching the top of the steps, he gripped the edge and heaved himself up till he stood on the warm earth of the 'Flatlands'.

Some of the 'Ash-Kids', who had followed Skyrover-Turquoise into the next-door cavern, stared in amazement as they saw Skyrover-Turquoise seem to vanish into the ceiling, running back to tell the others that Skyrover-Turquoise had been lost to an 'Air-Bubble' in the 'Heights'. At this, all the 'Ash-Kids' held their heads in their hands and moaned loudly, until the leader of the 'Ash-Kids' raised his hand, so that they all began to continue eating and enjoying the party.

Above ground, Skyrover-Turquoise noted, except for the volcanos, which blasted out their 'Fire-Dust' at regular intervals, there seemed to be no other activity, nothing moved on the face of the 'Flatlands'.

He turned in a large circle, looking for something which would give him a clue as to who lived in this land but there was nothing. Turning back to look towards the volcanos, Skyrover-Turquoise began to walk towards them, the red fire-smoke, seeming to change colours, getting even thicker as he drew nearer. He saw the small mouths at the bottom of each volcano, 'Cave-Doors' set into the bases and far too small for him to enter.

Wearily, he sat down, not knowing what to do, except simply sit and wait for anything to happen.

"Are you a 'Giant- Thing?"

Skyrover-Turquoise stood up, blinking his eyes, realising he had fallen asleep and not heard the 'Ladybird' draw up.

Skyrover-Turquoise stared at the 'Ladybird', it was Citrine in colour with large black spots to its body. Beneath its body were twenty little black legs, which seemed to run, though the insect did not move.

"Well...Are you a 'Giant-Thing'?" asked the 'Ladybird' again.

"Yes, I suppose I must be a giant, seeing as you're so small." answered Skyrover-Turquoise. It seemed so strange that he should be talking to this little 'Ladybird', Skyrover-Turquoise thought but, in this

strange 'Flatlands', one had to expect anything.
"But I can grow!" exclaimed the 'Ladybird' and
Skyrover-Turquoise stepped back as, suddenly, there
came a loud buzzing sound from the 'Ladybird' and
it grew to a much larger size. "Hop in." said the
voice and the wings of the 'Ladybird' opened up, so
that Skyrover-Turquoise could see the 'Ladybird'
was not an insect but some sort of mechanical car.
The driver, a small 'Gnome-Like' person, who
seemed to be neither child nor adult. He was dressed
in a Citrine suit, the same colour as the 'Ladybird'.
He had a red, warty, face and wore a cheery
expression.
"Hop in the passenger seat." he said again, inviting
Skyrover-Turquoise to sit next to him.
Skyrover-Turquoise seated himself, finding the
interior much roomier than he thought and, no
sooner had he sat, than the wings folded down again
and the 'Ladybird' sped off over the 'Flatlands'.
The machine seemed to have no controls, except
when the driver told it where to go, saying... 'Left,
or Right, Forwards or Backwards', whatever was
needed.
The driver leaned back in his seat and rested his
hands behind his head.
"Where do you come from?" asked the Gnome. "I
come from the world of Celestial Dream, it lies
above yours." replied Skyrover-Turquoise, trying to
see out from the machine, though no window was
visible.

"How can it lie above the 'Flatlands', when this is the top of the world?" said the Gnome.

"Ah, you see." answered Skyrover-Turquoise. "When I am in my own world of Celestial Dream, I am at the top of the world."

Skyrover-Turquoise stopped to think for a moment and then said… "Where I come from, your world is unknown to us. We call it the 'Endless Horizon', the land where earth meets the sky."

The Gnome wrinkled his brow, not completely understanding what was being said, then offered… "I am called 'Citrine-Junior'. I work for my Master, 'Citrine Miner'."

"What work do you do for your Master?" inquired Skyrover-Turquoise.

"All the 'Miners' have a 'Junior'. We make the 'Char-Tar Tea' and help mine the 'Fire-Dust'." replied 'Citrine-Junior'.

Skyrover-Turquoise mulled this information over in his mind, careful not to seem too inquisitive.

"Citrine-Junior?...That's a grand name. My name is Skyrover-Turquoise."

"That's funny! We have a 'Turquoise Miner'." exclaimed 'Citrine-Junior'!"

"Will I get to meet your fellow 'Juniors'?" asked Skyrover-Turquoise, hoping he would be able to meet them and, through them, get to meet the 'Miners', especially the 'Emerald-Fire Miner'.

"That's where we are going now." replied 'Citrine-

THE CHAR-TAR
TEA ROOMS

Junior'." adding… "We're going to the 'Char-Tar Tea Room' right now."

"The 'Char-Tar Tea Room'?" queried Skyrover-Turquoise.

"Yes… We 'Junior-Miners' meet every day at this time, to sit in the 'Char-Tar Tea-Room' and play cards until the hooter blasts. That lets us know it is time to pick up our Masters and bring them to the 'Tea-Room' for their 'Char-Tar Tea'."

Before Skyrover-Turquoise could ask any more questions, there came a small 'Beep' from the front panel and a green light came on.

"Turn left at the 'Rabbit-Hole' and stop outside the 'Char-Tar Tea Room." commanded 'Citrine-Junior' and Skyrover-Turquoise felt the machine swing to the left, then stop, the humming noise becoming quiet.

"Here we are." said 'Citrine-Junior', as the 'Wing-Doors' swung upwards.

Skyrover-Turquoise got out of the machine, his eyes roving over the large wooden hut, which seemed to stretch for ever and, following 'Citrine-Junior' into the hut, he saw that it only had a table and chairs, made of plain white wood, set out for twelve places. In the corner was a strange machine, which stood upright and whirred as 'Citrine-Junior' pressed a button on its side. Picking up a square plate with a small lip on one side, he held it beneath an opening on the bottom of the machine, saying… "Sit down while I make you a cup of 'Char-Tar Tea' to drink."

Skyrover-Turquoise sat and watched as 'Citrine-Junior' pulled a lever on the machine, which squeezed out a lump of black toffee, which immediately flattened itself into a hard black pancake.

"You have to pick it up and just sip it. It's very hot and can burn your tongue." warned 'Citrine-Junior', bringing the plate over and placing it on the table, before Skyrover-Turquoise.

Not wanting to upset 'Citrine-Junior', Skyrover-Turquoise picked up the black pancake and gently nibbled at its rim.

"Goodness!" he exclaimed, sitting up and looking at the place where he had nibbled. It was extraordinary, for where Skyrover-Turquoise had nibbled was melted and tasted just like hot sweet tea in his mouth.

"This is very nice." he said, beginning to nibble again.

"I can consider myself to be the very best of the'Junior-Miners', that's all." said 'Citrine-Junior', before going to one of the windows and looking out.

"Here they come." he said. "You go and sit over in the corner, by the 'Char-Tar Tea Machine', so all the 'Junior-Miners' can sit down to play cards."

Skyrover-Turquoise walked to the window, watching as all the different 'Ladybird' machines pulled up outside. There were another ten of them, all coloured to match the colours of the Crystal Moons.

The 'Junior-Miners' who alighted from the

machines, were all dressed in suits, the same colours as their machines.

Skyrover-Turquoise sat on the floor, over by the 'Char-Tar Tea Machine', as the ten all came through the door, laughing and pushing each other playfully. None of the 'Junior-Miners' seemed to take any notice of Skyrover-Turquoise, simply sitting in the chairs and calling for the cards to be dealt. Skyrover-Turquoise counted the 'Junior-Miners', noting that the only one missing was 'Emerald-Junior'.

The 'Junior-Miners' made a lot of noise, shouting, 'Snap 'N' Jack!' as they slammed down their cards on the table, scooping up the rest of the cards while others moaned at losing. This went on for some time as more and more cards were dealt out, so that the cards over-flowed from the table onto the floor. Suddenly there came a loud 'Hooter' blast and the 'Junior-Miners' jumped from their chairs, chasing each other out through the door.

"Can you collect the cards up and tidy around before we come back with our Masters'?" shouted 'Citrine-Junior', as he joined the rush, the 'Junior-Miners' racing to their machines and, with a whirring of engines, they raced off in the direction of the volcanos.

Skyrover-Turquoise rose from his seat and began to pick up the playing cards from the floor. As he picked the cards up, he saw that all the cards had no numbers on them at all, they were all blank!

'A most strange world this is', he mused, collecting the cards and pushing the chairs back into place. The 'Char-Tar Tea Room' was a most remarkable place, in that, from the inside, it seemed there was just enough room to house the table and chairs, plus the 'Char-Tar Tea Machine'. Yet, when Skyrover-Turquoise walked through the door and looked at the hut from the outside, the hut seemed to stretch back as far as the eye could see.

Even when Skyrover-Turquoise walked right around the hut, which took him some time, there was no other opening, no other doorways or secret openings. And when Skyrover-Turquoise went, peering through the last window on the end of the hut, all he saw was the table and chairs, nothing more.

Returning to the inside of the hut, Skyrover-Turquoise sat by the 'Char-Tar Tea Machine' and waited and it was not long before he heard the whirring sound of the 'Ladybird' machines, their different crystal colours shining as they raced towards the 'Char-Tar Tea Room'.

Skyrover-Turquoise watched them come, smiling at the rush of little black legs, which all moved together, like the legs of a Centipede, as the machines moved over the ground.

As they drew close, Skyrover-Turquoise moved back to the corner and sat waiting, hearing the 'Wing' doors of the machines open, then close, and the raised voices of the 'Junior-Miners' as they began to file into the hut, to form a queue by the 'Char-Tar

Tea Machine', each making a slab of 'Char-Tar Tea', then, putting the loaded plates on the table, they all filed out of the door.

"Excuse me, 'Citrine-Junior'… Where are the 'Miners'?" asked Skyrover-Turquoise, catching up with 'Citrine-Junior' before he left.

"They're 'Gabbling', speaking direction." explained 'Citrine-Junior'.

"Speaking direction? Gabbling? What is that?" asked Skyrover-Turquoise.

"It's how they talk, their language. If you don't have direction of 'Gabbling', you won't be able to understand them. All we 'Junior-Miners' had to go to school, to learn 'Speech-Direction', to get the 'Gift of the Gab', before we could work for the 'Miners'." said 'Citrine-Junior', now hurrying out, to join the other 'Junior-Miners', who then raced off, back the way they had come. Skyrover-Turquoise sat once more in the corner of the room, staring at the plates on the table, seeing the black pancakes of 'Char-Tar Tea', then realised the chairs had suddenly changed colour. They had just been ordinary plain white wooden chairs, yet now, each chair was the colour of a Crystal Moon, all except the end one, which had not changed to the colour of Emerald, neither was there a plate on the table before it.

It was while Skyrover-Turquoise pondered on this situation, when there was a 'Shushing' noise and he turned to see that a door had magically appeared in the wall behind the 'Char-Tar Tea Machine'. It had

'Swished' open and from it came a file of small 'Miners' each carrying a silver shovel and pick-axe, which they hefted over their shoulders. Each wore a suit of work-clothes, grimy with dust, yet shining in colours of each Crystal Moon. On their heads, they wore peaked caps, with the names of the Crystal Moons written across them.

They appeared to take no notice of Skyrover-Turquoise as they took their seats, sitting where the colour of chairs matched their clothes.

They seemed happy enough, 'Gabbling' away in a strange language, so that Skyrover-Turquoise listened for a little while, then, grasping the language, stood up and coughed loudly.

The 'Miners' stopped talking, their eyes opening wide as they stared at Skyrover-Turquoise, even wider when he started to speak in their language.

"Excuse me… Can you tell me where I can find 'Emerald-Miner', please?" he 'Gabbled'.

"That's the 'Giant-Thing', my 'Citrine-Junior' spoke about" said 'Citrine-Miner', staring at Skyrover-Turquoise intently.

"But how does he understand and speak our language?" asked the 'Pearl-Miner'.

They all looked at each other, shaking their heads and all began 'Gabbling' at once.

"My name is Skyrover-Turquoise and I have the 'Gift of the Gab', I can speak in 'Gabbling'. Now, will you please tell me where I might find 'Emerald-Miner'?... It's very important."

"It's no use trying to talk to the 'Emerald-Miner', he has gone insane and lost his mentality. He can't speak or understand us. All he talks is in 'Gobblygook' and 'Dribble'." said 'Sapphire-Miner', picking up the 'Char-Tar Tea' and nibbling at the edges.

"I can help him." said Skyrover-Turquoise. "If I can speak to him, I can give him the 'Gift' of the 'Gab', so he can be understood."

"A 'Gift' you say?" said 'Aquamarine-Miner', putting down his 'Char-Tar Tea'. Then, looking round at the others, who had also put their 'Char-Tar Tea' back on the plates, now looked at Skyrover-Turquoise with interest.

"Why should you give that mad 'Emerald-Miner' a 'Gift' and not us? After all, we are all sane and work hard to 'Fire-Dust' the Crystal Moons'."

"Yes." demanded 'Ruby-Miner', banging his fist on the table. "If you can give a mad 'Miner', who does not work, a 'Gift', then why not all of us?"

Skyrover-Turquoise held up a hand, so the 'Miners' fell silent.

"If I give each of you a 'Gift', will you promise to show me where the 'Emerald-Miner' is, so I can speak to him?" he asked.

"What kind of 'Gift' will you give us? I can't see any sack, or anything you have which will carry 'Gifts'." said 'Diamond-Miner', coming to where Skyrover-Turquoise sat and lifting his cloak, to see if Skyrover-Turquoise had anything beneath.

"See?" continued 'Diamond-Miner', lifting Skyrover-Turquoise' cloak, showing the other 'Miners'. "There's nothing there... Nothing at all. He doesn't have any 'Gifts' with him!"

"My 'Gifts' are special." explained Skyrover-Turquoise, moving over to the table.

"I promise to give each of you a 'Gift' in turn, so you all have something special."

At this, all the 'Miners' started shouting, each demanding to be first in line, to receive a 'Gift'.

"Stop!" shouted Skyrover-Turquoise, holding up his hands and causing the shouting to suddenly stop.

"I will deal with you all but I need to speak to you, one at a time... And I need to have you in line with your 'Birthed-Months', which means I need to speak with the 'January-Birthed', which is 'Garnet-Miner'!" declared Skyrover-Turquoise, pointing to 'Garnet-Miner', who stood up, looking around at the other 'Miners' with a wide smile.

"Why him?" demanded 'Peridot-Miner'. "Why should he get the first and best 'Gift' of all?" This brought shouts of agreement from the rest of the 'Miners', apart from 'Garnet-Miner', who put his thumbs into his jacket lapels and stood proudly upright.

"The 'Gifts' are all equal and you all will be able to share what you have with each other, once the 'Gifts' have been distributed amongst you!" exclaimed Skyrover-Turquoise.

This seemed to appease the 'Miners' who,

whispering amongst themselves, finally agreed to leave the 'Char-Tar Tea Room', so that Skyrover-Turquoise could be alone with 'Garnet-Miner'.

"We'll go to the 'Miner-Dormitory' and wait." said 'Opal-Miner', leading the others from the table and, as Skyrover-Turquoise watched, they walked to the far wall, behind where the 'Char-Tar Tea Machine' sat, continuing to walk through a Secret-Door which suddenly appeared. The door 'Shushed' shut and, just as mysteriously faded into the wall so that it disappeared completely.

Skyrover-Turquoise took his eyes from the wall and indicated that 'Garnet-Miner' sit opposite him at the table.

"Where's my 'Gift'?" asked 'Garnet-Miner', sitting and holding out his hands.

"My 'Gift' to you will be the 'Gift of Ambition and Aspiration'." replied Skyrover-Turquoise. "What kind of 'Gift' is that?" asked 'Garnet-Miner' beginning to look disappointed. "What is 'Ambition'?...And that other funny word you said?"

"Aspirations" reminded Skyrover-Turquoise, then asked… "Do you have a child?"

"Of course I do!... Well, not exactly my own but I have a 'Junior-Miner'. We all do, that is part of all 'Miners' lives, that we each take a 'Junior-Miner', to train so they follow us into the 'Mines', when it is time for the 'Senior-Miner' to go. When I first came from school, I was the 'Junior-Miner' and, when my 'Senior' went to 'Sleep', I took over and became the

'Senior-Miner', the 'Garnet-Miner'. That's how we live… So you can see that my child is 'Garnet-Junior'."

Skyrover-Turquoise understood what 'Garnet-Miner' had said.

"But what would happen if you wanted your 'Junior-Miner' to become, say, a Doctor, to leave the 'Garnet-Mine' and help those who are sick?" asked Skyrover-Turquoise.

"The 'Junior'…Become a Doctor? To not work as I have done… But who would keep the 'Garnet Crystal Moon' fired up with 'Fire-Dust'? You are talking foolishly!" exclaimed 'Garnet-Miner', becoming alarmed. Skyrover-Turquoise put out his hands, to pacify the alarmed 'Miner', who had never heard such talk before.

"You have to understand, 'Garnet-Miner', because you don't have any sense of 'Ambition' and 'Aspirations', you do not see what can lie ahead, in the future for your 'Junior', to be able to step up in class. Please understand, 'Garnet-Miner', once you receive the 'Gift' of 'Ambition' it will all become clear!" persuaded Skyrover-Turquoise.

"I don't understand what you are saying." said 'Garnet-Miner'. "Tell me this…If my 'Junior' went away to become a Doctor, then who will mine the 'Fire-Dust', with which to blast onto the 'Garnet Crystal Moon'? Who will take over from me, if my 'Junior' does not follow me in line?"

"Tell me, 'Garnet-Miner'…Who cleans the 'Ash-

Dirt' from the 'Under-Grating'?" asked Skyrover-Turquoise.

"The 'Ash-Kids' do, of course." quickly replied 'Garnet-Miner'.

"Then you can train the 'Ash-Kids' to mine the 'Fire-Dust' for you, so your 'Junior' can leave, to become a Doctor, or something higher in life."

"But the 'Ash-Kids' are stupid!" exclaimed 'Garnet-Miner'.

"You are wrong, 'Garnet-Miner'. The 'Ash-Kids' are very bright, it's just that all of you, living here in the 'Flatlands' have no 'Ambition' to elevate your positions in life and so you all stay in a 'Time-Warp'."

'Garnet-Miner' took off his peaked hat, scratching his head and not understanding anything at all.

"I don't understand." he said, replacing his hat. Skyrover-Turquoise leaned across the table, placing a gentle hand to the forehead of 'Garnet-Miner'.

"This is known as the 'Gentle-Touch', it is hypnotic and will allow you to see how your life will change, once you have 'Ambition' for the future." said Skyrover-Turquoise, softly.

'Garnet-Miner' closed his eyes, feeling all kinds of sensations flow through his body and, when Skyrover-Turquoise removed his hand, 'Garnet-Miner' opened his eyes, to beam broadly, realising the joy of having 'Ambitions' for his 'Junior', willing also, to teach the 'Ash-Kids' how to mine for the Garnet 'Fire-Dust'. Skyrover-Turquoise lifted up a sleeve and showed 'Garnet-Miner' a small tattoo and, with a finger-nail, peeled off the tattoo and laid it on the table, to become a gold stamp. "Pick it up and look at it." said Skyrover-Turquoise, watching as 'Garnet-Miner' did as he was told. "It's grown into a book, a photo album!" exclaimed 'Garnet-Miner', nearly dropping the album as it grew larger in his hands.

"Look inside." instructed Skyrover-Turquoise. "Look!" exclaimed 'Garnet-Miner', opening the album and staring at a photo. "There is a picture of my 'Junior', lining up with others, to receive his Doctor's Certificate. He is wearing a beautiful purple gown and golden hat and now waves to me. In his hand is the 'Certificate of Honour'. He is no longer a 'Junior-Doctor' but a full 'Senior-Consultant'." Suddenly, 'Garner-Miner' stopped talking, aware of the noise, of clapping and cheering, aware, too, that both he and Skyrover-Turquoise were actually within the photo, part of the cheering crowd who stood to applaud the Doctors who collected their 'Honours Certificates'.

"How did we get here? What magic is this?" 'Garnet-Miner' shouted in Skyrover-Turquoise' ear… "This is wonderful, all the feelings I am getting inside of me, as if I instigated all this. I am so proud, I feel myself bursting with pride and now understand that 'Ambition' is not only for the 'Self' but, more importantly, for the future of our 'Juniors'!" cried 'Garnet-Miner'. "What you see here, is down to your sense of 'Aspiration', that you have a hand in making a future for those who live in the 'Flatlands'." said Skyrover-Turquoise, moving aside as two aged Professors, dressed in 'Sasquash-Fur' cloaks and gold hats, who were followed by small Imps who rang small silver hand-bells, came towards 'Garnet-Miner'.

"May we congratulate you on your inovative ideas, 'Garnet-Miner', that you gave the 'Junior-Miners' the desire to study and become members of a 'New-Society'." spoke one of the Professors, in a very shaky voice.

'Garnet-Miner' blushed in embarrassment, not used to such praise and not knowing what to say. "All praise to 'Garnet-Miner'!" shouted one of the Imps in a huge voice, shaking his bell, so that the other Imps began calling out as they, too, rang their bells. This set everyone in the audience and all the 'Juniors' cheering loudly, 'Garnet-Junior' running over to raise his 'Master's hand high in the air. Skyrover-Turquoise smiled, seeing 'Garnet-Miner' in such a happy frame of mind and then took his hand away from 'Garnet-Miner's forehead, so the 'Miner' gently woke from his trance, the sight of his 'Junior' receiving a 'Doctor's Degree' and the delight of all those cheering him, still sharp in his mind.

Glancing down at the table, 'Garnet-Miner' looked at the small stamp. "That is part of your 'Gift', an

THE
GARNET-MINER

album which, when you want to, you can hold between both thumbs and it will become the 'Scene of Reality', to show you what 'Aspiration' can produce."

Sighing in happiness, 'Garnet-Miner' smiled happily at Skyrover-Turquoise and thanked him for such a wonderful 'Gift'.

"When I have given all of the 'Miners' a gift each, you will all know how to share your gifts, so you can begin to enjoy your lives." said Skyrover-Turquoise.

"I will tell the rest of the 'Miners' what a handsome gift you have for each of us!" exclaimed 'Garnet-Miner'.

"Please tell the others nothing, until I have given you all a 'Gift', because, until you all share the 'Gifts', no-one will understand what you say and will think you are speaking 'Gobblygook'!" 'Garnet-Miner' put his fingers to his lips, promising to say nothing to the others.

"Now go into the 'Bed-Dormitory' and ask the next 'Miner'… That is 'Amethyst-Miner', whose 'Birthed-Month' is February, to come and see me for his 'Gift'."

'Garnet-Miner' picked up the delicate gold stamp and, with a happy smile walked towards the far wall. The door appeared, to 'Shush' open, then disappear as it closed, once 'Garnet-Miner' had gone through into the 'Bed-Dormitory'.

'Amethyst-Miner' suddenly appeared from behind the door, looking rather apprehensive as he approached Skyrover-Turquoise.

Skyrover-Turquoise watched the Secret-Door, fascinated by the way it 'Shushed' to a close, then faded once more into the wall.   Taking his eyes from the wall to face 'Amethyst-Miner', smiling in assurance, offering the chair opposite.

"What have you done to 'Garnet-Miner'?" asked 'Amethyst-Miner', sitting himself and fidgeting in the chair before becoming comfortable.

"I have done nothing to 'Garnet-Miner', except give him a 'Gift' which he will share with all of you when the time comes… Just as you will share your 'Gift' with the other 'Miners' later." replied Skyrover-Turquoise.

"That all depends whether I want to share it or not." said 'Amethyst-Miner'. "I might just want to keep the 'Gift' for myself."

Skyrover-Turquoise leaned forward and spoke earnestly… "If you try to keep your 'Gift' a secret, after the others have shared their 'Gifts' with you, then you will lose the 'Gift', it will just disappear."

'Amethyst-Miner' scratched at his chin and sniffed loudly.

"So what is my 'Gift'." he asked, holding out his hands, his eyes searching.

Saying nothing, Skyrover-Turquoise reached inside the left-hand lapel of his cloak and drew out a blue Lotus leaf, to lay it on the table.

"Is that my present?" asked 'Amethyst-Miner', his eyes down, curiously watching the Lotus leaf as it shimmered and shone in the light.

Smiling, Skyrover-Turquoise, picked up the leaf, then dropped it into the grasping hands of 'Amethyst-Miner', who looked at it, closing a fist round it, squeezing, then opening his fist to examine the leaf, expecting to see it crushed flat. The leaf flared its colour, still in bloom. With furrowed brows, 'Amethyst-Miner' put the leaf into his mouth and bit a part of it, chewing the part of the leaf. Looking at the leaf again, 'Amethyst-Miner' was surprised to see there was no damage to the Lotus leaf, it had quickly grown another petal.

"What is it?... It doesn't do anything!" he said at length, putting the leaf down on the table and folding his arms crossly.

Skyrover-Turquoise picked up the leaf and folded it into two, then opened it again, to expose a small blue box seated in the middle of the leaf. Taking the box in his hand, Skyrover-Turquoise shook it and the box suddenly grew in shape, first in a triangular shape, then as a form of funnel, the large end becoming a six-sided diamond.

"What is that?" exclaimed 'Amethyst-Miner' in surprise.

"It's a 'Kaleidoscope of Dreams', you have to look through the small end, to see the pictures." explained Skyrover-Turquoise, holding out the Kaleidoscope. 'Amethyst-Miner' took the Kaleidoscope and put one eye to the small end.

"What do you see?" asked Skyrover-Turquoise. "Just some black and white little squiggly things!" exclaimed 'Amethyst-Miner' grumpily, laying the Kaleidoscope back on the table.

"Do you know what I see?" said Skyrover-Turquoise, picking up the Kaleidoscope.

"The same squiggly things?" asked 'Amethyst-Miner'.

"What I see is four coloured pictures, of rivers and mountains, of animals and a yacht on an ocean." replied Skyrover-Turquoise, collapsing the Kaleidoscope into the flat box again and putting in into a small pocket under his cloak.   "I don't know what animals are, nor a yacht…Or a river and mountains. What are they?... And what has that 'Kaleidoscope of Dreams' got to do with my 'Gift?'" demanded 'Amethyst-Miner'.

Skyrover-Turquoise leaned across the table, his hand gently resting on 'Amethyst-Miner's forehead, so that 'Amethyst-Miner' felt the 'Gentle-Touch', the influence of hypnotic sleep flow through his body.

"My 'Gift'." said Skyrover-Turquoise. "Is a 'Gift' which will allow you to 'Dream', to see magic pictures, to imagine scenes which will inspire you to draw and paint the pictures and to write stories and poetry, to see the world of 'Flatlands' as a magic place, where animals play and birds sing wonderful tunes, which you will be able to sing." explained Skyrover-Turquoise gently and added… "You will

THE AMETHYST MINER

see through the image of the 'Kaleidoscope' and make illusions and magic become a reality."
Saying that, Skyrover-Turquoise took out the flat box again and lay it on the table.

'Amethyst-Miner' smiled and picked up the box, shaking it, so that it reformed in shape, back into a Kaleidoscope. Peering into the small end, he suddenly felt himself being drawn into the funnel, so that he now seemed to drift in a sea of confusion, drowsy, as if he floated. Opening his eyes, 'Amethyst-Miner' found himself to be afloat on a large blue Lotus leaf, in a profusion of colours, with Rainbow and Angel fish swimming in company. On the banks of the pond, he saw strange animals, playing and leaping, Rabbits which sang in soft harmony with doe-eyed Deer.

'Amethyst-Miner' looked about him in wonder, his mind awash with soft lights of colour, of violet pages, on which appeared written poetry and pictures of strange lands.

" I can see... I can imagine all the pictures...I can see. I am floating in a 'Sweet-Water' pond... Now, I am breathing in clear 'Mountain Air'." whispered 'Amethyst-Miner', his eyes flickering, then closing as he drifted deeper into the experience of sweet 'Dreams', which infused his body and mind.

Skyrover-Turquoise could feel the magic of illusions flowing through his fingers, knowing the 'Dreams' which the 'Miner' felt. He smiled, keeping his fingers in 'Gentle-Touch', till he knew all that needed to be infused into 'Amethyst-Miner's heart and head.

He lifted his hand away and 'Amethyst-Miner' opened his eyes, seeming to be miles away but ever so happy. He cocked an ear to one side, as if listening to something and then rose from the table. He stood for a moment, his eyes on the blue Lotus leaf which had suddenly appeared on the table.

"Take your 'Gift'." said Skyrover-Turquoise. "And remember to fold the leaf, so that you open it to find the box, when you want to look through the Kaleidoscope, to visit the land of 'Dreams'."

'Amethyst-Miner' leaned, to take up the Lotus leaf with a gentle hand and smiled in a generous pleasure, thanking Skyrover-Turquoise for such a beautiful 'Gift'.

"Now... Go to sleep in the 'Bed-Dormitory', 'Amethyst-Miner'. Sleep well and promise me you will tell no-one of your 'Gift', till all the 'Miners' have a 'Gift' and are ready to share everything." said Skyrover-Turquoise.

"I will do as you say." promised 'Amethyst-Miner', dreamily, his mind full of inspired 'Dream-Time.'

"And will you ask 'Aquamarine-Miner' to come and see me." asked Skyrover-Turquoise, as 'Amethyst-Miner' left the table.

"Aquamarine-Miner' is next in line, with his 'March Birthed-Month'." finished Skyrover-Turquoise.

The Secret-Door 'Shushed' open, then closed as 'Amethyst-Miner' left the 'Char-Tar Tea Room'.

Skyrover-Turquoise sat and waited for the next 'Miner' to appear, staring at the back wall and, eventually, set himself the task of clearing up the plates which the 'Miners' had left.

It was as he had just put the plates into a tin bucket by the 'Char-Tar Tea Machine', the far wall opened its Secret-Door and the face of 'Aquamarine-Miner' peered round.

"Come in." said Skyrover-Turquoise, pointing to a chair.

'Aquamarine-Miner' continued to peer around the corner of the door, his eyes wandering around, a worried frown wrinkling his brow. "Please come in." said Skyrover-Turquoise, this time, rising and going over to 'Aquamarine-Miner', gently touching the 'Miner's shoulder, before returning to the table and seating himself. 'Aquamarine-Miner' moved away from the door, so that it 'Shushed' to a close.

Sitting opposite him, Skyrover-Turquoise noted 'Aquamarine-Miner's worried frown and the way the 'Miner' tapped his fingers on the table, keeping his eyes down.

"Are you afraid?" asked Skyrover-Turquoise softly.

"No… I just don't like people looking at me." replied 'Aquamarine-Miner' nervously, his eyes still down on the table.

"Is that why you keep the peak of your hat pulled down over your eyes?" asked Skyrover-Turquoise, adding… "So others can't see you, or because you don't wish to have clear sight of others, so that you can't see them looking at you?"

'Aquamarine-Miner' continued to look down at the table, though he nodded his head, to show he understood what Skyrover-Turquoise had said. "You know, 'Aquamarine-Miner', the problem is that you lack 'Confidence', that you wish not to have 'Clear-Sight' of whatever, or whoever you feel will judge you."

Saying this, Skyrover-Turquoise leaned across the table and raised his hand, laying it with soft fingers, to give 'Aquamarine-Miner' the 'Gentle-Touch'. "How do you feel?" asked Skyrover-Turquoise. "I feel so fine!" exclaimed 'Aquamarine-Miner', his eyes closed, though his face was wreathed in smiles and had lost all sense of aggression. "Come with me." whispered Skyrover-Turquoise, inducing 'Aquamarine-Miner' with soft words, so that the 'Miner' felt himself drift into another world, to hear singing and dancing. "Do you see the 'Hedge-Hog Folk'?" asked Skyrover-Turquoise.

'Aquamarine-Miner' nodded, his mind full of music and seeing a group of folk, all wearing cloaks of Hedgehog-Quills, who danced and sang around a camp-fire. He felt himself jump, to land amongst the 'Hedge-Hog Folk', so they looked at him as he began to twirl and clap his hands, throwing his hat into the air and sweeping the hair away fom his eyes. "Look at me!" he shouted… "I can see you all looking at me, clearly… And I can look at you all, with complete 'Confidence'!"

The 'Hedge-Hog Folk' danced around him, each peering closer in turn, so that he could see right into their faces.

"Do you feel the 'Gift' of 'Clear-Sight', of the 'Confidence', to project yourself out into the world, without fear of rejection?" asked Skyrover-Turquoise.

From somewhere, out in the distance, 'Aquamarine-Miner' could hear Skyrover-Turquoise speaking, yet his eyes were opened to the scene before him, of the singing and dancing, as the 'Hedge-Hog Folk' twirled and clapped, drawing him, closer, into the circle. He saw the faces, the laughing eyes of those who danced around him and knew he had never, in his life, felt so good.

Then a whistle began to play a tune, coming closer, shrill notes, to be followed by the appearance of a large Porcupine, who walked forward, playing a silver 'Penny-Whistle'.

The 'Hedge-Hog Folk' stopped dancing and sat down, forming a circle and leaving 'Aquamarine-Miner' and the Porcupine to stand in the centre. The music shrilled higher and louder as the Porcupine jigged to the music, causing 'Aquamarine-Miner' to go into a frenzy of dancing, then to be led by the Porcupine's music, out into a town full of 'Hedge-Hog Folk' who waved from windows and shouted from the rooftops at the dancing which was wild, for all to see.

Suddenly, the music stopped and 'Aquamarine-

THE PORCUPINE

Miner' realised he was standing in the village-square, completely alone, except for all the 'Hedge-Hog' towns-folk, who had gone quiet.

It did not matter any more. 'Aquamarine-Miner' lifted his head up and danced alone, so that the clapping and cheering began again.

"Are you happy, 'Aquamarine-Miner'?" asked Skyrover-Turquoise.

The images of the 'Hedge-Hog Folk' seemed to fade gently away and Skyrover-Turquoise took his hand away from 'Aquamarine-Miner's forehead, so that the 'Miner' slowly opened his eyes.

Rubbing at his eyes, he became aware and taking his hat from his head and pushing his hair from his eyes, 'Aquamarine-Miner' began to laugh with all the confidence in the world.

"What a marvellous 'Gift' you have given me." he cried out. "You have instilled such confidence in me that I feel I can go anywhere and do anything!" exclaimed the happy 'Miner', shaking Skyrover-Turquoise by the hand.

"As I have asked 'Garnet-Miner' and 'Amethyst-Miner'… Before you go from here, I ask that you return to the 'Bed-Dormitory', to say nothing of the 'Gift' you have, until all the 'Miners' have their 'Gifts' and are ready to share them with each other. And one more thing, 'Aquamarine-Miner', here is a 'Memory-Gift' to remind you of your experiences."

Saying that, Skyrover-Turquoise handed the 'Miner' a small silver 'Penny-Whistle'.

"Now…Please return to the 'Bed-Dormitory' and sleep well and with 'Confidence'. I also ask that you tell the next 'Miner', 'Diamond-Miner' who was 'April-Birthed', to come and see me." said Skyrover-Turquoise.

He sat and smiled as he saw 'Aquamarine-Miner' replace his hat in a cocky fashion, tilting it back on his head then, playing a shrill little note on the 'Penny-Whistle' and treading a little dance, he made his way to the far wall, vanishing as the Secret-Door opened, then closed behind him, to fade into the wall.

'Diamond-Miner' had no retiring shyness, coming out through the Secret-Door and walked straight up to Skyrover-Turquoise with an outstretched hand. The light seemed to shine and sparkle from the 'Dazzle-Razzle' of rings, bracelets and necklaces which 'Diamond-Miner' wore, jingling away merrily, each time he moved.

Skyrover-Turquoise smiled, remarking on 'Diamond-Miner's jewellery. "It's very bright." he said.

"Do you like it? Don't you think I have good taste?" asked 'Diamond-Miner', lifting the many necklaces, so that Skyrover-Turquoise could get a closer look.

"It is quite eye-striking." replied Skyrover-Turquoise, though not with much enthusiasm. The problem was, while all the gold and diamonds glittered with a real shine, Skyrover-Turquoise could see, with a first glance, the jewellery was all fake, cheap costume jewellery and not worth anything.

"Where is my 'Gift'?" asked 'Diamond-Miner', sitting opposite Skyrover-Turquoise and holding out his hands. "Is it a gold ring, or diamond brooch?" he demanded.

"Do you see what I have in my hand?" asked Skyrover-Turquoise, taking something from a pocket in his cloak and reaching out.

"What is that? Is it a 'Star-Diamond' for my forehead?" asked 'Diamond-Miner' staring at the shiny object in Skyrover-Turquoise's hand. "No." replied Skyrover-Turquoise. "It is the 'Sparkle of Flight', exactly what we need, so we can go to where you can gain a real sense of 'Good-Taste'."

'Diamond-Miner' looked crestfallen, now understanding he was not going to get a diamond ring. "I thought you would give me a 'Glitter-Comfort', something which would make me feel rich, so that I can afford to buy whatever I like." he said.

"You will have to learn, in life, that you don't have to wear your wealth to feel secure or that you can appear attractive to others." replied Skyrover-Turquoise, in a quiet voice and,

as he spoke, Skyrover-Turquoise reached forward, his hand soft as he gave 'Diamond-Miner' a 'Gentle-Touch'.

As 'Diamond-Miner' felt the 'Gentle-Touch', his

THE
DIAMOND-MINER

eyes closed and he felt as though he was flying, speeding across a red sky, seeing the space of the 'Flatlands' below. His eyes opened wide, his hands grasping the cloak of Skyrover-Turquoise. "Where are we going?" he shouted.

"We are going to a place where money, diamonds and gold mean nothing. But it is there, in the 'Ash-Pits', you will know exactly what 'Good-Taste' is." Skyrover-Turquoise answered as they began to descend.

"Hoity-Toity" shouted an 'Ash-Kid' when he saw Skyrover-Turquoise and 'Diamond-Miner' arrive, seeming to fall from the sky.

'Diamond-Miner' was not afraid, seeming to be in some sort of dreamy daze, although he was suddenly aware that all the glitzy jewellery had gone from his fingers wrists and neck and, strangely, he found he was quite relieved to be rid of such 'Bad-Taste'.

"Will you give 'Diamond-Miner' one of your lovely 'Ash-Cakes'?" asked Skyrover-Turquoise.

The 'Ash-Kid' laughed happily, quickly gathering up some of the ash and patting it into the form of a ball.

"Here." said the 'Ash-Kid', offering 'Diamond-Miner' the 'Ash-Cake'.

"Taste it, 'Diamond-Miner'." said Skyrover-Turquoise. "You will find, it's not how it looks but whether it has 'Good-Taste'."

'Diamond-Miner' bit into the 'Ash-Cake', finding it to be quite delicious and greedily gobbled the cake up.

"What I give you as a 'Gift' is the knowledge of what is 'Good-Taste'." said Skyrover-Turquoise. "That a small diamond is worth more than all the promise of cheap jewellery, that one needs nothing at all, to have 'Good-Taste'."

"I have never tasted anything so good and have also learned that all is not what it seems to the eye." answered 'Diamond-Miner'.

"Do you see these 'Ash-Kids' who work down here in the 'Ash-Pits'? They are dressed in only the clothes they were 'Birthed' in and spend all day, raking the 'Ash-Dust' which falls through the gratings of your 'Dust-Fires' above." explained Skyrover-Turquoise. 'Diamond-Miner' looked around at the 'Ash-Kids', who sat in a circle, their faces wreathed in smiles.

"Do you see them crying?" continued Skyrover-Turquoise. Then, turning his eyes on the 'Ash-Kids', he asked them the same question, asking if they were sad with their life. The leader of the 'Ash-Kids' stood up and began yodelling, so that the whole clan began to rise up, yodelling and laughing, till the noise deafened the ears of 'Diamond-Miner', who asked Skyrover-Turquoise to take him home.

"You are home, at the 'Char-Tar Tea Room'." whispered Skyrover-Turquoise.

'Diamond-Miner' opened his eyes, to find he had not moved from the chair, that it had all been some kind of dream, though he was minus all the 'Razzle-Dazzle' of imitation jewellery and now saw he wore a small but brilliant ring on his little finger, made purely of 'Ash-Dust'.

"That is your 'Gift-Ring', to remind you of how lucky you are, to be rich in life and to have 'Good-Taste'." said Skyrover-Turquoise.

"Thank you for my 'Gift'." said 'Diamond-Miner, to the smiling Skyrover-Turquoise. "For giving me the 'Gift' of 'Good-Taste'."

"I only ask that you keep your 'Gift' to yourself, only sharing it when all the 'Miners' have their 'Gifts' to share." said Skyrover-Turquoise, also asking that 'Diamond-Miner' tell 'Pearl-Miner' to come and see him in the 'Char-Tar Tea Room'. Skyrover-Turquoise watched 'Diamond-Miner' walk towards the far wall and saw, once more, the Secret-Door appear, to open, so that 'Diamond-Miner' went through, to close after him, then disappear.

Curiously, Skyrover-Turquoise rose, walking to the far wall and pressed with his hands, pushing against the wall, though nothing happened, no matter what he did or tried, there was no door.

Giving up, Skyrover-Turquoise returned to the chair and it was not long before the Secret-Door appeared, to 'Shush' open, to admit 'Pearl-Miner' who came to the table in a seemingly agitated state. At first, he seated himself, then rose quickly, to walk around the room, then sit again.

Skyrover-Turquoise watched as 'Pearl-Miner' rose once again, then sat once more.

"Do you have a problem in settling down?" asked

Skyrover-Turquoise.

"Indeed, I do." replied 'Pearl-Miner'. "It's always the same. No sooner do I feel comfortable than I begin to feel uncomfortable and have to move again."

Once more, as he spoke, 'Pearl-Miner' rose from the chair, walking round the table, to sit for a third time.

"Your problem is 'Settling-Down', being able to feel that you are comfortable in one place, so you keep trying out new positions and places." said Skyrover-Turquoise.

"Well, I am not sure what you mean by that." replied 'Pearl-Miner', getting up and moving again.

Skyrover-Turquoise waited till the 'Miner' sat again, then said... "A problem with the balance of your emotions, keeping them on an even keel." Before 'Pearl-Miner' could get up from the table once again, Skyrover-Turquoise leaned across and, giving 'Pearl-Miner's forehead a 'Gentle-Touch', he asked... "Do you see where we are now?"

'Pearl-Miner' had seemed to drift off and now opened his eyes slowly, becoming aware that he stood in some kind of magic 'Play-Ground'. There was no noise, although 'Pearl-Miner' could hear the sounds of laughter in his head. He looked all around, seeing that Skyrover-Turquoise, who stood next to him was more a ghostly figure than real. Again he looked at the scene.

"I can see a lot of animals playing." he almost whispered.

THE SEE-SAW

"Yes… Look, there are Monkeys on the 'Roundabouts' and an Elephant is on a swing, while another Elephant pushes him!"

"And what else do you see?" asked Skyrover-Turquoise.

"Look…There!" exclaimed 'Pearl-Miner'.

"I can see a Cat and a Dog. They are on a 'See-Saw', going 'Up' and 'Down' like a crazy pair, trying to make each other fall off!"

"They are not trying to make each other fall off, 'Pearl-Miner'." said Skyrover-Turquoise. "They are acting that way because they cannot get a balance, which will hold them steady and make the 'See-Saw' ride far more enjoyable."

"So what can anyone do, to make it a settled and comfortable ride?" asked 'Pearl-Miner', afraid the crazy ride on the 'See-Saw' would end up with the Cat and Dog falling off and getting hurt.

"What you have to do, 'Pearl-Miner' is to go to the 'See-Saw' and stand on the middle of it, your feet firmly on the centre, so the 'See-Saw' cannot move but stays perfectly balanced and still."

'Pearl-Miner' did as Skyrover-Turquoise bid, walking to the 'See-Saw' and, climbing on, moved to the middle, his feet just apart, so that, no matter how hard the Cat and Dog tried to swing the 'See-Saw' in a wild way, the 'See-Saw' stayed perfectly balanced and stable. Once the Cat and the Dog had felt the calmness of stability, they laughed as they began to enjoy the ride, riding the 'See-Saw' in a gentle way. "There, you see." said Skyrover-Turquoise as 'Pearl-Miner' jumped from the 'See-Saw' and returned, to stand by his side.

"Once a sense of balance is restored, then one can settle down and feel comfortable, able to be 'At Home' within themselves as they 'Ride' through life." explained Skyrover-Turquoise, taking 'Pearl-Miner' by the hand, leading him through some fields of calming violets and roses. "Where are we going?" asked 'Pearl-Miner'. "Back home, to where you can settle down." said Skyrover-Turquoise, gently shaking 'Pearl-Miner' by the shoulder.

'Pearl-Miner' seemed to blink a couple of times, then opened his eyes, to find that he still sat at the table, facing Skyrover-Turquoise.

At first, he was not aware he sat, calmly and without needing to move, feeling very much 'At Home' within himself and then, feeling the comfortable warm glow of calm, he smiled.

"I have given you the 'Gift' of 'Emotional-Calm'." said Skyrover-Turquoise, softly, before handing 'Pearl-Miner' a small silver brooch of a Cat and a Dog on a 'See-Saw'.   'Pearl-Miner' took the brooch and held it in both hands. "And please remember, 'Pearl-Miner'." said Skyrover-Turquoise. "That not one word must be spoken of this to the others, till all are ready to share what 'Gifts' have been given, to share with each other."

'Pearl-Miner' happily agreed with Skyrover-Turquoise, before walking to the far wall, his hands clutching the silver brooch, walking cool and very calm.

The Secret-Door opened, then 'Shushed' behind him.

'Ruby-Miner' had been birthed to a 'July Birth-Time' and came through the Secret-Door, into the 'Char-Tar Tea Room' with a face that shone with rosy glow, his ruddy cheeks seeming to give light to the surroundings. Bowing dramatically to Skyrover-Turquoise, he seated himself on the opposite side of the table, in the chair that Skyrover-Turquoise indicated, who watched with a smile as 'Ruby-Miner' first looked around the room and 'Clucked' his tongue, before saying… "This room can really do with brightening up. It needs colour and highlights, to give it a sense of romance, a sense of drama."

"You are quite right, 'Ruby-Miner', the room does look quite drab, indeed it does."

"I wish I could do something about it." said 'Ruby-Miner', sadly and sighed loudly… "But when I suggest the desire to give the room some colour, the other 'Miners' say I'm being overly dramatic!" he finished.

"There can always be a problem when one within a group wants to do or be different." said Skyrover-Turquoise.

"Yes, I do see things differently, though, when it comes to doing things, I tend to lose the sense of grandness and only do changes in a small way, nothing dramatic." said 'Ruby-Miner', then brightened as he added… "Will your 'Gift' be to have a sense of drama, create a dramatic effect?"

"That all depends on what you consider to be creative, drama can also be romantic and pleasurable, like creating a picture and not always to have a dramatic effect." replied Skyrover-Turquoise.

"Well, I try to give a softer interpretation to things but they always seem to be 'Over-The-Top!'" exclaimed 'Ruby-Miner', standing to present a dramatic pose.

"That is because you always allow your sense of drama to lead you into making a display." said Skyrover-Turquoise and, leaning forward, he signalled 'Ruby-Miner' to sit down, then put his fingers lightly to the 'Miner's head, giving a 'Gentle-Touch'. 'Ruby-Miner's' eyes closed, his cheeks beginning to glow a deeper red as his smile widened. His eyelids moved, flickering, as if he was watching a scene in a play.

"Do you know this land?" asked Skyrover-Turquoise, spreading his arms out.

'Ruby-Miner' opened his eyes, not understanding that what he saw was within a hypnotic sleep, induced by Skyrover-Turquoise. In this state, he saw the waste of the 'Flatlands', bleak, with just the shafts of the volcano 'Blast-Fires' smoking in the distance.

"This is the 'Flatlands', where we live." said 'Ruby-

Miner'.

"Now you have the 'Gift', to paint this land in a most dramatic and romantic way." said Skyrover-Turquoise, adding… "You can paint the whole scene."

'Ruby-Miner' threw out his arms, as if using a paintbrush, dipping the brush into different tins of paint and creating beautiful pastoral scenes, so that, where there was once just flat stony ground, now rose up trees, which shaded a 'Sweet-Water' stream and a 'Lovers-Lane', where lovers strolled hand in hand. Beyond the beauty of roses and blue heather, ran orchards of apple-blossom, so the scent of beauty hung sweet in the air.

"I am creating pure beauty and romance!" cried 'Ruby-Miner', waving his arms about. "This is what life should be about, beautiful colours and love, the beauty of creativity!"

Once more, 'Ruby-Miner' painted, beginning to run and touch the flowers with his brush, painting small petals and clear morning dew. Then he jumped as high as he could go, painting the sky a deep blue, with white puffy clouds.

Skyrover-Turquoise watched as the sense of creativity caused 'Ruby-Miner' to stand up and laugh in delight, allowing him to feel the sensation of having the power to create such scenes.

"This is real beauty!" shouted 'Ruby-Miner'… "Real drama!"

"It is time to leave these beautiful scenes you have

THE
RUBY-MINER

created." whispered Skyrover-Turquoise, reaching over, to gently wake 'Ruby-Miner' from the 'Dream-Sleep'.

'Ruby-Miner' shook his head, looking around the room before focusing his eyes on Skyrover-Turquoise.

"Was that a dream?" he asked. "Did I really have the 'Gift' of 'Creativity'? Can I give beauty and romance to the 'Flatlands'?"

"I give you this paintbrush." said Skyrover-Turquoise, handing 'Ruby-Miner' a small golden paintbrush. "Please use it well, when the time comes." he added. "I will use it to create all the beauty of nature!" exclaimed 'Ruby-Miner'. Skyrover-Turquoise smiled, then spoke… "You now have the 'Gift' and can use it, once all the 'Miners' have their 'Gifts'. Then the 'Gift' of creating beauty and romance will be yours, to share with all those who live in the 'Flatlands'. However, you have to remember, never to over-dramatise the nature of beauty by over-colouring the scene, nature has a very soft brush."

'Ruby-Miner' agreed to Skyrover-Turquoise' words and rose, his face wreathed in smiles, making his way to the far wall.

The Secret-Door appeared and, just as 'Ruby-Miner' was about to pass through it, Skyrover-Turquoise reminded the 'Miner' not to divulge to the other 'Miners' what his 'Gift' was and that he should ask 'Peridot-Miner' to come into the 'Char-Tar Tea

Room'.

"Thank you for my 'Gift'." said 'Ruby-Miner' holding the small paintbrush in the air. The Secret-Door closed as he walked through, into the 'Bed-Dormitory'.

The Secret-Door 'Shushed' in opening, to allow the grumpy face of 'Peridot-Miner' to appear and, 'Humphing' twice, as loudly as he could, the grumpy 'Miner' sat down opposite Skyrover-Turquoise and glared.

"I suppose you have some magic 'Gift' which can help me? Well, I can tell you here and now, nothing you have can help me, whatsoever!" declared 'Peridot-Miner'.

Skyrover-Turquoise smiled, seeing through the grumpiness and knowing exactly how to make this grumpy 'Miner' happy.

"I need you to help me." said Skyrover-Turquoise.

"You don't need me, nobody does!" shouted 'Peridot-Miner', rather annoyed.

Skyrover-Turquoise took no notice of the outburst, calmly speaking… "But you are needed, for your very good advice and in helping others."

"Helping others?" said 'Peridot-Miner' loudly. "Don't make me laugh! When I offer advice to the other 'Miners', they tell me to be quiet, that I am interfering and to leave them alone. That's why I am grumpy and don't talk to the other 'Miners' anymore… No-one likes me or will listen to me!"

"Have you ever heard of 'Good Co-Habitation'?"

asked Skyrover-Turquoise.

"No…What does that mean?" replied 'Peridot-Miner'. "It means to live peacefully with others, to 'Get along'." said Skyrover-Turquoise. "I've tried that but it doesn't work. When things went wrong, if one of the 'Miners' had a problem, I was always there, where I was 'Needed'. I always talked perfect sense and did everything by the book. But did I get any thanks for my help?...No, of course not!" shouted 'Peridot-Miner'. "You have to understand that some might not want your help, or want to work things out for themselves." soothed Skyrover-Turquoise. "Exactly! And that's why I am not needed, my advice is shunned!" continued 'Peridot-Miner', beginning to feel sorry for himself and starting to put his face into his hands as he sobbed.

"You are not useless, it is just that you need to realise when help is needed and how to be tactful when offering to help." explained Skyrover-Turquoise, reaching over to lift 'Peridot-Miner's face and, before he could move away or say anything, Skyrover-Turquoise gave the 'Miner' a 'Gentle-Touch' on the forehead.

"Let me show you something." said Skyrover-Turquoise, taking 'Peridot-Miner' by the hand. The 'Miner' felt a sudden sensation of flying through the clouds. Below, the ground grew green, with tall trees and streams which sparkled, reflecting the sunlight. "Where are we?" asked 'Peridot-Miner' in a calm voice. "And what is in that log hut… And all that noise coming from inside?"

"It's a 'Dolly-House'. Come with me and let's go inside." said Skyrover-Turquoise, leading the way up the path and opening the door, so that the noise grew to such a pitch that both Skyrover-Turquoise and 'Peridot-Miner' had to hold their hands over their ears. Inside the 'Dolly-House', everything was in uproar, with 'Dollies' lying all over the floor, some with only one eye, while others had lips on their foreheads. Some had one arm and three legs, others, with four fingers on one hand and six on the other. "You're doing it wrong!" shouted a red-faced Pixie, throwing a 'Dolly' at another Pixie, who threw a 'Dolly' back, so that it hit the wall and the head fell off. Another Pixie, dressed in a green costume and cape, put another eye on a 'Dolly' which already had two eyes, pressing the eye on top of the 'Dolly's head, after removing the hair.

"What are they doing?" shouted 'Peridot-Miner', above the noise of the shouting and arguing which was going on between the three Pixies. "They are making 'Dolls'. Christmas presents for the children of 'No-Hope Homes'." replied Skyrover-Turquoise, raising his voice.   "The children of 'No-Hope Homes'?" said 'Peridot-Miner', walking forward and waving his arms about, so the three Pixies stopped shouting and turned to look at him. "Go away!" shouted the Pixie in the green costume. "Yes, go away." said the Pixie in the red costume, who was now joined by the Pixie in the yellow costume, who also shouted… "Yes, go away and stop interfering with our work!"

"But you are making a mess of it all. Don't you see, you have to learn to work with each other, so the children from the 'No-Hope Homes' have beautiful 'Dollies'!" exclaimed 'Peridot-Miner', holding up a 'Dolly' and putting the eyes, nose and lips in the right places. "See how nice this 'Dolly' looks?" 'Peridot-Miner' asked, holding the 'Dolly' up.

"You are right!" exclaimed the Green-Pixie. Then, turning to the Red-Pixie and the Yellow-Pixie, he said. "I shall put the eyes on the 'Dollies' and one of you can put the nose on and the other can put the lips on the faces, then we can help each other put the arms and the legs on, so all the 'Dollies' are ready for Christmas." The three Pixies shook hands and clapped each other on the back, becoming very good friends and now knowing that things would work out well, now they had sorted out the perfect way to work, where co-operation made perfect sense.

"I have to leave you now." said 'Peridot-Miner' and smiled as the Pixies hugged him, thanking him for his help.

"Take me home, please." he said, turning to Skyrover-Turquoise.

"You are home." said Skyrover-Turquoise, touching the 'Miner's arm gently.

"You see how easy it is, when everyone works well together." said Skyrover-Turquoise, as 'Peridot-Miner' opened his eyes, to find himself still sitting at

THE BROKEN DOLLS

the table.

'Peridot-Miner' smiled with kind eyes, now having the 'Gift' of 'Co-Operation' and knowing that working with others in a good way, brings good results.

"Is that yours?" asked Skyrover-Turquoise, indicating the small gold 'Dolly' which lay on the table, continuing… "I do believe it is part of your 'Gift', to remind you of how well you are 'Needed'." 'Peridot-Miner' thanked Skyrover-Turquoise, picking up the 'Dolly' and putting it in his jacket pocket. Standing up, the 'Miner' began to leave the room.

"Remember, 'Peridot-Miner', to keep your 'Gift' to yourself, till all the 'Miners' are ready to share theirs, when you awake from your sleep." said Skyrover-Turquoise, as 'Peridot-Miner' rose to leave. "And remember to ask 'Sapphire-Miner' to come and visit me, please." he added.

"I shall remember to tell 'Sapphire-Miner' to visit you. And may I thank you for all you have done, for giving me such insight." replied 'Peridot-Miner', just before the Secret-Door closed behind him.

'Sapphire-Miner' had been birthed to the month of September and found an attraction to all that shone, that reflected the colour of gold. 'Sapphire-Miner' jangled as he walked, the bracelets and necklaces jingling together as he moved through the Secret-

Door, to sit opposite Skyrover-Turquoise.

"Is my 'Gift' made of gold?" he asked. "I do hope so…Is it a ring, or a bracelet, perhaps?" "Tell me why gold has such an attraction to you?" asked Skyrover-Turquoise, closing his eyes against the glare, the light hitting the gold of the necklaces and rings that 'Sapphire-Miner' wore.

"You don't understand." exclaimed 'Sapphire-Miner'. "Nor do any of the other 'Miners'. Gold is like a magnet, it will attract and draw only those who relate to riches… Can't you see that!" "But what good will your gold do you, if there is no-one else around, who finds gold attractive. You will be left on your own." replied Skyrover-Turquoise. 'Sapphire-Miner' rattled the gold on his wrists and round his neck, holding out his fingers, so the gold glistened.

"Look at the way I stand out, the way I shine!" he exclaimed proudly. "There has to be another who will be attracted to me!"

"Let me show you a picture, 'Sapphire-Miner', a wonderful scene." said Skyrover-Turquoise, leaning over to gently touch 'Sapphire-Miner' on the forehead.

"Where is this place?" asked 'Sapphire-Miner', staring at the picture which had lit up in front of his eyes. "Who are those strange men and what are they doing?" he asked.

"Those little men are called 'Gold-Grubbers' and they are picking up the chunks of gold which lie on the ground and putting them into the bags they have strapped to their backs." replied Skyrover-Turquoise. 'Sapphire-Miner' stared at the picture of the 'Gold-Grubbers', watching as the little men ran here and there, hastily picking up the shiny gold and filling up the bags on their backs.

"I want some of that gold!" cried 'Sapphire-Miner', overcome with greed and began to run forward.

"No!" cried Skyrover-Turquoise, in alarm, trying to stop 'Sapphire-Miner' from running forward. "If you run into the picture, you will not be able to get out!" But 'Sapphire-Miner' would not listen and, pulling away from Skyrover-Turquoise' grasp, he ran into the picture, snatching a bag from the back of one of the 'Gold-Grubbers', beginning to run all over the place as he snatched up the gold and filled his bag. Skyrover-Turquoise sat down on a rock and watched the picture, seeing all the 'Gold-Grubbers' begin to slow down as their bags got fuller and fuller, till the bags on their backs got so heavy, they lay on the ground and could not get up. 'Sapphire-Miner' continued to run, stepping over the helpless 'Gold-Grubbers', in his rush to collect the gold. Then, he too, began to get weary as the bag filled and began to slow him down.

At last, 'Sapphire-Miner' could struggle no more and crawled towards the outer light of the picture, to find he could not get out. He tried to remove the bag from his back but was too tired to unstrap it, so that he lay down, gasping for breath.

"Skyrover-Turquoise!" he cried. "Can you help me

THE
SAPPHIRE MINER

get out…I will share my gold with you!"
"I can't help you, 'Sapphire-Miner'." replied
Skyrover-Turquoise. "I am not attracted to gold as
you are."

'Sapphire-Miner' began to moan, tears springing to
his eyes then, suddenly, he felt a hand on his arm.
"It was only a dream, Sapphire-Miner." said
Skyrover-Turquoise, in a gentle voice and 'Sapphire-
Miner' realised he was still in the 'Char-Tar Tea
Room', seated opposite Skyrover-Turquoise.
"Was that dream to teach me not to be so greedy?"
asked 'Sapphire-Miner', very glad it was only a
dream and not real.
"It was not to teach you about being greedy." replied
Skyrover-Turquoise, smiling and continued, "It was
really all about 'Relationships', how to relate to
things in a proper way, to realise that not all people
will relate and be attracted to gold as you are. We all
find some things very attractive, though we don't
expect others to love those things in the same way."
'Sapphire-Miner' looked down at his fingers and saw
that his rings had disappeared, as had the necklaces
and bracelets also disappeared. He laughed aloud,
shaking his hands and showing Skyrover-Turquoise
that he wore no gold.
"Look, Skyrover-Turquoise." he cried. "You have
given me a most marvellous 'Gift', the 'Gift' of
relating to others, through the 'Love' for each other.

I now understand, it is not what I am 'Personally' attracted to, as far as wealth is concerned but what lies beneath the glitter that attracts me to others and they to me!"

"And here is a present which will remind you of that." said Skyrover-Turquoise, handing 'Sapphire-Miner' a small lead model of a Caterpillar.

"What does this mean?" asked 'Sapphire-Miner', looking at the Caterpillar. "It is to remind you that the Caterpillar and the Butterfly are one and the same, the change is only in the way a person sees them." replied Skyrover-Turquoise. "Thank you so much, you have given me a wonderful present." cried 'Sapphire-Miner', rising from the table. Skyrover-Turquoise clapped his hands and, wishing 'Sapphire-Miner' the best of his 'New-Found' wealth, bid him not to tell anyone until all the 'Miners' had their 'Gifts' to share… "And will you please ask 'Opal-Miner' to come through the Secret-Door, to see me." finished Skyrover-Turquoise.

The 'Secret Door' appeared in the far wall and 'Shushed' open, so that 'Sapphire-Miner', with a smile and backward wave of his hand, disappeared behind it, the door closing so the wall appeared solid once again.

Skyrover-Turquoise sat back in the chair, his eyes closed as he rested. It was quite tiring, giving each of the 'Miners' a 'Gift', even though he had all the 'Infused-Gifts' dazzling his body and mind.

The 'Shush' of the Secret-Door caused him to open his eyes and smile as he saw 'Opal-Miner' step forward, the door closing quietly behind him.

"Please come and sit down." said Skyrover-Turquoise, indicating the seat opposite.

'Opal-Miner' sat down with a sigh, a seemingly hopeless look in his eyes as he turned them upwards, to look at Skyrover-Turquoise. "Why are you so sad, 'Opal-Miner'?" asked Skyrover-Turquoise.

"Because, I do not think you can help me." replied 'Opal-Miner'. " I know…" he continued… "You have a 'Gift' for each of us and it most likely will make all the other 'Miners' happy but my problem lies deep inside me and I cannot show you what I want as a 'Gift'."

Skyrover-Turquoise looked deep into 'Opal-Miners' eyes and said…. "You wish to 'Worth-Share' what is within you."

'Opal-Miners' eyes widened in full surprise. "You are right, Skyrover-Turquoise, you can see into my soul. I do wish to 'Worth-Share', to share what I have with all who live in 'Flatlands'. The problem is, I have no idea what it is I wish to 'Worth-Share' and, because I do not know what is secretly tucked away inside me, I cannot share anything."

"May I take you to a 'Dream-Place'?" asked Skyrover-Turquoise.

"What is a 'Dream-Place' and what is there?" replied 'Opal-Miner', sounding dubious.

"The 'Dream-Place' is a magical scene and that is

where you will enter the 'Transformation-Chamber'."

"Will it hurt?" asked 'Opal-Miner', as Skyrover-Turquoise reached forward to give a 'Gentle-Touch'.

"No." was all Skyrover-Turquoise said as he saw 'Opal-Miner's eyes close.

'Opal-Miner' relaxed into a most fine 'Dream-State', drifting on clouds across a blue heaven. He felt no fear as he drifted, just a lovely sense of calm, allowing Skyrover-Turquoise to guide him as both flew into the joy of the 'Dream-Place'. Silently, the pair descended into a valley and further, into a cave with purple sides and silver sounds.

"What is this place?" asked 'Opal-Miner'.

"It is the 'Source of Wells', the endless stream of 'Emotional Water'." replied Skyrover-Turquoise, as they both stood, up to their knees in the soft pool of golden liquid.

"Where does the water come from?" asked 'Opal-Miner', now feeling a strange sensation deep inside, as if he felt like crying, then feeling such happy laughter bubbling up inside him. "The waters are a world of tears, that are cried from happy and unhappy children." said Skyrover-Turquoise.

"Yes... I can feel the tears, sometimes happy and sometimes sad!" exclaimed 'Opal-Miner', reaching down, to run his fingers through the water and feeling his fingers tingle.

"If you look upwards, you can see the children's faces." said Skyrover-Turquoise, pointing upwards, so that 'Opal-Miner' gazed up and saw hundreds of childish faces, all seeming to cry tears, so that the tears continuously dripped into the waters below.

"They all look so sad." said 'Opal-Miner' now feeling the hurt of sympathy causing him to cry. "Is there nothing I can do?" he asked.

"See how you 'Share' your sadness?" asked Skyrover-Turquoise.

"Yes… But that is because I feel the children's pain and sadness." replied 'Opal-Miner'.

"That is because you have not yet allowed yourself to 'Share'." said Skyrover-Turquoise… "And so cannot 'Transform' tears of sadness into 'Tears of Joy'." he finished.

"How do I learn to transform the 'Tears'?" asked 'Opal-Miner', in a sad voice.

No matter what passed through 'Opal-Miners' mind, he could not think of one way in which he could make changes.

"Can you give me the 'Gift', so that I can 'Transform the Tears'?" 'Opal-Miner' asked Skyrover-Turquoise, his eyes earnest.

"You already have the 'Gift'." replied Skyrover-Turquoise. "Though the 'Gift' I gave you is the 'Gift' of 'Sharing'." finished Skyrover-Turquoise.

"So what is the good of being able to 'Share' when I have nothing I can share with others?" cried 'Opal-Miner'.

"It is within yourself that you have the power to 'Transform', to make changes to emotions. All you

THE
OPAL-MINER

have to do is believe you have the power to do that, to exert enough emotion, that the force will change what you want to." said Skyrover-Turquoise and watched as 'Opal-Miner' began to allow his feelings to over-ride his mind, till he began to feel such a strong sense of feelings that his face began to change colour.

Skyrover-Turquoise watched, standing to one side as 'Opal-Miner' turned 'Opalesque', then a deepest 'Opal-Blue', then the colours of a royal sunset and a beauty of 'Autumn-Rain'.
The water beneath their feet changed into a run of glorious colours, rippling with laughter.
"It's happening!" laughed 'Opal-Miner' happily. "I can transform the 'Tears' from sadness, to 'Tears of Joy'!"
At that, the children's faces in the ceiling began to change, laughing in happiness as they wept tears of 'Joy'.
"Now." said Skyrover-Turquoise. "You have the power to 'Transform' and 'Share', to give happiness to all those who live in the 'Flatlands!'"
'Opal-Miner' stood in the multi-coloured waters and cried tears of happiness... And found himself still crying as he opened his eyes, to find himself seated opposite Skyrover-Turquoise, back in the 'Char-Tar Tea Room'.
"When I have given all the 'Miners' their 'Gift', then you can 'Share' your joy with all of the 'Miners'."
said Skyrover-Turquoise and gave 'Opal-Miner' a

small gift of rememberance, so that the 'Miner' would never forget to 'Worth-Share' what he felt inside, the happiness and joy. 'Opal-Miner' looked at the heart-shaped Opal in his hand and held it tight. "I shall never forget what you have given me." said 'Opal-Miner', rising from the table and turned to face Skyrover-Turquoise before leaving the room. "Thank you." 'Opal-Miner' said once more.

"I ask you, as I have the other 'Miners', not to divulge what you have received till all of the 'Miners' have their 'Gifts' from me." said Skyrover-Turquoise.

'Opal-Miner' assured Skyrover-Turquoise he would do as he asked, then added… "I will tell 'Citrine-Miner' you wish to see him, shall I?"

"Yes please, 'Opal-Miner'." replied Skyrover-Turquoise, as the Secret-Door appeared and 'Shushed' open and closed once 'Opal-Miner' had passed through.

It was not long before the door opened once more, to allow the figure of 'Citrine-Miner' to pass through, his whole bearing seeming to give a sense of apathy, as if 'Citrine-Miner' needed to find some enthusiasm, something to bring him enjoyment. "Well, I would be glad if you could help me in some way." began 'Citrine-Miner', slumping down in the chair, seeming not to care whether Skyrover-Turquoise could help him or not. Saying nothing, Skyrover-Turquoise lifted a small flap to a pocket in his waistcoat and, opening the pocket, thumbed inside and drew out a marble of red, blue and green swirling colours. Placing the marble on the table, Skyrover-Turquoise sat back, watching as 'Citrine-Miner' began to sit up taller in the chair, his eyes on the marble, which seemed to change colours.

"Is that my present, my 'Gift'?" he asked Skyrover-Turquoise, wrinkling his nose in some disappointment when Skyrover-Turquoise nodded.

"Is that all? Is that all it does, change colours?" The disappointment in 'Citrine-Miner's voice was obvious and he slumped back in his chair again.

"Spin it!" suddenly suggested Skyrover-Turquoise, a smile on his lips.

"Spin it?...What happens when I spin it?" asked 'Citrine-Miner', uncertain whether this was a trick or not.

"Go on, 'Citrine-Miner'. Take the marble between finger and thumb and simply spin the marble." ordered Skyrover-Turquoise.

"Oh, alright… If you insist." yawned 'Citrine-Miner', reaching over, to take the marble and spin it, so that it spun in quick circles on the table.

'Citrine-Miner' suddenly sat upright, his eyes widening as he saw the marble begin to grow, larger and larger, till it settled itself into a huge globe, set into a frame so that it could be turned whichever way one chose. Its surface was mostly blue, with ripples of greens and browns, of yellows and orange.

"What is it?" stammered 'Citrine-Miner' his eyes large and fearful.

"It's called a 'Round-The-World'." said Skyrover-Turquoise.

"Well, what does it do? What kind of 'Gift' is it…Is it magic?" asked 'Citrine-Miner' now more at ease and leaning forward, to peer intently at the large coloured globe.

"I can tell you that it is not a trick or a magic ball." replied Skyrover-Turquoise. "What it does is it has the power to 'Expand-Horizons'." "What do you mean, you really will have to explain that to me." said 'Citrine-Miner', now really interested.

"I can tell you this, 'Citrine-Miner', the reason you are so bored with life, so full of apathy, is because you have allowed your world, your mind, to close in on you, so that you cannot see beyond your work as a 'Miner'…There is no 'Expansion' in your life." replied Skyrover-Turquoise and, saying that, he reached right across the table, to touch 'Citrine-Miner's forehead with a 'Gentle-Touch'.

'Citrine-Miner' immediately felt a calmness come over him and smiled, though his eyes now gleamed with a new awareness, as though his mind had livened up.

"Now, 'Citrine-Miner', reach out and touch the 'Round-The-World' globe" said Skyrover-Turquoise, seating himself firmly into his seat, hands clasped across his front, as if expecting to be blasted off into space.

'Citrine-Miner' reached out and put his finger on one of the green places, then gasped as the globe began

THE
CITRINE MINER

to spin, the colours merging into a single purple, a loud 'Whirring' sound coming from high above and coming closer. It seemed that both, Skyrover-Turquoise and 'Citrine-Miner' were suddenly lifted and jetted off into 'Far-Away' space, through black clouds of smoke and 'No-Time' illusions, then slowly descending till they felt their feet land.

"Where is this place?" whispered 'Citrine-Miner'. "It's the land of 'Encompass'." replied Skyrover-Turquoise, walking forward, so that 'Citrine-Miner' followed.

"There…" said Skyrover-Turquoise. "Do you see those 'Ant-Like' people, with blades of grass?" "Yes…What are they doing?" replied 'Citrine-Miner', moving closer, behind Skyrover-Turquoise, who was now standing amongst the 'Ant-Like' people. "They are writing out the world's history and everything which is known about everywhere and all people of the 'Universe'." said Skyrover-Turquoise, adding… "If you pick up that special glass which lies on top of that daisy, you will be able to read what they write. And, remember this, 'Citrine-Miner'… Only you will be able to read the words the 'Ant-Like' people write… Only you are allowed to 'Expand' your mind and 'Broaden your Horizons'. That is your special 'Gift'!"

'Citrine-Miner' picked up the special glass, a form of 'Magnifying Glass' and began to read, his eyes widening as the 'Expanded' knowledge filled his mind with understanding.

"I will be able to share all this 'Expansion' with the other 'Miners'." he enthused. "I can help them 'Broaden their Horizons!" he laughed, jumping with joy.

"Yes." said Skyrover-Turquoise. "This is your world, your knowledge. And now, we have to return to the 'Char-Tar Tea Room'.

With that, Skyrover-Turquoise lightly touched 'Citrine-Miners' shoulder, so that they, once more, seemed to be lifted and sped through space.

'Citrine-Miner' blinked his eyes, not once but many times, then opened his eyes to a widest extent, as if he had been in a dream. Then he fixed his eyes, first, on Skyrover-Turquoise, who sat opposite him in the 'Char-Tar Tea Room', then his eyes fell upon the coloured marble, which sat on the table.

"Was that a dream?" he whispered.

"No, 'Citrine-Miner'. The 'Round-The-World' globe is yours to keep, it is your 'Gift' and you can always use it to 'Expand' your knowledge, through reading and travel." explained Skyrover-Turquoise.

'Citrine-Miner' gave a cry of joy, his eyes alight as he picked up the marble and, taking off his hat, placed the marble on top of his head and replaced his hat.

"Remember, 'Citrine-Miner'… To use the 'Gift', you just have to 'Spin' the marble." said Skyrover-Turquoise, adding… "You will also remember to 'Share' your knowledge with the other 'Miners', to enthuse them with 'Expansion'."

"Of course!" exclaimed 'Citrine-Miner', now fully enthusiastic and rising from the table.

"I will ask 'Turquoise-Miner' to come to you." said 'Citrine-Miner'.

"Thank you 'Citrine-Miner'.

'Turquoise-Miner' is the last 'Miner' I have to see before I can talk to 'Emerald-Miner'. At last, my journey is nearing its end and I can find out exactly why 'Emerald-Miner' is not working." replied Skyrover-Turquoise, as 'Citrine-Miner', with a last wave, passed through beyond the 'Secret Door'.

Skyrover-Turquoise sat and waited.

It was not long before the Secret-Door opened, to allow 'Turquoise-Miner' entrance into the room. Skyrover-Turquoise smiled to himself as he sensed the haughtiness of 'Turquoise-Miner' who stood, his eyes roaming, seeming to judge the personality of Skyrover-Turquoise, before seating himself opposite.

"I suppose you are giving me your sense of judgment." said Skyrover-Turquoise with a large smile.

"I judge you to be correct." replied 'Turquoise-Miner' adding… "But then, because you are also of 'Turquoise' nature, you would also be doing the same as me, that you are judging me." "Yes, it's a fact that we all share a certain wisdom, though how we use it is how we grow within ourselves." said Skyrover-Turquoise, then drew out a small gold coin from an inner pocket and placed it on the table in front of 'Turquoise-Miner'.

"So, that my 'Gift'." determined 'Turquoise-Miner'. "I must admit that someone with my reputation, as one who has 'Good-Judgment', would have expected more than just a shiny coin."

"I just wanted to test your attitude, to what is important." replied Skyrover-Turquoise.

Then, picking up the coin, Skyrover-Turquoise held it up, to catch the light.

"Let me tell you a story, about two friends who, standing at the top of a mountain, looked down and saw a shiny object far below." began Skyrover-Turquoise, still holding the coin up to the light. 'Turquoise-Miner' nodded, an indication that Skyrover-Turquoise should continue the story. "One man suggested they race down the mountainside and the one who reached the coin first should keep it." continued Skyrover-Turquoise. At this, both men raced down the mountainside, huffing and puffing until, finally, they reached the bottom, to find that the gold coin was nothing more than a large pool of water which had the golden reflection of the sun." finished Skyrover-Turquoise.

"What is the moral of this tale?" asked 'Turquoise-Miner', with interest.

"The moral is, one should not make any judgment until one is certain of the truth." replied Skyrover-Turquoise, handing the coin to 'Turquoise-Miner'. "The coin you hold is not the 'Gift' I have for you." added Skyrover-Turquoise. "Although you 'Judged' it to be so, on first seeing it. My 'Gift' to you comes

THE TURQUOISE-MINER

with a 'Gentle-Touch'." finished Skyrover-Turquoise, reaching across, to touch his fingers to 'Turquoise-Miner's forehead.

"Do we go up, or down?" inquired the man in the top-hat, his white-gloved hand poised over the buttons.

"We should go up." said 'Turquoise-Miner', not entirely sure how he and Skyrover-Turquoise happened to be inside a lift, which shone in gold and had this strange man, who demanded whether they go 'Up' or 'Down'.

"We can go nowhere, until one of you pays the price of the ride in this elevator." said the man, taking his top-hat off and bowing low, then placing the hat back on his head.

"Give him the coin." said Skyrover-Turquoise to 'Turquoise-Miner' who handed the man the gold coin.

"Going up!" shouted the man, his finger pressing one of the buttons. There seemed to be no movement from the lift, no sensation of rising upwards.

"All out at the top floor!" shouted the man.

"But we haven't moved!" exclaimed 'Turquoise-Miner', angrily.

"How do you know the lift has not moved?" asked the man, with a smile. "Because I felt no movement!" continued 'Turquoise-Miner', beginning to shout.

"So... Do you use what you feel, to make

'Judgments'?" asked the man, then urged Skyrover-Turquoise and 'Turquoise-Miner' out of the lift. "You really ought to give more time, more thought, before you make any 'Judgments'." said the man, before closing the door to the lift. "How strange." said 'Turquoise-Miner', still staring at the lift door and hearing the noise of the lift moving downwards. "I wonder where this corridor will lead us?" said Skyrover-Turquoise, his question drawing 'Turquoise-Miner's attention away from the man in the lift.

"I am not sure whether I am dreaming or all this is real." said 'Turquoise-Miner', beginning to follow Skyrover-Turquoise who had set off down the corridor.

It was hard to really determine what was real and what was not, for, as they came to the end of the corridor, the scene changed and 'Turquoise-Miner' wrinkled his nose at the smell.

The corridor led to the inside of a small and tired old house, which seemed to need a lot of repair work, before it fell apart.

"What are we doing here, this place really smells, it needs pulling down!" stated 'Turquoise-Miner', holding a handkerchief to his nose.

"We have come to meet the 'Tall-Tale'." replied Skyrover-Turquoise as he led 'Turquoise-Miner' up a set of old and rickety stairs.

"The 'Tall-Tale'? Is it a joke, or some kind of tramp?"

Skyrover-Turquoise smiled secretly at the questions from 'Turquoise-Miner', then opened the door to a bedroom which reeked of stale fish and eggs which had been left to rot for a thousand years.

"This." said Skyrover-Turquoise, indicating a little man who sat at the end of the bed. "Is 'Tall-Tale'."

'Turquoise-Miner' held the handkerchief tight to his face, his eyes taking in the ragged old figure who sat, wrapped in a dirty brown coat, which seemed to be alive, with mice that poked their small furry heads from every torn hole in the coat.

"Who on earth is that!" asked 'Turquoise-Miner', disdainfully, moving back, against the door, wanting to run away from the sight of the 'Beggar' and the smells, which seemed to get worse as the ragged old man stood up.

"Do you 'Judge' me?" inquired the old man in a shaky voice, looking directly at 'Turquoise-Miner', his eyes piercing out from under thick grey eyebrows.

"I 'Judge' you to be a dirty old, smelly tramp, who needs a bath and new clothes!" stated 'Turquoise-Miner', the handkerchief muffling his voice.

"Then... I am afraid you have misjudged me!" claimed the old man and, rising from the bed, he smiled. 'Turquoise-Miner' gasped in astonishment as the old man seemed to grow in stature, getting taller and younger, so that he seemed to fill the entire room, filling it with a golden glow.

"Now, do you dare judge the cover to my book!" he

exclaimed, his voice like thunder.

With that, the man threw open his coat, to reveal a suit made up of entirely golden coins, which shimmied and shivered in a blinding gold light, till both, Skyrover-Turquoise and 'Turquoise-Miner' had to hide their eyes from the glare, holding their hands to their faces.

'Turquoise-Miner' could stand the sight no longer, fully understanding his ignorance and that he should give 'Time', before making any judged consideration. He fell to his knees and begged that he be forgiven for his rudeness and, suddenly, the golden light went in a flash, leaving the room in total darkness.

"Get up, Turquoise-Miner'." said Skyrover-Turquoise, helping the stricken 'Miner' upright. The glow of soft lights began to reflect themselves in the room, which now smelled as sweet as any garden. There was no sign of the man in the golden suit, instead, there, on the bed, lay a shiny gold coin.

"Take the coin, 'Turquoise-Miner'… It is my 'Gift' to you, it buys you the 'Gift' of 'Good-Judgment'." said Skyrover-Turquoise, gently. As 'Turquoise-Miner' leaned in to take the coin, he was suddenly aware the coin he now reached for and picked up was the gold coin which lay on the table, the same one that Skyrover-Turquoise had placed there.

"It was a dream!" 'Turquoise-Miner' exclaimed, holding the coin. "We have not been anywhere at all!... But, I judge it to have helped me to make

'Good-Judgments'!"

Thanking Skyrover-Turquoise for his 'Gift', 'Turquoise-Miner' rose to leave.

"Before you go, 'Turquoise-Miner', can you tell me how I can talk to 'Emerald-Miner'? I have given all the 'Miners' the 'Gifts' as promised and now it is the turn of 'Emerald-Miner' to receive his 'Gift'."

'Turquoise-Miner' walked to the far wall, the Secret-Door appearing and turned… "I have no idea where 'Emerald-Miner' is." he said, before disappearing, the door 'Shushing' after him and fading.

Skyrover-Turquoise felt tired and so worried that, after all his work, having given each of the 'Miners' a 'Gift', there was no-one to show him exactly where to find the 'Emerald-Miner'.

He sat at the table, his head in his hands when, suddenly, there came a noise from outside and he saw, from the window, the arrival of all the 'Ladybird' machines, the coloured round bodies, with little black legs scooting over the ground, to pull up outside the 'Char-Tar Tea Room' then, with engines racing, the 'Ladybird' machines began to grow larger, the 'Wings' opening up, so that Skyrover-Turquoise could see the 'Junior-Miners' in the driving seats, all shouting and waving to each other.

Rushing to the door, Skyrover-Turquoise pulled at the handle, trying to open the door but it was locked tight. Urgently, he shouted out, banging on the door, to get the attention of the 'Junior-Miners' but they

could not hear him above the noise they made.
It was then, Skyrover-Turquoise saw, coming round
the side of the 'Tea Rooms', all the 'Miners',
walking in a line and, reaching their different
'Ladybird' machines, climbed into the passenger
seats, the 'Wing' doors closing and, as each machine
grew smaller, they took off, speeding into the
distance of the 'Flatlands'.
It was only then, that the door suddenly opened,
allowing Skyrover-Turquoise to dash out, shouting
and calling. But it was too late, the 'Ladybird'
machines had vanished into the distance.
Skyrover-Turquoise walked back into the 'Tea
Room', sitting himself dejectedly into a chair and
began to weep.
A strange noise, like the sound of a creaky, rusty,
spring bouncing along, caused Skyrover-Turquoise
to look up, to see through the open door a most
peculiar sight, for there, bouncing along on a small
green Pogo-Stick was an old and wizened Imp,
dressed in a green tunic with a yellow hat which kept
falling to one side. Skyrover-Turquoise watched as
the Imp bounded towards the 'Char-Tar Tea Room',
to keep coming until he bounced into the room, to
bounce on the spot as he looked at Skyrover-
Turquoise.
"I have never seen a 'Giant' cry!" he exclaimed in a
squeaky voice.
"I was not crying." said Skyrover-Turquoise,
defensively... "Just wiping some dust from my

eyes."

"Hmmm… A likely story." decided the Imp, still hopping on his Pogo-Stick, like a flea with an itch. "I'm called Jumpstick." suddenly said the Imp, climbing off the Pogo-Stick, although his small body continued to go up and down.

"Hallo Jumpstick… And I am called Skyrover-Turquoise, a 'Magi' from Celestial Dream." explained Skyrover-Turquoise.

"A 'Magi'? I've never heard of a 'Magi' before. When I think of it, I've never heard of Celestial Dream neither." said Jumpstick, studying Skyrover-Turquoise curiously, then climbing aboard his Pogo-Stick and beginning to bounce again.

"Well, I've never heard of an Imp called Jumpstick, who bounces on a Pogo-Stick." smiled Skyrover-Turquoise, his eyes going up and down as he spoke. Suddenly Jumpstick laughed, a high tingling sound.

"I suppose it takes all sorts!" he exclaimed. Then he stopped jumping, so the Pogo-Stick seemed to hang, suspended in the air.

"What are you doing here?" he asked of Skyrover-Turquoise, the Pogo-Stick suddenly coming down with such a thump that it bounced the little Imp high into the air.

"I'm trying to find out where the 'Emerald-Miner' lives. I desperately need to talk to him… But it seems no-one can help me" explained Skyrover-Turquoise, sadly.

"He lives in the back room, with his 'Junior'…

Though no-one can understand him, he talks 'Gooblygook' and 'Gibberish'… So does his 'Junior' so they can't even understand each other!" said Jumpstick, laughing and bouncing again.

"In the back room? In here!" exclaimed Skyrover-Turquoise excitedly, jumping to his feet.

"Of course he does…Didn't you know that?... Come with me and I will show you." said Jumpstick and, with a few hops, had reached the far wall and, as soon as the Secret-Door had 'Shushed' open, Jumpstick went through the opening, the door closing and disappearing before Skyrover-Turquoise had even managed to get near the wall.

In a fit of anger, he banged on the wall with his fist but there was no sound from the inner room, only the echo of his banging and so, seating himself once more, Skyrover-Turquoise, allowed himself to calm down, his eyes on the far wall, then jumping as the Secret-Door appeared, to 'Shush' open and the bouncing little figure of Jumpstick came through the door and into the room.

"Where were you?" he said accusingly to Skyrover-Turquoise. "I thought you were right behind me!"

"I tried to follow you, Jumpstick. But you move so fast on your Pogo-Stick, that I could not catch you." replied Skyrover-Turquoise, now so very glad that Jumpstick had come back for him.

"I have to go fast, otherwise I will fall off my Pogo-Stick and will not be able to move. I can only jump up and down, if I'm not on my Pogo-Stick." said

Jumpstick, almost apologising. "Well, let me go first, to be with you as we reach the door and we can both pass through at the same time…You just jump up and down." said Skyrover-Turquoise, hurrying, to be in front of Jumpstick.

"Oh, there's no need for that." laughed Jumpstick. "The door is a normal door now and you can come and go as you please."

Skyrover-Turquoise looked quickly at the wall, to discover there was a normal wooden door in its centre, with a big round brass handle and, turning the handle, he walked inside the room. "Welcome to my 'Sitting-Room'." said Jumpstick, hopping past and drawing the curtains from the window, so that light flooded in.

"But where are the 'Miners' beds? This was a Dormitory for the 'Miners'!" gasped Skyrover-Turquoise, staring around at the green sofa and table and chairs made of glass.

"Dormitory?... Oh, I see." replied Jumpstick, realising what Skyrover-Turquoise was talking about. Getting down from his Pogo-Stick and continuing to jump, he then collapsed into a heap onto the sofa, the Pogo-Stick left standing straight and still. Jumpstick giggled as he looked at the bemused face before him.

"When I go out." he explained. "The 'Miners' can come here to rest. This room becomes their Dormitory, with beds for each of them…That is, till I get back, then they have to leave and it becomes my home."

Skyrover-Turquoise nodded, not fully understanding, though too polite to say so.

"So, where does the 'Emerald-Miner' live?" he asked, looking round to see if there were any more doors, leading from the room.

"He lives in that room, the one we have just left." said Jumpstick, in a very matter-of-fact voice.

Skyrover-Turquoise did not allow his surprise to show, beginning to understand this was a very strange world to be in, so much different to his own world of Celestial Dream.

Without a word, he went to the door and opened it, half expecting to see the 'Tea Room'. Instead, he saw a simple bare room with, at its centre, 'Emerald-Miner' and 'Emerald-Junior', both with hands across their faces, hiding their eyes, as they lay on the floor.

Walking swiftly to where 'Emerald-Miner' lay, Skyrover-Turquoise lifted him up into a sitting position and whispered softly in his ear.

"I can understand you!" cried the stricken 'Miner', his hands reaching out to touch Skyrover-Turquoise's face.

"It is alright, I have the 'Gift' of 'Clear-Speech', so that I can understand what you say. I have come to help you and 'Emerald-Junior' get back to your 'Emerald Mine', to your work."

"How can you help me? You are the first to understand what I say. I have tried talking to the other 'Miners' but they locked me away and said that

'Junior-Miner' and I had gone mad."

"Why did you stop working at the 'Emerald Mine'?" asked Skyrover-Turquoise. "You must have known, without the 'Fire-Dust' covering the Emerald Crystal Moon, you would have lost the power of 'Clear-Speech', as would all who were birthed in the month of May."

"I tried to tell the other 'Miners'… I had lost my silver 'Pick' and 'Shovel' and only the Imp, Jumpstick knows where the spare tools are kept… And he could not understand me, so he had me put in here with 'Junior-Miner'."

"I will go and tell Jumpstick to get the tools for you, so you can get back to work." said Skyrover-Turquoise, beginning to rise, but 'Emerald-Miner' held him back.

"It is no good!" he cried. "… Jumpstick will only give the tools to the 'Miners' and no-one else!"

"Then lay quiet and calm." said Skyrover-Turquoise, placing his fingers on 'Emerald-Miner's forehead so that the 'Miner' felt the effect of the 'Gentle-Touch'. He lay quietly as Skyrover-Turquoise drew out a small emerald crystal, shaped like a heart. He opened it, like a locket and drew out a tiny book, which had the words 'Dictionary' on its front. Putting the miniature book back into the Emerald locket, Skyrover-Turquoise gently opened 'Emerald-Miner's mouth and placed the locket on his tongue.

"This is my 'Gift' to you… Just swallow the locket." Skyrover-Turquoise said gently. "It will open your mind to 'Clear Speech', once you have swallowed the 'Dictionary'."

'Emerald-Miner' did as Skyrover-Turquoise asked, swallowing the locket, sitting upright and, with a huge smile, stood up and spoke clearly. "This is marvellous!" he exclaimed, then saddened as he touched his face, his fingers gently feeling round his eyes.

"Although." he continued… "It will be much better once my eyes can see correctly." Skyrover-Turquoise pondered the problem, uncertain how to proceed.

"I think it is better that we see about getting you a set of tools, then set about getting you back to your 'Ash-Mine', to get you to work." said Skyrover-Turquoise, taking 'Emerald-Miner' by the hand and leading him to the door.

"What about my 'Junior?" asked 'Emerald-Miner'.

"I'm afraid I cannot help him at this time." replied Skyrover-Turquoise. "I could only give one person the 'Gift' of 'Clear-Speech', which I gave to you. But once you have the 'Emerald Ash-Fire' going, the magic of the Emerald Crystal Moon will return his sight and speech to him."

"Then we have to get moving." exclaimed 'Emerald-Miner'… "Though I have to ask Jumpstick to show me where the silver picks and shovels are kept."

"And then, there is the point of getting you back to your 'Mine', so you can start work again." said Skyrover-Turquoise, wondering how to set about this, how to get to the 'Mine' and, once getting there, how could 'Emerald-Miner' find his way about once he got to the 'Mine', because, whilst the 'Gift' gave 'Emerald-Miner' 'Clear-Speech', it did not give him his sight back until the Emerald Crystal Moon was covered in Emerald 'Fire-Dust'.

Skyrover-Turquoise voiced his concerns.

"Just let me have the pick and shovel and get me to the Mine and I will soon start work!" exclaimed 'Emerald-Miner', adding… "I know the Mine very well and, once there, I can work blindfolded!"

"Then just assure your 'Junior-Miner' all will be fine, then we can ask Jumpstick to show us where the Mining-Tools are kept." declared Skyrover-Turquoise.

'Emerald-Miner' knelt beside his 'Junior-Miner' whispering assurances, that all would be fine, then followed Skyrover-Turquoise, who had opened the door, entering the room, to find Jumpstick fast asleep in a small cot, his legs jerking up and down, so the blanket moved as if it were alive. Beside the cot, the Pogo-Stick danced up and down, in time with Jumpstick's legs.

"What goes on here!" exclaimed Jumpstick, angry at being woken from sleep and he rubbed at his eyes, to see Skyrover-Turquoise bending over the cot, with 'Emerald-Miner' holding onto Skyrover-Turquoise' coat.

"I want to know where you keep the silver picks and shovels." demanded 'Emerald-Miner'.

At first, in grumpiness, Jumpstick pulled the blanket over his head, refusing to come out, till Skyrover-Turquoise shook the cot vigorously, so that the Pogo-Stick bounced high into the air. "In the cupboard under the stairs!" shouted Jumpstick, poking his face out from under the blanket.

"Stairs? There are no stairs in this hut, it's a single storey!" exclaimed Skyrover-Turquoise in annoyance.

"Over there!" shouted Jumpstick in a shrill high voice, pointing to the far corner of the room. Skyrover-Turquoise followed the pointing finger and gasped in amazement, for there, in the corner, rose a flight of stairs which ended abruptly at the ceiling height, leading nowhere. Beneath the stairs was a small cupboard door, which opened into a large Gallery-Room wherein hung on silver hooks an assortment of silver picks and shovels. Taking a pick and shovel from off their hooks, Skyrover-Turquoise handed the tools to 'Emerald-Miner' who ran his hands over the tools with a fondness, feeling the sharpness of the pick and the grade of the shovel, nodding his head, a smile widening his mouth.

"Now, all we need is a way of getting you back to your 'Emerald Mine'." said Skyrover-Turquoise and returning to the cot, wherein Jumpstick had returned to his sleep, with loud snores, Skyrover-Turquoise shook the cot wildly saying... "Any ideas, Jumpstick?"

Jumpstick awoke with a start, not a very happy Imp

at all.

"What do you want now?" he shrilled.

"Have you any ideas as to how we can get back to the 'Emerald-Mine'?" asked Skyrover-Turquoise, giving the cot another rough shake as Jumpstick closed his eyes again and started to snore.

"You can borrow my Pogo-Stick!" declared Jumpstick, his eyes popping open, to glare at Skyrover-Turquoise.

"Just grasp the Pogo-Stick by the middle and it will grow to whatever size you want. All you have to do." continued Jumpstick, slowly and plainly, as if explaining himself to a baby… "Is you have to carry the 'Miner' on your back. Then tell the Pogo-Stick exactly where you want to go and it will take you there. Oh, and by the way… When you have finished with my Pogo-Stick, just tell it to come back to me… Do you need to know anything else… Or can I go back to sleep?" finished Jumpstick with a yawn.

"There is only one thing more, Jumpstick." said Skyrover-Turquoise. "Once 'Emerald-Miner' has got his 'Blast-Furnace' going, so that 'Junior-Miner' comes to his senses, please tell him to hurry and get back with his 'Ladybird' machine and help 'Emerald-Miner' to collect the 'Emerald Fire-Dust'."

"Yes, yes, yes!" shrilled Jumpstick. "I will remember… Now go away and let me sleep!" With that, the little Imp snuggled himself into the blanket once again and started snoring. Skyrover-Turquoise grasped the Pogo-Stick round its middle and,

THE POGO-STICK

suddenly, the Pogo-Stick grew to a size which suited Skyrover-Turquoise, who held on grimly as he felt the power of the Pogo-Stick, jumping up and down, in a quiver to be off.

"Quick, 'Emerald-Miner'… Climb onto my back as I kneel down and then hang on tightly with your arms around my neck."

Feeling the weight of 'Emerald-Miner' on his back and the firm grip of arms around his neck, Skyrover-Turquoise jumped with both feet landing on the pedals, shouting… "Take us to the Emerald Mine!" There was no telling how fast the Pogo-Stick went as it accelerated through the open door of the 'Char-Tar Tea Room', so that, within a blink of the eyes, the 'Char-Tar Tea Room' was lost to sight and they were hopping in speed across the open country of the 'Flatlands'.

"I can smell it…I can smell the smoke!" shouted 'Emerald-Miner' as the sight of the volcanos came into view.

The Pogo-Stick jerked to a halt outside the only volcano which was not puffing out smoke, continuing to jump up and down on the spot, then settling, to allow Skyrover-Turquoise to alight and help 'Emerald-Miner' down from his back.

"Go back to your Master, go back to Jumpstick." ordered Skyrover-Turquoise, at which the Pogo-Stick jumped high into the air, then hopped at great speed, back the way it had come, disappearing into the horizon.

"Lead me to the entrance of the volcano and I will go from there." said 'Emerald-Miner', holding onto Skyrover-Turquoise's coat as they made their way to the mouth of the volcano. "It's okay now." said 'Emerald-Miner' letting go of the coat and, feeling his way, passed through the small entrance and was lost to sight. Skyrover-Turquoise stood back and waited. He could hear the sounds of digging and a 'Hissing' sound, which came from inside the volcano. Then there was a sudden blast and clouds of 'Energy-Smoke' belched out from the opening at the top of the volcano, black at first, then clearing, to become the brightest Emerald-Green, to be seen anywhere in the Universe. From within, came shouts of jubilation as the 'Fire-Blast' exploded, then calmed itself, waiting. Skyrover-Turquoise watched as the Crystal Moons passed overhead, patiently waiting till he saw the pale globe of the Emerald Crystal Moon rise, to reach its zenith, directly over the top of 'Emerald-Miner's volcano.

The blast, the roar of the 'Emerald 'Fire-Ash' as it blasted out of the volcano took Skyrover-Turquoise completely by surprise, even though he was expecting it.

The cloud of Emerald-Green 'Fire-Ash' completely covered the surrounding air, causing the whole site to become fogged with the colour. Then it cleared, whisping away, to reveal the Emerald Crystal Moon in a blaze of coloured excitement, a deepest green which hurt the eyes to stare into its centre. From the entrance to the volcano came 'Emerald-Miner', his eyes as green as the Emerald Crystal Moon itself, laughing and crying at the same time as he ran to Skyrover-Turquoise, hugging him tightly.

"I can see again!" he cried "I can see and it is all thanks to you and I can speak again, my friend!" Skyrover-Turquoise hugged 'Emerald-Miner' back, then allowed the 'Miner' to return to work and wait for the appearance of his 'Junior-Miner'. Skyrover-Turquoise stood back, watching as the Emerald Crystal Moon moved on, pulsing its green ripples out, to merge into the other colours of the 'Rising' Crystal Moons.., then, laughing happily, he made his way back to where the pit opened, to where the 'Ash-Steps' descended into the grim and dark 'Work-Pit' of the 'Ash-Kids'. Peering over the rim of the 'Work-Pit', Skyrover-Turquoise could make out the distant sounds of laughter and shouting which came up from below.

Turning once again, to take a last look at the volcanos, seeing them 'Blast' their 'Fire-Dust' out in huge amounts, to cover and colour the Crystal Moons as they sailed high overhead, Skyrover-Turquoise smiled, then knelt down and, gripping the side of the rim, he lowered himself down until his feet touched the 'Ash-Step' beneath him.

It was Juniper-Emerald, who first saw him as he walked through the passage, into the big cavern, where the 'Ash-Kids' sat in a circle, eating and singing. Juniper-Emerald, his green eyes alive with excitement, his voice bubbling over in joy, ran to Skyrover-Turquoise, throwing his arms around him, thanking him over and over again, for saving him. Around him, the 'Ash-Kids' ran to and fro, laughing and yodelling, so the cavern echoed with their wild noise, till it grew to such a pitch that Skyrover-Turquoise shouted for them to stop. Immediately, the 'Ash-Kids' formed a circle around him, sitting quietly.

"How did you come back from the 'High-Heaven'?" asked the leader of the 'Ash-Kids', pointing up at the ceiling.

"Above the 'High-Heaven' is a world of light and colour." said Skyrover-Turquoise, trying to explain what lay above ground, though he could tell by the way the 'Ash-Kids' stared at each other and shook their heads, they had no understanding of anything other than their own dark and grim world.

"Come with me, both you and Juniper-Emerald. You both need to see what is above ground and how things are." said Skyrover-Turquoise, so that the leader of the 'Ash-Kids' and Juniper-Emerald climbed to their feet and followed Skyrover-Turquoise, through the passage, into the next cavern, where the 'Ash-Steps' led up to the 'High-Heaven'.

"Where are we going?" quavered the 'Ash-Kid', now feeling not so brave as he saw Skyrover-Turquoise start to climb the steps.

"Do not be afraid." said Skyrover-Turquoise. "No harm will come to you and, as the leader of the 'Ash-

Kids' you have to be the one who will lead your Folk up into the 'New-World'." Juniper-Emerald moved to be beside the 'Ash-Kid' and took hold of his hand. "I am with you." he said, giving the 'Ash-Kid' the confidence to climb the steps behind Skyrover-Turquoise. Reaching the top of the 'Pit', Skyrover-Turquoise heaved himself up and stood on the ground, to look, once more at the volcanos, which lazed different coloured smoke until the right Crystal Moon rose overhead.

Juniper-Emerald had climbed up and, helping the 'Ash-Kid' to climb to the top, stood with wide eyes as he saw the Citrine Crystal Moon rise high overhead, then jumped, startled as the volcano, directly beneath it, blasted a storm of 'Crystal Fire-Dust', which covered the Citrine Crystal Moon in a glorious colour, so that the Crystal Moon blazed in a brightness. The 'Ash-Kid' stared with large, frightened, eyes, afraid of the light and sound, of this new world which blazed with light. He clung to Skyrover-Turquoise, shaking with fear.

"Do not be afraid." said Skyrover-Turquoise, gently. "Look around you and see this 'New-World', where you and your 'Ash-Kid Folk' can live in, how you will be able to have fun and learn to help the 'Miners' with their digging for 'Fire-Dust'. Some of your folk will grow to be important in this 'New-World'."

The leader of the 'Ash-Kids' came out from behind Skyrover-Turquoise's back, standing straight, feeling the new sense of importance and feeling the wonder of the 'New-World'.

"It will be up to you, as the leader of the 'Ash-Kids', to bring your folk up here, to stand unafraid of this change." furthered Skyrover-Turquoise. As they stood, there fired, one more blast of 'Fire-Dust' from one of the volcanos, covering a Crystal Moon with a brilliant cloud of colour and misting the 'Flatlands' below.

"It is beautiful." whispered Juniper-Emerald.

"Indeed, it is." agreed Skyrover-Turquoise. "And remember all you see here, Juniper-Emerald, for it will be your job, to return here at times and become good friends with all the 'Miners', the 'Junior-Miners' and the 'Ash-Kids', so that we all live in safety and happiness."

"I will always be your very best friend." laughed the leader of the 'Ash-Kids', putting an arm round Juniper-Emerald's shoulder, starting to yodel softly.

"Then let's go back down the steps and you can tell your friends in the 'Ash-Pit' what to expect." said Skyrover-Turquoise.

"Yes... They will not believe me till I bring them up here to see for themselves. They will be frightened at first but I will lead the way!" exclaimed the leader of the 'Ash-Kids'. "Then it is time for Juniper-Emerald and I to return to Celestial Dream, our own world, to tell our people of all we have seen and heard." said Skyrover-Turquoise.

"Look!" exclaimed Juniper-Emerald, excitedly.

"One of the volcanos is about to burst and shower the Peridot Crystal Moon with 'Fire-Dust'… Can we stay and just watch this one before we go!" he begged. The three of them watched as the blast from the volcano belched pure Peridot dust, of vivid green with soft touches of gold that enveloped the Crystal Moon and clouded the sky around.

"Oh!... It's like a firework display!" said Juniper-Emerald, watching in wonder.

"Come along…It's time to go." said Skyrover-Turquoise, starting to descend into the 'Ash-Pit', careful how he went down the steps.

"Let's have a party before you leave!" shouted the leader of the 'Ash-Kids', then began yodelling loudly as he saw other 'Ash-Kids' crowded round the bottom of the steps, all pointing up, laughing and starting to join in the yodelling.

"Oh, can we stay for just a short while, Master? Just for a little party?" asked Juniper-Emerald. "Only for a little while." agreed Skyrover-Turquoise, reaching the last step, so the crowding 'Ash-Kids' moved aside to allow him through.

"A party! We're having a party!" shouted the leader of the 'Ash-Kids', his shouts causing the rest of the 'Ash-Kids' to go running into their 'Cave-Holes' and returning with arms full of 'Ash-Dust' which they lay in a pile on the floor, seating themselves in a circle and began to roll the 'Ash-Balls', as they laughed and yodelled. Skyrover-Turquoise sat between the leader of the 'Ash-Kids' and Juniper-

Emerald, rolling the 'Ash-Balls' and enjoying the taste of bananas and apple pie.

The 'Ash-Kids' fully enjoyed their party, listening as their leader told them about the wonders of the world above. He talked of the light and the volcanos which belched out clouds of beautiful colours, which clouded the big Crystal Moons that passed high overhead. The 'Ash-Kids' listened with wide eyes, some starting to demand that the leader take them up, beyond the 'High-Heaven', to see the wondrous sights.

Skyrover-Turquoise whispered to Juniper-Emerald that they should begin to leave, to make their way home. But Juniper-Emerald was so enjoying the 'Ash-Cakes' that he pretended not to hear.

"I think." said Skyrover-Turquoise, standing up... "That your leader should take you up the 'Ash-Steps', to go above the 'High-Heavens' and see the volcanos as they blast out their beautiful coloured 'Fire-Dust'.

At this, all the 'Ash-Kids' stood up and began chanting and yodelling, demanding to be taken above to the 'High-Heavens'.

"Come on then...Let's go and see your 'New-World'!" shouted the leader, walking fast towards the passage and into the other cavern, calling back so his words and yodells echoed from the cavern's walls. All the 'Ash-Kids' rose and began to run through the passage, shouting and laughing, to follow the leader.

"Come." ordered Skyrover-Turquoise, tapping Juniper-Emerald on the shoulder so that his Assistant rose, his mouth full and followed his 'Master', who began to make his way back down towards where the 'Magnetic-Machine' sat idle.

Climbing into the machine and making sure Juniper-Emerald was strapped in securely, Skyrover-Turquoise set the controls to travel on the 'Lay-Lines' towards the 'Magnetic-South'. "Make yourself comfortable, Juniper-Emerald." said Skyrover-Turquoise, adjusting his own straps.

"When I start this machine, it goes with such force that it takes the breath away. On the way here, you were very frightened but you are far more confident now because you have a 'Clear-Mind' and your sight back. Even so, you have to be calm and expect the speed to make it a bit uncomfortable."

"I am ready, Master." replied Juniper-Emerald, confident and very excited to be going back to his home in Celestial Dream.

"You will also feel the heat as we go through the core of this planet, the hot molten core will get hotter as we approach the centre, though it does not take long before we are through and entering the 'Zone' of our 'Crust', coming up to our land." With that, Skyrover-Turquoise pressed the buttons which caused the engine to 'Whirr' into life, then roar as the energy pulsed, then projected the 'Magnetic-Train' forward in such speed that, even though both, Skyrover-Turquoise and Juniper-Emerald, were expecting the propulsion, the force caused them both to gasp as they fought to get their breath.

"Take deep breaths and keep calm!" shouted Skyrover-Turquoise, between gasps.

Juniper-Emerald gasped in the air, breathing deeply, then relaxed as he felt the 'Magnetic-Train' begin to smooth its journey and race forward without hardly any sound at all. The air became warm, then warmer still, until the heat caused Juniper-Emerald to wipe at his brow. His eyes took in the view from the window, seeing the molten core,firing its streams of red and yellow 'Energy-Heat', turning in on itself and melting its own colours to a fierce purple. Just as the heat became almost unbearable, it began to get cool, then cooler, as Skyrover-Turquoise said…

"We're nearly home now, just a bit more till we come out through the crust of the planet and then to breath our pure air once more."

"I will be so glad to get home again, Master." replied Juniper-Emerald, then shouted in excitement as the 'Magnetic-Train' surfaced from the earth and docked under the light of 'Celestial Dream's sky.

"Look, Master!" exclaimed Juniper-Emerald, pointing upwards as they alighted from the train.

"Look at the Crystal Moons. See how beautiful the Crystal-Colours are as they pass overhead!" "Yes." replied Skyrover-Turquoise… "And do you see how the 'Emerald Crystal-Moon blazes its colour now, so wonderful!"

For a while, both stood, watching as the Crystal

Moons gracefully made their journey around the sky, each one, in turn, 'Rising' above the horizon.

"Now." said Skyrover-Turquoise, turning to his Assistant... "I must return to the 'Infusion-Chamber' and reverse the 'Infusion', giving back the 'Gifts' of power the other 'Magi' have loaned me. And you, Juniper-Emerald, have to return to the 'High-Dome', to mark down the 'Elements' that you see through the telescope, till I get back from my duties."

"Yes, Master." replied Juniper-Emerald and, with a last look at the open sky, hurried away to the 'High-Dome', which housed the telescope. Skyrover-Turquoise stayed for a little while longer, the experience of the 'Flatlands' running through his mind, then he too turned away, hurrying down the flights of stairs and along the corridors which took him to the 'Echo-Hall', to where the 'Infusion-Chamber' sat.

As Skyrover-Turquoise hurried past, he could see the white faces of the sleeping 'Magi' through the portholes of the chamber. Climbing swiftly into the front part of the 'Infusion- Chamber', he switched on the machine, stirring and bringing it to life, then placed the headpiece firmly on his head. The chamber began its throbbing pulse, then louder as the green light flooded the compartment. Skyrover-Turquoise sat, waiting for the green cloud to drift away, knowing it was time to wake the eleven 'Magi', in the rear chamber, time to give back the powers they had allowed him to 'Infuse'.

THE EMERALD VOLCANO

Pressing the main button, which allowed 'De-Fusion', Skyrover-Turquoise picked up the microphone and began to talk, raising his voice above the noise of the machine.

"As each of you wake to this time, you will feel the 'Gift' of life liven your senses. I have completed my mission and now start the process of exchange, the return of your 'Power-Gifts'." Saying this, Skyrover-Turquoise closed his eyes and settled himself, then touched at the buttons to the side of the headset, feeling the quick sharp prick of injection.

He slumped, feeling some of the 'Power-Flow' leave his body, understanding that the power-source was being sent back to those it rightfully belonged to. There was a strange sensation of weakness as each 'Gift' was taken from him, transferring itself through the medium of 'De-fusion', Skyrover-Turquoise allowed this flow, knowing that it would take him some hours, till his mind and body adjusted to the loss of power, the 'Gifts' had provided.

In the back chamber, the eleven 'Magi' began to waken, feeling the surge of life-giving 'Gift-Force' being seeped into their bodies. Eyes began to open and thoughts started to whirl themselves into the minds of the 'Magi', so that memories began to flood in, memories of the 'Alarm', the reason why they were all seated in the 'Infusion-Chamber'.

"I can see clearly!" cried Articulate-Emerald, staring round to look at the others with a wide smile, remembering the loss of sight and the covering of

'Fire-Dust' which had been lost from the 'Emerald Crystal Moon'.

"And you have your voice back, clear speech, 'Articulate-Emerald'!" said Skyrover-Turquoise, speaking into the microphone.

"So… Tell us what happened!" exclaimed 'Dramaticus-Ruby'.

"Yes… What happened when you left us, Skyrover-Turquoise!" demanded 'Welltogether-Peridot'.

"I would suggest." replied Skyrover-Turquoise.

"That we all go to our homes and rest, that we allow ourselves to let our 'Gifts' reassert themselves for the 'Twelth-Hour' as is ordered. Then we can all assemble in the 'Great-Hall', where I will tell you all about the trip and what happened and who I met, how the whole of the 'Cycle of the Crystal Moons' work, so we all survive."

"I agree." said 'Worthwhile-Diamond', removing his headset, so the rest of the 'Magi' did the same. Alighting from the 'Infusion-Chamber' and starting to move away from the 'Echo-Hall', feeling that he needed to rest,

Skyrover-Turquoise switched off the engine and sat for a while, a smile playing on his face as he thought about what he should do. Nodding his head, having made his mind up, he climbed out of the front compartment and shut the door. Leaving the 'Echo-hall', he hurried his way through the corridors and passages until he entered the 'High-Dome', where he saw his Assistant, Juniper-Emerald seated before the telescope, his eyes staring up at the Crystal Moons as they circled the sky above.

"The 'Emerald Crystal Moon' is still in 'Full-Blaze'!" he cried in pleasure, on seeing Skyrover-Turquoise enter the room.

"That's good." replied Skyrover-Turquoise, waving his hand, ordering that his Assistant stay at his post, keeping an eye on the Crystal Moons.

"Tomorrow." he said, sitting himself at his desk. "The 'Magi' are to meet in the 'Great Assembly Hall' and I want you to accompany me there." Juniper-Emerald took his eyes from the telescope, to stare round. "Me, Master?" he said, his eyes wide…

"Why do you need me to be with you. It is not allowed for 'Non-Magi' to enter the 'Great Assembly Hall', especially the junior rankings!" he exclaimed.

"Do you remember, Juniper-Emerald, when we climbed the 'Ash-Steps' and you saw the volcanos? Do you remember how I told you to be aware of all you saw at that time?"

"Yes, Master, I do remember." replied Juniper-Emerald.

"Then, you will also remember how we got to the 'Flatlands'. Later today, at 'Eves-time', I will take you down to the 'Docking-Bay', to show you how to set the 'Magnetic-Train' on the 'Lay-Lines', so that you will be able to go to the 'Flatlands' by yourself."

"But…Why, Master? Why me?" cried Juniper-Emerald in alarm.

"Tomorrow, I will explain it all to you, at the 'Grand assembly'." said Skyrover-Turquoise, closing his eyes and beginning to sleep.

Juniper-Emerald knew better than to wake his 'Master' and turned his attention back to the giant telescope, wandering it across the Celestial Dream sky.

The next day morning, Skyrover-Turquoise led his Assistant down to the 'Docking-Bay' and explained the intricacies of setting the wheels in motion, of setting the course, so that the train would basically drive itself through the core of the earth, to end up at the terminal, in the caverns near to where the 'Ash-Kids' lived. Juniper-Emerald allowed himself the fact that the 'Magnetic-Train' almost drove itself, once it was set to 'Magnetic-North' on the 'Lay-Lines'. Returning back to the 'High-Dome', Skyrover-Turquoise left, after telling Juniper-Emerald to be outside the 'Great Assembly Hall', after he had seen the Emerald Crystal Moon was about to Rise.

Skyrover-Turquoise made his way back to his own quarters and allowed himself time to dress in accordance with the rules, of long flowing black robe and scull-cap of Royal Turquoise. Around his waist was the gold chain of the 'High-Magi' and hanging from his neck was the emblem of the Turquoise Crystal Moon, a large Turquoise Crystal, encased in gold. He dressed slowly and carefully, knowing the other 'Magi' would all be dressed in their 'High-

Robes' as befitted the meeting in the 'Great Assembly Hall'.

The earlier danger was over, that meeting being a confusion of noise, with no time to 'Dress in Code', all the 'Magi' wearing simple 'Day-Gowns' and no royal regalia.

Now was the pleasure of time and, dressed in fashion, Skyrover-Turquoise paused once, to motion his Assistant, Juniper-Emerald to wait outside until he was called. Skyrover-Turquoise opened the large door and entered the 'Great-Hall'.

The eleven Celestial Dream 'Magi' sat behind the big curved desk, dressed in official robes and impatient to hear exactly what had happened to Skyrover-Turquoise and his Assistant…And how they saved the Emerald Crystal Moon from going out completely.

Skyrover-Turquoise strode to the front of the desk, walking up and down as he spoke… "What I am about to tell you will sound totally fantastic and, even though it does seem to be unbelievable, you will have to know what lies in the land which we call the 'Lands of the Horizon', that land which is beyond the horizon and is known as the 'Flatlands.'"

The 'Magi' sat quiet as Skyrover-Turquoise continued to talk, to explain to them about the 'Miners' and the 'Ash-Kids', the 'Char-Tar Tea Room' and the 'Ladybird' machines.

"The outcome was…" continued Skyrover-Turquoise… "That I set the wheels in motion and when the 'Junior-Miners' become socially advanced, owing to the 'Gift' of 'Ambition', there will be social changes to their life-structure."

"And what can we do about that?" asked 'Dreamteller-Amethyst'.

"The point is, while we have no right to interfere with another nation's life, because I was the one who started it all off and we are the advanced nation, I feel we have to have someone who will visit the 'Flatlands' from time to time, just to act as mediator, to make sure things are running fine and the Crystal Moons are a priority to us. In this light, we all owe the people of the 'Flatlands' for our lives."

"And which one of us do you propose should visit this 'Flatlands' from time to time?" asked 'Looksharp-Aquamarine'.

Skyrover-Turquoise did not answer.

Walking to the door, he opened it and brought in Juniper-Emerald.

"This is Juniper-Emerald, my Assistant." said Skyrover-Turquoise in introduction. "And he is the one who will be our 'Emissary', the one who knows the 'Ash-Kids' and how the volcanos work." he finished.

There were no arguments about Juniper-Emerald taking such a position and he was given the 'High Chain of Office', a large pendant with the word 'Emissary' emblazened in Emerald across it.

"Now I want to make a proposal." said Skyrover-Turquoise, having sent his Assistant back to the

'High-Dome'.

The 'Magi' leaned over the desk to listen as Skyrover-Turquoise spoke.

"Before each of you, on the desk is a small box. Now I want you to open it and take out the tablet."

"What is it for?" queried 'Softfeeling-Pearl', taking out the tablet and looking at it. Her gaze turned back to Skyrover-Turquoise, who also held up a tablet for all the 'Magi' to see.

"This tablet, the same one as each of you have, is a 'Forget-All' pill, which will cause all of us to forget everything I have shared with you about the people of the 'Flatlands'."

"Why should we all forget what you have told us?" shouted 'Dramaticus-Ruby', followed by shouts from the others.

"Because…" explained Skyrover-Turquoise, holding his hands up for silence… "If we have no knowledge of what is going on in the 'Flatlands', then none of us is tempted to interfere with their lives."

"But your Assistant, Juniper-Emerald will be the only one to know about the world beneath us!" shouted Dramaticus-Ruby.

"That's just it." replied Skyrover-Turquoise. "As a 'Junior', he will understand what a young country will need and not interfere unless asked for help."

At this, all the 'Magi' agreed and, holding the tablet ready to swallow, Skyrover-Turquoise shouted out… "Are we ready?...Now…Swallow!"

In this way, all the Magi forgot everything, all except Juniper- Emerald, who was forever after, very important and known as the…

'KEEPER OF THE EMERALD FIRE.'

JUNIPER EMERALD

THE END...

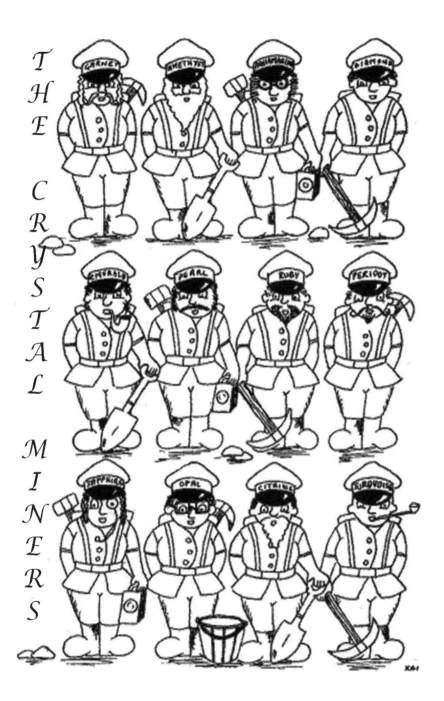

THE CRYSTAL MINERS

THE CHAR-TAR
TEA ROOMS